Mistletoe
Kiss

Just One
Mistletoe
Kiss

Just One
Mistletoe
Kiss

**Scarlet
WILSON**

**Janice
LYNN**

**Lucy
CLARK**

Published in Great Britain 2016
By Mills & Boon, an imprint of HarperCollins*Publishers*
1 London Bridge Street, London, SE1 9GF

JUST ONE MISTLETOE KISS... © 2016 Harlequin Books S.A.

After the Christmas Party... © 2013 Janice Lynn
Her Firefighter Under the Mistletoe © 2013 Scarlet Wilson
Her Mistletoe Wish © 2013 Lucy Clark

ISBN: 978-0-263-92688-0

9-1116

Our policy is to use papers that are natural, renewable and recyclable products and made from wood grown in sustainable forests.
The logging and manufacturing processes conform to the legal environmental regulations of the country of origin.

Printed and bound in Spain
by CPI, Barcelona

AFTER THE CHRISTMAS PARTY...

JANICE LYNN

To my parents, James and Brenda Green,
for making all my Christmases so full of
good times, good food, and lots of love.
Love you both very much!

Janice Lynn has a Masters in Nursing from Vanderbilt University, and works as a nurse practitioner in a family practice. She lives in the southern United States with her husband, their four children, their Jack Russell—appropriately named Trouble—and a lot of unnamed dust bunnies that have moved in since she started her writing career. To find out more about Janice and her writing visit janicelynn.com.

CHAPTER ONE

IF THE PRETTY little blonde were a chameleon, Dr. Riley Williams was positive she'd have blended into the hotel ballroom wall long ago.

Who was she? Obviously not someone's date as only a fool would have left her alone. She had to be a hospital employee he just hadn't had the pleasure of meeting.

She sipped on a glass of what appeared to be rum punch and nervously surveyed the room as if she'd rather be anywhere than at the Pensacola Memorial Hospital Christmas party.

He took a sip of his soda and continued to listen to Dr. Sanders discuss an upcoming heart program the hospital was sponsoring while Riley's attention was really on the blonde.

Never had he seen a less likely wallflower. Although she did seem as delicate as one of the orchids his mother loved to grow. Fragile even.

Every bit as beautiful.

Looking almost hopeful, she smiled at a group of women that passed by but they never paused in their hee-hawing to say hello. If anything, she seemed to wilt further. A pity because he'd liked that brief glimpse of a smile.

The need to see that smile again hit hard. Surprisingly hard. He liked women. A lot. Always had. He imagined he always would but he didn't envision himself ever settling down. The long hours and demands of his career would keep him from ever tying a woman to him. A family deserved time and attention.

A plump pink lower lip disappeared between white teeth. Every muscle in Riley's stomach contracted and he'd swear the air in the room had thinned.

Never had he had such an instant, strong reaction to a woman.

He placed his half-full glass on a passing waiter's tray. "Excuse me, gentlemen, but I just spotted what I want for Christmas."

Several of his colleagues followed his line of vision and grinned.

"Trinity Warren. She just started last week," a cardiologist who was one of his partners informed him. "On the cardiac unit. I'm surprised you haven't already noticed her."

With the way his insides were stirring, so was he. Then again, he hadn't been around the hospital much this week. He'd taken a few days off work to spend some time helping his mother with odds and ends of Christmas decorations and shopping. For too long since his father's heart attack sadness had filled her at the holidays. Seeing her renewed joy in the festivities did Riley's heart good.

"Trinity Warren..." He let the blonde's name roll off his tongue, wondering at the way his pulse pounded at his throat. "She works on our unit?"

He didn't usually become involved with women he worked with. Too messy.

"She's been in orientation with Karen this past week. Quirky sense of humor, great smile, patients like her, seems to really know her stuff."

Yeah, well, he'd really like to know her stuff too. Up close and personal. Plus, that glimpse of her smile had been great. He could only imagine what her full-blown one would be like. His imagination was working overtime at the moment.

He studied her, watching as she cast her big brown eyes downward to stare into her glass before taking another sip. Her tongue darted out to lick punch from her full lips. He swallowed. Oh, hell. Without even trying, she was sending his blood pressure through the roof.

How much he wanted to see her pretty mouth curved into a smile stunned him, to see her eyes dancing with pleasure. Want was the wrong word. He needed to see her smile, her pleasure.

"You want me to introduce you?"

He glanced at his best friend and one of the several partners in their cardiology group. "Have you ever known me to need you to introduce me to a beautiful woman?"

"Figured you needed all the help you could get," Trey teased.

"Besides, I'm onto you," Riley continued, hesitating just a little longer, feeling his friend's interest in the woman too. "You're just looking for an excuse to talk to her yourself."

Trey grinned. "If I'd spotted her first tonight, I wouldn't have needed an excuse to talk to her. I'd be over there now, rather than talking to your ugly mug."

"But now?"

"Now I've seen the determined look on your face."

Trey shrugged. "She doesn't stand a chance and neither does any other man in this room. Go for it."

Relieved his friend didn't have a vested interest, Riley didn't deny his claim. Besides, Trey was right. Trinity Warren didn't stand a chance when he turned on the charm. Before long she'd be smiling and enjoying her evening—with him.

Nurse Trinity Warren was smart enough to know that facing her fears was the best way to move on, to put her ho-ho-ho hang-ups to rest. But, seriously, had she really had to come to this Christmas party?

Leaning against the hotel ballroom wall, she took a sip of her third cup of fruit punch. Was she nuts or what? By coming here, she was sticking her neck under the proverbial guillotine. Two years ago she'd vowed to never attend another Christmas party, to ban Christmas for ever. Bah, humbug! That had been her motto.

Only she'd relocated two weeks ago and her new nursing director had said she needed to attend. So here she was, pretending she was having a good time and that she wasn't contemplating a dash to the ladies' room to toss the liquid-only contents of her fluttery stomach.

She smiled at a group of women who worked in the billing department as they paused near where she held the wall up. She didn't personally know them. She knew very few people outside the cardiac care unit. But she had seen the trio around. Waving their hands with animation and talking a mile a minute, they didn't notice her.

"He is so hot," one of the women said, fanning her face with a bejeweled hand decked out with rakish long manicured fingernails and a sparkly ring so big it had to be fake.

"He's yummy in his scrubs, but in those dress slacks and fitted button-down open just right at his collar…" a heavy-chested blonde gave an exaggerated sigh "…he's outright lickable."

Trinity followed their line of sight to see who had their tongues wagging. Oh, my. Um, yeah, they were right.

He was hot.

And lickable.

And a lot of other things that had her looking away really fast so her retinas didn't start smoking.

Startled at her tongue-slurping reaction, she glanced back toward the object of their admiration. Her gaze collided with his. Wow. Something about him made her burn. Probably because he looked as if he'd walked straight out of every woman's fantasy. The mischievous gleam present in his blue eyes said he was well aware of his many manly charms and that she threatened to spontaneously combust any moment just from his visual perusal. He knew he was that hot.

She gulped back another sip of punch, hoping it would cool the burn. It didn't.

Which didn't make sense because she'd banned men right along with Christmas two years ago. Especially a man like the one grinning at her. A man like that one would incinerate the already shattered bits of her heart.

"Oh! Shh! He's coming this way," one of the women squealed, slapping the other's arm and sloshing a little of her Cosmopolitan onto the ballroom floor. All three of the women struck we-weren't-just-talking-about-you poses and one gave a fake laugh as if whatever they were discussing was of the utmost interest and batted her lashes flirtatiously.

Really? Trinity wanted to roll her eyes. She glanced Mr. Lickable's way again to see if he'd caught onto the women fan-girling him.

Yet again her gaze collided with electric blue and this time didn't let go, couldn't let go, as if there was some magnetic force at play that held her eyes in place.

She forgot how to inhale. Literally and figuratively. She couldn't breathe.

Wow. He really was a beautiful man. Dark brown hair that had just a touch of golden curl and looked invitingly soft. Tanned skin that hinted he spent a lot of his time outdoors and, living next to the Gulf of Mexico, he probably did. He had a face and body gorgeous enough to give any movie-star hunk a complex.

Then there were those eyes.

So intensely blue that they had to be contact lenses, because no one's eyes could really be that blue. Or that full of mischief. No doubt he'd been one of those kids who'd stayed on Santa's naughty list.

Yes, the women were right. He was hot, so hot her mouth felt like the Sahara but the rest of her rivaled a rainforest and was probably putting damp spots on her dress. Great. Managing to shift her eyes, she took another sip of her punch, draining the clear plastic cup. Oops. Now what was she going to do with her nervous hands?

"Do you want something else to drink?" Mr. Hotness himself asked, walking past the we-weren't-just-talking-about-you women and planting himself right in front of Trinity.

She glanced to either side, expecting to see some

parched Delilah close by. He couldn't be talking to Plain Jane her, right? And if he was, *why*?

The trio was staring at her in dropped-jaw surprise. She was surprised herself. She wasn't chopped liver, but she didn't kid herself that she was the model type this guy most likely dated either.

The last swig of punch had done nothing to help her dry mouth, which was problematic. Her tongue stuck to her palate, refusing to budge. She was positive anything she attempted to say could and would be held against her.

"I'll be happy to get you more punch," he added, causing a wave of eyebrow rises from their spectators. "Or anything else you might want." One corner of his mouth lifted in a sexy grin. "I'm a man who aims to please."

If the heavy-chested blonde had fallen into a fit of vapors right then and there, Trinity wouldn't have been surprised. She was about to need resuscitation herself.

He was flirting.

With her.

Eyes narrowing suspiciously, brain reeling, she peeled her dry tongue free of the roof of her mouth. "Then perhaps you should aim elsewhere."

Because, really, what would be the point of encouraging him? She wasn't interested in a relationship, or anything else.

Rather than take the hint and move on, his devilish grin widened, digging dimples into his cheeks. "You don't like to be pleased?"

Darn it. He was quick tongued and she'd set herself up for that one. No matter how she answered, he'd twist her words. The mischievous gleam in his eyes assured that.

She shoved her empty cup toward him. "Punch."

Fantastic. She sounded as if she had a mouthful of peanut butter and the IQ of a rock, but at least letting him get her punch would give her a reprieve.

Taking her cup, he laughed. "Then punch it is, but don't think I'm letting you off the hook. We'll discuss what gives you pleasure when I get back." His eyes sparkled. "I could make a few suggestions even."

Heat washed over her body, melting her from the inside out at the thought of just what those suggestions might be.

Not that it mattered. She so wasn't having that conversation with him.

"I wouldn't hold my breath if I were you," she mumbled.

She didn't meet his gaze and earn another laugh from him and an "Is she crazy?" from one of their billing-department eavesdroppers.

They probably thought she was, but the reality was that she didn't want to attract a man like him. Chase had been as high octane as she went and look where that had gotten her. Burnt. Burnt. Burnt.

"Who needs to hold their breath when you've already stolen mine?" he quipped with another flash of his perfectly straight pearly whites, sending her up in a puff of smoke. Then, in a decent imitation of a famous movie line, he added, "I'll be back."

The women sighed then giggled as if he'd said something super-romantic then brilliantly funny. Trinity just stared. Her gaze zeroed in on his retreating figure.

"You go, girl," the heavy-chested woman told her,

stepping closer and giving a thumbs up. "I'm pea green with envy. You're tonight's lucky girl."

She winced that the women had obviously overheard his pleasure comment. Great. She didn't want gossip. Lord knew, she'd dealt with enough of that during her lifetime already. Especially at work. And, seriously, although he was the hottest man she'd ever set eyes on, she didn't want a man in her life. Not ever again. Maybe she should leave before he returned. If her director got upset that she'd left too early, she could always claim she hadn't felt well. With her nervous stomach, she'd be telling the truth.

Glancing around, she easily spotted him in line to refill her punch and chatting with a few people whose faces she recognized but didn't recall which hospital department they hailed from.

Who was he and why had he sought her out?

What did it matter?

She was not getting involved. Especially not with someone who worked at the hospital or had anything to do with the hospital. Been there, done that, had the gaping hole in her chest to prove it.

A sick feeling took hold in her stomach, like she might really lose its contents. Time to go. Fast.

Eyes locked on the exit, she made a beeline for the ballroom door, intent on making her escape. Just after she stepped into the long hallway that would lead her to the hotel's over-decorated foyer, a hand grabbed her elbow. She jumped.

"You okay?"

Him. Great. No doubt there would be scorch marks where his fingers burned into her skin. She grimaced and started to say she was heading to the ladies' room, but why lie?

She turned, faced him, felt her breath hitch again at just how lickable he really was, then inhaled deeply because she was strong. "Look, I appreciate the offer of more punch and boring conversation, but I've had enough and I'm headed home."

His forehead creased. "You're leaving? Because of me?"

"No." Heat infused her face. Hadn't she just asked herself why she should lie? "Look, I'm not a party girl. You should go talk to someone else."

Understatement of the year.

"I don't want to talk to someone else. I want to talk with you. Besides, you're problem is that you've been partying with all the wrong people." His wink told her exactly who she should be partying with.

Determined not to be swayed by his outrageous charm and the way him saying he wanted to talk to her warmed her insides, she arched a brow. "I suppose you're my right person?"

A full-blown smile slashed across his handsome face. "I've been called a lot of things in my life, but I'm not sure Mr. Right is one of them."

She started to correct him, to let him know that she hadn't been implying that he was calling himself Mr. Right, but before she could, he reached out and ran a tingle-inducing fingertip across her cheek. Hello, lightning bolt!

"There's always a first so, sure, I am the right person for you to be partying with tonight. I'm Riley, by the way." His smile cut dimples into his cheeks again and he stared straight into her eyes. "I don't want you to go."

Not offering him her name, she closed her eyes. It was all she could do not to lean towards him, be seduced by the appeal in his voice. Was he like the Pied Piper of women or what, because she just wanted to follow him wherever he led.

"Stay. Dance with me," he whispered near her ear in an enchanting tone that made her want to dance to his tune in more ways than one.

Mesmerized, she stepped towards him, her body almost pressing to his.

He inhaled. "You smell amazing. Good enough to eat."

Um, no. She was not going to let her mind go where his words threatened to take her. Not going to happen. Only her mind went exactly where it wasn't supposed to go. *Bad mind.*

Keeping her eyes squeezed shut, she parted her lips to say no, that she was leaving and couldn't be tempted by visions of sugar plums and whatever else he dangled in front of her. Apparently, he took her movement and open mouth as an invitation. Without hesitation his lips covered hers.

Shocked at the unexpected kiss, Trinity's eyelids flew apart, startled to find his intent blue eyes open, watching her, as his lips gently brushed over her mouth. Tasting. Tempting. Teasing. Rocking her world to the very core. Wow.

Shockwaves rippled to the tips of her toes and she questioned if time was standing still because the hotel seemed to fade away to just the two of them, just his eyes searching hers, his lips branding hers.

When he pulled away, reality immediately sank in. Hospital Christmas party. Surrounded by new coworkers. The most gorgeous man ever had just kissed her. Hello, had she lost her mind?

"Why did you do that?" She took a step back, wiping her lips as if trying to clear away his kiss. Sandpaper couldn't have erased his kiss. Riley. Riley's kiss. He'd permanently branded her lips, her entire body. The man started fires.

He pointed up to the doorway she'd stepped beneath.

"Had to." He shrugged nonchalantly, as if the kiss had been no big deal. To him it probably hadn't been. His knees weren't the ones shaking. "Tradition."

She glanced up, eyed the large clump of mistletoe tied with a red ribbon that hung over the doorway. Her gaze dropped back to him suspiciously. "You're a traditional kind of guy and just couldn't resist?"

"Absolutely, just ask my mom. She'll tell you I'm the apple of her eye." He grinned. "Now that we know I'm a traditional kind of guy, that you smell and taste like the sweetest candy, and the pressure of our first kiss is out of the way, let's go party. I guarantee a good time. Plus, you can tell me all about you while I hold you in my arms on the dance floor, Trinity." His eyes sparkled with devilment.

Feeling oddly out of sorts that he knew her name despite the fact she'd purposely not told him, that he was piling on the charm, she felt what little resistance she had to him ebbing away. "Do you always get what you want?"

One side of his mouth curved upward. "Not always, but it is Christmastime and I've been a very good boy."

She doubted that. Besides which there was nothing boyish about his broad shoulders and testosterone-laden aura.

"I'm hopeful there will be something sweet under my Christmas tree this year. An angel." He raised his brows. "You have plans? We could start a new holiday tradition."

She should go. She knew that. Her tattered heart was no match for this man's charisma. But the thought of going back to her lonely apartment just didn't appeal. Not even with Casper there, waiting for her. Her cat might love her but, whether Trinity wanted to admit it or not, she craved the temptation Riley waved in front of her.

An escape, albeit temporary, from the deeply embedded loneliness that had taken hold of her soul from the moment Chase Langworthy had dumped her publicly at their hospital Christmas party two years ago and plunged her into depression and Scrooge-dom.

Darn him for doing that. Darn her for letting him.

She took the punch glass Riley still held and downed half the contents as if she were chugging a shot of whiskey. Ha, she never drank alcohol, but she needed something to give her the push to do what she suddenly wanted to. She'd pretend the punch was liquid courage. She'd pretend that she was the kind of girl used to men like him flirting and wanting to dance with her. She'd pretend she was the life of the party.

"Okay, Riley…" She drawled his name out. She would do this, would have fun. "I'll dance with you, but I should warn you that I dance much better than I kiss so you might struggle to keep up."

She had no clue how she managed the confident words, the brilliant smile, or where they had even come from. The only time she ever danced confidently was around her living room with only Casper around to yawn at her antics. Still, head high, she headed back into the ballroom.

Riley's pleased laughter behind her warmed parts of her insides that hadn't felt sunshine in a long, long time.

CHAPTER TWO

WHAT A PLEASANT enigma, Riley thought of the woman he held loosely in his arms. She really did dance like an angel. But she was crazy if she thought she danced better than she kissed.

No one danced better than this woman's lips had felt against his. A meeting of their lips that hadn't been an angelic kiss but one that lit hot fires all along his nerve endings. He still burned. Of course, that might be because her curvy little body swayed next to his and every cell in him had an apparent surge of testosterone.

What other excuse could there be for that brief brushing of his mouth against hers to have set him on fire the way it had?

If he didn't quit thinking about how much he'd wanted to deepen that kiss, about how he wanted to take her somewhere private and kiss her again and again and on places other than her juicy mouth, she was going to know exactly what he was thinking. He was intuitive enough to recognize she wasn't the kind of girl who went for one-night stands.

And he wasn't the kind of man who sweet-talked a woman into doing something she'd regret.

Exactly what he did want wasn't entirely clear, but he sure wanted something.

Her.

He brushed his cheek across the top of her head, the light touch sending shockwaves of awareness through him. Yes, he wanted to know her in every sense. He'd always been the kind of person who'd known what he wanted and had gone after whatever that might be. He wanted Trinity with an intensity that made his head spin.

"How long have you been a nurse?"

Tilting her head back, she blinked her big brown eyes at him. Most of the women he knew would have had make-up accenting their large almond shape, would have made the most of the naturally thick lashes rimming her lids to lure some unsuspecting man into her snare. Not Trinity. As best he could tell, Trinity had nothing on her face except the light sprinkling of freckles across her nose and a little mascara coating those already long lashes. Her hair was clipped back with loose springs, framing her heart-shaped face. She looked as if she could be sweet sixteen.

"Trinity?"

Her beautiful face had become pinched, as if she were troubled by his question. "Long enough that I know about men like you."

Her instant defensiveness confused him. "Men like me?"

"You shouldn't get ideas about me." Her face flushed a pretty shade of pink, but she held his gaze. "I'm just here to dance, nothing more."

Riley liked the spunk shining on her upward-tilted face and had to fight the urge to kiss her mouth again.

"You shouldn't get ideas about me," he warned. "I'm simply making conversation with the beautiful woman I'm dancing with. Nothing more."

Her gaze narrowed. He grinned. After a moment she sighed in resignation. "Fine. You win." A sly smile slid onto her mouth. "This round."

He looked forward to future rounds. "And?"

"I've been a nurse for four years," she admitted, as if giving away some top secret. That would likely make her around twenty-six.

"Where did you nurse prior to coming to work for Pensacola?"

She tensed in his arms and stopped moving. "You don't have to play Twenty Questions or even make conversation at all. For the record, I'm a girl who appreciates silence in a man."

Riley chuckled. Oh, yeah, he liked this woman. "Shut up and dance, eh?"

She nodded.

"Problem is, I want to know more about you." Lots more. "Where did you nurse prior to coming to Pensacola?"

She sighed. "How about I save us a lot of time and send you a copy of my résumé?"

He stared at her stubborn expression.

"Oh, all right," she relented, and pushed his chest, motioning for him to start dancing again. "I went to school at University of Tennessee in Memphis and went straight to work at one of the hospitals there. I worked in the cardiac unit until I took the job here in Pensacola."

"Now, was that really so painful?"

"Excruciating." But a smile played on her lips. He

really liked her smile. And the sparkle of gold in her brown eyes.

"Now, be quiet and dance."

He laughed at her order. Talking with her was like a breath of fresh air. Stimulating. Fun.

"I have a friend who went to medical school in Memphis. He says it's a great place. What brought you to Pensacola? Family?"

With a look of what he hoped was feigned annoyance that he hadn't taken her order of silence seriously, she shook her head.

"Friends?" he persisted, despite her glare.

"Nope," she answered after a moment's hesitation.

The music picked up tempo. When she went to pull back he tightened his hold. "Boyfriend?"

"Ha. Exact opposite."

No hesitation there. He frowned. "You have someone in Memphis?"

"Not any more."

There was enough sadness—or was it regret?—in her voice that he felt a little guilty at just how much relief flowed through him at her denial.

"I'm glad there's not someone waiting for you in Memphis. Or anywhere else, for that matter." Because he hadn't liked the thought that she might belong to someone else. "Very glad."

For the first time since they'd started dancing she mis-stepped and caught his toe. "Sorry. I didn't mean to hurt you."

"You didn't," he assured her, thinking that as petite as she was she could stand on his toes and not hurt him. She was like a pixie. A curvy pixie. He couldn't recall ever having the urges that rushed through him when he looked at Trinity. There was something about her. Something intriguing that had him hooked. Was it just that she wasn't the type of yes-girl he was used to? "Recent break-up?"

She gave an ironic laugh and shook her head. "Forever ago. If you insist on talking, let's talk about something else. Anything else."

As much as he'd like to know more so he could understand what made her tick, Riley didn't push. Instead, he loosened his hold and caught her unawares by spinning her out and back to him. "Fine, we'll save the talking for later and dance now," he told her as he caught her.

Looking more than a little relieved, she smiled, then caught him unawares by dipping backwards in his arms and laughed as if she'd been set free. "Deal."

Trinity felt light-headed. Giddy almost. Despite her boisterous claim about her dancing skills, she stepped on Riley's toes more than once. He didn't seem to mind, just kept smiling at her and making silly little comments that made her laugh.

For once she relaxed enough to just enjoy the music, to let loose and move to the beat even if she looked ridiculous. Something about the way Riley looked at her, the way every bit of his attention was focused solely on her, boosted her confidence and let free her love of music.

Riley. He smelled so good. Spicy. Musky. Heavenly.

Her gaze dropped to his lips.

Somewhere in her brain she registered that something was wrong with her thought processes, that she wasn't thinking clearly. Still, she licked her lips, wondering if the flavor of him lingered there from his impromptu kiss. *She wanted to taste him again.*

"You're killing me, princess."

"Princess?" Had anyone ever called her princess? *And had she really just giggled?*

A kiss under the mistletoe and a few fancy steps to one of their coworker's karaoke singing "Rocking Around the Christmas Tree" and she'd morphed into someone she didn't even recognize. Who knew that pretending to be the life of the party could be so much fun?

"Well, you have me royally torn up so, yeah, princess." He grinned, his gaze going to her just-moistened lips. "Don't tease me, Trinity."

He'd said her name. She liked him saying her name. Her cloudy mind registered that she hadn't officially introduced herself. "I'm Trinity, by the way." Which seemed a really dumb thing to say as he'd called her by her name repeatedly. She grimaced at her lapse and wondered what was wrong with her brain.

He smiled indulgently at her. "Trinity Warren. I know."

"How?"

"I asked about you before I came over."

She blinked, wondering if she'd misheard. "You did? Why?"

His hand pressed against her lower back. "I wanted to know more. I've never dated a woman who works at the hospital. Too messy."

"Dated a woman who works…" Was he saying he wanted to date her? Or just letting her know that he didn't date women at the hospital so she wouldn't take any of tonight the wrong way?

"Messy?" she prompted, then added, "Not that I'd date you."

He grinned at her comment. "I am going to prove you wrong but, yes, messy. If things don't work out, there's a mess to deal with when the two people involved work at the same place."

"Ha. Tell me something I don't know." She was an expert on that particular mess. Chase had worked as the IT manager for the hospital where she'd worked in Memphis. She knew all about dealing with messes. Especially when he'd made their break-up so public.

"You'll have to explain that comment," Riley commented close to her ear.

"Not likely." Because she had no intention of ever telling anyone in Pensacola of her humiliation. She'd come to forget things, not to rehash them.

His hold at her waist tightened a fraction. "You're a really private person, aren't you?"

None of her personal business had been private in Memphis. Chase had dumped her for another woman in front of the whole Christmas party. He'd been drunk and had… She grimaced, not letting the memories take hold. "Generally, I prefer to blend in than be center stage. If that means I'm a really private person, you're right."

He pulled back enough to stare into her face. "Funny, because when I look at you I can't picture you anywhere but center stage."

His kind words sounded so sincere that her knees threatened to buckle. She wanted to throw her arms around his neck and…actually, her arms *were* around his neck. She leaned closer, breathed in his musky scent.

He pulled back, stared into her eyes. "You're a leading lady, Trinity. You could never blend into the background."

Heat infused her face and she started to point out that earlier tonight she'd blended in quite well until he'd made an entrance into her life. Now lots of people were looking at her and trying to figure out why he was dancing with her. Didn't they know? Tonight she was the life of the party. Tomorrow she'd go back to the real world.

"You're smooth with the lines, Casanova."

His hand moved across her lower back, holding her close. "No Casanova and no lines. Honest. I'm just telling you the truth. You're a beautiful woman."

"I think you're a player."

"You think wrong."

The woman's comment about her being tonight's lucky pick ran through her mind. "You're telling me you're as pure as snow?" She gave him a skeptical look. "I'm not buying it."

"Not sure how pure snow is these days but no one would label me as pure anyway other than my mother, who thinks I hung the moon, of course." He winked.

Trinity rolled her eyes. "Okay, snowflake."

Her nickname obviously caught him off guard and he stared at her a moment then shook his head, laughter shining in his eyes. "I enjoy spending time with the opposite sex and I'm no saint, but you can call me 'Snowflake' if you want to. But for the record, I don't say things I don't mean."

"No red-blooded man ever does."

"Suspicious little thing, aren't you?" He grinned. "Fortunately, I'm an open book and you don't have a quiz in the morning. So how about for the rest of the night you don't analyze this and just enjoy yourself?"

"With you?"

He tightened his hold at her waist. "That was the idea. I'd be very disappointed if you left me to enjoy yourself with someone else."

Despite her uncertainty, the giddy feeling was still inside her so she just shrugged as if she couldn't care less one way or the other. "So long as you don't suggest we sing karaoke."

That naughty look twinkled as brightly as the colored lights adorning the Christmas tree in the corner of the ballroom. "Too bad, because my number is coming up two songs from now and I plan on you joining me."

"You plan wrong."

He reached into his dress pants pocket and pulled out a slip of paper. "Due to the time constraints, the Christmas committee had interested parties draw numbers earlier this evening." He waggled his brows. "This interested party got a winning number."

"I'd ask if you ever don't win, but having to get up in front of all these people and sing doesn't sound like a prize." Grimacing, she glanced at the duo currently belting out a number. "Not a good one, at any rate."

He laughed and touched his finger to her nose. "You're funny, Trinity. I like that."

"Not really." She wasn't funny. She hadn't been since…since Chase had broken her heart and she'd withdrawn into her shell, trying to protect her tender inside.

Why had she done that? Why had she let him steal so much from her? Why was she still letting him steal so much of her life? For goodness' sake, she had moved to a beach town because she'd assumed the locals wouldn't put so much emphasis on a holiday associated with snow. Pathetic.

"Fine, I'll sing with you, but just to warn you, I'm an even better singer than I am dancer and we both know how I excel at that." She stepped on his toes, hard, to prove her point.

"My ears can hardly wait." He grinned down at her. "Like I said, fun girl."

CHAPTER THREE

TRINITY'S HEAD HURT. Not just a little. Her mouth felt as if something had crawled inside and died. Her stomach warned she might just upchuck.

She rarely ever got full-blown, miserable sick, but this morning she just felt bleh. Thank goodness she wasn't scheduled to go into work today, just to take call. Maybe she'd get lucky and her phone wouldn't ring.

Digging deeper beneath her covers, she groaned and snuggled up next to the warm body beside her.

Warm body? Hello. There wasn't supposed to be a warm body in her bed!

"Good morning, sleeping beauty," an unexpected voice broke into her haze.

An unexpected and very male voice.

A voice she immediately recognized, even though she'd only met him the night before. Why was he rambling on about sleeping beauty being a princess and her looking like one? Right. Because, like all fairy princesses, her hair and make-up remained perfect while she slept. *Not.*

She twisted to look at him. "Riley."

"You were expecting someone else?" A lazy brow rose beneath sleep-tousled hair and he looked way too sexy for first thing in the morning. Apparently fairy princes really did remain perfect while sleeping.

She was in bed. Her bed. Between the covers. With Riley. Her heart pounded against her ribcage. Not good. She scooted away from his warmth until she reached a cold spot on the sheet. Too bad half her butt was now hanging off the edge of the bed.

"I wasn't expecting anyone." Her words came out half-croak, half-cry.

Pulling the covers tighter around her, she tried to register the fact that she was in bed with Dr. Riley Williams. Even more confusing, she tried to remember how she'd gotten there. How he'd gotten there.

"What are you doing here? You shouldn't be here."

He shouldn't. She barely knew him. She didn't do one-nighters. Not ever. She didn't do anything. Not before or after Chase.

At her accusing tone, Riley's grin slipped. "You asked me to stay."

That threw her. "I did?"

"You did." His confident tone and coolly assessing blue gaze brooked no denial.

She'd asked him to stay. They were in her bed. Although her black dress was gone, as were her hose, she still wore her panties. But no bra.

In bed with a sexy cardiologist with nothing on but her granny panties. Awesome.

She closed her eyes, took a deep breath and asked the twenty-million dollar question that kept echoing through her throbbing head.

"What did we do?" She sounded accusatory again, but she wasn't able to control the rising panic within her.

What had she done? She'd finally broken away from

the chains that had bound her to Memphis, had moved to Pensacola to make a fresh start, and she'd ended up in bed with the first man she'd stood under mistletoe with? How could she?

Christmas.

It was the blasted holiday that wreaked havoc in her life. Always had. Always would. She really should go to some remote location every December and not come home until well after New Year. If only.

Riley had the nerve to look offended. "You don't remember last night? Our coming here? What we did after we got here?"

"If I remembered, would I be asking?" Really, she'd thought him smarter than that. Or maybe she was just cranky because a thousand things were running through her mind and not one of them good. "Did we have sex?" she demanded, while her throat still worked because, seriously, the tissue threatened to swell shut any moment.

From where Riley lay next to her, he stared, not saying anything at first, just watching, making her wish she could pull the covers over her head, making her wish her stomach didn't churn.

"I can assure you—" confidence and perhaps annoyance oozed from his words "—that had we had sex, you'd not only remember, you'd have woken up with a smile on your face and not that look of horror."

Face aflame, relief flooded her, as did curiosity because sex up to that point in her life hadn't been that memorable. There had just been Chase but, still, she had been practically engaged to the man. Sadly, she had never woken up with a smile on her face. Quite the opposite. So maybe Riley thought she'd remember if they'd had sex, but maybe she wouldn't have remembered. Maybe she just hadn't been impressed and had blocked the experience from her mind.

"You're saying we didn't, um, you know?"

Cool amusement at her lack of ability to say the actual words shone in his eyes. "We didn't have sexual intercourse last night, if that's what you are attempting to ask."

No sexual intercourse. His tone mocked her question but, come on, they were in bed and she was only in her skivvies. Which meant that they had done something, right? The way he was looking at her said they'd done something. But what?

Letting her gaze run over his face, his lips, the strong line of his jaw, his throat, his bare shoulders, his chest, his... She gulped. Had she touched him? Kissed him? Run her fingers over those broad shoulders? Those washboard abs? Had she seen him naked? Face afire, she glanced back up, met his gaze, and winced. He so knew what she was thinking and he liked it.

An inferno burned her cheeks.

"Riley, I..." She pulled the covers even tighter around her, holding on in case the material got a sudden urge to slip below her neck and put her chest and abs on display for his inspection. No washboard anywhere in sight at her midsection. More like a laundry basket. Taking a deep breath, she tried to pull her thoughts together and away from their bodies. "I don't do this."

"This?" His face was unreadable, his eyes dark. She didn't like the look and found herself wishing things were different. That she was different. That she could have woken up in bed with him and not freaked out but reveled in a night full of passion. That she really had woken up with a smile. That she could have been good enough that he could have woken up with a smile. That instead of lashing out at him with accusatory questions she could have teased him awake with kisses and had a morning full of passion.

A morning she'd remember always.

A morning he'd always remember.

A morning that would leave them both exhausted and smiling.

But that wasn't her. She was a woman who disliked Christmas, disliked men, was terrible at sex, and although she'd come to Pensacola to forget her past, she could only handle confronting one hang-up at a time. She seriously had her work cut out for her even with that.

"What is it that you don't do?" Riley prompted when she failed to elaborate.

Everything. She sighed, took a deep breath and went for broke.

"Wake up in bed with a man and not remember how I got here and what we did while here." She grimaced. She sounded horrible. Waking up next to him was horrible. He probably thought she was horrible—in bed and out of it. "I don't do that. Ever."

"I just told you, we didn't do anything, not really. We ended up here because I drove you home from the Christmas party and you invited me in. And, although there's another bedroom, there is no bed."

Which meant he must have at least considered sleeping elsewhere.

"I wasn't doing the floor," he said matter-of-factly, "and I'm too tall to comfortably sleep on your girly sofa."

She did have a girly sofa. A plush Victorian piece

that she loved because it had been the first piece of furniture she'd ever bought for herself, but it really wasn't that comfy. Not that comfort mattered so much, because she never had company or spent much time there.

Trying to recall the previous night's events, she closed her eyes, thought back. The Christmas party. She'd danced with Riley, sung one silly reindeer song with him, celebrated that he'd won one of the door prizes when random names had been drawn from a stocking, then they'd left. He'd driven her home. They'd walked into her house and then he'd kissed her. No mistletoe required. Just a simple good-night kiss that had somehow morphed into something more, something hotter, something that hadn't been simple at all.

Wow, if his kiss had been that amazing she might have really woken up with a smile had they had sex. Then again, had they had sex he'd know how lame her lovemaking actually was.

Her panties weren't the only thing she was wearing.

She reached up, touched the door prize he'd won and given to her. "You won this."

He shrugged, causing the covers to slip a little lower at his waist. "I gave it to you."

He'd taken the pearl necklace out of the velvet box and fastened it around her neck. There had been something mesmerizing about him putting the necklace on her. Something erotic and gentle and totally captivating.

Kind of like his abs.

No wonder she'd asked him to stay. He'd been the perfect date.

Only they hadn't been on a date.

"You can have it back if you want it," she offered, in case he regretted having given her the piece. Maybe he'd expected bodily payment for the beads. Ha, had they been out of a gumball machine he might have gotten his money's worth, but that's about it if Chase's claims about her skills could be believed.

Riley's brows formed a V. "Why would I want them back? Don't you like the necklace?"

"It's lovely."

"Not nearly as lovely as you are."

He was smooth with the lines. Too smooth perhaps. She swallowed.

"You told me I was beautiful last night."

Actually, he'd repeated the compliment several times.

"You were." His eyes bored into hers. She didn't have to be looking directly at him to feel his stare. He stirred beneath the covers, but he didn't reach for her. Somehow she knew he wanted to.

"You are," he continued. "Very beautiful."

Last night, in her haze, he'd made her feel beautiful. Like the most beautiful woman in the world. This morning she felt like a woman who'd gone to bed without washing her face or brushing her teeth. She was rank and knew it.

"Why would you say that?"

"Because it's true."

The sincerity in his voice told her that he was either the world's greatest liar or he believed what he said. Maybe he really did have fantastic blue contact lenses and they were blurred with sleep, leaving him blinded to the truth.

Making sure to keep the covers pulled over her almost bare body, she rolled over to face him directly. She could feel his body heat, could feel the magnetic pull of him. She wanted to touch. Really really wanted to touch. His sheer physical perfection robbed her of thought. Or maybe it was his bare chest that made her brain waves frazzle. He was the one who was beautiful. Eye-poppingly, mouth-wateringly, finger-itchingly, body-twitchingly beautiful.

It occurred to her that the happy trail leading beneath the covers didn't appear to have anything material impeding its path. At least she was wearing underwear.

No sexual intercourse, he'd said. That left a lot of possibilities. Oh, my.

"What happened to your clothes?" she choked out, more and more flustered that he was naked in her bed.

Although she recalled the removal of her clothes, she didn't recall how he'd gone from fully dressed to whatever he still wore beneath her covers.

He was wearing something. *Wasn't he? Just because she couldn't see any outlines, it didn't mean boxers or cotton briefs weren't there, right?*

His eyes glittered. "You don't recall ripping them off me with your teeth, princess?"

She'd taken them off him? With her teeth? Her jaw dropped then clamped shut in case her teeth got any fresh ideas.

"Okay, it was bad of me to tease you." His grin turned devilish. "You didn't use your teeth."

She'd... She closed her eyes and tried to recall the events of the night before. "We had sex, didn't we?"

"I already told you that we didn't have sex." He sounded annoyed that she'd asked again, that she hadn't taken him at his word.

Unable to resist a moment longer, she reached out beneath the covers to touch his chest. His bare chest. To see if the feel of his skin was familiar, to see if touching him would cause a rush of memories.

"Then why are we naked in my bed?"

"I wasn't planning to spend the night anywhere so I hadn't packed any pajamas…not that I normally wear anything to bed. But I'm not naked. I'm wearing boxers and would be happy to show you if you'd like proof." He covered her hand with his, brushed his thumb across her skin. "Besides, you looked as if you needed me to stay. My guess is that you don't drink often."

Still reeling from his offer to show her his underwear and just how tempted she was to take him up on that offer, she focused on the other part of what he'd said. "I don't drink at all and I didn't drink anything last night except fruit punch."

"That was rum punch you were drinking, Trinity. It had alcohol in it."

"The punch was…but…" Hadn't she felt funny? Hadn't she noticed that the more she'd drunk the less nervous she'd been? *Dear Lord.* "I was punch drunk."

Looking as if he wanted to laugh, he just grinned. "You were a bit inebriated but no worries, you were a cute drunk."

A cute drunk. As if such a creature existed. No one was a cute drunk. At least no one Trinity had ever had the misfortune of seeing drunk. Her mother had certainly never been cute. Chase had not been cute.

"I didn't know there was alcohol in the punch."

"It's okay, princess." His thumb paused and he gave her a sympathetic smile. "I figured out that you weren't at a hundred percent. That's why nothing happened."

She tried again to remember the events of the night

before, but only bits and pieces came back to her. "You wanted something to happen?"

He gave her a look that questioned if she had really asked that. "Of course I wanted something to happen."

"Why?"

He laughed but the sound came out a little stilted. "That's a question with a very obvious answer."

"Because you're a guy?"

"Despite what the female population may believe, not every guy wants sex to the point of doing so with any willing woman."

Which meant she'd been willing but he hadn't been. Urgh. What was she thinking? Of course she'd been willing. The man was hot and got under her skin to probe places she'd rather keep locked away. She'd been under the influence to where her fears wouldn't have come into play to remind her of yet another reason why she should keep her legs closed.

"I'm confused. You wanted something to happen, but even though I was willing, nothing happened?" Even as she said the words, the reality that they were almost naked, lying in her bed, hit her. That he could have taken advantage of her and he hadn't. She liked that. A lot. Possibly because most of the men in her life had taken advantage at every opportunity presented. Not sexually, necessarily, but in any other way they could.

Riley made a sound that she wasn't sure was a low laugh or a growl. "Yes, princess, I wanted something to happen. A lot of somethings. Had you been sober, this morning would have been very different."

She didn't doubt that the morning would have been different. Had they had sex, he probably would have snuck out at some point during the night. Or perhaps he wouldn't have bothered to sneak, he'd have just gone, and left her to her non-sexual self. She knew her strengths and weaknesses and if she hadn't, Chase had done a really bang-up job of pointing them out to her and anyone else who had cared to listen. Sexual prowess wasn't in her bag of tricks.

"I'm sorry."

"I don't want you to be sorry," he surprised her by saying. "What I want is to see you smile."

She bared her teeth in a semblance of a smile because, really, he deserved a smile. He was unlike any man she'd ever known and that made her want to know more…and terrified her, too.

"Not exactly what I had in mind, but it's a start." He smiled so warmly at her that the nausea within her actually eased. "Now, the most pressing question is whether you have any food in this joint so I can cook us something or would you like to go out for breakfast? I'm starved."

In reality they did neither. Not long after she'd draped the comforter around her shoulders and rushed into her bathroom to clean up her mess of a face, he tapped on the door.

She cracked the door open to peer at him. He was fully dressed in his clothes from the night before.

"I've got to head to the hospital. I'm on call today, and they've had several chest pains come into the emergency room. Apparently the cath lab is a madhouse. Dr. Stanley is going to be tied up there for some time and there are two more chest pains on their way by ambulance."

Trying not to look too disappointed that whatever

their morning had been going to bring had been interrupted, she nodded. "I understand."

Apparently she didn't do such a good job at hiding
her doubts.

He tilted her chin toward him so he could fully see
her face. "For whatever it's worth, I don't want to go."

His fingers on her face were so warm, so tender that
she sucked in her breath. "What is it you want?"

"To spend the day with you. Maybe help you drag
out your Christmas decorations because your apartment
is sadly lacking in Christmas spirit. Or, for that matter, we could decorate my tree. It's been delivered, but
I haven't had a chance to trim and decorate it."

He had a live Christmas tree? Who did that in these
days of commercialized Christmas? Not that she'd be
doing either of his suggestions. She'd had her fill of
Christmas spirit the night before and preferred to stick
her head in the ground until the season passed. Just look
what happened when she tried to get into the spirit of
things. She'd ended up drunk and waking in bed with
a man she barely knew. No, thank you.

"Honestly, what we did wouldn't matter so much just
as long as I got to spend some time with you."

From somewhere in her bedroom her cellphone
started buzzing.

"If that's who I think it is, you'll probably get your
wish. I'm on call today, too, and if you've been called
in, I'm likely to be as well," she mused, pulling her
robe tight around her while she dashed toward where
her phone had ended up the night before.

"The hospital?" he asked the moment she disconnected the call.

She nodded.

"Maybe the chest pains will end up gastro related rather than cardiac and we won't have to stay long. We could grab lunch," he suggested.

"Maybe," she replied, dropping the phone back into the small black evening bag she'd carried the night before.

"Trinity?"

She glanced towards him.

"I like you."

She wasn't sure what to say.

"I'd like to see you again."

Was he a glutton for punishment or what?

"Despite whatever impression I gave you last night, I'm really quite boring," she said, wondering if she should also warn him about how much baggage she carried. The airport's claim area had nothing on her.

"I don't believe you."

"You should," she warned. "I've known me a lot longer than you have."

He laughed then glanced at his watch. "I could never be bored around you, funny girl. Unfortunately, I have to get moving and your car is still at the hotel where the Christmas party was held. You'll have to ride with me to the hospital so get hopping. We have lives to save."

"Sure thing, snowflake."

CHAPTER FOUR

ALTHOUGH RILEY HADN'T been on the schedule, he still spent most of the day at the hospital.

Fortunately, so did Trinity.

He'd been able to easily maneuver her into the cardiac lab with him. Right or wrong, he wanted her near him. The panic he'd seen in her eyes that morning worried him. Plus, she was going to need a ride to pick up her car at the end of her shift. He was way too smart to miss out on the opportunity to play white knight and give her a lift.

Doug Ryker, a fifty-three-year-old, had woken up with chest pain that had increased as the sun had come up. When he'd started clutching his chest, his wife had called 911. An ambulance had brought him to the emergency room. His cardiac enzymes had been elevated and, at the minimum, he'd needed an arteriogram.

That's where Riley came in.

He'd met the gentleman's family very briefly while the patient was being prepped. Now Riley was scrubbed and ready to proceed. Trinity was his nurse.

He stole a look at her. If she noticed, she ignored him and focused on their patient.

Too bad there wasn't a sprig of mistletoe around because he'd love to pull down her mask and kiss those plump lips of hers. Did she remember their kiss beneath the mistletoe or had she blocked it from her mind along with the rest of the night? Just how much did she remember about their evening together?

'Twas the season for good tidings and cheer. Riley couldn't think of anything that would cheer him more this Christmas than getting to know the lovely woman he'd spent the night holding and had developed a fascination for that he couldn't quite explain, much less understand. Maybe it really was the season?

He loved Christmas, everything about it. The sounds, the smells, the spirit of giving, all of it. If someone popped a bow on top of Trinity's head and set her beneath his tree to unwrap, he'd be a very happy man.

He glanced over at the angel monitoring Mr. Ryker's vital signs.

She caught him looking. Instant hot pink tinged what he could see of her upper cheeks peeking out from behind her surgical face mask. He winked and her color deepened.

Something warm and fuzzy, like the smell of cookies baking, filled him. Something that just made him feel…happy.

Odd that the feeling felt strange, because he couldn't think of anyone he'd label as happier than him. He was totally happy go lucky. Yet he couldn't deny that the feeling felt alien.

And addictive because already he knew he'd want more when the feeling waned.

Maybe everything would go well with Mr. Ryker's arteriogram and the man wouldn't need anything beyond a few stents. Then, Lord willing, Riley would ask Trinity to go to a late lunch.

"Vitals are good," she said, probably more just to say something rather than to actually inform him.

After she'd prepped Mr. Ryker's groin, Riley numbed the area with an anesthetic and made a penciltip-sized incision. Carefully, he threaded the cardiac catheter through the femoral artery and up into Mr. Ryker's heart.

Mr. Ryker's elevated enzymes had already conveyed that there was cardiac tissue not getting proper perfusion. Riley had hoped he'd find a single small blockage that could be fixed easily with a stent to restore blood flow. He found much more than that. Unfortunately.

Mr. Ryker's mammary artery had a large area of calcification and stenosis. Plus, there were other areas of calcification scattered throughout the arteries. Riley carefully positioned the catheter tip and placed a stent, then another, corrected the blockages that he could via an artificial material holding the artery open. Unfortunately, the stents weren't nearly enough to restore blood flow to the tissue. He withdrew the catheter.

"He's going to need a coronary artery bypass graft," he told another nurse, while Trinity applied pressure to where the catheter had been withdrawn. "Find an available vascular surgeon stat and let's get Mr. Ryker into the operating room."

So much for taking Trinity out to eat any time soon. They'd be here for several hours yet.

Trinity wasn't sure how she'd gone from being in the catheter lab to the operating room as that wasn't usual protocol. At least, it hadn't been standard at the hospital where she'd worked in Memphis, but there she was. In the operating room. With Riley.

She was working as his assistant and blowing CO_2 into Mr. Ryker's open chest. That helped keep blood from interfering with Riley being able to readily see where he was making the anastomosis in the mammary artery to loop the vessel into the right coronary artery. While keeping the CO_2 blowing at just the correct angle, she watched him carefully cut away a pedicule and reroute the artery. Painstakingly, he sutured the arteries together, making sure not to damage the vessels.

Another nurse dabbed at his forehead. Trinity found herself wishing she was the one touching him. Silly really. They were at the hospital. Working to save a man's life. Touching the cardiac surgeon while he performed a procedure should be the absolute last thing on her mind.

She'd touched him the night before.

On the lips under the mistletoe and again on the dance floor and again this morning when she'd reached out to touch his magnificent chest. Who knew where else she'd touched him during the night? After all, she'd woken up spooned against that long, lean body of his.

She swallowed back the knot forming in her throat and refocused her attention on the CO_2.

After what seemed like hours she snuck a peek. His blue eyes, which were normally so full of mischief, were focused intently on the job at hand, on how he meticulously placed sutures, making sure the vessel remained patent, that every movement of his hands were precise.

He'd been full of fun and teasing the night before, and even this morning. Now he was as serious as serious could be. Which one was the real him? The mischievous player who'd stolen a kiss from her under the mistletoe or the brilliant, intense heart surgeon attempting to save his patient's life?

"How late do you have to stay?" Riley asked Trinity later that day, hoping she wouldn't have to pull a full shift.

"I'm not sure. If nothing else has come into the emergency room, I expect the charge nurse will let me go soon." She gave him a suspicious look. "Why? Do you need me to help you with something? Another procedure?"

"I do need your help with something. Have dinner with me."

Her brow lifted. "You need help with dinner?"

"I'll be lonely if you don't join me."

"I seriously doubt you're ever lonely."

He thought about her comment. He couldn't really say that he recalled ever being lonely. He had a full life that he enjoyed a great deal, but the thought of not spending the evening with Trinity, as crazy as it was, did leave him feeling oddly bereft. "You might be surprised."

"I don't think going to dinner together is a good idea."

Why had he known she'd refuse? "Because of last night?"

Her cheeks blushed a rosy pink and she shook her head.

"No?" One eyebrow rose. "Because you don't want to encourage an incorrigible bloke like me?"

Looking torn, she took a step back. "That's not it."

He waggled his brows. "Then you *do* want to encourage an incorrigible bloke like me?"

If her cheeks had been pink before, now they were blood red. "You are incorrigible, but…"

He took her hands in his. "Then you'll help me?"

"You don't understand."

"You have other plans?"

"No, but—"

"No worries, I'll let you choose where we go. I'll even splurge for dessert."

"I don't want dessert."

He shrugged. "Okay, I'm easy. No dessert for you. If you're nice I'll share mine, though."

She let out a long breath. "You really are incorrigible."

He wouldn't deny it.

"What time should I pick you up? You need a ride to your car and it's my responsibility to get you there."

"I'm not your responsibility."

He studied her a moment then rubbed his knuckles across her cheeks. "We're talking dinner and a ride to your car, Trinity, not for ever. Smile and say, 'Thank you, I'd love to go to dinner with you, Riley.'"

Her face screwed up with doubts, she bared her teeth. "Thank you. I'd love to go to dinner with you, Riley."

He laughed and tweaked her nose. "Atta girl."

How had Riley finagled Trinity into doing this?

Going to the hospital Christmas party one night and going on a dinner date the next was just too much for her bah-humbug to digest.

Oh, yeah, she didn't have her car, she justified to herself.

"Jingle-bells, jingle bells," he sang, looking way too

amazing in his jeans and lightweight sweater as he maneuvered through traffic.

Urgh. The only thing worse would be if he was wearing an ugly Christmas sweater.

He glanced her way and grinned. "Penny for your thoughts."

"You don't want them."

"Sure I do."

"I was imagining you in an ugly Christmas sweater. I bet you have a closet full."

Laughing, he arched one brow. "Ugly Christmas sweater?"

"You know, the ones that sport more decorations than a department store."

"Oh, those ugly Christmas sweaters." He grinned. "I might have a few prime specimens tucked away from years past. You wanna borrow one, or are you just making your Christmas gift request?"

"Hardly." But she ruined the effect by laughing at the thought that he might really have a few. Surely not. Covering his shoulders and chest with a knit sweater with sparkly dangly things all over it would be awful.

"Speaking of department stores, do you mind if we swing by and pick up a few strands of lights for my tree before we go eat? I should have grabbed some last week but didn't realize mine were shot at the time."

She bit the inside of her lip. He'd been so kind to her that could she say no?

"I guess that would be okay."

Not really, but maybe she could sit in the car to avoid the hustle and bustle. If he insisted on her going inside the store, she could surely find a happy place in her mind somewhere for however long it took him to get his lights.

"Don't sound so enthusiastic," he teased.

She didn't want to seem ungrateful. He'd transformed the night before into a fun memory…at least the parts she remembered had been fun. He'd not taken advantage when she'd been at his mercy. He'd been gracious and kind, offering to take her to dinner and to get her car. He made her smile. Whether she wanted to or not, she liked the man.

"Sorry, I guess I get a little cranky when I get hungry."

Pulling into a parking spot, he turned off the ignition and reached across the car to take her hand. "If it's okay, I'll do a quick run for the lights while you grab us some sandwiches from the place there." He handed her a couple of twenties and pointed to a sandwich shop. "I'll make it up to you by taking you to my place so you can help decorate my tree. Deal?"

Before she could tell him that decorating his tree would be more like punishment, he got out of the car. "I'll take a club loaded with everything…hold the onions."

A sinking feeling in her gut, Trinity watched him rush toward a seasonal store in the strip mall.

Dinner and decorating a tree? Not what she'd signed up for, but apparently what she'd be doing, all the same, with a forced smile for Riley's sake.

Trinity had to admit the sandwiches were delicious or she really had been hungrier than she'd thought. The tree decorating, well, she was still holding back her opinion on that.

Not that she enjoyed the decorating but she'd have to be blind not to appreciate the view. Standing on a stepladder, Riley leaned and made another snip from the live blue spruce tree that towered several feet over her head. After clipping a few more twigs, he inspected the tree to see if it met with his approval.

From where she stood at the bottom of the ladder, she had to admit he definitely met her visual approval. The man was hot.

"What do you think? Look good?"

Did he have a crystal ball to see into her mind or what? "Oh, yeah."

"Now, that's the enthusiasm I've wanted to see all evening. To think, if you'd had your car you'd have found some excuse to say no."

Trinity closed her eyes and winced. He'd meant the tree, not his rear end. Duh. Of course he hadn't meant his rear end.

"I did say no," she reminded him. The man was persuasive. She'd better be careful or he'd have her agreeing to dress up in a red suit and climb down a chimney proclaiming, ho, ho, ho and a merry Christmas to all.

"You have to admit this is more fun than going home alone." His forehead wrinkled as he inspected the tree and stretched to straighten a branch, giving her another great view of his rear end. "You think I need to take a little more off the top? I want this tree to look amazing when we're done."

What she thought was that no amount of trimming was going to make the tree come anywhere near to how amazing his bottom was. Someone should stick him at the top of the tree and her views on Christmas might brighten more than a little. Definitely, she could get into unwrapping his package.

Urgh. What was wrong with her? Perhaps Riley had placed a spell on her beneath the mistletoe because she'd really like him to climb down that stepladder, take her in his arms and kiss her until her lungs were so deprived of oxygen she had to pull away just to keep from losing consciousness.

Then she wanted him to kiss her some more. More. More. More.

Crazy. She wanted to be kissed right now. And not because of some silly song coming over his surround-sound system about a kid seeing momma kissing Santa either. Riley's belly could never be compared to a bowl full of jelly and the dusky five o'clock shadow gracing the strong lines of his jaw were sexy, not fluffy white tufts that would tickle her face.

"Are you hanging mistletoe?" Oops. Had she really just asked that out loud? Who needed the cozy fire that he must have also turned on to keep the room temperature comfortable? Her face had to have just sped up global warming with a single embarrassing moment.

He glanced down at her, his grin positively lethal. "Would you like me to hang mistletoe, princess?"

How did any good girl in her right mind answer that?

"Um, no, I was just wondering if you were going to, not suggesting you do so, *snowflake*. I mean, if you were going to that would be okay, but if not…" Okay, time to zip her lips because she was rambling and just fanning the flames.

The dimple in his left cheek dug deeper. "You know, I'm a traditional kind of guy so I do have mistletoe. It's in that box over by the sofa if you want to dig it out."

Just to have an excuse to move away from his gaze, she went to the plastic storage container and searched through the labeled boxes inside. When she lifted the lid off the properly labeled one she wrinkled her nose. "You insist on a live tree but have plastic mistletoe?"

"I know. A travesty." He gave a faux devastated shrug. "We should go shopping tomorrow evening to buy me the real deal."

"I wasn't hinting for an invitation."

"I didn't think you were."

"I have better things to do."

"Than to enjoy the spirit of Christmas?" He gave her a horrified look. "What could be better than that?"

"Just about anything and everything."

"Don't you like Christmas?" Obviously he found the possibility that someone might not like Christmas so absurd he didn't wait for an answer, just climbed down the ladder to survey his handiwork.

"It's not my favorite holiday," she muttered under her breath, glad that at least for the moment she didn't have to stare up at his amazing butt.

Her answer caught his attention and he glanced at her. "Which holiday is your favorite, then?"

Not that she'd ever discussed her aversion to Christmas with anyone, but no one had ever asked her which holiday was her favorite. She thought for a moment.

"New Year's Day." She blinked at the man standing right in front of her.

"Why's that? You like making resolutions no one ever keeps?"

"And people think I'm cynical?" Smiling, she shook her head. "No."

Besides, she tended to keep the few New Year's resolutions she made each year. Somehow she'd bet Riley did his best to keep any resolutions he made too. He just seemed like that kind of guy.

"After New Year is when everyone takes all their Christmas decorations down and gets on with their real life, instead of wasting a month dreaming dreams about a man in a red suit bringing them their heart's desire."

"Ouch." He placed his hand over his heart and took a step back as if she'd struck him a vital blow. "You're a mean one, Miss Gr—"

She held up her hand and squinted at him. "Don't you call me names, snowflake." She tossed a loose piece of mistletoe at him, smiling when he easily caught it and blew her a kiss.

She puckered up and kissed the air. Electricity sizzled between them and she clung to their conversation to keep her mind away from just how much she wanted to feel his lips against hers for real. "Not liking this superficial holiday that's a bunch of marketing hype to get people to spend money that they don't have does not make me a bad person…or a green one."

His lips twitched, as if he knew what she was doing, as if his lips had a few wants of their own. "Agreed, but I'd really like to know why someone who's as sweet as you wouldn't like the most wonderful time of year."

"First off, whether or not Christmas is the most wonderful time of the year is a matter of opinion." Was he moving closer or was she imagining that the distance between them was shrinking? Oh, please, let the distance be shrinking because if he didn't kiss her soon, she might just bury herself in mistletoe and present herself to him. "Obviously," she continued, as if her heart wasn't pounding in her chest, as if every cell within her didn't leap toward him, "I am not of that opinion."

"Second?" He'd definitely moved closer. A lot closer. She could feel his body heat, could feel his breath brush across her lips, could smell his musky male scent that sent her senses into hyperdrive.

"Second..." she stared into his eyes, her lips parted, her pulse throbbing "...you don't know me well enough to know how sweet I may or may not be."

"I disagree." He covered her mouth with his, moved his lips in a caress that was teasing, tasting, erotic and sensual. Hot and demanding. Everything she'd just been longing for. Him. His kiss made her feel as if someone had strung lights on her and she twinkled from the inside out.

"Oh, yeah, you're sweet," he whispered against her lips when he pulled back. "Sweet as candy canes and gumdrops."

"Right," was all she could manage, because what she really wanted was to pull his mouth back to hers. Desperately she wanted another kiss, wanted him. That terrified her. "Let's get this tree decorated so I can go home."

After a brief pause, in which he studied her, Riley threw his head back in laughter. "You know, princess, if I didn't know any better, I'd think you like me even less than you profess to like Christmas."

"Good thing you know better, then, eh?" she retorted, handing him one of the new strings of lights. "Get to hanging or I'm out of here."

Because at the moment she was having a difficult time recalling all the reasons she shouldn't want him and needed not to trust in him.

"Yes, ma'am." With a wicked gleam in his eyes he reached for the mistletoe and went to hold it above her head. "I'll start with your favorite decoration."

"No!" But she ruined her denial by having to suppress a laugh. She pointed to the tree. "Decorate."

He gave an exaggerated sigh. "I didn't know you were such a slavedriver."

She gave him the sternest look she could muster when he looked so darned cute and remorseful with his mistletoe. "Like I said, there are a lot of things about me you don't know."

"Yet," he clarified, with what she was quickly realizing was his usual optimism. Or was stubbornness a better label? "Don't worry," he continued. "I plan to know everything there is to know about you, princess."

Lord, she hoped not. She'd come to Pensacola to escape people who knew everything there was to know about her.

"You'll be coming to me to find yourself," he added, his expression way too confident.

She hoped not on that too because she never wanted to let anyone that close ever again.

"Here, you save this for later." He tucked the loose piece of mistletoe she'd tossed at him into her scrub top pocket. "Any time you get the urge, you just wave that and I'll pucker up."

She rolled her eyes but couldn't keep her fingers away from the cheap plastic greenery in her pocket. "Like a red flag in front of a bull?"

He chuckled. "I hope I have a little more finesse than that." His brow furrowed in mock concern. "I do have more finesse than a stampeding cow, right?"

She gave a little shrug. "Maybe."

His brow rose.

"Okay," she confessed. "A little."

"I'll settle for that for now, but later we'll renegoti-ate your thoughts about my finesse."

If that meant he planned to kiss her again, she should find a reason to leave, but instead she just smiled and secretly hoped that was precisely what he meant.

Prior to placing the lights on the tree, they plugged the strands in to make sure each bulb lit up. Each one shone a brilliant color, sparkling against the tiled floor-ing. Then she held the lights while he went back up the stepladder. They worked together to string them around the tree, starting at top and working their way down.

Every time she started to enjoy herself a little too much, she reined herself in because he made her feel a little too happy, a little too comfy, and that could only lead to heartache, right? She couldn't deal with more heartache so it was much better to keep her defenses high.

Telling herself she really did not like the woodsy scent filling her nostrils and that she'd probably have a rash on her hands from handling the branches, Trinity frowned. "Why do you have such a big tree?"

He waggled his brows, covering the last of the branches with lights. "You know what they say about men with big Christmas trees."

The man was a certifiable nut. She must be too be-cause she almost giggled. So much for her defenses. "They have big trees to compensate for their wee lit-tle...minds?"

He gave her a scolding look. "I could show you my wee little mind and put that theory to rest."

"You wish," she teased, before thinking better of it.

He reached for the snap at his waist.

"Fine." She didn't bother suppressing her eye-roll but tried really hard to keep her blush in check. "Please, tell me, oh great ginormous tree owner, why is your tree so big?"

His eyes sparkled and his grin almost knocked her off her feet. "The bigger the tree, the better to light up her world."

"Her?" He hadn't brought anyone with him to the hospital Christmas party, had spent the evening with her, had spent the night afterwards in her bed and flirted outrageously with her. He'd better not have a "her".

"Your world?" he corrected, looking sheepish.

"I don't need your compensatory huge tree lighting up my world. My world is just fine the way it is."

Even as she made the bold claim, she wondered if perhaps she did because when he clicked a button and his tree sparkled to life, she had to admit, something inside her felt better. Warmer.

Lighter.

As if the button had turned on something inside her too that had been stuck in hibernation.

"Wow," she gasped, unable to quash her surprise. "I have to admit, that's beautiful."

Exactly, Riley thought, but he wasn't looking at the tree. He couldn't drag his eyes away from Trinity.

She was beautiful.

He wanted to light up her world, to see a permanent sparkle in her eyes and a smile on her lips.

Too bad he didn't have a remote control that he could click and turn her on.

To turn her on in more ways than one.

Because he was turned on.

Had been from the moment he'd first noticed her at the Christmas party. Something about her got under his skin and made his body go haywire. Big time. Was it just that instead of chasing him, like most women did, she seemed intent on keeping him at arm's length?

"Just wait until you see it after we've finished decorating," he promised. "My tree, which I refuse to label as compensatory and would still be more than happy to set the record straight once and for all, will steal your breath, guaranteed."

"I..." She glanced away then her lips tightened. "I seriously doubt that, but I do like the lights." She wasn't going to touch his offer apparently. Not that he'd really expected her to. "Let's hurry and finish."

"So you can leave?"

She met his gaze, her lips twitching lightly, letting him know she was fighting back a smile. "So I can have some of that dessert you promised but have totally failed to deliver."

"Touché." He laughed.

Yes, he really liked this woman, even if she professed not to like his favorite holiday. There had to be more to her claim than just a dislike of Christmas.

A more that he wanted to know every detail of so he could prove her wrong and show her the magic of the holidays.

CHAPTER FIVE

TRINITY DIDN'T LIKE Christmas at all and doubted she ever would. But when they'd finished decorating, she did think that Riley's Christmas tree was beautiful. Magical even.

Plus, she had concluded that she did like the woodsy pine smell filling his living room. Why had she practically gagged on the scent for the past couple of years, comparing the outdoorsy aroma to spruce-scented household cleaner?

Because she didn't like this holiday, she reminded herself.

From childhood this holiday had only ever held bad memories. Nothing good had ever come out of Christmas. Not for her.

She'd do well to remember that.

Riley's constant smiles and holiday good cheer made her forget that she didn't like a single thing about the season. Still, she was doing something to help someone who had helped her. Someone she genuinely liked and who hadn't taken advantage of her.

"Thank you."

"For?" he asked, studying her way too intently for her comfort.

She wanted to squirm, like a kid sitting on Santa's lap. "Last night."

"Nothing happened last night for you to owe me any thanks for."

Was that how he saw the night?

"Had something happened," she admitted, "I wouldn't have been thanking you."

"You might have," he teased, but when she didn't smile, he relented. "For the record, I prefer my bed partners to be sober and just as into me as I am into them. Whether or not we were going to have sex last night was never an issue."

"I wasn't into you?" That she had a hard time imagining because the man made her burn from head to toe. Even now she wanted to rip his clothes off him and lick him all over. She squeezed her eyes shut, trying to clear the image of her doing just that.

He shrugged. "We've already established that you drank a little too much."

"Did I want you?" she said, more insistently. What was she saying? Of course she'd wanted him. She still wanted him.

"You said you did."

"Oh." A vague memory of her telling him he could do whatever he wanted so long as he didn't leave her ran through her mind. Fire spread across her cheeks. She had made a complete and utter fool of herself. "I'm sorry." She turned to go, wishing her car was in his drive so she really could escape.

"I'm not." He turned her to face him. "I wanted you, Trinity. I'm not ashamed to say so."

She blushed and he grinned.

"I wasn't inebriated, except by your smile."

"I've said it before but it bears repeating, you're smooth with the lines, Riley."

"No lines," he said. "Just the truth."

"Right."

"Seriously."

"Seriously, I want that dessert now." Anything to get away from this conversation.

"Chicken," he accused, apparently reading her well enough to know exactly what she was doing.

"Bok bok, Mr. Big Tree," she replied, wondering at her sparring back and forth with him verbally when really she should be embarrassed at her out-of-character behavior.

His laugh made her feel warm inside.

"Like I said, fun girl."

"Like I said, give me dessert."

Trinity had expected Riley to insist on coming into her apartment when he'd followed her home, but he didn't. He walked her to her door, kissed her forehead, saw her inside, then left without setting foot into her place.

Go figure.

Staring at the closed door, she wanted to open it, to yell to him that he could have at least kissed her good-night properly.

'Meow.' Casper brushed up against her leg, reminding Trinity that she'd like to be fed.

"I know. I know. I rushed off this morning without paying you much attention." She glanced down at the solid white cat that she'd rescued from an animal shelter when she had been nothing more than a tiny pitiful-looking kitten.

Casper mewed again, staying practically beneath her

feet as she walked towards her small pantry to get a can of cat food. She opened the can, put the contents into Casper's dish and watched the cat dive in with gusto.

"You'd think you were starved," she teased. "But I am fully aware that Riley fed you this morning while I threw on my scrubs."

That he'd been thoughtful enough to do so had impressed her, even if she hadn't made a big deal of him having done so. The man was thoughtful all the way round. He was just a little too good to be true.

Well, all except for the not having kissed her goodnight part. That he could use some work on.

Or maybe it was her sanity that could use some work, because she shouldn't want him to kiss her. She didn't want a relationship, didn't want to set herself up for another fall, like the one Chase had delivered.

"I know you aren't starved," she informed the cat.

Casper's blue eyes cut to her for a brief second as if to say, So what?

Trinity laughed then jumped when her phone rang. She glanced at the number. It wasn't one she was familiar with, but she knew who the caller was as sure as she lived and breathed. Should she answer?

Could she not?

"Did you forget something?" she said by way of greeting, because "Hello" seemed all wrong when he had just left.

"Apparently." He sounded confused, frustrated. "I'm standing outside your front door."

Trinity's stomach flip-flopped. Had he ever left? Or had he just come back? Did it matter?

"The usual protocol when standing outside someone's door is to knock, not phone." Her heart pounding in anticipation of whatever was to come, she headed towards the front door.

"I didn't knock because I don't want to come in."

Her hand paused in the process of reaching for the doorknob. "You don't?"

Her stomach knotted. Was he playing some sick game with her? Teasing her? Toying with her emotions?

"I do, but…Trinity, tell me to go home."

If this was his idea of a game, it was cruel and twisted. She wasn't amused.

"Go home," she ordered, and meant it. She'd been hurt enough in the past. She wouldn't let someone sour her future. Not even someone who seemed as wonderful as Riley.

Then again, most of the time when something seemed too good to be true, it really was. So why was she still on the line, waiting for him to say something? Hoping he'd say something. Something brilliant and wonderful that would make her smile instead of feeling as if her eyes were about to spring a leak.

A low laugh sounded in her ears. "That was way too easy for you, princess."

"You have no idea," she muttered, wondering at the silence that followed. She wanted to tear the door off its hinges and drag him inside her apartment and demand he explain himself.

Instead, she leaned her forehead against the cold metal doorframe, wishing she could see through it to the other side, wishing she knew what he was thinking, why he was standing outside her door when she was inside, why he'd called her instead of knocking.

Why was he there at all?

Why wasn't she hanging up?

Urgh. Her head hurt with all the questions plaguing her mind.

"If I knocked, would you let me in, princess?" His voice was barely above a whisper but she heard just fine.

Her hands shook. "I guess you'll have to knock to know the answer to that question, won't you, snowflake?"

Taking a deep breath, he laughed again. "If you had any idea how much I want to rip through this door because I know you're standing just the other side..." He paused, and she'd swear she felt his forehead bump against the door. Was he trying to knock some sense into his head? How was it he kept putting her thoughts into words that came from his mouth?

"As much as I want you," he admitted, "what I want more than anything is to not mess this up."

"Knocking on my door would mess this up?" What was "this", she wanted to ask, but held her tongue. She doubted he knew any more than she did. That he admitted there was a "this" was monumental, had her brain undoing every wall she'd just attempted to erect between them. Didn't he know he should leave those walls alone? She needed them.

"It might. What if you didn't open the door?"

He had a point.

"True, but what if I did?"

Or would that be messing things up even worse?

Riley ground his forehead against the cold, hard metal of Trinity's apartment door and prayed for the knowledge to know the right thing to do.

He wanted to knock.

Whether she would admit to it or not, she wanted him to knock. He could hear it in her voice.

Every instinct warned he shouldn't, that, despite their mutual desire for one another, she wasn't ready to consummate that desire. Not really.

As much as he hated listening to that voice of reason, he trusted his instincts more than the body part that had him wanting to he-man his way into her apartment.

To do that would only satisfy him in the short term and although he had no clue exactly what he wanted with Trinity, he knew that one night would not be enough. If he rushed, she might shut him out for ever. Despite the tough front she attempted to put on, she was vulnerable in ways that made him want to fight every dragon that had ever taken a swipe at her. Although he didn't understand or like how protective he felt about her, he refused to be yet another dragon for her to fend off, even if a well-intentioned one.

"We both know you shouldn't open your door to me. Not tonight." He straightened from the door before he gave in to temptation.

"Then why did you call?" She sounded irked, which pleased him because it meant she wasn't immune to the chemistry between them. That he wasn't wrong.

"Why call?" He loved her logic and her sass. Despite the rebellious throb in his body, he couldn't help but smile. "To hear your voice. For you to tell me I'm crazy."

"You're crazy," she replied, without hesitation.

"About you," he admitted, knowing it was true, that she was different from any woman he'd ever known, and not just because she didn't fall at his feet.

Which was why he'd leave, and smile while doing so. Yeah, he'd like to be on the other side of her door but there was no rush. He'd take his time, woo her, have her begging for more, and then give her more for however long the sparks between them flew.

"You don't even know me," she insisted, much as she'd done previously.

"A problem I intend to remedy."

But not tonight.

Forehead against the door, Trinity held her breath. Surely, any second now he'd knock. He had to knock, right?

He was there.

Just on the other side of her door, teasing her. No, not teasing really. More of a temptation to reach out and take what she reluctantly admitted she wanted.

He did tempt her. Like fresh-baked cookies tempted a starving dieter.

She wanted a bite.

A big bite.

Before she could have biter's remorse, she undid the chain, undid the deadbolt and flung the door open.

"Riley?"

"Hmm?" His response buzzed in her ear.

"Where are you?" Stunned, she glanced down the hallway.

The empty hallway.

"My car."

His car?

He'd left?

Her heart sank.

"You were never really on the other side of my door?"

She might kill him. He'd gotten her all worked up for nothing, had...

"I was there."

Frowning, fighting disappointment she didn't quite understand and definitely didn't want, she went back into her apartment. She should hang up now, before she incriminated herself.

Why was she surprised? Disappointed? She should be glad he'd left, that he'd had reason when she'd temporarily lost her mind. Her stomach knotted and her eyes watered. Great.

Why was she not telling him where to go and turning off her phone?

"Trinity?"

"Yes?" She slumped back against the door, fighting a sniffle. Was he seriously whistling? She might just throw her phone at him for real.

"I like you."

Were they in grammar school or what?

Eyes squeezed closed, she sighed. "So you keep saying, but at the moment, Riley Williams, I don't like you one bit."

He surprised her by bursting into laughter. "There's my funny girl."

"Are you dating Dr. Williams?"

Putting her stethoscope into her scrub pocket, Trinity spun around to look at her coworker. Karen Mathis, Trinity's favorite coworker by far—usually—grinned at her and waited with an expectant look that said she wasn't going to be easily distracted.

"Why would you ask me that?"

"I saw you at the Christmas party," Karen pointed out. "I'd been looking for you because I knew you didn't know many people yet and I was going to have you join the group I was with. I didn't spot you until you were all cozied up with the only cardiologist on staff who makes women's hearts beat faster with just a flash of his smile."

Trinity's heart was beating pretty fast without the benefit of one of his smiles. "We just danced. It wasn't a big deal."

"And sang together," Karen reminded her. "Plus, I hear you arrived at work with him yesterday morning when you both got called in. You rode home with him yesterday at the end of your shift. Despite many females' valiant efforts, I don't know of him ever dating anyone who works here. This all sounds like a big deal to me. So, are you two an item or what?"

Inwardly, Trinity cringed. The hospital gossip mill had sure been busy. How did she answer a question she didn't know the answer to? Because saying he liked her just sounded a bit second grade to her. She didn't really know what they were other than that she liked him too.

"Did you also hear that she's going to eat with me after work tonight?"

Both women turned at the newcomer to their conversation.

"Dr. Williams." Karen's cheeks flushed almost as bright as Trinity imagined hers were.

"Riley," she gasped, her eyes devouring the man before her, searching his eyes for some trace of the man who'd spent hours on the phone with her the night before. Hours and hours. He'd blown her away. They'd talked long into the night without awkwardness or long bouts of weird silence. The man was way too easy to talk to. "Anyone ever tell you it isn't polite to eavesdrop?"

She almost called him "snowflake" but caught

herself just in time. Yeah, that would have had some tongues wagging all over the cardiac unit.

"Never. Most people like having conversations with me." He waggled his brows, his eyes not leaving Trinity's. The twinkle there said everything. That he knew what she was thinking, was thinking the same thing himself. "Good morning, ladies."

Trinity mumbled a good morning, glancing away because all she could think was that this was the man with whom she'd fallen asleep while on the phone with him the night before.

He'd stayed on the phone with her because he'd said he really did want to get to know her without the physical getting in the way. Honestly, she just didn't know what to think about him. He was unlike any many she'd ever met.

Chase sure hadn't worried about the physical getting in the way.

Sex had gotten in the way of their relationship.

Big time.

Not because they'd rushed into a physical relationship. They hadn't, despite Chase's constant pressure to do so. Perhaps she should have held out longer. When she'd finally given in, it had been the beginning of the end. She'd flopped in bed.

Chase had had no qualms announcing that juicy little tidbit to the world.

So a man who put emphasis on getting to know her rather than on her bedroom performance was good. Raised her odds of success, right? Or just set up her expectations to where her failure would sting all the more?

"Trinity?" Riley interrupted her thoughts. "We *are* going to eat after work today?"

She blinked, thinking him too good looking for his own good. He was so used to getting his own way that she almost said no just to be difficult. But that wasn't any way to start a relationship. Or to maintain one.

A relationship. Was that what they were doing? What she wanted?

"Yes," she agreed, knowing she wasn't going to deprive herself of spending the evening with him, even if she still didn't trust him. "Just as long as we don't do anything Christmassy."

For answer, he just grinned. "Would I ever ask you to do that?"

"Never." Trinity couldn't keep a smile from curving her lips. She tried. Really, she did. After all, she had sworn off men, but there was something about Riley that couldn't be ignored. Okay, so everything about him refused to be ignored.

Karen stared back and forth between them. "So the gossip is true?"

Trinity blushed.

Riley grinned. "If they're saying that I'm pursuing the hottest nurse at Pensacola Memorial then, yeah, it's true."

Had he really just said that? Trinity's face caught fire and her mouth dropped. Chase had always been so private, not wanting anyone to know how much he cared about her, saying that with them both working for the hospital they should keep their relationship on the quiet. Ha, he'd sure blown that at the end.

Then again, had he really cared about her at all? She'd certainly thought so. They'd dated for nine months. She'd thought she was going to get an engagement ring for Christmas. Instead, she'd gotten a horrendous public humiliation and a reminder about why she disliked the holiday so much. Or perhaps it was Christmas that disliked her. Maybe she should ask Riley for a rain check until New Year.

Karen smiled. "I'll be sure to let everyone know you're off the market, Dr. Williams."

"I didn't know I was ever on the market. But you do that. My free time is definitely going to be occupied by this little lady so long as she'll let me hang around." Riley winked and nodded towards the cardiac care patient rooms. "How's Mr. Ryker this morning? Holding his own?"

Still not quite believing how he'd just essentially given Karen permission to tell everyone that he belonged to her, Trinity shook her head in wonder.

Take that, Christmas party trio who'd called her "tonight's lucky pick".

She was this week's lucky pick.

Or something like that.

Then again, she had to wonder just what he had to gain by hanging out with her. Why he'd want to. Ultimately, how much did they have in common? Was he so used to women chasing him that he had to dazzle her so she'd follow suit?

Sure, she'd enjoyed talking to him into the wee hours, but everything was different when you were bone tired, right?

Still, she'd be lying if she said she hadn't enjoyed spending time with him the evening before, despite what he'd had her doing. She'd definitely be fibbing if she said she hadn't derived deep pleasure from falling asleep to the sound of his voice, to his breathing on the other end of the phone, to him asking her thoughts and dreams.

No one had ever asked her those things.

"Oxygen sats are staying at 97-98%, but he's still on two liters per minute," she told him, referring to the patient she'd just finished checking prior to Karen's inquisition. "Cardiac monitoring is normal. His vitals are stable. Ins and outs are normal. A physical therapist had him up walking not long ago."

"That's what I like to hear."

It's what she liked to report. No nurse wanted to deliver bad news regarding a patient.

"Come round with me?"

He was her superior so of course she'd go round with him if that's what he wanted. Based on the past couple days, she'd do a lot of things with him if that's what he wanted. If he could get her to decorate a Christmas tree, she was pretty much at his will to command.

Lord, she hoped that wasn't really so.

"Y'all have fun and don't do anything that will get Mr. Ryker's heart racing," Karen teased, looking quite pleased at Riley's admission.

He laughed and Trinity didn't say a word. Honestly, as impressed as she was at Riley not caring who knew he was interested in her, she hated the thought that she was the focus of hospital gossip. Even if it was positive gossip regarding her and Riley, because all good things came to an end and then what? She'd once again be poor pitiful Trinity who'd been dumped, because realistically she acknowledged that he'd be the one to end their relationship.

Would he humiliate her publicly, the way Chase had?

Of course, to give him credit, Chase had been drinking too much. Would he have otherwise announced her shortcomings so cruelly at their hospital Christmas party? Probably not, but once done he'd been unable to take back his words, couldn't stop the teasing that had ensued at Trinity's expense. Why had she stayed in Memphis so long after that horrible Christmas? Had she purposely been punishing herself for being so stupid as to put her hopes in a man? At least she hadn't started drinking, the way her mother had after being deserted by Trinity's father.

She should have removed herself from the situation much sooner. She hadn't wanted to run but, really, after her mother's death she'd had no ties. She should have left. Next time she'd know.

Next time?

Was she already planning for the demise of any relationship between her and Riley? Whatever that relationship might be. She really didn't have a clue what he wanted from her.

If he'd just wanted sex, wouldn't he have knocked the night before instead of talking to her into the wee morning hours?

Riley tapped on the patient's door then entered the private cardiac room. "Good morning, Mr. Ryker."

The man stretched out in his bed smiled at Riley and then at Trinity. A clear tube ran around his face with a nasal cannula delivering oxygen. Multiple wires and leads were attached at various points to his body.

"Your nurse tells me that you're ready to dance a jig and you want to blow this joint as soon as possible. That so?"

Not her exact words.

"If it would get me home earlier, I'd dance a jig or

two," the heavy set man admitted, raising the head of his bed and scooting up, wincing a little as he did so. "Other than the pain in my chest and leg from being cut open, I feel great."

"If all goes well today, I'll release you to go home tomorrow morning and see you back in the office in a week or so."

The man's wife, who'd been sitting quietly in a chair next to his hospital bed, got wide-eyed. "You're going to let him go home that soon? Is that safe?"

"If everything goes as expected today, yes, I am. It's safe for him to go home. Actually, the sooner I can get him home, the less risk there is of secondary infections such as a resistant strain of staph or C. diff."

"Oh," the woman blanched and she pushed a heavy-framed pair of glasses up the bridge of her nose. "What if something else happens? I won't know how to take care of him."

"If it's a problem, we can have a home health agency come out and dress his chest wounds and the surgical site on his leg. But, honestly, he should be fine as long as he doesn't overdo it."

The woman's relief was evident.

"But the first thing we have to do is get you through today." Riley placed his stethoscope on the man's chest, moving the diaphragm from spot to spot to listen to the man's heart sounds.

"Can you tell if the bypass is taking, based on what you hear?" the man asked, looking concerned. "I keep wondering what I'd do if my heart rejected the graft."

"That's unlikely to happen as it's your own tissue. But no worries, we'll take another look at the blood flow via an echocardiogram to make sure everything is working properly. You're in good hands."

Trinity wouldn't argue with Riley's claim. He did have good hands. Expert hands that worked magic with hearts.

Which, of course, made her wonder about what those hands were going to do to her heart.

Or should she even worry about that since Chase had tattered it to shreds and despite her move she knew there were only broken pieces where once a strong heart used to beat?

Maybe she was immune to Riley hurting her because she didn't have a heart left to be broken.

Somehow she doubted that because already she knew she'd miss him terribly if he left her life.

That scared her more than she cared to admit. Maybe she should run while she still could.

Only could she, even if she wanted to?

CHAPTER SIX

"This isn't dinner," Trinity pointed out when Riley pulled into the crowded mall parking lot that evening. Although he looked handsome in khakis and a polo and was in way too good a mood to have worked all day, she was still in her scrubs, hungry, tired and really didn't want to fight the crowds. She'd told him she'd have dinner with him, so dinner they would have.

Somehow she hadn't envisioned him taking her to a shopping center for a slice of pizza or Chinese. Then again, she knew next to nothing about his eating habits and they had eaten sandwiches the night before.

"True," Riley admitted, not looking one bit guilty as he parked the car in a just-vacated parking spot.

One more thing to not like about Christmas. Everywhere was packed. Parking lots, shops, streets. It was as if every person came out of hibernation and crowded every public place, searching for that great deal on the perfect gift that they'd spend money they didn't really have to spend. Trinity would much rather be at home with a good book and Casper curled up in her lap than dealing with all the holiday hoopla.

Her car door opened and she glanced up at the man

waiting for her to get out of the car. Really? She'd rather be with her cat than with this gorgeous man?

Okay, so not really. But hanging with Casper would be a lot easier on her emotions in the long run.

Please, don't hurt me, she silently pleaded. All day she'd questioned why he'd taken an interest in her when there were so many women out there who would gladly kiss his rear end and had to be more suitable than her. She was just Trinity Warren from the wrong side of the tracks, so to speak. He was a cardiac surgeon who'd obviously led a privileged life. They couldn't be more different.

"Come on, princess." A big smile on his face, he motioned for her to get out of the car. "We're just going to do a little shopping before we eat."

What? He wanted her to go in there and face the shopping frenzy? Had he lost his mind?

"I don't think so. You didn't mention anything about shopping."

"Didn't I?" He pretended to look repentant. "Must have slipped my mind." He took her hand and laced their fingers together. "No worries, princess. I promise to feed you, too."

As if skipping a meal or two would hurt her.

Still, the last thing she wanted was to go into a mall all decked out with Christmas decorations and sales. Maybe she really was a Scrooge.

"I don't like shopping." Had she sounded petulant? It hadn't been her intent, but she felt like digging her heels in and refusing to budge. Seriously, the man did not have to have his way on everything.

"Every woman likes to shop."

She snorted. How stereotypically male!

"Shows how much you know about women," she countered, chin high at his arrogant comment.

He stopped walking and gawked at her. "How can you not like shopping? Especially at this time of year? Every store is a smorgasbord of treats just waiting to make someone happy."

Her stomach roiled. "It's especially at this time of year I don't like shopping and my guess is that that smorgasbord of treats causes more problems than happiness. Someone has to pay for all that stuff bought that no one really needed to begin with."

Wow. She sounded a lot like her mother.

Which she really didn't want because, God rest her soul, Trinity didn't want any similarity between herself and the woman who'd given birth to her. Still, facts were facts. People went crazy at Christmas.

"Bah, humbug."

"Make fun of me all you like, but I prefer if we eat and then you take me home before you do your shopping." If his lower lip stuck out any further she'd swear he was pouting. "Or you can just take me home now and you can come back and do your shopping. We can do dinner some other time."

"We're not doing my shopping and no way am I taking you home without feeding you first."

This time she was the one who stopped walking. She stared at him as if he was making no sense. Actually, he wasn't making any sense.

"Whose shopping are we doing?"

"Yours."

Her face squished and her nose curled in disgust. "Mine?"

He nodded, tweaking her nose to unfurrow the wrinkles.

"I don't need to do any shopping." Her needs were simple and she wasn't running low on anything. Who would she buy something for? She barely knew anyone in Pensacola and as much as she liked Karen, she wasn't sure they were at a buy-each-other-Christmas-gifts point in their friendship. Although she did like the woman and Karen had seemed happy for her regarding Riley's interest, so maybe… Trinity usually just ordered a few gift cards online to have on hand in case she needed a quick gift. Last year she'd used most of them herself come January because she just hadn't had anyone to give them to.

"Sure you do," Riley countered with so much confidence that her insides heated a little.

She blew out a frustrated sigh. "Riley, I don't like it when you assume things about me."

A serious expression slid over his face. "Noted. I don't mean to railroad you into doing something you don't want to do, princess. But I also feel it my personal responsibility to get you into the Christmas spirit."

His personal responsibility? Poor guy. He had no clue what he was in for.

"Good luck with that."

"Thanks."

She shook her head, not surprised her sarcasm had fallen short. Riley only seemed to see the positive, regardless of what she did or said.

Still, Christmas was pushing it. Why couldn't they have met at a Halloween party? Or, better yet, a New Year party? Anything but Christmas because taking away the fact that he was a gorgeous doctor and she was just her, the fact they'd met at a Christmas party spelled doom from the start.

So far as she was concerned, nothing good had ever come out of Christmas.

But the sooner they got this shopping ordeal over with the sooner they could eat and the sooner she could go home and over-analyze the past few days yet again. "What am I shopping for?"

"It's less than two weeks until Christmas Day and you don't have a single decoration up or a single wrapped present in your apartment."

That was a problem why? Her apartment was the one place she could escape from all the holiday craziness.

"I hate to burst your bubble, Riley, but most single people without kids don't go all out with decorations and presents. They have better things to do with their time than decorating for themselves."

Like take out the trash and give the cat a bath. Important things like those.

He shook his head in mock disappointment, his eyes twinkling. "I bet you were one of those kids who never believed in Santa and took joy in telling other kids that he wasn't real."

Although she doubted he'd meant his comment to hurt, she felt a sharp sting in her chest and a defensive shield popped up. "I never told other kids Santa wasn't real."

He stared at her incredulously. "But you never believed in Santa? In the magic of Christmas? Not even as a kid?"

Swallowing the lump in her throat at memories she didn't want rising to the surface, she shook her head.

"Then who did you think climbed down your chimney and left all the Christmas morning goodies? The tooth fairy?"

She didn't think anything. Not about the tooth fairy or Santa. Or the Easter bunny or any other mythical creature who was supposed to do something good for her. Why would she?

"Apparently your Christmas mornings were very different from mine." At her house Christmas had just been another day. No big deal. Actually, if she'd made the mistake of mentioning the holidays, Christmas morning had been worse than other days because her mother would go into a bigger than normal rant. New Year had never been able to get there soon enough.

"Were you so naughty that Santa didn't visit?" His tone was teasing, but Trinity had to look away because she'd swear something had blown into her eyes. Probably a bit of fake snow off the ginormous tree gracing the entryway of the shopping mall.

Stupid tree. Stupid fake snow. Stupid shopping trip. Stupid her for coming here and dredging up all these memories.

She was not going to let him see her cry, had learned long ago to hide her pain. Most of the time, at any rate. So she slid her game face on, the same one she'd worn year after year.

"Apparently so, because he never did."

Riley stared at Trinity, trying to decide if she was joking. The pale undertones to her skin and tight set to her mouth before she'd turned away from him said she wasn't but that she would just as soon he thought she was.

He'd really stuck his foot in his mouth on this one. He'd been teasing her, wanting to make her smile, wanting to make her reveal more about herself, and she had. But he felt awful. Surely, she was over-exaggerating?

"Not even once?"

Her eyes downcast and expression somber, she shrugged. "It's not a big deal, Riley. We've been through this already. Christmas is just a commercial gimmick to make people spend money. I didn't need Santa bringing me presents. Not then or now."

The lift of her chin declared she didn't need anything and dared anyone to claim she did. Was that what she really believed? If so, shame on her parents.

"Didn't your parents believe in Christmas? In the joy of giving?" He couldn't imagine his own parents not making a big deal out of the holidays. It was the one and only time of the year his father took time away from work. His mother had barely been able to wait to get her house decorated. Pretty much the minute she had removed the remains of the turkey from the table at Thanksgiving, she'd have him and his brothers start carrying down precisely labeled totes of decorations. Despite whining, those times were some of his best memories.

Although he hadn't given it much conscious thought, he was carrying on in her footsteps right down to how he stored his Christmas goodies.

"Oh, my mother believed in the joy of giving all year long." But the way Trinity said the words conveyed a very different message from the one Riley had meant.

Poor Trinity, not having similar holiday traditions. As crazy as his family was, his Christmas memories were all good ones, except for those first few following his father's death when his mother had seemed lost and forlorn. Riley had vowed to give her back her Christmas mojo and he had. Their shopping and decorating spree the previous week was proof enough of that.

Trinity rubbed her hand across her forehead, sucked in a breath and stared into an electronics store window as if their display was the most fascinating thing she'd ever seen. For a brief moment he thought her eyes watered, but not a single tear fell so he might have been wrong.

But he doubted it.

"What about your father?"

She gave a low laugh. "I have no clue about my father's thoughts on Christmas, or anything else for that matter. He left before I was born."

That he could relate to on some levels, because although his father had lived in the same house he'd rarely been home. Except at Christmas.

He'd wanted to know more about Trinity and her comments had revealed more than any other statement that she'd ever made. Yet all it had really done was to pose more questions. Questions that he didn't think walking in a shopping mall was the right time to ask. But someday he wanted to tear down the walls she hid behind.

"Well, Trinity Warren, this is your lucky year, because this Christmas is going to be your best ever." He squeezed her hand, knowing if he'd brought joy back to his mother's holidays he could do so to Trinity's too. "I promise."

"It's really not a big deal." But the no big deal had her voice choking a little beyond what she was able to hide. Maybe her eyes really had watered.

"Christmas is just another day," she continued, protesting a little too much perhaps. "I usually volunteer to work. I really don't mind and really don't need a 'best ever' Christmas."

In years past, he'd volunteered to work as well so that others with children could be at home with their loved ones. He imagined he'd do the same this Christmas Day, too. His family all understood that he could be called away from celebrations at any time, but fortunately he'd always been at the family get-together for at least most of the day.

He loved the craziness of his family under one roof, of kids running around everywhere, shaking packages, wanting to know what Uncle Riley had bought them this year, and his mother warning that he'd better not have bought them anything that was going to cause a ruckus in her house. And, of course, he always did.

"My mom cooks a big Christmas lunch. My whole family goes. And I do mean the whole family. There's a bunch of us—aunts, uncles, my mother, two brothers and two sisters, and more nieces and nephews than I can count these days." He smiled at the thought of his family. "It's a bit of mayhem, but in a good way. Maybe you'd like to go with me?"

Her gaze cut to his and a panicky look shone in her eyes. "Why?"

Why? Good question because Trinity going with him would raise all kinds of questions and expectations in his family's minds. He'd never brought a woman home for the holidays.

"Because I'd like to take you with me." Despite whatever teasing and questions her presence triggered, he knew he'd never spoken truer words. "I want you to spend Christmas Day with me, to be there with me and my family, to see what Christmas is really like."

Because no way could she go with him and not be enchanted with the holidays.

Her eyes definitely a little misty, she sucked in a deep breath. "Like I said, I'll probably be working, so I shouldn't make any plans. Thanks, though."

That was a cop-out if he'd ever heard one. Why was she being so stubborn when he was offering to include her in his life? Something past girlfriends had begged for. He was offering to take Trinity to his most important family get-together, one he cherished and had never risked an outsider disrupting, and she was tossing it back in his face?

"But if you're not working, you'll go?" He resented having to push when she should be happy to be invited, but he wasn't going to let her be vague with her answer. She'd wiggle out of going if he let her.

"I'll be working."

He arched his brow. If having to work was all that stood in the way of her going with him, he'd find a way to get someone else to work in her stead. Even if it meant slipping someone a nice fat Christmas bonus out of his own pocket. He wanted Trinity with him and, as crazy as it was, he'd do almost anything to ensure she was. She needed to experience the magic of Christmas and what better way than with his family?

"Fine." She relented at his look.

He could tell she was only agreeing because she didn't think that whether or not she'd be working was an issue. She planned to work, would probably beg to work. A spark of annoyance flashed through him. Surely she didn't think he'd let her get away with that?

"If I'm not working, I'll go with you to Christmas dinner with your family." She gave him a stern look.

"But the next time you ask me out to dinner, there had better actually be food involved rather than shopping because, in case you couldn't tell by looking at me, I'm not one of those girls who skips meals."

He threw his head back in laughter. "Funny girl. You're perfect just as you are, princess, and should never skip meals. No worries. I will feed you. Right after we buy your decorations."

CHAPTER SEVEN

THE LAST THING Trinity wanted in her apartment was Christmas decorations. She certainly didn't want to waste her hard-earned money on glittery, glowing fake trees and wreaths and garlands. Just having to walk through the aisles of ornaments and bows made her skin crawl.

She fought the urge to throw her hands into the air and run out of the store. This was pure torture.

Telling Riley the truth about her childhood had been torture. Why had she done so?

She'd never told anyone. Not even Chase. She'd not wanted to see the look of pity in his eyes, hadn't wanted anyone's pity. She was doing just fine, had a good life overall. She didn't need some man coming along and stirring up all kinds of childhood hang-ups to go along with the new ones Chase had hand-delivered two years ago.

She hadn't liked the sympathy in Riley's eyes. She didn't need his sympathy. She hadn't needed him to invite her to spend Christmas with his family out of pity.

"What about this?" Riley asked, pointing out a box of red glass balls. He'd already pointed out more than two dozen decorations, all of which she'd turned down.

She could tell he was losing patience with her. Good. Hopefully, he'd soon take the hint that she really didn't want to be doing this. Maybe she could fake a stomach growl to speed things along. She willed her stomach to let loose with a loud rumble, but didn't even manage a tiny one.

Great, the one time she wanted loud body noises around a hot guy and she couldn't even force one out. It figured.

Barely glancing at what he held, she shook her head. "No, thank you. Not interested. Besides, I really don't need any decorations. Just dinner."

"I've never met anyone who needs decorations more than you." His frustration was obvious and rubbed her wrong.

"I think I'm offended by that comment." She hadn't asked him to take her shopping, had only agreed to dinner, not a stroll down holiday horror lane.

He raked his fingers through his hair, glanced around the aisle then faced her. "I didn't mean it in a bad way."

"Because there's a good way to say someone needs plastic garland, fake glass balls and gaudy red velvet bows?"

"Precisely." Obviously having whipped his frustration into control, he grinned and held up a box of horrid cheap plastic candy canes for her inspection. "What about these? Awesome, right?"

Hoping he'd take the hint, Trinity didn't hide her boredom, just yawned. "If I pretended that my blood sugar was bottoming out, could we go and eat? Please?"

His gaze narrowed suspiciously. "Is your sugar dropping?"

She grimaced then shook her head. "No, but I could fake it."

He touched her chin, tilted her face towards him. "As long as I have breath in my body, I don't ever want you faking anything. I don't want you to even have need of faking anything." His lips twitched. "And I do mean *anything*."

His fingers burned her skin, singeing her flesh with the feel of him. She stepped back before she did something stupid. Like say she wanted to buy mistletoe. Bunches and bunches of mistletoe. Barrels of it.

"Okay, deal," she agreed, hoping he didn't see how his touch had made her pulse race and her breath catch. "Feed me, so I don't have to fake interest in shopping."

He shook his head in obvious displeasure. "If you really want to go, we'll go, but I'm disappointed that we didn't find a single thing you wanted."

She wanted him to touch her again, and in more places than just her chin. Did that count? It should because it was a really big want.

Then she saw it.

At the end of the aisle on a platform. A ten-and-a–half-foot blue spruce fake tree decorated with snow-flakes and angels and silver ribbon that twined back and forth between the branches. A toy train set was wound around the base and a few packages assured hidden delights but were probably nothing more than empty promises. No matter. It was what was at the very top of the tree that had caught her eye.

A big shiny star that looked absolutely magical and just like the one she'd seen at her elementary school when she'd been five.

That Christmas she remembered well.

That Christmas she'd gotten caught up in the excitement of her classmates, in the whole spirit of Christmas. Prior to then she hadn't even been sure if she'd known what Christmas or Santa had even been about. She'd written a rudimentary letter to Santa and even crawled up in his lap when he'd come to her classroom. Packed back in her things she had a Polaroid photo of that moment that she'd kept hidden away over the years for some crazy reason. Probably a reminder of what lay ahead when one got one's hopes up and believed in things that weren't real.

With excitement she'd told Santa of what she'd wanted more than anything and he'd told her to be a good girl and come Christmas morning she'd find her surprise under the tree.

She'd been as good as gold. Better than any five-year-old had ever been, surely. She'd gone to bed on Christmas Eve full of hope and had barely been able to sleep because she'd been sure she'd wake up to a pile of goodies but mainly to the pair of new sneakers she'd desperately wanted. Her others had been hand-me-downs and had grown too small. A new pair of stylish pink hightops for school was going to be a breeze with how good she'd been.

Only there had been no surprise. Or even a tree. Her mother had claimed the entire holiday was nothing more than a scam and she wasn't spending hard-earned money on something as ridiculous as putting a tree inside their tiny apartment.

When her mother had found her crying, she'd complained that Christmas was a rich man's holiday invented to make poor parents like her look bad and that

Trinity should feel ashamed for making her feel bad. Then she'd gone off and drunk until she'd passed out.

The same as she did the other three hundred and sixty-four days of the year. Only without Trinity having set herself up with false hopes that the day might bring something different.

She had stopped believing. Right then and there at five years old she'd quit believing in Christmas and Santa. Sure, she'd still gone through the motions at school and, after she'd graduated from college, at work. But she'd never believed the holiday to be anything more than commercialized hype meant to build false hopes and to disappoint. How absolutely fitting had it been that Chase had broken her heart at a Christmas party?

"Stars are magic," Riley said from beside her, pulling her back from the past to the present, obviously clueless about where her thoughts had gone. How could he know? Although she'd revealed more to him than to any other person ever, she'd rather die than have anyone know the true depth of her shame.

"Just like the star that led the wise men and the ones that guide sailors through the sea," he continued, his voice low, mesmerizing. "They lead us where we need to go if only we'll follow. Anywhere in particular you'd like to go, princess?"

Trying to keep her cynicism to a minimum and any dream of going somewhere magical well tamped down, Trinity looked at him. "It's just a cheap piece of glass and tiny light bulbs."

"Use your imagination."

"I don't have one."

"Sure you do." He laced their fingers. "Close your

eyes and picture that star, Trinity. Picture it leading you where you want to go."

"That's the most ridiculous thing I've ever heard." So why were her eyelids so darned heavy all of a sudden?

"Do it," he ordered in his Dr. Williams voice.

"You're crazy."

"About you."

That was twice he'd implied he had feelings for her. Trinity glared. "You're not going to run off when I close my eyes, are you?"

"You couldn't run me off. I'm right where I want to be."

"At the mall, shopping?" She gave him a doubtful once-over. "You sure you're straight?"

"With you," he clarified, shaking his head at her. "And if you'd like me to give a demonstration of my straightness, I'll gladly do so."

She gulped back the image of Riley proving to her that he preferred the opposite sex. Even when she was tired and irritated at him, the man could send her libido through the roof. Wow.

"Fine." She closed her eyes and did as he said. Or tried to. The image of his straightness refused to budge from her mind.

"Do you see where you want to go?"

"Oh, yeah, I see where I want to go and you offered to take me there, but for some reason I'm still quite hungry and there's no food in sight."

He laughed then surprised her by leaning forward to drop a kiss on her lips. Just a quick peck, but a kiss all the same. Had he read her thoughts?

"Come on, Scrooge," he relented, not sounding angry

but definitely not his usual happy-go-lucky self. "I'll feed you."

Guilt hit her. He was trying to be nice. It wasn't his fault she was being so otherwise.

"Hey." She feigned surprise, wanting his sparkle back. "I take back everything. That star thing worked!"

After staring at her a brief second, he grinned. "I never thought it wouldn't. Glad to know you were imagining me kissing you."

Wondering if he'd just played her with his probably feigned disappointment, she shook her head. "Keep telling yourself that, lover boy, but it's the promise that you're finally going to feed me that I referred to."

His grin way too endearing, he lifted her hand to his lips and kissed her fingertips. "You keep telling yourself that you weren't imagining my arms as where you want to be but I'm going to prove otherwise to you."

Unfortunately, Trinity couldn't argue with him because she feared he was right.

Trinity managed to make it through the next week without Riley dragging her shopping again. Thank goodness.

However, that didn't keep him from dragging her to the local soup kitchen where everyone greeted him by name. They helped serve over a hundred meals and whether it was in the name of the Christmas spirit or whatever, Trinity felt good about doing so and promised herself that she'd sign on to help on a regular basis. Not only that, she'd look for other charitable places where she could volunteer.

Of course, with Christmas being only a week away she couldn't escape the festivities. Who would have guessed that people who lived at the beach would be so into the ho, ho, ho swing of things?

At work, everyone was wearing Christmas print scrub tops and a few of the docs had Christmas ties, Riley included.

Having just returned to the nurses' station and spotting him, she rolled her eyes at the tie currently around his neck. "Seriously? You have a reindeer with a light-up nose on your tie? That's what you wore while you saw patients at your office all day?"

Waggling his brows, he grinned. "Yep, I'm quite disappointed that no one asked me to guide their sleigh tonight." He shifted to where he could look behind her at her bottom. "How about you, princess? You want me to light up your world and guide your sleigh tonight?"

That he could light up her world she had no doubt. In the past week she'd smiled and laughed more than she had...well, maybe ever. The man was a nut. And brilliant. And kind. And generous. And...

She was getting way too dependent on him. It was barely a week since he'd kissed her under the mistletoe at the hospital Christmas party and every free waking hour had been spent with him. When she wasn't with him, she was thinking of him, dreaming of him.

"Sorry, I'm fresh out of sleighs and there's not a bit of fog in sight."

If spending a week with him could have her feeling so clingy, she really needed to get a hold of herself before she did something silly. Like fall in love with him. That would be nothing short of a tragedy.

And something she needed to guard against.

"This Santa is flexible. How about we grab a bite to eat then catch that new Christmas movie?"

"Not tonight."

His smile morphed into a frown. "You have other plans?"

Trying to keep a straight face because he read her way too easily, she nodded.

"Am I invited?"

Was he invited? What kind of response was that to a woman saying she had other plans? Really, the man was too much.

"Do you want to be invited?"

"If you're going to be there? Yes, I want an invitation. A VIP pass even."

Although she was pretty sure she'd just scolded herself for being so dependent on him, she found she couldn't say no, didn't really want to because to say no would mean depriving herself of the twinkle in his eye, the mischief in his grin, the wit in his words.

"Fine. You can go with me."

He grinned and she wondered if that meant he'd known he'd get his way all along. "Where are we going, princess?"

She had no clue because she'd just made up that she had other plans in a panicky moment. She should have known better.

"It's a surprise." To her too since she probably would have just gone to her place for grilled cheese sandwiches and a rerun of some TV series. She still might.

"Aw, are you taking me caroling?" he teased.

She squinted at him in a forced glare. "That would be a surprise, now, wouldn't it? But, no, I'm not a caroler. That would contradict that whole don't-like-Christmas thing I have going."

"But you do sing," he pointed out, leaning against the counter.

"In my shower doesn't count."

"I'd like to be the judge of that for myself. You could give me a private viewing tonight. Now, that would be a surprise."

She rolled her eyes again and ignored him and the images of them in the shower flashing through her mind.

"You also sing karaoke," he reminded her.

"Only under the influence of alcohol, which I'd never knowingly do." She made a pretense of being busy.

"It's okay to let loose every once in a while and just enjoy yourself."

"I don't need alcohol to enjoy myself." She winced at how harsh her voice had been. She hadn't meant to bite his head off, yet she definitely had. Unable to just stand still, she headed to a patient room. Anything to escape him.

Unfortunately he followed her, catching her just outside the door. "I didn't say you did. I was just saying it was okay for you to relax and enjoy life. Talk to me."

She didn't want to talk. They were at work. Only Karen was near, but anyone could see them, could hear them if they wanted to eavesdrop. Even if they'd been in private she wouldn't have wanted to have this discussion, but she sure didn't here. She closed her eyes, took a deep breath. "Sorry."

"Okay." He sounded confused. "You want to explain why you jumped down my throat on that one?"

She shook her head. No, she didn't want to go there. Not at any point in the next century or so.

He appeared to weigh his options. "Okay, I'll let it slide."

They both heard his unspoken "for now".

Trinity pulled the covers off Jewel Hendrix's legs to asses them for edema.

"They're only swollen a little compared to what they were when I checked into this joint," the seventy-two-year-old woman with end-stage congestive heart failure said a bit breathily. "I can actually move my toes again."

She wiggled them back and forth.

On arrival in the emergency department, she'd been retaining so much fluid that her skin had been too tight for her to flex her toes. She'd had weeping from her skin on her shins and calves and had had crackles in her lungs. Had she not been brought to the hospital, she would have drowned in her own body fluids.

"There's still enough fluid that I can't make out your pedal pulses, though." Hopefully after another round of diuretics the swelling would go down even more.

The woman glanced at her feet. "Honey, this is a good ankle day in my book." She paused to catch her breath. "I'm pretty sure if y'all would let me up out of this bed, I could even get these boogers into a pair of shoes. Most days I feel like one of Cinderella's ugly stepsisters trying to shove my monstrosity into a glass slipper."

Trinity smiled at her patient. She really liked Jewel. The older woman had spunk.

"What about you? Some lucky fellow slip a glass slipper onto your foot and make you feel just like a princess?"

Why was it that the elderly felt they had a right to

ask questions about one's private life? Why was it that Trinity felt obligated to answer the feisty older woman?

Hoping her face was unreadable, she raised her foot up from the floor to display her solid white nursing shoes. "No glass slipper for me."

"A pity."

"Not really." Trinity slipped the skin protectors back around Jewel's feet to prevent skin breakdown and positioned her feet on the pillows to keep them elevated. "I don't need a man to slip my foot into a glass slipper. I'm way too practical for that. Besides, with my luck a glass slipper would only shatter and cut my foot up anyway."

Trinity smiled at the woman, but Jewel's face was pinched into a frown.

"Maybe the wrong quality of men have been attempting to slip glass slippers onto your feet. You need to upgrade."

Ha. No man had been attempting to slip a glass slipper onto her foot, but she wouldn't admit that to Jewel. Besides, she had no right to complain. Riley treated her as if she really were the princess he often called her. She had to admit that most of the time she liked the attention he showered on her. Who needed glass slippers and a Prince Charming when you had a handsome cardiologist trying to woo you into Christmas cheer?

Trinity tucked the bed sheet and white blanket around her patient's elevated legs. "I'll keep that in mind the next time a Prince Charming asks to see my feet."

The woman chuckled. "I like you."

Trinity shot the woman another smile. "You can sweet-talk me all you want, but I'm still going to give you your medication."

"I never thought you wouldn't." The woman practically cackled. "When's that handsome doctor of mine going to be here?"

"Dr. Williams should be by any time. He was here earlier, but got called to the cardiac lab for a procedure." She'd only caught a glimpse of him, but a glimpse had been all it had taken to get her heart racing. Especially with how he'd winked at her when their eyes had met. Karen had teased her on that one, but Trinity hadn't really cared. Most of the time he made her feel good. And confused.

Although everyone at the hospital had accepted that they were a couple, Trinity just wasn't sure exactly what they were. Other than a few brief kisses and holding her hand, he barely touched her. What was his game? "I expect he'll be finishing up some time soon."

Did she mean with the patient or with her?

Jewel sighed. "I'd like to be home for Christmas. Maybe he'll let me leave this evening."

"Maybe," Trinity said, adjusting the setting on Jewel's intravenous pump. The woman wasn't receiving any fluids currently as her problem was fluid overload. However, her diuretics were being given intravenously and Trinity had just hung a new bag of the medication. "But I doubt it. You were a really sick lady when you got here yesterday morning. We really need to get more fluid off before you can go home."

Jewel eyed the bag of medication. "But I'm a lot better than I was and that stuff there is going to help even more."

"True, but you're also heavily medicated and Dr. Williams will want to keep a close check on your electrolytes for at least another day, probably longer. Your medication can deplete your potassium and if that happens, a whole new set of problems could occur."

"We can't have that."

"Which is why I don't think he'll discharge you any time soon. Or at least not until after you've had your echocardiogram."

Jewel sighed. "That's the ultrasound thing with the sticky stuff on my chest?"

"Yes, ma'am. No pain involved." Trinity entered the data from her assessment of Jewel into the in-room computer and that she'd begun administration of the medication ordered.

"How's my most beautiful patient doing this evening?"

The old woman's brow rose. "I'm your only patient? A brilliant doctor like you? That's surprising and a bit worrisome."

Riley laughed and winked at the older woman. "You're a quick one, Jewel."

"That I am." The woman beamed.

Trinity smothered a smile and clicked to save and sign the data she'd entered.

"You going to let me go home today?"

Riley shook his head. "Now, why would I do that when your nurse just told you the reasons why you should stay?"

Jewel shrugged her heavy shoulders. "I was just checking."

"Anyone ever tell you what a testy thing you are?" Riley teased the older woman, pulling his stethoscope from his pocket and cleaning the diaphragm with an alcohol swab.

"Only my husband." The woman's face took on a happy glow. "God bless him."

Riley laughed and placed his stethoscope on Jewel's chest.

The breathy woman watched his every move. Glancing up, she noticed that Trinity also watched his every move.

Jewel motioned towards Riley then waggled her drawn-on eyebrows.

Noticing the movement, Riley glanced up, caught just enough that he glanced back and forth between them. "Okay, you two, what are you cooking up?"

Trinity shook her head. No way was she going there. Jewel would have to do her matchmaking elsewhere because as sweet as Riley was to her and as fine as he seemed to be with everyone thinking they were a couple, she didn't fool herself that he was a Prince Charming who was going to slip a pair of glass slippers onto her feet.

Or even a pair of pink hightop sneakers.

She'd do well to remember that.

CHAPTER EIGHT

LETTING HIS GAZE soak up the sight of Trinity in her dark navy scrubs, Riley stepped up beside where she worked at the nurses' station. "Dr. Stanley is having a small impromptu get-together tomorrow night, just dinner and drinks, to celebrate the holidays."

Trinity looked briefly at Riley then went back to studying the computer monitor.

"Would you like to go?"

"No, thank you," she immediately replied, without another glance his way.

Tempted to scream with frustration, Riley sighed. "Do you know any words other than those?"

"Yes."

"Great." He rubbed his hands together in glee. "You really do. We should get you in the habit of using them more often. Let's practice. Trinity, will you go to a Christmas dinner party with me tomorrow night?"

She arched a brow at him. "You want me to be a yes-girl?"

Did he?

"I want you to be an open-minded girl who answers questions based on more than her preconceived notion that she doesn't like Christmas and wants no part of any celebration of it."

"You're missing the point completely."

He leaned against the desktop and stared down at her. "Which is?"

"That I really don't like Christmas so why would I purposely choose to celebrate it?"

Had a more stubborn woman ever walked the face of the earth?

"Okay, fine." He sighed. "We won't go to my boss's Christmas party that he invited me to and mentioned bringing you with me." Was it wrong that he was laying on the guilt as thick as could be? "What would you prefer to do tomorrow night?"

"Just because I don't want to go, it doesn't mean you can't go, Riley. You go ahead and have enough fun for both of us."

Ouch. "You want me to go to a party without you?"

"If it's a Christmas party? Yes." She put a lot of emphasis on the word. "I do."

What woman wanted her man to go to a party without her? Or maybe she didn't think of him as her man? He'd purposely fought to keep the physical side of their relationship at bay because she was so obstinate she'd be likely to use them having sex against him. If he went to a party without her, she'd likely do the same.

He shook his head. "What if I'd rather be with you?"

"Then maybe we could go for a walk on the beach," she surprised him by suggesting. He'd expected her to insist on him going, on her insisting she had other plans. She rarely said yes without him having to sweet-talk her. He didn't like it and kept waiting for her to quit playing such games. Maybe she finally had.

"To be so close to the Gulf," she continued. "I've barely been there."

"My place okay?"

Without looking at him, she nodded. "Yes." She put great emphasis on the word. "That would be fine."

Wow. Maybe they really had reached a turning point. Good, because keeping his hands to himself was growing more and more difficult. He wanted her.

"You want me to grill some salmon fillets? We could walk on the beach afterwards then sit on my deck and enjoy a glass of wine?"

Make love under the stars, in his bed, his shower especially, because ever since he'd mentioned her giving him a private viewing he hadn't been able to get the image from his mind. Or maybe they'd just sit on his deck and talk. Just so long as she let her guard down long enough for them to enjoy the night, he'd be a happy camper, sex or not.

"I don't drink," she said, but at least she hadn't said no.

"Cool. We'll sip juice on my deck." Other than the occasional glass of wine, he generally didn't drink either, so wine or juice wasn't a big deal to him. Plus, he wanted a completely clear mind if and when they touched. "I'll pick up some fillets on my way home and let them marinate tonight. You want a spinach salad? Maybe some sautéed asparagus in butter sauce?"

Trinity blinked up at him. "Are you for real? I just made you grilled cheese for your surprise dinner the other night."

"Pinch me and see." He waggled his brows, feeling lighter than he had in days. He hadn't realized just how frustrated he'd grown. "I'll pick the spot."

Her lips twitched with a smile she couldn't hold back and his entire insides warmed. Finally they were making real progress.

"I should do just that. Only I'd have to pick the spot."

"I'm game. Anywhere in particular you'd prefer to start? I could offer a few suggestions. Maybe give you a few pointers on my preferences?"

She looked up as if she was going to roll her eyes, but her smile was now full blown. "You really are crazy, you know?"

He thought about reminding her of exactly what he was crazy about, but just grinned, happier than he should be that she'd agreed without him having to talk her into doing so.

"I don't want to keep you from your boss's party, Riley," she relented, but he could tell she wasn't enthused at the prospect. "Not if it's something you want to go to."

"Not a problem." His insides felt light. "I like our plans better anyway."

Her smile made her eyes sparkle with the brilliance of twinkling green Christmas lights. "You're sure?"

"Positive."

"I feel guilty that you're going to cook for me. Is there something I can do?"

He nodded.

She arched a brow.

"Come with hunger in your belly and a smile in your heart."

She hesitated a moment then met his gaze head on, making his heart stutter a time or two.

"That's all you want me to bring?"

A dozen different responses ran through his mind.

An open mind. A spirit full of Christmas. Open arms
to embrace him. A willing heart. He settled for something simple.

"For now."

Okay, the man was really too good to be true. Because
Riley had not only cooked for her, he'd lit candles.

Candles.

At no point in her life had a man given her a candlelit
dinner. Actually, never had a man cooked for her either.

Riley had done both and was merrily singing while
he did so.

What was this? A romantic seduction? Didn't he
know he could have had her at any point over the past
week?

She'd like to think not, but truly, had Riley pushed,
she'd have invited him into her bed any of the nights
that he'd seen her into her apartment then left with little more than a kiss.

Not only were there candles on the dining table, but
they were scattered around the room as well. Plus, his
tree sparkled with the thousands of lights they'd strung
around the branches. Garlands hung over the doorways.
Gorgeous burgundy and gold ribbon bows accented
the centers and twined outwards. A nativity scene was
spread out over a coffee table. His sofa cushions had
been replaced with ones with a smiling Santa on them.

He even wore a "Kiss Santa" apron tied around his
waist.

Leaning against the deck railing, she shook her head.
"I do have to wonder how old you are sometimes."

A breeze ruffling his hair, he glanced up from where

he stood at the grill. "A person is only as old as they feel so I'm about...thirteen."

Smiling, she glanced through the glass windows making up the back of his house and door leading into his open living and dining area again. Her eyes caught on the toy train set on the floor beneath the Christmas tree. Her lips twitched. "Gee, I was thinking more along the lines of six. Maybe seven."

"Nah." He shook his head, moved away from the grill long enough to plop a kiss on her lips. "Six- and seven-year-old boys couldn't care less about girls and I definitely am into girls. Specifically, I'm into you."

Trinity's belly did a few somersaults. "Point taken, and I'm glad."

Because as scared as she was of getting hurt, she was honest enough to admit that she wouldn't have wanted to miss out on being the center of his attention. For however long it lasted, Riley was into her and that was a glorious thing. Her defenses might warn she should run while she still could but another part of her admitted that it was already too late.

Perhaps it had been too late from the moment at the Christmas party when she'd looked into those devilish blue eyes and he'd assured her he was a man who aimed to please. No one had ever made her feel the way he did. Worthwhile. Wanted.

"You look beautiful, by the way."

Point in case. Trinity's cheeks burned. He was always complimenting her, making her look in the mirror and wonder what he saw that she didn't. That no one other than him had ever seen. Because despite their nine-month relationship, Chase had never called her beautiful. Neither had he ever made her feel as if she was.

Why had she fancied herself in love with him?

Because she hadn't known any better? Hadn't known what a good man was really like and she'd been settling for what had been right in front of her rather than looking for something more? Something real?

Something like Riley.

No, she wasn't in love with him, although it would be so easy to fall in love with him. The man was a phenom. She didn't know how any woman could spend any amount of time with him and not fancy herself in love with him. He was that kind, that considerate, that witty, that sexy, that everything.

"I hope you're hungry, princess." He lifted a tin-foil-wrapped salmon fillet off the grill.

"Starved."

Starved for food, but maybe for much more than she'd bargained for. Nothing in her life had prepared her for Riley. She was supposed to be taking charge of her life, learning to deal with her Christmas aversion. She was not supposed to be becoming so entangled with a man she'd have a difficult time ever letting go of, and yet she didn't regret being here with him. She cherished every precious second of his company, of his attention.

She'd given up pretending otherwise.

"Starved?" He grinned. "That's my girl."

His girl. He didn't care who knew, who saw them together, or who saw him brushing his knuckles across her cheek or just giving her hand a quick squeeze. If anything, he acted possessive, as if he wanted everyone who saw them to know they were together. As if he was proud she was with him.

It had been months before Chase had wanted anyone

at the hospital to be aware that they were dating and then he'd acted more embarrassed than proud.

"Why are you so nice to me?" she mused out loud.

"Huh?" Obviously, he had no clue what she meant. Which made her happy inside. He wasn't putting on airs or trying to impress her, just being himself.

"I'm just curious why you're so nice to me."

"I already told you the answer to that, princess. More than once."

"What's that?"

"I like you." He smiled and she deep-down knew he believed what he said. He liked her. "A lot."

"This is good," Trinity praised twenty minutes later, the lemony grilled salmon practically melting in her mouth. "Much better than my grilled cheese the other night. I think you missed your calling."

"I happened to like your grilled cheese the other night, although perhaps not the butt-kicking at chess that followed." He grinned. "You really think I should give up cardiology and cook for a living?"

She snorted. "When you word it that way, probably not, but you are a very talented man and I am well aware that I barely won that chess game."

"Glad you noticed and appreciate my efforts."

"Oh, I notice." Every detail about him. She took another bite. "You have a beautiful place, Riley."

"I like it. When I was looking to buy, I knew I'd make an offer on this one the moment I stepped inside, even though it's a little further from the hospital than I'd intended. It felt like I was coming home."

She glanced out the windows towards the sea. "Great view."

"It's better tonight than usual."

But when she turned to him, he wasn't looking at the gulf. He was looking at her.

Heat infused her entire body. "You don't have to say things like that, you know."

"I know. I want to."

"Why?"

"Why?" He sounded confused. "Why wouldn't I?"

"I don't know. You're just always complimenting me and I don't want you to feel it's necessary."

"But complimenting you is necessary. Very necessary."

She wanted to ask why again, but didn't want to sound like a broken record. So she smiled. With Riley, when in doubt about what to do, smiling seemed to work best. "This house suits you. Functional, beautiful—"

"Christmasy?" he interjected, grinning.

"Christmasy," she agreed, unable to deny his claim. He was everything Christmas should be. Everything that Christmas had never been. Not for her. But everything he did made a long-suppressed part of her memory pull forward.

Enough so that she experienced a twinge of panic, but the evening was too nice to let doubt ruin it.

They finished eating and together cleared away the dishes, stacking them in the sink. Trinity tried to load them into the dishwasher, but he shook his head.

"Not now. Let's go for that walk on the beach. I've been looking forward to it since you first mentioned doing so earlier."

"Okay." She set her plate down on the marble countertop and picked up the jacket he'd set out earlier for their walk as the wind was brisk. "You talked me into it."

Putting on his own lightweight jacket, he laughed. "That's my girl."

As much as she kept telling herself that she wasn't in love with this man, that she wouldn't fall in love with him, she couldn't argue with his statement.

She was his girl.

Indisputably.

Hand in hand, Riley and Trinity walked along the beach. Ignoring how much he wanted Trinity was getting more and more difficult. He didn't want to rush her, didn't want to make wild assumptions, but from the moment she'd arrived all he'd wanted to do was pull her into his arms.

Her mind stimulated him.

Her quick wit stimulated him.

Her curvy little body stimulated him.

It was the latter that was currently tearing his resolve into bits. He felt as if he was in a constant state of stimulation.

He couldn't recall ever feeling this way. Not even when he'd been a randy teenager.

Letting go of his hand, she'd ran ahead of him, laughing as the waves lapped at her bare feet. She turned to beckon him to join her. Wind whipped at her hair.

Temptation whipped at his soul.

What he wanted was to push her down in the surf, rip her clothes off and make love to her right then and there, with the waves crashing around their naked bodies.

He swallowed, watched her dance around in the white foam.

"Riley, hurry," she called. The water crashed around

her ankles and she laughed, looking and sounding freer than he recalled ever seeing her.

Like a child set loose to play.

Like the most tantalizing woman to ever tempt man.

"I ate too much to hurry," he called, enjoying watching her play too much to rush.

"Right." She laughed then plopped down just beyond the water's reach, her toes stretched out towards the sea, tempting the water to move closer and closer.

"You know you're going to get wet, right? Then you'll be cold."

She shrugged. "At the moment I don't care. This is wonderful."

He glanced out to sea then back at the smiling woman leaning back as if offering herself to the moon shining above them.

If so, he was jealous of the moon.

Because he wanted her to offer herself to him that way.

Every way.

He wanted her to come to him, for her to initiate their lovemaking, for her to have no regrets and for him to have no worries that he'd talked her into something she hadn't really wanted.

He'd thought himself a patient man, but looking at her body stretched out under the bright moonlight, the surf nipping at her toes, he had none.

"Besides, if I get cold, you'll warm me up, right?"

He hadn't realized she was watching him. He gulped back the knot her words caused to form in his throat and willed the one forming in his pants to go away.

"Riley?"

"Hmm?"

"Are you afraid to join me?"

Terrified. Because getting close to her might mean losing control and seducing her right out of her panties. What would his neighbors think? Although, honestly, he wasn't sure how many were even home at this time of year. A lot of the houses along this stretch were owned by wealthy snowbirds looking for an escape.

"Scared you'll get wet?" she teased, digging her fingers into the sand beside her.

"Nope." To prove his point, he sat down next to her on the sand. "But I should warn you that I'm very turned on and perhaps you should get up and run while you can because what I really want to do would get me arrested."

Arrested? Trinity blinked, wondering if she'd misheard him over the waves. "Do what?"

"You heard me. Just what I said. You're beautiful and totally do it for me. I look at you and I want you. I have wanted you from the first moment I set eyes on you propped up against that hotel ballroom wall. Tonight, here on the beach, I want you so badly I may explode from it. I feel weak. If I did with you what I want to do with you, I'd be arrested."

He wanted her. Really wanted her. A heady sensation, but the other thing he'd said played in her mind.

"I make you weak?" She didn't want to make him or any man weak. Especially not when he made her feel strong, stronger than she recalled ever feeling.

He picked up her hand, pressed it to where his heart beat. "Does that feel as if you make me weak?"

His heart pounded beneath her fingertips. She shook her head.

"My resolve is what's weak. You make me feel alive,"

he clarified. "As if everything I do is bigger, brighter, more than anything I've ever done."

That she understood because it's how he made her feel. It amazed her that he could possibly feel the same. How could he when that seemed so unlikely? "I do?"

He nodded.

"I want you, Trinity, but I didn't mean to tell you like this."

She glanced around at the beach. Although there were other houses along the stretch of beach, they were essentially alone. The moon shone bright above them. The sea crashed foamy white waves that played a perfect love song. He'd just cooked her a delicious dinner and he'd lit candles. She couldn't imagine anything more romantic, more seductive.

"What's wrong with this? With this very moment?"

"Earlier I thought..." he shook his head. "It's too soon."

He was probably right. Less than two weeks was too soon. Still, they'd been together every night and if you put that on regular dating terms of weekend dates, they'd been seeing each other for months. Or was she just reaching?

Probably.

Because her hand had moved from his chest to his face. The grit of sand still lingered on her fingers but his skin was smooth, perfect.

"It's not too soon," she whispered, knowing it was true, especially when she heard his intake of breath above the crash of the waves. "But I should warn you that if we did, you'd be disappointed."

"Never."

She laughed ironically at his faith. If only. "I wish that was true, but I'm not very good at…well, you know."

"Sex?"

Staring at where her hand caressed his jaw, she nodded. "I can pretty much guarantee that you won't want me any more once we do."

This time it was he who laughed. "You'd be wrong."

"Again, I wish that was true."

"Why?"

Could she write him a thesis on all the reasons why? Things like that he made her feel good about herself? That he made her believe in things that she shouldn't believe in? That he'd taken away the loneliness that had iced her insides for so long that she'd believed the coldness was a permanent part of who she was?

"Because I like you," she said instead, using his usual response to sum up all the emotions bubbling inside her. "A lot."

In the moonlight, she saw his mouth curve upwards.

"Good to know," he admitted, taking her hand. "I was beginning to wonder if this relationship was one-sided."

"Is that what we're doing? Having a relationship?" Not that it didn't feel like a relationship. It did. Plus he carried on at the hospital as if they were. But, still, there was no one around but the two of them and she wanted a straight answer from him.

"If you have to ask me that, I'm doing something very wrong," he teased, scratching his head as if trying to figure out what that something might be.

"I…I just wasn't sure." Which sounded quite lame at the moment, with how his eyes searched hers. Even in the moonlight she could see desire flickering in the blue depths.

"After the past two weeks you aren't sure that I'm totally fascinated by you and want to spend every second of my time with you?"

Wow. That's all that her brain could register. Just wow. Wow. Wow. Riley's words seemed so foreign, so far-fetched, yet she heard his sincerity, saw the truth in the way he looked at her. He looked at her as she'd never been looked at, as if she was the most precious being on earth.

"I'm scared," she heard herself say, knowing her words were as true as his, shocked, though, that she was admitting her fear to him. Wasn't that exposing just how vulnerable she really was?

"Don't be scared of me, Trinity. I'd never intentionally hurt you."

Intentionally. Which meant she likely would be hurt at some point down the line. Her life had taught her to expect no less. But she wasn't going to hold back, wasn't going to let the past or fear dictate who she was. Not when it came to Riley. Was she?

At this moment she was a woman sitting on a romantic beach, touching a fantasy man who was quickly encompassing her whole world.

He wanted to be here, with her. He thought she was beautiful, he wanted her, and he didn't mind telling her, showing her.

When he was with her she didn't get the impression that he wanted to be anywhere except right with her. When he looked at her she didn't get the impression that he wished she were someone else.

He wanted *her*.

He lifted her hand to his lips, kissed her fingertips.

"I have sand on my fingers." And tears in her eyes. Why was she crying?

"Doesn't matter." He kissed the top of her hand, gently turned her arm to press his lips to her wrist, then he kissed her there. Gentle kisses where his lips lightly brushed across the tender skin, heating her blood. Brilliant kisses that made her mind go in thousands of directions, all of which involved him.

She shivered and scooted closer to him, grazed her knuckles across his clean-shaven jaw. "Smooth."

He chuckled. "The better to kiss you without worrying about scratching you."

"I'm not a dainty flower that easily wilts."

"You want scratched?"

"I want kissed."

"I'm a man who aims to please."

When his lips covered hers, he didn't kiss her with the gentle pressure he'd kissed her goodnight with each night. No, he kissed her with the mouth of a man who was hungry. Hungry and wanting to devour her.

As if he wanted her so much he couldn't not kiss her that way.

The sensation was heady.

Trinity's head spun she felt so light, so good, so unreal.

Riley was unreal.

Because no way was such a beautiful man kissing her as if he couldn't get enough, as if he wanted, no, needed, everything she could give him.

She wanted to give him everything.

But if she did, would it be the beginning of the end, the way it had been with Chase?

Would Riley find her so lacking between the sheets that he wouldn't want her any more and would wonder why he'd ever thought he had thought her something special?

Or did sex even matter that much to him?

His mouth moved lower, to her neck, trailing hot kisses, making love to her skin.

Um, yeah, this was a man who cared about sex. No doubt about it.

Which meant she was in big trouble.

CHAPTER NINE

RILEY FELT THE difference in Trinity's response and pulled back. "You okay? Am I coming on too strong? I didn't mean to move too fast."

He'd known better than to rush things, but he'd thought… No matter what he'd thought. The reality was they'd only known each other for two weeks and he had moved too fast. She was scooting away from him, standing, brushing the sand off her clothes, and was a million miles away from him.

"You're fine."

Fine? Not the adjective he wanted to be called when he was on fire for her and had just been kissing her with a great amount of gusto.

Mindless kisses that had been all about feeling and emotion and had had little to do with thought or intentions.

"The wind just felt a little chilly. That's all. I want to finish our walk now."

Just what every man wanted to hear when he was on the verge of making love to a woman he was crazy about. When he'd been overcome with passion and she'd…she'd decided she wanted to finish their walk. Oh, yeah, he'd pushed too soon. Only had he really?

She'd wanted him, too. Had he done something wrong? Or was she playing games with him?

"Okay, we'll walk." He stood, brushed his clothes off, and took her hand.

He wasn't sure she wanted him holding her hand either, but he wasn't going to let her shut him out after the kiss they'd just shared.

She'd told him she was scared. Was that why she'd pulled away?

She'd also told him that she wasn't very good at sex.

Based on how she kissed him, he'd say she couldn't be more wrong.

But maybe she really believed otherwise. He was reaching, but there had to be some reason why she was now lost in thought instead of in his arms, and he sure didn't want to believe it was that she was a tease. The vulnerability he sensed within her assured him that wasn't the case.

"You're a very good kisser."

Her head jerked toward him.

"An amazing kisser," he added, seeing the doubt in her eyes. Hell, someone had really done a number on her.

"You're the one who's a great kisser." She shrugged as if it was no big deal, but he could see that his praise pleased her. "I just follow your lead."

"Thanks for saying so, but you don't give yourself enough credit. You drive me wild, Trinity."

She gave him a weak smile and squeezed his hand. "Thank you."

"You're welcome." As much as his body urged him to pick up where they'd left off, to take her in his arms and kiss her until she was breathless and begging for the release he craved, he just clasped her hand in his and walked.

Patience might not be his virtue, but some things were worth the wait. He had no doubt that when he and Trinity made love, and they *would* make love, the wait would be worth having the patience of Job.

How could her schedule have been changed? No one ever wanted to work on Christmas, so surely she wouldn't have been randomly taken off the schedule?

She stared at the holiday work schedule. Her name was not on the twenty-fifth anywhere. Christmas Eve, yes, but not the big awful day itself.

She had been on that list. How had her name been taken off?

"What are you looking at?" Karen asked, stepping up behind Trinity and looking over her shoulder to see what had her so captivated.

"There was a message in my inbox about last-minute holiday schedule changes and for everyone to recheck the hours they'd be working."

"Yeah, I saw that."

"I'm no longer scheduled for Christmas Day."

"Lucky girl."

"Not lucky girl." Because if she wasn't working, she had to go with Riley to his family dinner. Not that there wasn't a teeny tiny part of her that wanted to go, to meet the people he spoke of with such love, but the thought of a Christmas Day dinner was too much. Plus she'd have to buy them presents. Not that she was such a tightwad that she minded spending the money, but what the heck would she buy people she'd never met and who were from such a different social background from her own?

"You sound as if having Christmas Day off is a bad thing." Karen grinned at her. "Enjoy yourself, spend some time with family."

Time with family? Ha. Her only family had been her mother and she'd died several years ago from liver problems.

But Riley's family?

"Or that good-looking man you're dating. Now, there's a way to spend Christmas Day. Unwrapping really great packages." Karen waggled her brows.

Panic tightened Trinity's throat. She glanced at the schedule again. "You're supposed to work. Let me take your place."

Karen looked at her as if she was crazy. "Why would you do that?"

"Because I moved here from out of state, remember? I don't have any family. I'll be by myself if I'm not working. I should work and you go enjoy your day with your family."

Karen shook her head. "No way. Pay for Christmas Day is always double time and I need the extra money. I'd put in to work and was glad for the schedule change as I'm helping put my kid sister through school. Besides, I seriously doubt Dr. Williams is going to let you spend Christmas Day alone."

Okay, so convincing Karen to swap with her wasn't going to work. Maybe one of the other cardiac nurses would swap with her.

No such luck.

Trinity couldn't work out why not a single one of the nurses scheduled to work on Christmas Day preferred to have the holiday itself off. Not a single one of them was willing to let her work instead of them. Unbelievable.

What was up with this hospital anyway? Didn't they have any Christmas spirit? They were supposed to want to be at home, to be with their families, to…not be like her.

Annoyed at herself, she went into a patient room and forced a smile onto her face for Jewel's benefit.

"Not working."

"Huh?" she asked, confused by her patient's immediate comment. "What's not working?"

"That fake smile." Jewel pursed her lips. "I take it you still haven't found that pair of glass slippers?"

"If you recall our conversation, you'll remember that I don't want glass slippers. Way too impractical for a practical girl like me."

Jewel snorted. "You can talk big all you want, but when I look at you I see the truth."

Scary thought, but somehow she believed Jewel really did see more when she looked than most people did. As if age had given her insight beyond the surface.

"What truth would that be?"

"That you're a romantic through and through."

Trinity made a face then put her hand across Jewel's wrinkled forehead as if taking her skin temperature. "Uh-oh. I think we'd better call your doctor because you're delirious."

"And you, my dearie, aren't fooling this old gal. You crave romance."

Wondering at why she sounded as out of breath as her patient, Trinity shook her head. "Wrong. Pink hightops were my dream shoes, not glass slippers. I run from romance."

Riley paused outside Jewel's door, fascinated by the conversation he was overhearing. Perhaps he should feel guilty for eavesdropping, but he didn't. He needed an edge with Trinity, something to push him in the right direction where she was concerned, because she confused him.

And frustrated him.

Since the night on the beach she'd gone right back behind her wall, and had also erected a barrier between them. A new barrier because he wasn't convinced there had ever been a point where she hadn't had a protective wall between them.

Except perhaps for a few moments there on the beach when she'd been touching his face. When she'd looked at him, touched him, she'd been unguarded.

He'd liked what he'd seen, what he'd felt. A lot.

He wanted that woman, that unguarded Trinity, all the time.

The one he knew was buried within her who claimed to not like Christmas, to not believe in the magic of the season. He wanted to see her laugh as she had in the surf, to let herself loose with him and just embrace life.

Not for her to beg every nurse on the schedule to let her work for them on Christmas Day so she could get out of spending the day with him.

That had almost had him losing his temper. Even now the idea that she'd do that got his hackles up. Then again, perhaps he couldn't say a thing because he'd already ensured none of them would swap with her, and without bribery.

Just because Trinity claimed not to be a romantic, it didn't mean the other nurses on the cardiac floor were immune to romance. When he'd told them he'd planned a Christmas surprise for Trinity, they'd all oohed and ahhed. Yeah, the other cardiac nurses were as much suckers for romance as…as he was.

Because he wanted to give Trinity romance and lots of it. He wanted to show her what Christmas was all about.

"Why on earth would you run from romance? Especially in a pair of pink hightops?" Jewel sounded as confused by Trinity's claim as Riley himself was.

"Because romance is all about building up expectations and making promises that won't come true, not in the real world, so of course I run."

That's exactly how she described Christmas.

"Honey, like I said before—" Riley could just see Jewel's head bobbing back and forth "—you've been hanging out with the wrong Prince Charming."

Riley frowned.

She'd been hanging out with him.

Was he the wrong Prince Charming for Trinity?

For that matter, did he even want to be a Prince Charming? It wasn't a role he'd ever envisioned for himself. He worked long hours, was dedicated to his career and would never want to do to a wife and family what his father had.

He wasn't looking for happily-ever-after, but there was something about filling Trinity's world with goodness and dreams come true that made him long for the ability to wave a magic wand and give her the world, to slip that glass slipper on her foot and be her Prince Charming.

"I like the man I've been hanging with. He's a great guy."

Riley's chest puffed out a bit at her admission. Oh,

yeah. That was him she was talking about. She liked him and thought he was a great guy.

"If he's such a great guy, where's the glass slippers on your feet and the dreamy look in your eyes?"

Leave it to Jewel to point out the harsh reality.

Trinity laughed, the sound sparkly and warming something inside Riley.

He wanted to make her laugh that way.

"He tries, Jewel, he really, really tries, but I'm damaged goods."

"Damaged goods?"

"Lots of baggage. Plus, Christmas isn't my favorite time of year."

"Not a crime, but why not?"

"Long, long story, but the most recent installment would be that my boyfriend dumped me quite publicly a couple of years ago at our hospital Christmas party. I wasn't much on the holiday prior to that, but gave up completely at that point. Nothing merry about a day that only reminds you of bad memories."

"Sounds to me like I was right. You have been dating the wrong Prince Charming." Jewel made a sound that could have been her clearing her throat or could have been her faking a gag. "Let's hope this current guy you say you like has more sense."

"Let's hope."

Trinity's voice held a dreamy quality that could only be defined as real hope. She hoped he had enough sense to be her Prince Charming? Was that it? Was he not giving her enough romance? He hadn't really tried to be romantic, just himself. Although most men would say that cooking a candlelit dinner for her should have won him more than a few romance brownie points. He'd done more for her than he'd ever done for any woman. Was it not enough?

Still, she'd given him food for thought.

He'd planned to go in, check Jewel and see if sending her home for the holidays was a remote possibility.

Instead, he walked away from the room wondering what one had to do to be Trinity's Prince Charming? Her *right* Prince Charming?

And wondering why making sure he did just that was so important when he wasn't a happily-ever-after kind of guy.

Christmas Eve. Only a few more days of this nonsense and then the world would be focused on out with the old and in with the new and how many resolutions could everyone make that they didn't really intend to keep.

Trinity could barely wait.

Sure, so far she'd made it through the holiday season with a lot fewer tears than last year.

Actually, she hadn't cried much at all, and she knew why.

Riley.

Since the Christmas party they'd been together pretty much non-stop and she hadn't had time to dwell on Christmases past.

Just Christmas present.

No way would she even consider Christmas future. She had to make it through the rest of the current holiday season first.

As in, what the heck was she going to buy his family? She'd forced herself into a few shops and hadn't found one thing that said, *Buy me because Riley's family will love me.*

How the devil was she supposed to know what to purchase for people she'd never met? She'd considered buying everything from gourmet cheese and fruit to the latest bestseller. She'd even done several late night frantic internet searches on gifts for people one didn't know.

Nothing had seemed just right.

She'd yet to see Riley today as the cardiology group he was a part of had closed up shop for the next two days, but she knew he'd be by at some point to check on his hospital patients. He was the kind of doctor who would do a round on his own patients rather than have the on-call doc do so.

"Hey, before you leave today, make sure you find me," Karen said as she came around the nurses' station. "I have a little something for you."

"You do?" Trinity asked, thankful for the little something she'd picked up for her coworker while searching for Riley's family something. The small gift was stuck inside a Christmas bag with Karen's name on it inside her purse.

"Well, yeah." Karen gave her a "duh" look. "We are friends, aren't we?"

"Well, yeah." She mimicked Karen's tone, mostly to cover the odd emotion moving through her chest. Karen had gotten her a Christmas gift. And just called them friends. "But we never discussed gifts, so I didn't expect you'd get me anything."

"What? You didn't get me anything? Guess that rules out that new Corvette I've been wanting." Karen feigned a sigh. "There's always next year."

"I didn't say I didn't get you anything," Trinity pointed out, "but you're right, there's not a Corvette sitting out in the employee parking lot with a big red bow and your name on it. At least, if there is, I'm not the one who got it for you."

Karen grinned. "Maybe we should check the parking lot out to see."

They both laughed.

"So what are your Christmas Day plans?" Karen asked, but sounded as if perhaps she already knew the answer.

"Well, unless I can convince you to let me work in your place, I'll be going with Riley to his family Christmas lunch."

"Wow. I figured you'd be spending the day with him but a family get-together? Are you two that serious?"

Heat infused Trinity's face. That serious. How did she answer that when she didn't know the answer herself? "It's just a meal."

"When a man takes a woman with him to a family holiday meal, it's never just anything. It's a big deal."

"Maybe he just felt sorry for me because I'm new in town." Yet another reason why she didn't want to go. She didn't want his pity.

"Are you kidding me? I have seen the way that man looks at you. He is smitten."

Which sounded good but also a little too good to be true. She kept expecting him to snap out of whatever spell he'd fallen under. Then where would she be? Lost.

"What are you wearing?"

Trinity shrugged. She hadn't even thought about what she'd wear. What was wrong with her? She should have thought about it. Only she was so used to just wearing hospital scrubs that she didn't give much thought to anything else.

Laughing, Karen shook her head. "Okay, so you've

no clue what you're wearing. How about gifts for Riley's family?"

If her face had been hot moments before it was deathly cold now.

"I wish I knew. I've been searching for something from the moment I realized I was going to have to go to this dinner, but what do you buy for people you've never met?"

Karen paused a moment then shrugged. "Nothing big or fancy, just some token of appreciation that says thank you for including me and, no, I'm not a total loser that your son's dragged home to meet you."

"Maybe I am a total loser when it comes to Christmas, because I don't have gifts for them and don't know what to buy."

Karen looked thoughtful then waggled her brows. "Anything at home you can re-gift?"

Re-gift? As in give away something that someone had given her once upon a time? That would be assuming that she'd received gifts over the years. She rarely had.

She winced and met her friend's gaze. "What am I going to do? I'm running out of time. Tonight, after work, is the last chance I have."

Shaking her head in mock sympathy, Karen laughed. "I guess you are going to join the throng of last-minute shoppers who are hitting the stores the minute they get off work tonight and pick something from whatever is left on the sales rack."

Trinity closed her eyes.

Go shopping for Christmas gifts on Christmas Eve.

Oh, joy to the world.

CHAPTER TEN

RILEY HAD PLANNED to spend Christmas Eve with Trinity, but obviously she'd had other ideas because when he'd asked her to come over for dinner, she'd refused.

Something she hadn't done for a while so she'd caught him off guard. He'd just assumed they'd spend Christmas Eve evening together and hadn't even considered any other possibility.

He paced across his deck, staring out at the sea. The wind was up a bit and held a chill. The waves crashed noisily against the beach, the pounding sound matching his mood.

What if Trinity refused to go with him tomorrow? What if she refused to see him on Christmas Day, period?

What kind of glass-slipper-wielding Prince Charming could he be if she wouldn't even let him have a go at her feet?

Besides which, he wasn't quite sure how he was going to pull off everything he had planned. His sports utility vehicle was packed to the brim with what he'd planned to give her, but the reality was that he might have put a whole lot of effort into something he wouldn't even be able to pull off. It wasn't as if she even had a chimney for him to shoot down. Besides, breaking and entering with her asleep in her bedroom seemed a little too stalker-ish.

He closed his eyes, breathed in the salty scent of the sea.

Where was she? What was she doing?

Surely not mourning over the idiot who'd dumped her? Ever since he'd overheard her conversation he'd wanted to strangle the guy.

And to hold her tight and never let go.

At least he understood the walls she hid behind a bit better.

Raking his fingers through his hair, Riley sighed. He didn't like feeling at a loose end. They'd only started spending time together two weeks ago. A single night away from her had him antsy?

Maybe Trinity was missing him as much as he was missing her. Only one way to find out.

He slid his hand into his pants pocket to call her. His phone started ringing before he could even press a single key.

The number on the screen had him letting out another sigh, this one full of relief and something akin to pleasure that she'd taken the initiative.

"Trinity." No hello, just her name. "I need your help."

His help? Panic hit him. Was she in trouble?

"Anything." There were few things he wouldn't do for this woman.

She told him what she needed and he burst into laughter.

"Okay, princess, I have everything you need. I'll save your royal hind end."

* * *

From the corner of her eye Trinity watched Riley trail a long curly ribbon across the floor, enticing Casper to pounce, which the cat quickly did, only to have Riley tug the string a little further away.

"She'll never tire of that, you know," she warned, liking it that he was a cat kind of man. That he hadn't minded that she'd brought Casper with her. Chase had been more into dogs. She liked both. "She likes to play."

"Smart cat." He dangled the ribbon out in front of the cat, causing Casper to swat at a curl.

"Because she likes to play?"

"Every good girl should take time to play."

"That a dig at me?"

"No, ma'am, but if the shoe fits."

If the shoe fit? Ha, if he only knew that Jewel was hoping he'd shove her feet into a pair of glass slippers he wouldn't be making jokes about shoes fitting.

He nodded then glanced at where she was attempting to fold wrapping paper around a box. "Are you sure you don't want me to do that for you?"

"I can wrap a present."

His gaze dropped to the box and he scratched his head. "I'm sure you can, but maybe I could help you. It's not a crime to accept help from time to time."

She glanced down at the bunched-up paper and then at the previous package she'd wrapped. "They certainly don't look like the ones in the store," she mused, casting a longing eye at his perfectly wrapped present then onward to his Christmas tree. "Or the ones under your tree."

"They don't have to look any certain way," he assured her, helping her straighten the wrapping. He gently pushed Casper out of the way when the cat attempted to pounce on the paper, obviously not finished with having Riley's attention. Her cat really was smart. Brilliant, even.

"It's not the packaging that matters, Trinity," he continued, smoothing the paper Casper had managed to crinkle. "Like a lot of things in life, it's what's inside that counts."

"Yeah, well, I'm not sure about what's inside either." She gave the packages a skeptical look, handed him the string so he could occupy her cat while she attempted to wrap presentable gifts. "It wasn't easy buying something for someone I've never met."

"You did fine. My mom will love her gift and that you brought her something. She loves presents." He tugged on the string again, sending Casper into another pouncing fit. "For that matter, she's going to love you."

"Let's hope so."

She was nervous about meeting his family, wanted them to like her, had gone out on the worst evening to Christmas shop and fought the crowds to buy them gifts. She'd even picked up little gifts for his nieces and nephews. Her, Christmas shopping. Whatever had come over her?

And then there was Riley's gift. Something silly and ridiculous and so emotionally expensive she hadn't been sure she could pay the price. Yet the moment the idea had struck her, she'd known that's what she wanted to give him.

Something she hoped would have meaning to him and make him smile.

She pulled off a piece of tape and stuck it to the box she was working on. She managed to get all the box covered with paper, but she used a lot of tape in the process. At the rate she was going, they'd have to make a tape run soon.

Much to Casper's delight, Riley tossed the curled string of ribbon onto the floor. Grinning, he scooted over beside her and cut a new sheet of the wrapping paper the stores she'd been at had sold out of. Thank goodness, he'd been more than willing to not only share, but to help out with all the other things she hadn't even thought of asking him if he'd had, such as tape, name tags, and ribbons.

"Here." He set another box in the center of the cut paper. He placed his hands on her face and forced her to look at him. "Let me show you how I do this then you can develop your own technique."

Trying to ignore the bolts of electricity zooming through her at his touch, she grimaced at the roughly wrapped package sitting beside her. "I certainly need to lose my current technique. I'm horrible at wrapping."

At lots of things. Things she wanted to be good at. To be mind-blowing at.

"You just need a little guidance and then some practice." He stroked his thumb across her cheek. "I'm more than happy to oblige."

"Is sex that way, too?"

That had his eyes bulging and her grimacing.

"What do you mean?"

Her and her big mouth. Why had she had to say anything? Then again, she really did want to know. Because she thought about sex with this man a lot. Sometimes in a good fantasy way and others as in a scary way that would have him changing his phone number and running when he spotted her in the hospital hallways.

"I told you I'm horrible at that, too," she admitted, wondering if she was like the worst woman ever in making her admission. Then again, if she'd thought she could fake it successfully, they'd have gotten naked on the beach the night he'd cooked for her. She'd wanted to but had been scared of losing him, something she hadn't been ready to admit, much less risk. "Is sex something you'd instruct me in and then help me practice?"

"Princess, happy doesn't begin to convey how I feel about helping you with sex, but I've kissed you and know how wonderfully sensual you are. My guess is that you're better than you think."

If only. She knew she wasn't. She'd been there. And if she hadn't been, well, Chase had told her and the entire Christmas party how awful she'd been in the sack.

"No, I'm not."

Twisting a piece of ribbon around the package, he frowned. "Not that I believe for one minute that it's true, but what makes you say that you're not any good at sex? Are you a virgin?"

"No," she said quickly. Did he think she'd just made up that she lacked bedroom skills? That wasn't exactly the kind of thing a woman went around tooting her horn about. At least, none she'd ever known. "My ex told me how terrible I am."

"Your ex was an idiot." His words were immediate and matter-of-fact.

"Well, yes, he was." Chase had been. She could see that now. "But, unfortunately, on that matter, he was right. I didn't enjoy sex and won't be winning any Oscars for my bedroom performance."

"If you didn't enjoy sex, then he was the one who was lacking, not you." Riley's gaze bored into her, making her want to squirm. "It's his job to see to it you're enjoying sex, Trinity. If you weren't and he blamed you, he was an even bigger idiot than I thought."

Than he thought? She'd barely mentioned Chase to him, because mentioning her ex just brought her down, made her worry that Riley would move on as well. Riley was so much more than Chase had ever been. Why wouldn't he move on?

"What do you know about Chase?"

For once, it was he who averted his gaze and started wrapping the present, but as if he realized what he'd done and didn't like the action, he met her gaze head on. "Just what little you've told me…and what I overheard you tell Jewel Hendrix."

"You were listening to my conversation?" Her cheeks heated. That would teach her to have inappropriate conversations with older women who went on and on about glass slippers and Prince Charming.

"Perhaps I shouldn't have, but I did."

She digested that, trying to recall just what all she and Jewel had said about Chase…and Riley himself. "What else did you overhear?"

"That he dumped you at a hospital Christmas party. Sounds like a jerk."

"He did and he was."

"He didn't deserve you," Riley said immediately, with such conviction that she had to stare at him in wonder. He believed that. He believed in her. The question was, could she believe in him?

"No, he didn't." Warmth lit inside her and spread through her chest. "Funny that it's taken me two years to realize that."

Riley paused from wrapping the present to take her

hand and kiss her fingers. "Is he why you don't like Christmas?"

"Partly."

"And the other part is the lack of Christmas while growing up?"

She wasn't sure she liked him knowing so much about her, the real her beneath the surface. Riley and Jewel had a lot in common.

"Not in the way you probably mean," she admitted softly, wishing they could just not have this conversation.

"Which is?"

"It's not that I expected grand presents or anything, it just would have been nice to have had a little bit of normalcy during my childhood."

Wow. She couldn't believe she was saying the words out loud, that she was admitting that her life wasn't perfect, because to make that admission just begged for someone to want to dig deeper.

For Riley to dig deeper.

She knew he would. So why hadn't she shut this conversation down? Instead, if anything, she'd encouraged it.

His hold on her hand tightened then he let go, started working on the present again. "By normalcy, you mean like a Norman Rockwell painting?"

"Not really." Normalcy, as in a Norman Rockwell painting? As in a mother and a father making a big deal over her, over having a brother or a sister to squabble with over who got to open the first gift. She hadn't ever really thought of normalcy that way, but perhaps, if she had, that's exactly how she would have envisioned an ideal childhood Christmas. "Maybe."

"I should warn you, my family is very non-normal. Christmas with us is more along the lines of a madhouse. The whole bunch are touched in the head."

She could hear the love in his voice and was honestly more than a little jealous. "Must run in the family."

"Must do," he agreed, holding up the wrapped gift for her inspection. *"Voilà!"*

"Nice." Every angle was perfectly aligned and taped down. "Do I have to be a heart surgeon to achieve something similar?"

"Nope, just need a little patience and a whole lot of practice. Here." He cut off a piece of paper and flattened it out on the floor, then placed the box in the middle. "Your turn."

Trinity wrapped the remainder of her presents with Riley's help. The packages weren't as neat as the one he'd done alone, but by the last one she was impressed with the progress she'd made.

"Look!" she exclaimed as she ran the edge of the scissors over the length of ribbon, causing a perfect curl to form. "I did it!"

His eyes were warm, full of praise. "I knew you could."

His faith in her was so evident, so real as to almost be palpable. "You did, didn't you?"

"It was a no-brainer."

When no one her entire life had believed in her, why did he? What did he see that no one else did? "Why's that?"

"You're a smart woman who can do anything you set your mind to."

"Thank you, but you're giving me more credit than I deserve."

"I don't think so. I just think you don't give yourself enough credit. Not where a lot of things are concerned. You really are the most amazing woman, Trinity."

Not knowing what to say to his comment, she made a show of surveying the assembly of presents. "I hope they like them."

His gaze stayed on her rather than the presents. "They will. They aren't picky. They're used to dealing with me, remember?"

He was so close to perfect it wasn't real. His family would see right away that they were from two different ends of the spectrum. A bubble of panic rose in her throat.

"What if they don't like me?"

"They will like you. Weren't you paying attention? They aren't picky." He grinned while he said the last and she knew he was attempting to ease her concerns. His easy smile and confidence did go a long way to dismantling her anxiety. The man's constant good humor was contagious.

She slapped his arm playfully. He had such a way of making her feel better. "Shame on you, Riley."

His eyes twinkled with merriment. "For?"

"Teasing me when I'm nervous about meeting your family."

"No worries, princess. I know they are going to love you. Besides, turnabout is fair play and you can tease me when I meet your family."

Which was yet another reason why she should have shut this conversation down a long time ago. She bit the inside of her bottom lip. "Won't happen."

His brow rose. "You don't plan to keep me around

long enough to have need to introduce me to your family?"

His tone was teasing, but a real question shone in his eyes.

"It's not that. We both know you'll be the one to get bored with me and walk away. Not vice versa." She hated the thought of him doing so. If she'd felt a panic bubble before, she felt a panic volcano now. "If you think back, I told you that I don't know my father, and my mother died a few years ago." Right before she'd started dating Chase, actually. "There's no family for me to introduce you to."

"No uncles or aunts or cousins?"

If there were she'd never met or heard of any of them. She shook her head.

"Oh, princess, that's terrible. Come here." He wrapped his arms around her and hugged her close, much as a parent would a child.

Trinity couldn't say her lack of family was terrible, just her reality, but Riley's arms around her felt good so she wasn't going to argue with him. Instead, she snuggled against him and rested her cheek against the hard plane of his chest, soaking in his strength.

"I'm sorry, honey. I didn't know."

"It's okay." How could he have known? How could anyone have known when she kept all her emotions bottled up inside her? Even now she wondered if she'd made a mistake, letting him know so much. "Does it matter?"

He pulled back to stare down at her. "Of course it matters. Family is one's support system and you've had to face life without that."

Her mother had been her only family and, honestly,

she hadn't been supportive, at least, not that Trinity could recall. More that Trinity had been an unexpected nuisance that had come along and interrupted her buzz.

"Not all families are supportive."

"True, and there are times mine drive me crazy, but I wouldn't trade them for the world." He kissed the top of her head. "Well, you'll see what I mean after you meet them tomorrow."

With that, a renewed dread of meeting his family, of having to endure a Christmas dinner and be smacked in the face with what all she didn't have in her life hit her. A renewed fear of what this Christmas Day would bring because, seriously, Christmas was never good for her. "You're really going to make me go?"

"You know I am. You gave me your word."

She nodded. She'd expected no less. "What should I wear?"

"Clothes. If you don't, my mother will be highly upset with me," he said with a deadpan expression that was unlike him.

"Okay, smartypants, what kind of clothes? A dress or just something casual?"

He grinned and she realized he'd once again purposely tried to distract her. "Casual. There's a lot of us, and I do mean a lot, and we're very informal. Just dress in whatever you're going to be most comfortable in."

"Okay." She leaned her head against him, drawing on his strength yet again and hoping she didn't disappoint him. "Thank you, Riley."

"For teaching you to wrap presents?"

"That, too, but I meant for just being here with me, period."

"With you is where I want to be. I was a bit lost without you tonight. I've gotten quite accustomed to eating dinner with you and hanging out afterwards. Being without you left me at a loose end and I didn't like it."

"I feel the same."

He tilted her chin to where she had to face him. "You do?"

With everything else she'd already told him, what was one more admission? "I think about you from the time I wake up until the time I go to sleep and all the time in between."

Okay, so maybe that had been a big admission.

"And your dreams? Am I there, too?" He spoke so close to her mouth that she could feel the warm moisture in his breath.

Her own breath caught, held, and blew out in an excited little burst of anticipation of his lips touching hers. He was going to kiss her. She knew he was. She wanted him to. Needed him to.

"Oh, yes, Riley, you are in my dreams." She lowered her lids then met his gaze head on, not trying to hide what she knew was in her eyes. "You and mountains of mistletoe."

CHAPTER ELEVEN

THINKING HIMSELF THE luckiest man alive, Riley accepted the invitation she'd just tossed out. He wanted to kiss her more than he wanted his next breath.

Her lips were hot and met his with a hunger that surprised him.

A hunger that matched his own.

His hands were in her hair.

Her hands were in his hair.

Threading through the locks, pulling him to her, grasping tightly as if she never wanted to let go.

His mouth left the lushness of her lips to travel down her throat, to sup at the graceful arch of her neck. She smelled of heaven, she tasted even sweeter.

Her hands had gone to his waist, were running over his lower back, pulling him towards her with an urgency that had his head spinning.

He groaned. He wanted her more than he'd thought it possible to want someone. He wanted her to the point his body ached with need, but more than that his mind craved her. Craved knowing what she looked like with pleasure on her face, craved knowing how she sounded when she experienced full and total release, craved the knowledge that he'd put that look on her face, made that sound escape her perfect plump lips.

He kissed and supped and touched.

She rubbed and massaged and arched against him, exposing the beauty of her neck more fully. He took full advantage, moving lower and lower.

He didn't consciously consider cupping her breasts, but his hands did so as if they had a mind of their own and had taken charge. No wonder. Her breasts were amazing and made him want her all the more, which he'd have thought impossible as he already wanted so much.

"That feels good."

Had she said the words or him?

His mouth must have developed an agenda of its own, too, because when his hands pushed away her top and bra, his lips covered the perfection of her creamy breast. His gut clenched.

He'd changed into jeans when he'd arrived home. Now he longed for the comfort of his loose slacks because his jeans had grown way too snug.

As if she'd read his mind, Trinity's fingers undid his jeans and slid beneath the material of his shirt. She ran her fingers along his abs, tracing lightly but with the effect of lightning bolts, before moaning and pulling him close enough that their bodies molded together.

"More," she demanded, her fingers going into his hair and pulling his mouth to hers. The moment his mouth covered hers, they both began to make haste with his shirt buttons, with her pushed-aside shirt, until they both stood bare chested against each other.

More sounded just about right. He wanted more. Lots more.

* * *

Somewhere in the recesses of her mind a small voice warned Trinity that she needed to stop. Sure, everything was going just fine at the moment but she really wasn't any good at this. If she didn't stop, Riley was soon going to discover that fact for himself, and then what?

But her body wasn't listening to her brain. Her body was way too busy discovering new and wonderful sensations that his mouth and hands were distributing all the way through her.

In a minute she'd stop, but for now she just wanted to feel everything he so generously gave. Surely that wasn't so wrong? After all, it was Christmas Eve.

So rather than cover her breasts when her shirt fell to the floor, she dropped her head back and basked in the absolute glory of his eyes feasting on her. They did. As if her body was the most beautiful thing he'd ever seen. Wow. How did he do that? Make her feel so good without saying a word?

So when his hands and mouth returned to work, she wasn't surprised that the rest of her body wanted to get closer, to get in on the action. Her hips ground against him, marveling at the hardness pressing against her, marveling at how he breathed raggedly, at how absolutely turned on he was. By her.

His hands sliding her pants down her hips felt natural, like the most perfect thing ever. Standing before him, his eyes eating up the image of her in only her peach-colored panties could never be wrong as long as he looked at her with that light in his eyes. He wanted her. More than she'd ever been wanted, Riley wanted her. Being the object of his desire was a heady high.

One that left her wanting more. And more. And more.

Unable to stand still another moment, she moved to him, kissed him, ran her fingers over the beauty of his shoulders, his chest.

Strong, chiseled, the way a man's body should look. He was so beautiful. So much so she should probably feel intimidated, but how could she when he was so obviously affected by her, when his eyes had been soaking up the sight of her body like a starved man? When he now touched her with that same urgency?

The open snap of his jeans dug into her belly, reminding her they were in her way. She slid her hands down over the hard planes of his abdominal muscles and into the edges of his waistband. She gave a hard tug. His hands immediately joined hers in removing his clothes.

Then they stood in front of each other, he in navy boxer briefs, she in panties that were growing more and more damp.

"You're beautiful."

She shook her head. "You are."

He smiled.

She smiled back and nodded. She knew better than to do this. Especially at Christmas, but she wasn't stopping.

Trinity sighed with contentment in her sleep, rousing herself. Without opening her eyes, she smiled.

Really, really smiled.

Because Riley had been right. Chase had been wrong. She hadn't been horrible at sex. She'd just been having sex with the wrong man.

And Riley was the right man.

A bubble of panic flitted through her, but her body glowed with contentment and her joy was too great to let doubt take hold. Not now. Now she wanted what she hadn't had the first time she'd woken up with Riley. She wanted to wake him up with kisses, make him smile.

Then, she hadn't believed herself capable. Now, she knew better. He'd woken a siren within her. And not one who was horrible either.

Smiling, she rolled over, only to come shockingly fully awake.

She was alone.

Alone.

She reached out and touched where Riley had been in the bed beside her, her hand running over the cool sheet. Apparently he'd been gone for some time. Was he in the other room? Or perhaps out on the deck? Regardless, he wasn't in this bed next to her.

Where she wanted him to be. Where he should be.

Her heart twisted in grief. Had she been wrong? No, he had enjoyed the sex as much as she had. She knew he had. She might not be the best he'd ever had, but she had given him pleasure. A lot of pleasure.

But maybe sex was all he'd wanted from her and now that he'd gotten it, he was done. Perhaps having left her in his bed was his way of telling her not to get too attached, that they wouldn't be waking up in each other's arms.

Really, she'd known better. Had known that when she'd had sex everything would come to a screeching halt. She hadn't needed it to be Christmas to achieve that feat, but she doubted the day of the year had helped any.

Would she never learn?

Recalling all the touches she and Riley had shared, the way their bodies had melted as if made to fit together, the way she'd seen stars flash in front of her eyes and cried out his name, the way he'd growled hers in a torrent of release, she couldn't regret the night before. Whatever Riley's reasons for not being in this bed, it wasn't that she had been horrible in bed and for him giving her that knowledge, freeing her from that burden Chase had saddled her with, for that she was grateful. Not only had he shown her otherwise, he'd given her the greatest experience she'd ever known.

Not just the sex, though. Every moment in his company was precious. He was precious.

She loved him.

Despite all the reasons she knew better, she loved Riley Williams.

She should leave. She should go let her cat out of his guest bathroom and she should leave.

Instead, she closed her eyes and pulled the pillow that his head had once rested on over her head, cursing her stupidity for falling in love with a man who was so far out of her league and who could never really be her Prince Charming, even if he did call her princess.

Had the past taught her nothing?

The tears that burned her eyes were nowhere near as hot as the ones that seared her heart.

His mind racing, Riley carried the last box of his supplies into Trinity's apartment. He hit the front door with his hip, wincing when it closed a little more loudly than he'd intended.

No one might be home but he didn't want any of her neighbors calling the law on him either. Then again, maybe they'd just think it was Santa making all the noise. He felt like Santa.

He'd worried how he would be able to pull off her Christmas gift without her knowing what he was up to. Leaving her warm, sexy body naked in his bed hadn't been easy, but her surprise would be worth it.

He couldn't suppress the grin on his face.

He'd promised Trinity the best Christmas ever and he was going to deliver.

She'd already given him the best Christmas ever.

The best night ever.

The best everything ever.

She'd rocked his world. In so many ways. Trinity had certainly knocked him for a loop. A good one. Like a carnival ride that thrilled and made you want to just keep coming back for more.

He glanced around her living room, smiling at his efforts. What would she think?

She professed to not like Christmas, but he'd never seen anyone more starved for the magic of the holidays. He wanted to give her that magic. He wanted to make all her dreams come true.

To make her day feel as if she lived a fairy-tale. He wanted to make every day of her life feel like a fairy-tale.

Which struck him as odd. His thoughts were those of happy-ever-after, not those of a man who knew he couldn't do to a woman what his father had done to his mother. Yet he couldn't bring himself to think of a future without Trinity.

Because he loved her.

Oh, hell.

He couldn't love her.

But he did.

Yet what kind of Prince Charming could he be when he'd forever be called away from her for his career?

With shaky hands and a heavy heart he finished what he'd snuck her keys out of her purse and driven to her apartment to do.

No Prince Charming had ever done better.

Too bad he was a Prince Charming who couldn't give a happy-ever-after.

Maybe if she didn't open her eyes, she could just pretend she wasn't awake and could sleep straight through Christmas. Darn whoever had changed the schedule at work and left her home alone today.

Only she wasn't at home.

She was at Riley's. In his bed. Alone.

She tugged on the covers, trying to pull them over her head, but they wouldn't budge. Which had her eyes popping open to see why.

"Good morning, princess."

"But…" She stared in shock at the man sitting at the foot of the bed, looking sexy as all get-out with only his jeans on. Wow. Maybe she *was* dreaming.

She stared at him, trying to reconcile the fact that he was here, that he was smiling and teasing her. Had she dreamed waking up in his bed alone? Dozens of conflicting emotions swirled inside her.

Last night had hurt. A lot. But he hadn't left because he was right here in front of her.

Of course he hadn't left. She'd been in his bed, in his house.

"Why?"

He looked confused. "Why what?"

"Why are you here?"

His brow arched. "Is that a trick question? I live here." His expression darkened. "Don't you want me here?"

How did she answer that? Did you tell a man that you'd woken up and found the bed empty and had assumed the worst? That you'd cried yourself to sleep and erected a hundred new walls to replace the ones he'd torn down because she'd realized she was in love with him?

"I woke up and you weren't here." Did she sound whiny?

She'd thought he would take a hint and tell her why he'd left his bed, but he just shrugged, as if his absence was no big deal. Only he didn't meet her eyes and he wasn't smiling.

"Sometimes a man has to do what a man has to do. Now, out of bed. Time's awasting."

He might convince her to get out of bed except there was an itsy bitsy tiny problem. "I'm naked."

"Good point." His smile was lethal and he suddenly seemed intent on lightening the mood between them. "Forget getting out of bed. I'll get back in with you. Much better idea." With that he dove towards her, tugging on the covers she had tucked beneath her chin.

"No." She wiggled and squirmed, trying to prevent him from uncovering her body. "No, I don't want you to see me like this."

He stilled. "Like this? I saw everything there was to see about your body last night. Up close and personal from all angles. Have your forgotten?"

"No, but..." How did she explain that when she'd woken and he hadn't been there she'd felt such devastation and had grieved and erected those walls to where she just didn't trust letting them back down. She didn't want to let them back down. Right or wrong since he obviously hadn't really left, she still felt defensive.

Or perhaps it was her other realization during the night that had her so defensive. She didn't want to be in love with him.

"Riley, I don't want to do this today."

"This?"

"You know."

He blinked and tugged at the covers again.

Holding them tight, she shook her head. "No."

He let go of the comforter. "What are you saying?"

Her grip on the comforter tightened. "Last night shouldn't have happened."

"Because?"

What could she say? That she was so damaged by her past that she couldn't bear any more pain? That she'd fallen in love with him and although she'd thought she was strong enough to be with him and survive when he got bored with her crazy hang-ups, last night had shown her otherwise?

"Fine," he agreed between gritted teeth. "Last night was a mistake."

She couldn't tell if he was being sarcastic or angry.

"At least get out of bed and come and see what Santa left you."

Her heart dropped somewhere to the pit of her stomach. "Please, don't."

Because she just couldn't take such comments this morning. She just couldn't pretend she was the same as him, that she could spend the night in his bed and go and be all jolly with his family. She couldn't pretend that she didn't love him and that she was terrified of that realization.

"Don't?" He raked his fingers through his hair then scooted up beside her, gently forced her to look at him. "Talk to me, Trinity. I thought you'd wake up smiling this morning, not looking at me as if I'm the Grinch who stole Christmas."

"No, that would be me. I'm the one who dislikes Christmas, remember?"

"That's just because you're so stubborn and refuse to give Christmas a chance. Quit being otherwise, get out of bed, and let's enjoy our Christmas morning together before it's time to leave for my mom's. We'll discuss last night some other time, but for now I promised you the best Christmas ever. Accomplishing that does require some effort on your part."

A sick feeling settled in her stomach. "What have you done?"

Because she didn't want him going and setting a precedent that every other year would have to live up to and never would. She didn't want him being nice to her because he felt sorry for her that her mother just hadn't been into Christmas. That Chase had messed with her head and heart. She didn't want to be another of Riley's charity cases.

"I didn't say I did anything. But maybe you were a very good girl this year, and Santa came to see you last night."

She didn't want him making her depend on him even more than she already did. That was becoming more and more difficult each day and after last night... She shook her head. He probably thought her a charity case all the way round. Maybe that's what the past few weeks had been about. She was this year's Christmas project. "No, whatever it is you've done, just undo it."

His jaw tightened. "You want me to undo your Christmas morning?"

She nodded. "I don't want you being nice to me."

"Now I'm really confused."

"Don't you see?" She fought sniffling. "You've got to stop doing this."

His eyes filled with concern. "I don't see at all. You've stumped me. What exactly do I have to stop doing?"

"Making me want to believe."

He reached over, ran his finger across her face and tucked a hair behind her ear. "Now, why would I want you to stop believing when the whole idea is to make you believe in Christmas?"

Only she hadn't been talking about Christmas.

She'd been referring to him.

CHAPTER TWELVE

RILEY SCRATCHED HIS head in total confusion while Trinity got out of the bed without his assistance and with the comforter wrapped around her delectable body. He'd have liked to have woken her up with kisses, but he hadn't wanted her to get the wrong idea.

Which meant there was a right idea.

He wasn't exactly sure what that was, but he figured he had some time to figure it out. To figure them out because he wasn't a forever kind of man and she deserved her own happy-ever-after.

At least he'd thought he had time and had told himself he just wouldn't think about the future today, that he'd focus on the holiday and giving Trinity a day to remember always.

He just didn't understand why she'd be back to bah-humbugging after the night they'd shared. He'd thought the night amazing, had expected all smiles and happiness on his favorite day of the year. Instead, she'd seemed determined to be contrary. Did she want to ruin their day? To fight?

Frowning, he slipped his shirt from the night before back on and went into his living room, surveying the room and trying to see it as she would.

He hadn't gone overboard at his house, just hung on his fireplace mantel a stocking with her name in glitter on it. Plus a few presents. He'd wanted her main gift to be a complete surprise. Had he not done a little something for her, she'd definitely have suspected.

He wanted to catch her off guard and blow her mind.

"Riley?"

He hadn't heard her step up behind him.

"What is all this?"

She'd put on one of his T-shirts and a drawstring pair of shorts that came down past her knees. She'd combed her hair and tied it back with a rubber band. Her face was freshly washed and ethereally beautiful. She looked like an angel.

One he was now afraid to touch for fear of upsetting her further. For fear that his feelings might show and set up expectations he couldn't follow through on.

"Christmas morning."

She glanced around the room, taking in where he had their breakfast cooked and waiting on the table, taking in the small package sitting beside her plate, taking in all the details of the room but not smiling. Instead, she looked distraught. "Why?"

He could list any number of reasons and all of them rang with truth. The panicky paleness to her face warned he might have miscalculated who she really was. "Because I want to make you happy."

But had obviously failed miserably.

Her face pinched with obvious disappointment. "You think you have to give me things to do that?"

"No." He frowned. She was taking all his efforts the wrong way. Not at all how he'd envisioned. "Haven't you ever heard it's more blessed to give than to receive?"

Without saying anything, she walked over to the fireplace mantel, ran her finger over the red velvet stocking with her name on it.

"There are presents inside."

She glanced down at the bulges in the stocking. Her face was still pinched. "I see that."

"They're yours." He'd wanted to watch her tear into the presents with excited gusto, wanted joy to sparkle on her face and laughter to curve her lips. He'd wanted her to throw her arms around him and wish him a merry Christmas. Instead, she appeared to be somewhere between starting to cry and darting out of the room.

"I...I'm not sure."

She didn't intend to open his gifts? What the...? He sucked in a deep breath. "Fine. If you don't want to open your presents, we can eat breakfast first."

"I'm not really hungry."

Determined that he was somehow going to lighten her mood without letting her ruin his, he waggled his brows. "If you don't want to open presents and you aren't hungry, then whatever do we do to pass the time until we go to my mom's house?"

Her gaze narrowed. "Not what you're thinking."

Yeah, her "Last night was a mistake" had clued him in that she wouldn't be dangling any mistletoe over her head any time soon. He crossed his arms. "You don't know what I'm thinking."

"Sure, I do."

"Then you should be ashamed of yourself."

She didn't crack a smile.

"Come on, Trinity. Lighten up. It's Christmas and

we're young and healthy and have a lot of things to be thankful for. I've done my best to give you a special Christmas morning. Why are you acting this way?"

Trinity felt like a grade-A heel. She was being an ungrateful pain when he was doing his best to make the most of the morning. She realized that.

Just as she realized that she wanted to give in to his cajoling. But what would be the point?

Last night had blown her away then blown her to bits.

She was in love with him. Just look at how she'd fallen apart when she and Chase had ended. Chase had been nothing compared to Riley.

Nothing.

She'd given her word she'd go with him today, but beyond that she couldn't do more. Couldn't risk more.

He was a good man. He deserved more. Deserved better than she could ever be.

He deserved someone who could look around at the effort he'd made to make her Christmas morning special and express her appreciation, not clam up with fear and panic. Someone who could give him good things in return.

Casper mewed at her feet and she bent over to pick up the cat, stroking the silky fur.

"I fed her some tuna. Hope that's okay and that I didn't do something else wrong."

Ouch. Usually he was so patient, but he must have reached his limit. She couldn't fault him for that.

Walking over to the table where he'd prepared a small feast, she sat in a chair, putting Casper in her lap. The cat nuzzled her a brief moment then jumped down to rub against Riley's leg. She didn't blame her cat. She'd choose rubbing against Riley's leg over her lap, too.

She and her cat could mope over him together when he was gone.

Her gaze fell on the brightly wrapped present next to her plate. "I don't have your present with me."

"You got me a present?"

Embarrassed, she nodded. "It's not anything big. Just a little something that you will probably think silly."

"Not a problem. We'll go by your place on the way to my mother's. I figure you will need to shower and change anyway."

"Actually, I have a bag in my car and could grab a quick shower here if that's okay." Because if she went home, he might not prise her back outside the door to go to his mother's. She might be a coward, but she wasn't a liar. She'd told him she'd go, so she would go. If he still wanted her to. "I keep a change of clothes in my car because of never knowing when I'm going to get off work."

"Whatever is fine. Can I get it for you?"

She shook her head. "Sit down. You've obviously worked hard this morning getting all this together. The least I can do is co-operate."

She could tell he was disappointed. By her words and her actions.

She just wanted this day over.

"Will you please open your presents?"

Glancing at the package, she nodded. Really, how could she say no?

With shaky hands she unwrapped the present, her breath catching at what was inside. An angel tree-topper.

"Thank you." She didn't point out that she didn't have a tree.

"You're welcome." He sounded as awkward as she did.

That the packages inside her stocking contained various Christmas ornaments didn't surprise her. Not really. What an optimist he was.

Part of her knew she'd treasure the gifts always. Another part wondered if she'd ever be able to look at them without remembering that the day he'd given them to her had been the beginning of the end.

Apparently, he was going to fail at giving Trinity a magical day. Not that he wasn't trying, but he could only do so much when she wouldn't look him in the eye and even her smile was fake.

Maybe he should have just taken her home instead of torturing himself with failure for the remainder of the day.

He didn't deal well with failure.

Especially when he didn't know why he was failing. He loved this woman and wanted to make her day special. Why was everything coming out wrong?

Because he was the wrong Prince Charming?

"You can take me home if you've changed your mind about wanting me with you today."

"Hell, no," he snapped, knowing he sounded harsh, but seriously, if that was her game and she'd purposely been aloof all morning to get out of spending Christmas with him, she could think again.

"Fine, but just remember that I did offer."

He tried to hold her hand as they walked around the car, but she pulled away under the pretense of helping him carry packages. He frowned but figured that her refusing to hold his hand was par for the course today.

Fine. She could act all weird if that's what she wanted, but today was Christmas and he was going to enjoy the day if it killed him.

His mother's house was in chaos as usual, being Christmas Day. There were easily more than thirty people present. They all looked to be having a great time and happy to be there. Except Trinity didn't want to be there and was doing a poor job of hiding that fact. Several times on the trip from the car to the house he'd thought she might make a run for it.

"Please, don't make me do this."

Frustrated beyond belief, he stopped walking to glare at her. "You act as if being here is making you a martyr."

She winced. "I'm sorry. It's just that I—"

"Uncle Riley is here!" Timmy, his sister's oldest, screamed, and came racing toward him. The seven-year-old launched himself at Riley, cutting off whatever Trinity had been going to say. "Did you bring presents?"

"Have I ever come to Christmas without presents?" he snapped, and regretted it even before Timmy's face fell. "Sorry, bud," he apologized to his favorite nephew, who stared at him as if aliens must have invaded his body. Riley sighed, gave the kid a hug, then sat him down on the pavement. "There are more in the car if you want to round up a posse to help unload."

Still looking at him as if trying to figure out what was up, Timmy and several of his other nephews, who seemed to appear out of thin air, ran towards his car.

Setting down the presents that he held, he turned

to face Trinity. "I know you don't want to be here, but Christmas is special to my family and I don't want the day ruined for my mother. She's been through a lot. Try to at least pretend you want to be here with me, okay?"

Looking pale, Trinity just nodded and was then over-whelmed by his mother and sisters. Being cornered by the Williams women could be compared to nothing less than an all-out assault.

"Oh, look at you, honey. What a pretty little thing you are!" his mother said, her hands on Trinity's shoulders as she studied her.

"Mom, you're embarrassing her," said Riley's younger sister, who then proceeded to do the same but pulled Trinity into a hug that she remained stiff through.

"Nah," said his sister, who was currently eight months pregnant and looked as if she was about to pop. "All women like to be called pretty and little."

"Hey, pretty little sister," Riley greeted her, stressing *pretty* and *little*. He kissed her cheek. "Mom, Becky, this is Trinity. We work together at the hospital."

Because what more could he say?

"You more than work together or she wouldn't be here with you." That had come from his brother, who'd joined them and slapped Riley across the shoulder.

Riley wanted to laugh, to shake his brother's hand and make a joke of his comment, but instead he just shrugged. "It's no big deal, really."

"Right," his older sister said, wrapping her arms around him and kissing his cheek. "Great to see you, little brother. And Trinity." She turned to a pale Trinity and did the same. "We're so glad that Riley has finally brought a woman home with him. We've all been plac-ing bets as to what you looked like."

"Bets?" Trinity's eyes resembled those of a doe in headlights. Her skin was pasty white and her posture stiff as a board.

Riley winced. "Sis, you're scaring her."

"Nah, if she's with you, she isn't easily scared."

His siblings all burst into laughter but Trinity remained quiet, and regret filled Riley. He'd made a mistake, bringing her here.

After the disaster of a morning they'd had, maybe he should just admit that everything about them was a mistake. He couldn't give her what she deserved and she didn't want anything he tried to give.

Maybe she really didn't like Christmas.

Or him.

Ending things as soon as possible was inevitable.

Trinity had made a mistake in coming here with Riley. Seriously, she should just hibernate through Christmas each year. She'd be a happier person if she did.

Those around her would be happier because she knew she was ruining Riley's day and that was a shame, but she felt unable to snap out of her melancholy.

She'd had sex with him the night before. Amazing, beautiful sex where they'd not held anything back from each other. Today she could barely look at him for the panic filling her mind.

Would he dump her on Christmas, as Chase had? Perhaps publicly do so in front of his family? His affluent family? She might not know the actual values of cars but the cars in Riley's mother's drive weren't at the low end of the market.

They couldn't be more different.

They'd probably all lost their bets because she

doubted any of them had bet on Riley bringing a charity case.

"Jake here thought you'd be tall and a buxomy redhead." A woman who looked a lot like Riley clarified her earlier comment, oblivious to Trinity's inner torment. "I thought you'd be tall, thin and blonde. Becky thought you'd be brunette."

"And I thought you'd be the luckiest girl in the world to be here with my wonderful son," Riley's mom butted in, shooing them all further into the house. "Come on in so we can say a blessing for our meal." The kids came running through with more packages. "Boys, y'all put those under the tree for now. We'll open presents after we all have full bellies."

"But, Nana!"

"Don't Nana me. You heard me." But her voice was full of love, rather than threat.

They were all being friendly, trying to include her, had smothered her with hugs and attention.

But Trinity felt the difference in Riley and knew she had no one to blame but herself. She'd known better than to come here, to become involved with him from the very beginning, and yet she had.

Because she had felt something when she'd looked at him that she hadn't been able to resist and she'd made the mistake of falling in love with a man she could never have.

"Don't pay them any mind." A very tanned, very blonde woman who looked like she'd stepped off a vacation ad for Florida advised her. "The whole Williams clan are nothing but troublemakers."

Trinity just blinked at the gorgeous woman.

"Hi, I'm Casey, Jake's wife. You must be Trinity.

Come and sit by me. I'll protect you from the Williamses."

"Hello," Riley interrupted with a scowl, stopping Casey from taking Trinity's arm. "In case you've forgotten, you are one of us Williamses now, too."

The woman flashed pearly-white teeth that contrasted brightly with her tanned skin. "Happiest day of my life."

Jake wrapped his arm around her waist and planted a kiss on the woman's mouth right there and didn't stop with just a quick peck either.

Blushing, Trinity glanced around, but no one was paying the couple any heed. Apparently showing affection was the norm at the Williamses' house. No mistletoe required.

"Uncle Riley, will you sit with us?" the little boy Riley had called Timmy asked, jumping up and down near Riley as if he had ants in his pants.

"At the kids' table?" Riley scratched his jaw. "Not this year, Timmy. I've brought a guest with me. She needs me at the adult table with her. I have to protect her from the big people."

Not hiding his disappointment, the boy gave Trinity a disgusted look. "She's just a girl, Uncle Riley."

"Just a girl, he says." Riley ruffled the boy's hair. "I'll have to remind you of that in a few years."

Trinity found herself watching Riley's family interact, watched the open affection, the laughter, the genuine gladness to be together, and she tried not to feel envious. She also tried not to feel guilty that Riley frowned more than smiled. She wasn't the only one who noticed and, unfortunately, various family members would shoot them curious looks from time to time, but no one asked what the problem was.

They had to be wondering, though. Why would he bring someone who so obviously didn't fit in with their wonderful lives? Why did it even matter? After all, she wouldn't be seeing these people ever again. Riley wouldn't want her to.

He'd given in to his nephew's repeated requests to come and check out the new video game Santa had brought him or he'd just given up completely on her. Either way, he'd disappeared some time ago, which was probably for the best because something his brother had said to him had made him almost growl earlier.

In a room full of people, yet oddly alone at an open archway leading into the foyer, she took a sip of hot cinnamon apple cider, liking the mix of sweet and tangy flavors and wishing it would settle her nerves.

Wishing her insides didn't twist, her mind didn't doubt, her stomach didn't roil. That she really was a part of this family and could go and play video games with Riley and the kids. Or even lounge comfortably with the crew that was settling in to watch a football game and talking back and forth about which team was going to win.

She wished she could be a glass-half-full kind of girl, rather than what stared back at her in the mirror. How did one go about changing one's reflection?

She rested her head on the archway and wished she could blend into this love-filled family.

"She doesn't seem to be having a very good time. Neither do you, for that matter."

Ouch. Was she supposed to have been able to overhear Riley's youngest sister? The pregnant one. She couldn't remember her name. She'd met so many different people today. Easily more than forty, although it might as well have been hundreds for how they'd made her head spin.

"We are a bit much to take in," Riley said defensively. Trinity's heart lurched at his defense but then crumbled at his next statement. "But you're right. I shouldn't have brought her here today, but she doesn't have any family and I didn't want her to be alone. Not on Christmas Day." He paused and she couldn't hear what his sister said. "Maybe, but, regardless, I made a grave miscalculation where she was concerned. One I dearly regret."

He wished he hadn't brought her? Well, duh, of course he wished he hadn't brought her. She was ruining his day with his family. What a Christmas-killer she was.

Determined not to dampen his day or this lovely family's day any more than she already had, she forced a smile onto her face and joined the closest group of adults to her.

Somehow she'd fake her way through the rest of the day.

Christmas couldn't end soon enough. Was she doomed to feel this way for ever?

Taking a quick glance toward Trinity as he pulled the car out onto the highway, Riley sighed. "You're quiet."

She'd been quiet most of the day. With him, at any rate. When he'd come out from trying to make up to Timmy for snapping at the boy, Trinity had joined a group playing cards. She'd laughed and had seemed to enjoy herself. Except when he'd come near. Then the silent treatment had rolled in.

"Sometimes it's better to say nothing at all."

"Than to say something bad?" On the day after they'd first made love. Christmas morning. The entire day should have been filled with smiles and happiness. She'd clammed up and shut him out rather than embrace the goodness of what they could have shared on what was probably the only Christmas they'd spend together.

"You think I would say something bad?"

Why was it he stuck his foot in his mouth so easily where she was concerned? He loved her. He didn't want to pick a fight with her. Not really. Or maybe he did because he felt so frustrated by the whole situation. At this point he wasn't sure what he wanted.

"No, I don't think you would say anything bad. What I think is that you'd sit quietly and answer a thousand questions as politely and concisely as you possibly could then go right back to being quiet, as if you'd taken a vow of silence rather than make any effort to make conversation."

Her face flushed pink. "I made an effort to talk to your family."

Keeping his eyes on the road and one hand on the steering-wheel, he raked his other hand through his hair. "I wanted you to like my family. To not have to make an effort to talk to them, but for it to flow naturally. I wanted them to like you."

"I did like them."

He heard her swallow and figured he'd said too much. That he should have held in what he wanted, because what he wanted didn't seem to matter.

"Did they not like me?"

A damn of emotion broke loose within him and he failed to hold his irritation in.

"They knew something wasn't right between us. I finally brought a woman home and they all kept asking me if we were arguing. I was embarrassed." He knew he should stop, that he should just zip his lips and not say a word more, but his insides felt raw from walking on eggshells for most of the day. "And I guess we are, because from the moment I woke you up this morning you've been determined to fight with me. Thank God you only ruined my day and not my family's."

"I ruined your day?" Her hands were folded neatly in her lap and she stared straight ahead through the windshield, not even bothering to look his way.

This was the woman he'd made love to, the woman he had wanted to give a special Christmas to. Instead, everything had gone horribly wrong.

"I can honestly say this wasn't how I envisioned us spending Christmas Day together."

"I imagine not." Now she glanced toward him, her eyes full of emotion that he wished was focused on the positive instead of whatever had occupied her mind all day.

"Which means what? That you've deliberately needled me because you didn't want to go with me to my mother's? That you've deliberately undermined our day together?"

Because he'd had that impression all day, but why she'd do that made absolutely no sense to him. No sense whatsoever.

"From the moment of the hospital Christmas party you've refused to listen when I tell you something about myself and you claim it means something else, something that's what you want to hear. Then, when, like today, I'm not what you envisioned, you don't understand why I'm not. Well, hello, Riley, but I am a woman with real needs and real wants and real desires. If I say I like something or don't like something, guess what? That means I like something or don't like something. And you want to know something else?"

"You're obviously going to tell me whether I want to know or not." He pulled his car into his driveway and parked beneath the covered awning.

"I don't like you after all." Trinity jumped out and headed to her car.

He felt a first-class jerk. How had the day gone so wrong? Why was he going after her when it would be better to just let her leave? They had no future. Yet he couldn't let her go.

"Where do you think you're going?" he asked, putting his hand over the car door to prevent her from being able to open it.

"Anywhere you aren't," she spat at him.

"Trinity, why are you doing this?"

Her? Trinity fumed. He was trying to blame this on her? Him and his goody-two-shoes, perfect, rich, Christmas-loving family could just get over themselves. Okay, so she'd liked his family, had enjoyed playing cards with his sisters, mother and aunt, had found herself thinking that this was how families should be. How Christmas should be.

She'd longed to be a real part of his family, had been saddened that she would always be on the outside of such family moments, of real Christmas joy.

But that didn't give Riley reason to blame her for the day going wrong. She'd told him she hadn't wanted to go and he'd finagled her into doing so and then blamed her when things hadn't gone as he'd hoped. Why was that her fault?

She'd taken blame for enough things during her life. For her mother's problems. For her father leaving. For Chase finding her lacking. For Chase leaving her. She refused to take blame any more for not being what someone thought she should be.

"Because I don't want to be here. I don't want to be with you. I didn't from the beginning but I got caught up in this fairy-tale you tried to create. Well, guess what, Riley? Fairy-tales don't exist. They don't come true. Not everyone gets a Prince Charming or a happily-ever-after or even a pair of pink hightops. The whole concept of happily-ever-after is as fake as...as Santa Claus himself."

"You really believe that?"

She nodded, saw the look of disgust in his eyes, the disappointment. No doubt she'd been one big disappointment for him. From last night through today.

"I also believe that I don't want to see you any more. Just leave me alone, please. We're finished." She shoved past him and got into her car.

This time he didn't try to stop her.

CHAPTER THIRTEEN

THROUGH HER TEAR-CRAZED haze, Trinity realized she'd left her cat at Riley's. How could she have forgotten Casper?

Then again, she couldn't exactly be faulted for not thinking rationally. She'd just had a crazy few hours.

She'd had sex, amazing sex that had proved at least on one count Chase had been wrong. She wasn't frigid. She might not be a dynamo in bed, but she at least now knew what all the fuss was about.

She'd met Riley's family. She'd liked them, regretted that she'd probably never see again the wonderful women she'd come to know.

She'd realized she was in love with Riley and then proceeded to fight with him all day.

Christmas. What a blasted day! A day when everything seemed to always go wrong. Only could she really blame everything that had gone wrong today on the holiday?

She'd expected everything to go wrong and had pretty much rejected his sweet, thoughtful gifts. He was right.

She'd been the problem.

How could she have been so blind?

How could she have dirtied something so good? Because Riley was good to her. Good for her. He'd genuinely liked her. Genuinely wanted her. Thinking back to how he'd looked at her, how he'd held her and touched her, she had to wonder if maybe he genuinely loved her.

She'd acted immature, scared, prickly. All because she'd fallen in love and didn't want to be hurt again. In the process she'd been the catalyst that had set the disastrous domino effect into play.

Today she'd been a one-woman demolition crew.

She would see him again. He had her cat. They worked together.

But before she saw him again, she needed to get her head straight. Needed to figure out who she was and what she wanted.

She went up to her apartment, still lost in thought about what she needed to do next. Was she woman enough to trust Riley? To trust in him? Because if she wasn't, then she just needed to let him go, let this be the end rather than continually looking for problems and dragging him down in the process.

If she was woman enough to trust him, if he'd forgive her for today, which was questionable, then what? Where did they go from there?

Distracted, she unlocked her apartment door and stepped inside, only to rub her eyes in disbelief at what she saw.

A nine-foot tree dominated her living room.

A gorgeous tree decorated with twinkling white lights and silver and glass ornaments.

Perhaps he'd meant the angel ornament he'd given her at breakfast to go at the top, but she didn't see how as the tree was amazingly decorated. At the top, brushing against her ceiling, was the silver star they'd seen at the shopping mall. The one that was so reminiscent of the one from her childhood classroom when Christmas had been magical to her.

Riley paid attention to details.

She walked over, touched a clear plastic ornament. A princess ornament. The entire tree was decorated with various princess paraphernalia. Cartoon princesses. A pumpkin coach. Tiny glass slippers. A magic wand. A crown.

A single medium-sized package was under the tree.

How had he done this?

When had he done this?

Last night. When she'd woken up and he hadn't been there. He'd been here. At her house. Decorating. Trying to bring the magic of Christmas into her life.

He'd played Santa.

A tear slid down her cheek.

She plopped down on the floor, picked up the package. A tag read, "Don't open until December 25th".

Being careful not to tear the paper, she undid piece of tape after piece of tape. A shiny silver box was inside. She lifted the lid, moved away white tissue paper.

Her eyes widened at what she saw. "Wow."

She kicked off her shoes. Holding her breath in anticipation, she slipped her foot into one pink hightop and admired the perfect fit. Oh, yeah, the man paid attention.

"I had to guess your size."

"Riley." She spun towards the door. Her open door. She'd been so distracted when she'd stepped inside that she hadn't closed it. He stood there, filling up the doorway with her cat in his arms.

"Sorry, I didn't mean to interrupt, but the door was open."

Her cheeks flushed. With joy that he was there. She didn't need the magic of Christmas in her life.

She needed Riley, because he made every day magic. He *was* magic.

"You're not interrupting. Not really." Not at all. Never had she been happier to see anyone. Would he think her crazy if she ran and threw herself at him? Wrapped her arms around his neck? Her legs around his waist?

"I brought Casper." He glanced around, looked awkward then set the squirming cat down. Casper took off towards the tree, intent to check out the new items invading her space.

They both watched the cat sniff and check out the tree, the open package, and then settle into the box lid as if it was the most comfortable of beds.

Riley put his hands in his pants pockets. "I won't keep you."

He turned to go. Every fiber of her being screamed to stop him. To risk everything and fight for this man. Whatever came, pain, loss, suffering, a single moment in his arms was worth taking that risk.

"Please do," she called out to his retreating back.

He turned, his forehead wrinkled. "What?"

She stood, took a deep breath. "Please do keep me, Riley."

She wanted him to keep her for ever.

"I don't understand."

She took a step towards him then another, until she stood right in front of him, one shoe on, one shoe off. She stared up into his beautiful blue eyes.

"I want you to keep me, Riley. For ever."

He regarded her for a moment. "What are you saying, Trinity?"

"That I'm an idiot who is so scared that you won't love me, that you will leave me, that I've made it impossible for you to love me and all too probable that you'd leave."

"You pushed me away."

She nodded.

"Why?"

"Because I was scared of how I feel about you."

"Which is?"

"I feel as if I can't breathe when you aren't around."

Some of the tension around his eyes started to ease. "And?"

"And as if I can't breathe when you're around because you take my breath away."

"Keep going," he insisted, crossing his arms over his chest. But his eyes had lost the cloudiness that had hidden away the sparkle she loved. Now that sparkle had come back and gave her strength. If she wanted this, wanted him, she was going to have to confront her fears, not let them overpower her the way they had for the entire day, for years. "You aren't going to make this easy, are you?"

"Lady, when I finally have you admitting that you care about me and want me in your life, you'd better believe that I'm going to keep pushing."

"I…" She shrugged. "I didn't know why you were so nice to me, why you wanted me, why you chose me. I thought maybe I was just another charity case."

"Why wouldn't I choose you? You're everything to me. All day I've kidded myself that we were a mistake, that we should just call it quits, that I could let you go because I'm not a forever kind of man. But from the time you drove away, I knew I couldn't ever call it quits with you." He ran his fingers through his hair. "I don't know what to do, Trinity. I never saw myself as marrying or having kids. Not with my career. I didn't want to be one of those dads." He paused. "I didn't want to be my dad."

"Your dad?" she asked, reeling at all he'd admitted, reeling that he'd said he loved her.

"He worked all the time, was always gone. That's why Christmas is so special to my family. It was the one and only time of the year that my dad didn't work. We had a day of him being with us, playing with us, with us being the center of his attention for an entire day. When the holiday was over, he was back at work and we rarely saw him until the following Christmas. I don't mean to whine. I know I was blessed. He was a good man, provided a good living for his family." Riley shrugged. "It's just that it seemed he was only there as part of our family at Christmas."

"Him working so hard allowed your mother to always be there for you kids, though."

"You're right," Riley agreed. "I know that in my head."

"But in your heart?"

"In my heart, I don't want to be like him."

"Which is?"

"A husband whose wife was lonely. A father whose children longed for his presence. A man I only have good memories of from Christmas."

"I'm sorry," she said, and meant it. "But at least you do have those memories. And now I understand why Christmas is so important to you, to your family."

Riley nodded. "The first few Christmases after he'd

died, my mother was devastated. My brother and sisters and I decided we were going to make sure to always be there for Christmas, to spend a good portion of the day with her, to bring her as much joy as possible."

"I'd say you were a success. She couldn't stop smiling and laughing today."

"But the other woman I wanted to bring as much joy as possible to wasn't smiling and laughing today. Not with me."

She wrapped her arms around his neck, hugged him tightly to her. "I'm sorry, Riley. I was confused, and last night…last night blew me away."

"Last night blew both of us away." He touched her cheek. "I've been doing all the chasing, Trinity, and you've been doing a lot of running." He gestured to her gift. "You said you weren't a glass slipper kind of girl, that you wanted pink hightops so you could run. When you need to run, run to me, Trinity."

Her eyes misted and she put her palms against his face. "It may take me a while to get my head on straight at times, but I will always run to you. You're my star."

He stared down at her in question.

"The star that leads me where I need to be."

He smiled. "I hope so."

She took a deep breath, rested her forehead against his chin. "For however long you want me, I'm yours, Riley."

"Then you're going to be mine for ever." He took her in his arms, kissed her. "Please, don't ever shut me out again the way you did today. My youngest sister could tell I was in love with you. She commented on how much when we were talking today."

That was what his sister had said?

"You told her that you'd made a mistake, that you regretted bringing me."

"You heard that?" He hugged her. "Our timing was off. We needed today, just you and me figuring out what happened last night and making sure we didn't do anything to mess up it happening again and again. But I couldn't cancel Christmas with my family. I just shouldn't have coerced you into going with me."

"I understand. I wouldn't have wanted you to have canceled. As a matter of fact, what I kept thinking was that I wanted what you had. That I wanted to be a part of that family, to experience the warmth and love of what Christmas should be." She stood on tiptoe and pressed a kiss to his lips. "You are what Christmas and love should be."

Riley kissed her long and hard. "My heart is yours, princess. I don't have all the answers to our future, but I'm yours every day for the rest of my life."

Her breath caught. "Really?"

"Really." His eyes catching on something behind her, he swept her up off her feet, carried her over to the tree then sat her down. "There's something I want to do."

Seeing what his gaze had caught on, she knew what he was going to do. Her heart swelled.

He pulled a chair over and she automatically sat down. He dropped to one knee and picked up the other hightop.

"Thank you for this." She spread out her arms towards the tree. "You make a great Santa."

He shook his head. "Wrong guy."

She arched a brow, not quite sure what he meant.

"I'm not going for Santa in your life."

"What are you going for in my life?"

He grinned and slipped the other shoe onto her foot. "I'm your Prince Charming, of course. Your right Prince Charming."

"My one and only Prince Charming," she assured him, touching his arm.

"I like the sound of that."

"But, Riley, I should tell you."

"Yes?"

"You're my Santa, too."

"Oh?"

She nodded. "Every day I'm with you is like Christmas."

"You're the one who is a gift, princess. You've made my life better."

"Hey, I have a gift for you, too," she recalled, jumping up and rushing to the drawer where she'd stashed his gift.

Smiling, she handed him the bag.

He eyed it suspiciously. "You used a bag rather than wrapping paper?"

She grinned. "I bought this before my wrapping lesson."

He pulled out the paper and lifted out a box about the size of his hand. What was inside made him burst out laughing.

And had his eyes shining brightly.

"It's perfect."

"I thought you'd think so, snowflake."

Holding the ornament as if it was the most precious treasure, he smiled at her, love in his eyes. "I love you, Trinity."

Her heart swelled with Christmas joy, with love. She leaned forward and planted a kiss on his lips. "I love you, too. Thank you for my best Christmas ever."

He grinned. "Until next year's."

EPILOGUE

CHRISTMAS DAY A year later, Trinity wasn't so sure Riley had topped the previous year's Christmas. As a matter of fact, at the moment she wasn't even sure she liked him. Or that she'd ever allow him to touch her again.

She moaned with pain.

There was just something about this day.

"Come on, sweetheart, you're almost there."

Okay, so she probably would let him. After all, she did love him with all her heart and was loved by all of his heart.

"Breathe, honey."

She was breathing. Trinity grimaced at her husband, who dabbed at her sweaty face with a washcloth. Her calm, patient, always-positive husband who had brought so much joy into her life. So much happiness. So much security and magic.

He'd given her Christmas.

And so much more.

"When the next contraction hits," the obstetrician said, "and when I tell you, I want you to push as hard as you can."

She felt as if she'd been pushing for hours, but in reality not that much time had gone by. She'd woken up during the middle of Christmas Eve night, had found Riley missing from bed and had gone to look for him. Not surprisingly, she'd found him beneath their Christmas tree, playing Santa.

What had been surprising was that before she'd been able to say anything she'd felt a gush of liquid between her legs. A gush of amniotic fluid as her waters had broken.

According to the clock on the wall, it was barely nine on Christmas morning. She was in the hospital. With her husband, The pink hightops she'd insisted on wearing digging into the stirrups. With their soon-to-be-born baby on its way. And their family anxious in the waiting area. The entire Williams clan.

"Push, Trinity," Riley encouraged, clasping her hand and focusing on her. "Look at me and push."

She tried to look at him but kept squeezing her eyes closed in pain as she attempted to turn her insides out.

"Breathe, baby. Breathe."

Breathe. Push. Pant.

Trinity felt a gut-wrenching pain then horrendous pressure.

"The baby's head is out," the doctor praised. "There's lots of hair."

Another contraction, a few more pushes and Trinity cried.

"You have a baby girl," the obstetrician informed them. "Congratulations."

"A girl." Riley said the words with absolute wonder. "We have a daughter."

Exhausted, but amazed at the man smiling at her with all the love a man had ever felt for any woman shining in his eyes, Trinity nodded. "A girl, born on Christmas Day."

"The most precious gift anyone has ever given me."

Trinity tried to point out that Riley was the one who'd given her the precious gift of their daughter.

"Joy Noelle Williams."

Trinity glanced down at the baby in her arms. "I have this feeling that my role as princess is going to be booted by this little sweetheart." She smiled at the man who'd brought so much joy into her life. Who'd made her part of his family, given her a family of her own. "I think you may have a hard time topping this year."

"Perhaps in your delicate condition you've forgotten, but I'm a man who aims to please, so just you wait and see."

Her eyes widened because she recognized that determined look on his face.

He just grinned. "Merry Christmas, darling."

* * * * *

HER FIREFIGHTER UNDER THE MISTLETOE

SCARLET WILSON

*This book is dedicated to my good friends
Jane Bell, Kirsten Gallacher
and Lorna McCririe who all enjoy
getting into the spirit of Christmas!*

Scarlet Wilson wrote her first story aged eight and has never stopped. She's worked in the health service for twenty years, trained as a nurse and a health visitor. Scarlet now works in public health and lives on the West Coast of Scotland with her fiancé and their two sons. Writing medical romances and contemporary romances is a dream come true for her.

CHAPTER ONE

Bzzz...bzzz...

The noise jerked Jess out of the delicious tranquil state that had been enveloping her.

Her eyes blinked at the bright light outside, the fuzziness of her brain trying to adjust and make sense of it all.

Her pager usually woke her in the dark of the night—just like it had three times last night. Having it wake her in the middle of the day was an entirely new experience.

A baby with RSV had kept her awake most of the night in Paediatric ITU, and when the ward had finally quietened down around an hour ago, she'd brought her coffee in here to do some paperwork.

Fat chance. She touched the coffee cup on her desk. Stone cold. Had she even managed a sip before she'd wiped out?

How long had she been asleep? She wriggled in her chair, rolling her shoulders back and trying to ease the knots out of her back.

Bzzz... Bzzz...

She glanced at the number. A and E. Another admission. Probably another respiratory problem.

It was Glasgow, at the start of November, but it felt like the middle of winter. The temperature had dropped dramatically in the last few days and paediatric emergency admissions had soared. Trips and falls on the slippery pavements had resulted in a whole host of strains, fractures and head injuries. Asthma and respiratory complaints were through the roof. Infections and nondescript viruses were causing mayhem with new babies and toddlers.

Just as well she didn't have anyone to go home to. She hadn't seen the inside of her house for days.

She picked up the phone and dialled A and E. 'It's Dr Rae. You were paging me.'

The voice was brusque, skipping over any pleasantries and getting straight to business. 'Assemble a flying squad. Nursery minibus in the Clyde on the city outskirts. Unknown number of casualties. We're waiting for more information from emergency services. You need to be ready to leave in five minutes.'

She was on her feet in seconds and throwing open the door, her tiredness, sore muscles and fatigue instantly forgotten. 'I need a flying squad,' she yelled, glancing down the corridor as the sister of the ward hurried towards her, 'Where's Jackie? I want her with me.'

Jackie appeared at her side in an instant. 'What is it?'

'Nursery minibus in the Clyde.'

The experienced nurse's face paled. 'In this weather? In these temperatures?'

'Go!' The ward sister waved her hand at them. 'Leave everything else to me.'

Jess started jogging down the corridor, heading for the stairs. It took less than a minute to reach A and E and one of the staff thrust a green suit into her hands. She climbed into it immediately, noting the fluorescent 'Doctor' sign on the back. It was essential that all staff could be picked out easily in an emergency. One of the paramedics thrust a pair of gloves towards her. 'Take these, you'll need them out there.'

She glanced at her watch. It was only two-thirty in the afternoon. At least a few hours of daylight left. She prayed they wouldn't need more than that.

'Let's go!'

The shout came from the front doors. Jackie appeared at her side again, similarly clad in a green jumpsuit with 'Nurse' emblazoned across the back. They picked up the pre-packed paediatric emergency kits and headed outside.

Jess climbed into one of the emergency vehicles and fastened her seat belt as the sirens sounded and they headed out onto the motorway. She turned to the man sitting next to her, 'I'm Jess, paediatric consultant. Have you heard any more?'

He nodded. 'Stan, emergency service co-ordinator. Lots of problems. Someone sideswiped the minibus and sent it down a thirty-foot slippery bank and straight into the Clyde.'

Jess tried to stop the sharp intake of breath. Her brain was into immediate overtime, imagining the types of injuries the children could have sustained.

'How many?'

He shook his head. 'Still waiting for confirmation. Three adults, at least ten kids.'

'Age range?'

'From two to five. We're getting more information all the time. The other nursery minibus missed everything. They didn't even know there had been an accident. The police are there now, collecting details of all the kids.'

Jess swallowed, trying to ignore the huge lump in her throat. The flying squad wasn't called out too often. She was the consultant on call—it was her job to be here.

But that didn't mean her stomach wasn't churning at the thought of the scene she was about to face.

Yes, she could appear calm. Yes, she could use her skills and clinical expertise. Yes, she would do everything that was expected of her and beyond.

But would she sleep tonight?

Probably not.

There was a crackle of the radio and some voices she couldn't distinguish. The driver turned his head. 'Five minutes. They've called out the rapid response and specialist rope rescue team. They should arrive just before us. Let's hope Callum got out of bed on the right side today.'

'Who is Callum?'

The words were out of her mouth automatically, before she even had a chance to think. 'And what's the specialist rope rescue team?'

None of this sounded good. All she could think about was the children involved in the crash. What did this mean for them?

Stan's face was pale. 'It means that the banking is too dangerous for our crews to work on, that, plus the added complication of being in water means we need the specialist crew.'

'Will it delay me getting to the children?'

Stan averted his eyes, obviously not wanting to give her the answer. He hadn't answered the other part of her question. He hadn't mentioned Callum. And the driver's comment had made her ears prick up. *Let's hope he got out of bed on the right side.*

The last thing she needed right now was a prima donna firefighter getting in her way when she had kids to attend to. 'Is Callum a bit on the crabbit side, then?' she asked as they pulled over to the side of the road. A bad-tempered

man she could deal with. As long as he didn't interfere
with her job.

'Only on a good day,' muttered Stan as he jumped from
the rescue vehicle.

Jessica opened the door carefully, to avoid the passing
traffic on the busy road. The police had cordoned part of
it off as best they could. But the constant flow of traffic
was unnerving.

The cold air hit her straight away. Biting cold, sneaking under the folds of her jumpsuit, made her wish she
was wearing a hat, scarf and fleece and not just the thin
gloves she'd been handed.

She flinched at the sight of the crash barrier, twisted
beyond all recognition and lying like a useless piece of
junk at the side of the road.

There were raised voices to her left. She turned just in
time to see a broad-shouldered man snap on his harness
and disappear down the side of the banking, with the vain
words 'Risk assessment' being shouted after him by his
colleagues.

A sense of unease came over her body. A vague awareness trickling through her. Callum—that's what they'd
said. It couldn't possibly be Callum Kennedy, could it?
She hadn't seen him since school and had no idea where
he'd ended up. But there was something vaguely familiar
about the body that had just disappeared over the edge.

Her footsteps shortened as she reached the edge of the
steep bank. Someone touched her shoulder, looking at the
sign on her back. 'Oh, good, the doctor. Let's get you harnessed up.'

She lifted her legs as she was clipped and harnessed
and talked through the motions of the descent. Her bag

was sent down ahead. A burly firefighter appeared next to her. 'You'll go down with me. Have you done this before?'

She peered over the edge again. Thirty feet of steep descent. How many times had the minibus rolled on the way down?

She could see it now, lying on its side in the Clyde, the icy cold water surrounding it. There was a flurry of firefighters around it. Some on top, trying to get through the windows, some on the banking, surrounded by other pieces of equipment.

'Get me down there.' Her eyes met the firefighter's and the whispered words grew more determined. 'Get me down to those children.'

He nodded and spoke into the radio clipped to his shoulder. 'The doc and I are on our way.'

She took a deep breath and turned with her back towards the water, edging down the side of the bank in time with the firefighter. It was slippery work. A thin layer of frost had formed over the mud at the side of the bank, her simple shoes giving her literally no grip. The firefighter's firm hand in the small of her back kept her from slipping completely. Even through her gloves the biting cold was already making her fingers numb.

She looked over her shoulder. 'How much further?'

'Keep your eyes straight ahead, please.'

Her anxiety was building. She wanted to get down. She wanted to help those kids. But she needed to get down there in one piece.

'Who is Callum? Is it Callum Kennedy?'

The firefighter's eyes gave a spark of amusement. 'Know him, do you?'

She wrinkled her nose. 'I'm not entirely sure. I think so. I went to school with a Callum Kennedy, but I didn't get a good look at him before he went over the edge.' She shrugged her shoulders, 'I'm not even sure he would recognise me now.'

The firefighter gave her a little smile, 'Oh, I'm sure he would.'

'What does he do exactly?'

'He's the head of the rope rescue unit. He'll be in charge down here.' They were inching closer and closer to the bottom.

'And is he any good?' She bit her lip. It might seem a little cheeky, but Stan had already mentioned he could be crabbit. She needed to know that he wouldn't get in her way. That he wouldn't stop her doing her job with these kids.

'Put it this way—if me or my kids were stuck anywhere that a rope rescue was needed?' He lifted his eyes skyward. 'I would be praying to the man upstairs that Callum would be on duty that night. He's the safest pair of hands we've got—particularly near kids.' He caught her around the waist. 'That's us. Let me just unhook you from this line—but we'll leave your harness on. You'll need it to get back up and they'll hook you up to another one if you're near the water.'

'Where's the doc?' came the shout.

Jess swivelled around, looking for her bag. 'I'm here. I'm coming.'

Several of the firefighters were forming a line, passing two little kids along to the edge of the bank. Jackie appeared at her side. 'Let's go.'

They reached the kids just as they were placed on warm blankets on the ground. Jess worked quickly, gently feeling over their little bodies for signs of injuries as she spoke to them in a quiet voice.

'Need some help?'

She nodded at the firefighter next to her. 'Heat them up. There are no obvious injuries. But they're in shock.' She turned back to the minibus. Now she was closer she could see every dent, every bash, every hole in the metalwork.

It made the chill seem even worse. 'Are these the first two?'

The man next to her nodded. 'Do we have a number yet? How many kids are injured?'

'Twelve. That's the figure we have for the moment. Just awaiting confirmation.'

She moved over to the side of the slippery river's edge as an adult was passed along and dealt with by the paramedics. She could see the hive of activity going on within the bus, hear the whimpering cries of the children.

'Can I get over there? Do you need me to get into the bus?' Her anxiety was building. She couldn't stand here and do nothing. It just wasn't in her nature. She needed to be at the heart of the action. It was her job to prioritise, triage and treat the sickest kids. She needed to be next to those children.

Her voice must have carried in the cold air, because a head whipped up from the bus. The man was lying across the windows, reaching down to grasp a squirming child, and his eyes connected with hers.

'Stay *exactly* where you are.'

Callum. Callum Kennedy. Absolutely no mistake.

She saw him flinch visibly as his brain made the connection of who was standing on the riverbank.

He'd recognised her? After all these years?

The cold hard air hit her lungs. She must have sucked in a bigger breath than normal. Her skin prickled.

How did she feel about seeing Callum Kennedy thirteen years on?

Unprepared.

Like a seventeen-year-old again, standing in a dark nightclub and willing herself not to cry as they broke up. It had been the right decision. The sensible decision. They had both been going to university, she in Glasgow and he—after a wait of a few years—in Aberdeen. Their relationship would never have worked out. It had been best for them both.

It just hadn't felt that way.

She pushed her feet more firmly into the ground, trying to focus her attention. Callum's gaze hadn't moved. It was still fixed on her face.

She could feel the colour start to rise in her cheeks. It was unnerving. But why the flinch? Was she really such an unwelcome sight after all this time?

Or maybe she was imagining this—maybe he'd no idea who she was at all.

Callum couldn't believe it. He was holding a child firmly by the waist, while a colleague released him from his seat belt.

But Callum's eyes were fixed on the flyaway caramel-coloured hair on the riverbank. Running up and down the thin frame that was in no way hidden by the bright green jumpsuit.

A sight he hadn't seen in thirteen years.

A lifetime ago.

His childhood sweetheart, here on the banks of the Clyde, at the scene of an accident.

He'd always wondered if he'd come across her sometime, some place.

As a firefighter he'd been in and out of most of the A and E departments in the city. But in all these years he'd never glimpsed her, never seen her name on any board.

He knew that Jessica had gone to university to do her medical training, but had no idea where she'd ended up, or which field she'd specialised in.

And now he knew. She was somewhere here in Glasgow, specialising in paediatrics. Why else would she be here?

Would she even remember him? It looked as though she had—even though he'd filled out considerably since the last time they'd met. She, on the other hand, looked as if she'd faded away to a wisp.

Although he could see her slight frame, the most visible changes were around her facial features and structure. And it wouldn't have mattered how many clothes she was bundled up in, he would have noticed at twenty paces.

It struck him as strange. The young Jessica he remembered had had an attention-grabbing figure and a personality to match. Every memory he had of her was a happy one. And for a second he felt as if they could all come flooding back.

There was a tug at his arms, followed by a sensation of relief and a lightening of the weight in his arms. He pulled upwards automatically. The little guy's seat belt had been released.

He pulled him up and held him to his chest, capturing the little body with his own, holding him close to let a little heat envelop the shivering form. The little boy wasn't even crying any more. He was just too cold.

He held the boy for a few seconds longer. He looked around four, just a year younger than his own son Drew. He couldn't help the automatic paternal shiver that stole down his spine at the thought of something like this happening to his son. It didn't even bear thinking about.

His only relief right now was that he hadn't signed a consent form for the school to go on any trips this week, meaning that his little Drew was safely tucked up inside the primary school building.

The temperature in the minibus was freezing, with water halfway up its side-on frame. They were going to have to move quicker to get these kids out in time.

'Callum! Callum! Pass him over, please.'

Oh, she'd recognised him all right. The authoritative tone made no mistake about that.

'Okay, little guy, we're going to get you heated up now.' He ruffled the little boy's hair before he passed him over to the arms stretched out towards him. He didn't have time to think about Jessica Rae now. Too much was at stake.

He thrust his head back inside the minibus. 'How are we doing?'

John, one of his co-workers, lifted his head. 'I'll have two more for you in a second. But I need some more light in here.'

Another voice shouted from the darkness, 'I think I've got one with a broken leg and another unconscious. Can we get a paramedic or a doctor in here?'

Callum lifted his head back up. The light was fading quickly, even though it was only afternoon. Winter nights closed in quickly—by four p.m. it would be pitch black. He didn't think twice. 'I need a paramedic or a doctor over here, please.'

He could see the quick confab at the side of the river. Jess was issuing instructions to the nurse with her and the paramedics and ambulance technicians at her side. Things were going smoothly out there. Two of the children and one of the adults had already been transported back up the slippery bank. The latest little guy was still being assessed.

Jess moved to the side of the bank. He could see the impatience on her face as she waited for her safety harness to be clipped to the harness point on the shore. She shook her head at the waders she was offered, grabbed at a hand that was offered and started to climb towards the minibus.

It was precarious. The Clyde was not a quiet-flowing river. It was fast and churning, the icy-cold water lapping furiously at the side of the minibus as it penetrated the interior.

The minibus was moving with the momentum of the river and Jess slipped as she climbed over the wing of the minibus, the weight from her pack making her unstable. She was just within Callum's reach and he stretched out and grabbed the tips of her fingers with a fierce, claw-like grip.

'Yeowww!' Her other hand flailed upwards then closed over his, and he steadied her swaying body as she thudded down next to him.

The red colour in her cheeks was gone, replaced with the whiteness of cold. 'Thanks,' she breathed, the warm air forming a little steamy cloud next to them.

'Fancy seeing you here,' he murmured, giving her a little smile. It had been impossible to spot from the riverbank, but here, up close, he had a prime-time view of the thing he'd always loved most about Jess—her deep brown eyes.

The smile was returned. That little acknowledgement. That in another time, another place...

The memories were starting to invade his senses. Jessica in his arms throwing back her head and laughing, exposing the pale skin of her neck—skin that he wanted to touch with his lips.

His brain kicked back into gear. This was work. And he never got distracted at work.

'Have you done anything like this before?'

She pulled back a little. It was the tiniest movement, a flinch almost, as if she was taken aback by his change of tone.

She shook her head and her eyebrows rose. 'An overturned minibus in a fast-flowing river with lots of paediatric casualties?'

The irony wasn't lost on him. He might do this sort of thing day in, day out, but Jess was usually in the confines of a safe, warm, comfortable hospital.

She hunched up onto her knees and pointed at the harness. 'I've never even had one of these on before, let alone abseiled down a hillside.' She wiggled her hips and tried to move her tether. 'These things aren't too comfortable, are they?'

It struck him—almost blindsided him—how brave she was being. The Jessica Rae he'd known at school hadn't even liked contact sports. He closed his eyes as an unguarded memory of other activities of a physical nature swam into his mind.

Focus. Focus now.

He knelt upwards and grabbed her around her waist, trying not to think about how it felt to be touching Jessica Rae again after all these years. Trying not to remember how her firm flesh used to feel beneath his fingers. What had happened?

'I'm going to lower you down, Jess.' He peered through the side window next to them, which had been removed. 'Your feet will get a bit wet because there's some water on the floor. Are you okay with that?'

She nodded. She didn't look scared. She didn't look

panicked. But there was a tiny little flicker of something behind her eyes. She looked in control.

He shouted down into the minibus. 'John, I'm going to lower the doc down. Can you take care of her?'

She started. 'Take care of me?' It was almost as if he'd just insulted her. 'Don't you mean take care of the kids?'

But Callum wasn't paying attention. He was back in rescue mode. 'There are two kids in the back who need your attention. One unconscious, the other with a broken leg. It's too cramped in there to take your bag down. Shout up and tell me what you need.'

Their eyes met again as she shrugged off her pack. 'Ready?' She nodded and he lowered her down slowly into the waiting arms of the firefighter below, praying that things would go to plan.

'Sheesh!' Her feet hit the icy cold water and it sent the surge of cold right up through her body. No one could stand in this for long.

It took her eyes a few seconds to adjust to the gloom inside the minibus. The mottled daylight was still sending shadows through one side of the bus, but Callum's body and those of the other firefighters lying across the windows was blocking out the little light that was left.

A flashlight was thrust into her hands. 'Here you go, Doc.' She turned it on immediately. The first sight was the way the water was lapping quickly around them. She felt the vaguest wave of panic. 'Is the river rising?'

John nodded. 'Not quickly enough for us to worry about.' His eyes didn't quite meet hers.

Work quickly.

She noticed his black trousers ballooning around his

ankles and gave him a little nod. 'Did you say no to the waders too?'

He smiled. 'No room for waders in here, Doc. Space is limited.'

She nodded and she shuffled around him towards the kids. 'Are any of the kids in water?' Her feet were already numb. There was a real danger of hypothermia setting in for any kid exposed to these temperatures.

'Four.'

'Four?' She could feel a flare of panic. She was one person. How could she attend to four kids?

Callum stuck his head in the gap. 'Start with the two at the back, Jess. As soon as you've stabilised them and they're safe to move, my men will get them out. The other two don't appear injured.' He pointed to the front of the bus. 'My men are getting them out as quickly as possible.' He looked towards the back of the bus. 'The little girl is called Rosie.'

His voice was calm, authoritative. The kind of guy in an emergency who told you things would be okay and you believed him—just because of the way he said it.

She pushed her way back to a little girl with masses of curly hair, still strapped into her seat. Her leg was at a peculiar angle, and it hadn't taken a doctor to make an accurate diagnosis of a fracture. The little boy behind her, strapped into the window seat, was unconscious, but she couldn't possibly get to him until she'd moved this little girl. She took off her gloves and put her hand round the girl, feeling for a pulse at his neck and checking to see he was still breathing. Yes, his pulse was slowing and his chest was rising and falling. But in these cold temperatures hypothermia was a real risk. She had to work as quickly as possible.

The water was lapping around their little legs and would be dropping their temperatures dramatically.

She shouted up to Callum, 'I need you to pass me down the kit with analgesia—I need to give Rosie some morphine. It's in a red box, in the front pouch of the bag.' She waited a few seconds until the box appeared then shouted again, 'And an inflatable splint.'

She spoke gently to Rosie, stroking her hair and distracting her, calculating the dosage in her head. It was too difficult to untangle the little girl from her clothes and find an available patch of skin. The last thing she needed to do was cause this little girl more pain. She took a deep breath and injected it through the thick tights on her leg, waiting a few minutes for it to take effect. 'Pass me the splint,' she whispered to John.

The positioning on the bus was difficult. 'I'm sorry, honey,' she whispered, as the little girl gave a little yelp as she straightened her leg and inflated the splint around about it to hold it in place.

'Is she ready to be moved?'

'Not quite. Can you get a collar? In fact, get me two. Once I've got that on her, you can move her.'

It was only a precaution. The little girl didn't appear to have any other injuries apart from her leg. She seemed to be moving her other limbs without any problems, but Jess didn't want to take a risk.

It only took a few seconds to manoeuvre the collar into place and fasten it securely. The cold water was moving quickly. It had only been around the children's legs when she'd entered the vehicle—now it was reaching their waists. Time was absolutely of the essence here.

She was freezing. How on earth would these children

be feeling? Kids were so much more susceptible to hypothermia because they lost heat more quickly than adults.

Another firefighter had appeared next to John, and they held a type of stretcher between them. Space was at a premium so Jess pushed herself back into the corner of the bus to allow them to load the little girl and pass her up through the window to Callum.

Time was ticking on. The sky was darkening and the level of the freezing water rising. She squeezed her way into the seat vacated by the little girl and started to do a proper assessment on the little unconscious boy, who was held in place by his seat belt.

'Anyone know his name?' she shouted to the crew.

'It's Marcus.' The deep voice in her ear made her jump.

'Where did you come from? I thought you were on the roof?'

'The water's too cold to have anyone in it for long. I told John to go ashore and dry off.'

'Tell me about it. Try being a kid.'

There was an easy familiarity in having Callum at her side. It didn't matter that she hadn't seen him for years, it almost felt as if it had been yesterday.

Callum had changed, and so had she. The skinny youth had filled out in all the right places. His broad shoulders and muscled chest were visible through his kit. The shorter hairstyle suited him—even though it revealed the odd grey hair. They were only visible this close up.

'What do you need?'

He was watching as she checked Marcus's pulse, took his temperature, looked him over for any other injuries and shone a torch in his eyes to check his pupil reactions.

She shook her head. 'This is going to have to be a scoop and run. He's showing severe signs of hypothermia. His pulse is low and I can't even get a reading with this thing.' She shook the tympanic thermometer in the air. 'So much for accurate readings.'

She placed the collar around his neck. 'I don't want to waste any time. I can't find an obvious reason for him being unconscious. His clothes are soaking—right up to his chest. We can't waste another second. Can you get me some kind of stretcher so we can get him out of here?'

Callum nodded. 'Get me a basket stretcher,' he shouted to one of his colleagues. He gestured his head to the side as the stretcher was passed down. She stared at the orange two-piece contraption, watching while he took a few seconds to slot the pins into place and assemble it. It had curved sides, handholds, adjustable patient restraints and a lifting bridle.

'This is the only way we'll get the casualties back up the steep embankment. Jump back up, Jess, we need as much room as we can to manipulate this into place.' A pair of strong arms reached down through the window towards her and she grabbed them willingly. It pained her to leave the little boy's side, but there wasn't time for egos or arguments here.

The cold air hit her again as she came back out into the open. If she'd thought standing in the icy water had been bad, it was nothing compared to the wind-chill factor. Her teeth started chattering.

'How…many more patients?' she asked the firefighter next to her.

'We've extricated all the adults. There's another two kids stuck behind the front seat, but their injuries are minor and they're not in contact with the water. We'll get to them next.'

'Has someone looked them over?'

He nodded. 'Your nurse and one of the paramedics. They had another kid who was submerged. She'll be in the ambulance ahead of you. We've just radioed in.'

The minibus gave another little lurch as the currents buffeted it. 'This thing had better not roll,' came the mumble from next to her.

Jess wobbled, trying to gain her balance. She hadn't even considered the possibility of the bus rolling. That would be a nightmare. There was a tug around her waist, and she looked to the side of the riverbank where one of the rope crew was taking up some of the slack in her line. The stretcher started to emerge through the window. At last. Maybe she'd get a better look at Marcus out here.

Callum's shoulders appeared. He was easing the stretcher up gently, guiding it into the arms of his colleagues.

The minibus lurched again. Callum disappeared back down into the depths of the minibus with a thud and a matching expletive. The firefighter next to her struggled to steady the weight in his arms, the stretcher twisting and its edge catching her side-on.

She teetered at the edge of the bus, losing her footing on the slippery side.

It seemed to happen in slow motion. She felt herself fall backwards, her arms reaching out in front of her. The firefighter who'd knocked her with the stretcher had panic written all over his face. There was a fleeting second as he struggled to decide whether to decide to grab her or maintain his hold on the stretcher.

What was it that knocked the air from her lungs? The impact of hitting the water? Or the icy water instantly closing over her head? Her reaction was instantaneous, sucking inwards in panic, instead of holding her breath.

The layers of clothes were weighing her down, as were her shoes. She tried to reach for the surface. The water hadn't been that deep, had it? She was choking. Trying to suck in air that wasn't there—only murky water. Then the overwhelming feeling of panic started to take over.

CHAPTER TWO

CALLUM HIT THE bottom of the river-filled minibus with a thud, the icy water doing nothing to slow the impact. What little part of him had remained dry was now soaked to the skin.

There was a splash outside, followed by some panicked shouts. Callum was instantly swept with a feeling of dread. The jolt had been a big one. *Please, don't let them have dropped the stretcher.*

He was on his feet in seconds, his arms grabbing at the window edge above him and pulling himself up onto the side of the bus.

The stretcher was steady, the child safe and being passed along the line. The crew around him, however, was panicking.

'Where's her line? Wasn't she wearing a line?'

Oh, no. His head flicked from side to side, searching frantically for any sign of Jess. She was the only female river-side. Everyone else was safely ashore. They could only be talking about her.

'Can you see her? Can anyone see her?'

Callum didn't hesitate. Not for a second. He saw where the outstretched fingers were pointing and jumped straight into the Clyde.

The water closed around his chest, leaving him up to his

neck with barely a toehold on the river's bed. Even after
the water in the minibus, being fully submerged in the fast-
flowing Clyde was a shock to the system. Every part of
his body seemed to react at once. Everything went on full
alert, hairs on end, trying to pull heat back into his centre.

He looked around him, shouting at the guys still on top
of the bus. 'Where? Here?' He pointed to the riverbank.
'Tell them to pull in her line!'

The Clyde was murky and grey and several pieces of
ice, broken from the river's edge, floated past.

He swept his arms around under the water. He couldn't
see a thing. Not even a flash of the bright green jumpsuit
she'd been wearing. The water wasn't too deep as he was
on tiptoe. But he was a good foot taller than Jess, with a
lot more bulk and muscle. Even he could feel the hidden
currents pulling at his weight.

Every man working on the minibus had been wearing
a line—except him. He took a few seconds to follow the
lines from the riverbank to the bus, until he located the
one that led directly into the river.

The firefighters on the bank were having the same problem. It took a few moments of frantic scrambling to ascer-
tain which line belonged to Jess. They started to reel it in
and Callum waded through the water towards it.

There! A flash of green as she was tugged nearer the
surface.

He grabbed, lifting her whole body with one arm, raising her head and chest above the water's surface.

For the briefest second there was nothing, just the paler-
than-pale face.

Then she coughed and spluttered, and was promptly
sick into the river. He fastened one arm around her chest,
pulling her back towards him, supporting her weight and

lifting his other arm to signal to the crew to stop pulling in her line.

'I've got you, Jess. It's okay.' He whispered the words calmly in her ear. The cold wasn't bothering him now. There was no heat coming from her body, but he could feel the rise and fall of her chest under his hands. He could feel her breathe.

Relief. That was the sensation sweeping through him. Pure and utter relief.

He always felt like this after a rescue. It was as if the anxiety and stomach-clenching that had been an essential part of his momentum and drive to keep going just left him all at once. More often than that, after a rescue he would go home and sleep soundly for ten hours, all his energy expended. Building reserves for the next day so he could do it all again.

Even Drew understood. And on those nights his little body would climb into bed next to his father and cuddle in, his little back tucked against Callum's chest—just the way Jess's was now.

She coughed and spluttered again. He could hear her teeth chattering. She still hadn't spoken. Was she in shock?

There would be an investigation later. An investigation into why the paediatric consultant helping them had ended up in the middle of a fast-flowing icy river.

But right now he wanted to make sure Jess was okay. He started wading towards the riverbank, keeping Jess close to his chest. Several of his colleagues waded in towards him, sweeping Jess out of his arms and wrapping them both in blankets.

One of the paramedics started pulling out equipment to check her over. Callum pulled his jacket and shirt over his head. The cold air meant nothing to him right now—

he couldn't be any colder anyway. He gratefully accepted a red fleece thrust at him by one of his colleagues.

He pulled it over his head. There was instant heat as soft fleece came into contact with his icy skin. Bliss.

Two basket stretchers with a firefighter on either side were currently being guided up the steep, treacherous slope. The two kids with hypothermia. He could see the ambulance technicians waiting at the top of the bank, ready to load them into the waiting ambulances.

'Stop it!'

He turned, just in time to see Jess push herself to her feet and take a few wobbly steps.

'I'm fine. Now, leave me alone.' She pulled the blankets closer around her, obviously trying to keep the cold out.

He turned to one of his colleagues. 'See if someone will volunteer some dry clothing for our lady doc.'

Jess stalked towards him. Her face was still deathly pale, but her involuntary shivering seemed to have stopped. She pointed to the stretchers. 'I need to get to the kids. I need to get them to hospital.'

Callum shook his head. 'Jess, you've just been submerged in freezing water. You need to get checked over yourself. The kids will go straight to Parkhill. One of your colleagues will be able to take care of them.'

She shook her head fiercely. '*I* will take care of them. I'm the consultant on call. Neither of my junior colleagues has enough experience to deal with this. Two kids with hypothermia? It's hardly an everyday occurrence. Those kids need me right now.'

One of the firefighters appeared at his side with a T-shirt and another jacket. Callum rolled his eyes. 'You've still got a stubborn streak a mile wide, haven't you?'

He handed the clothes over to her. 'Get changed and

I'll get you back topside.' She shrugged off her jump-suit, tying the wet top half around her middle, hesitating only for a second before she pulled her thin cotton top off underneath.

In just a few seconds he saw her pale skin and the outline of her small breasts against her damp white bra. It was almost translucent. She pulled the other T-shirt over her head in a flash. But not before he'd managed to note just how thin she was.

Jess had always been slim. But slim with curves. What had happened to her?

She zipped the jacket up to her neck. Meeting his eyes with a steely glare. Daring him to mention the fact she'd just stripped at a riverside, or to mention her obviously underweight figure.

Callum knew better.

He'd learned over the last few years to pick his battles carefully.

Now wasn't the time.

He signalled and a couple of lines appeared down the side of the steep incline. He leaned over and clipped her harness. Her whole bottom half was still wet—as was his. Spare T-shirts and jackets could be found, but spare shoes and trousers? Not a chance.

'You do realise we go back up the way we came down?'

She sighed, but he couldn't help but notice the faint tremble in her hands. An after-effect of the cold water? Or something else?

He stepped behind her and interlocked their harnesses. 'The quickest way to get you back up is to let me help you.'

He could see her brain searching for a reason to disagree.

'You want to get back up to those kids?'

She nodded. Whatever her reservations, she'd pushed them aside.

'Then let me help you. It's like abseiling in reverse. Lean back against me.'

She was hesitating, still keeping all the weight on her legs, so he pulled her backwards towards him. He felt a little shock to feel her body next to his.

It had felt different in the water, more buoyant, the water between them cushioning the sensation. But now it was just clothes. Wet clothes, which clung to every curve of their bodies.

Her body was tense, stiff, and it took a few seconds for her to relax. He wrapped his arms around her, holding onto the lines in front of them, and gave them a little tug. His lips accidentally brushed against her ear as he spoke to her. 'We let the lines take our weight. If you just lean back into me, I'll walk up back up the incline. Just try and keep your legs in pace with mine. It feels a little weird, but it'll only take a few minutes.'

He let her listen, digest his words. He could feel her breathing sync with his, the rise and fall of their chests becoming simultaneous. She put her hands forward, holding onto the same line as he was, reaching for a little security in the strange situation.

He wrapped his hands around hers. His thick gloves were in place, to take the taut strain of the line.

He felt the tug of the line and started to walk his legs up the slope, taking her weight on his body. He looked skyward. Praying for divine intervention to stop any reactions taking place.

It was the weirdest sensation. The last time their bodies had been locked together she'd been seventeen and he'd been twenty-one. A whole lifetime had passed since then.

A marriage, a divorce, a fierce custody battle—and that was just him. What had happened to her?

His eyes went automatically to her hand. He'd always imagined a girl like Jess would be happily married with a couple of kids by this age. But even through her wet gloves he could see there was no outline of a wedding band. Not even an engagement ring.

Something clenched at him. Was it curiosity? Or was it some strange thrill that Jess might be unattached?

His head was buzzing. He couldn't even make sense of his thoughts. He hadn't seen this woman in years. He hadn't even *heard* about her in years. He had no idea what life had flung at Jessica Rae. And she had no idea what life had thrown at him.

Drew. The most important person in his world.

A world he kept tightly wrapped and carefully preserved.

Drew's mother, Kirsten, had left after the divorce and costly custody battle. She was in New York—married to her first love, who she'd claimed she should never have left in the first place, as he was twice the man that Callum was. Callum had been a 'poor substitute'. Words that still stung to this day.

By that point, Callum couldn't have cared less about her frequent temper tantrums and outbursts. He had only cared about how they impacted on Drew.

Drew was the best and only good thing to have come out of that marriage.

He didn't intend to make the same mistake twice.

He'd never introduced any woman to Drew in the three years following his divorce. No matter how many hints they'd dropped.

But his immediate and natural curiosity was taking

over. He didn't have a single bad memory about Jessica Rae. Even their break-up had been civilised.

Seeing her today had been a great shock, but her warm brown eyes and loose curls took him straight back thirteen years and he couldn't resist the temptation to find out a little more when it was just the two of them. They were around halfway up now. 'So, how have you been, Jessica? It's been a long time since we were in a position like this.'

He was only half-joking. Trying to take some of the strain out of her muscles, which had tensed more and more as they'd ascended the slope. Was Jessica scared of heights?

Her voice was quiet—a little thoughtful even. 'Yes. It has been, hasn't it?' She turned her head a little so he could see the side of her face. 'I'd no idea you were a firefighter. Didn't you do engineering at uni?'

She'd remembered. Why did that seem important to him?

'Yes, three years at Aberdeen Uni.' He gave a fake shudder. 'These would be normal temperatures for up there.'

'So, how did you end up being a firefighter?'

Was she just being polite? Or was she genuinely curious? He'd probably never know.

'There was a fire in the student accommodation where I stayed. We were on the tenth floor.' He tried to block out the pictures in his mind. 'It gave me a whole new perspective on the fire service. They needed to call out a specialist team and specialist equipment to reach us.' He didn't normally share this information with people. But Jess was different. Jess knew him in ways that most other people didn't.

'That must have been scary.'

Not even close. There was so much he was leaving unsaid.

The terrifying prospect of being marooned on a roof with the floors beneath you alight.

The palpable terror of the students around you.

The look on the faces of the fire crew when they realised you were out of reach and they had to stand by and wait, helpless, until other crew and equipment arrived.

'Callum?'

'What? Oh, yes, sorry. Let's just say it made me appreciate the engineering work involved in the fire service's equipment. I joined when I finished university. It didn't take me long to find my calling at the rope rescue unit. I still do some other regular firefighting duties, but most of the time I'm with the rescue unit.' He wanted to change the subject. He didn't want her to ask any questions about the fire. 'What about you? Are you married with four kids by now?'

It was meant to be simple. A distraction technique. A simple change of subject, taking the emphasis off him and putting it back on to her.

But as soon as the words left his mouth he knew he'd said the wrong thing. The stiffness and tension in her muscles was automatic.

They were nearing the edge of the incline and he could see movement above them. The flurry of activity as the stretchers were pulled over the edge and the paramedics and technicians started dealing with the children.

'Things just didn't work out for me.'

Quiet words, almost whispered.

He was stunned into silence.

There was obviously much more to it than that but now was hardly the time or the place.

And who was he to be asking?

He hadn't seen Jessica in thirteen years. Was it any of his business what had happened to her?

The radio on his shoulder crackled into life. 'We've got the last two kids. Minor injuries—nothing significant. There's an ambulance on standby that will take them to be checked over.'

'Are all the ambulances heading to Parkhill?' She sounded anxious.

He lifted the radio to his mouth. 'Wait and I'll check. Control—are all paediatric patients being taken to Parkhill?'

There was a buzz, some further crackles, then a disjointed voice. 'Four classified as majors, eight as minors. Two majors and six minors already en route. The adults have gone to Glasgow Cross.'

'Give me your hand!' A large arm reached over the edge and grabbed Jessica's wrist, pulling them topside. Someone unclipped their harnesses and tethers, leaving them free of each other.

'Doc, you're requested in one of the ambulances.'

Jess never even turned back, just started running towards the nearest ambulance, where one of the hypothermic kids was being loaded.

Callum watched her immediately fall back into professional mode.

'Scoop and run,' she shouted. 'Get that other ambulance on the move and someone get me a line to Parkhill. I want them to be set up for our arrival.'

Callum looked around him. The major incident report was going to be a nightmare. It would probably take up the next week of his life.

He grabbed hold of the guy next to him. 'Any other problems?'

The guy shook his head. 'Just waiting to lock and load the last two kids. The clean-up here will take hours.'

Callum nodded. 'In that case, I'm going to Parkhill with the ambulances. I want to find out how all these kids do. I'll be back in a few hours.'

He jumped into the back of one of the other ambulances, where the paramedic and nurse were treating the other hypothermic kid. 'Can I hitch a ride?' He glanced at the nurse, who was balanced on one leg. 'Did you hurt yourself?'

The paramedic nodded.

'Ride up front with the technician. We're going to be busy back here.'

The nurse grimaced, looking down at her leg. 'I'm sure it's nothing. Let's just get these kids back to Parkhill.'

Callum jumped back down and closed the doors, sliding into the passenger seat at the front. Within seconds the ambulance had taken off, sirens blaring. Great, the paediatrician had ended up in the Clyde and the nurse had injured her ankle. The major incident report was getting longer by the second.

It wouldn't take long to get through the city traffic at this time. He pulled his notebook from his top pocket. It was sodden. Useless, soaked when the minibus had tipped and he'd landed in the water.

'Got anything I can write on?'

The technician nodded, his eyes never leaving the road, and gestured his head towards the glove box, where Callum found a variety of notebooks and pens.

'Perfect. Thanks.' He started scribbling furiously. It was essential he put down as much as could for the incident report, before it became muddled in his brain.

The number of staff in attendance. The number of victims. The decision to call out the medical crew. Jessica. The descent down the incline. The temperature and depth of the water. Jessica being called onto the minibus. His first impression of the casualties. The way the casualties had been prioritised. The fact that Jessica had landed in the water.

The feeling in his chest when she'd disappeared under the water.

He laid the notebook and pen down in his lap.

This was no use.

He wasn't thinking the way he usually did. Calmly. Methodically.

He just couldn't get her out of his head.

It seemed that after thirteen years of immunity Jessica had reclaimed her place—straight back under his skin.

CHAPTER THREE

THE AMBULANCE DOORS were flung open and Jess heaved a sigh of relief. Her team was ready and waiting.

The A and E department would be swamped. There were twelve kids with a variety of injuries to look after, as well as all the normal walking wounded patients and GP emergency admissions that would have turned up today.

Everyone would be on edge. The place would be going like a fair.

Her team sprang into action immediately as she jumped down from the ambulance.

'Is the resus room set up for these two kids?'

'All prepared, Dr Rae. Fluids heating as we speak. Harry Shaw, the anaesthetist, and Blake Connor, the registrar, will help you run these kids simultaneously. You're drookit, Jess. Wanna get changed?'

A set of scrub trousers were thrust into her hands and she gave a little smile. Her team had thought of everything.

Harry appeared at her side. 'I take it it was freezing out there?'

'Baltic.' The one-word answer told him everything he needed to know.

The second ambulance arrived and both kids were wheeled into the resus room and transferred to the trolleys. Jess ducked behind a curtain and shucked off her soggy jumpsuit, replacing it the with the dry scrub trousers. If only her underwear wasn't still sodden.

Her team was on autopilot, stripping the freezing-wet clothing from both kids and bundling them up in warming blankets.

She walked out from behind the curtains. Harry Shaw was standing at the head of one of the trolleys, doing his initial assessment. 'What can you tell me?'

She looked up as Callum appeared at the doorway and handed her a sheet of paper. 'Thought this might be useful,' he said as he walked away.

She stared at what he'd scribbled for her. *Temperature of the Clyde is currently minus five degrees centigrade. Moving water takes longer to freeze.*

It was just what she needed. The temperature to which these kids had been exposed was very important.

She walked over to Harry. 'This is Marcus, he's four. He was unconscious at the scene but I can't find any obvious sign of injury. Showing severe signs of hypothermia. As far as I know, his head was always above the water, but we couldn't get the tympanic thermometer to register on-site.'

Harry nodded. 'I need baseline temps on both these kids. Has to be a core temperature, so oesophageal temperatures would be best.'

More paperwork appeared in her hand from the receptionist. 'Nursery just called with some more details.'

Her eyes scanned the page and she let out a little sigh. 'This is Lily. She's four too. She was submerged at the scene—but no one can be sure how long.'

Harry was one of the most experienced paediatric anaesthetists that she knew. He'd already realised that Lily was the priority and left Connor to take over with Marcus. He was already sliding an ET tube into place for Lily. He took a few seconds to check her temperature. Both cardiac monitors were switched on and the team stood silently to watch them flicker to life.

Jessica's heart thumped in her chest. What happened in the next few minutes would determine whether these kids made it or not.

'Marcus's temp is thirty degrees. Moderate hypothermia,' shouted Connor.

She watched the monitor for a few more seconds. 'He's bradycardic but his cardiac rhythm appears stable. Any problems with his breathing?'

Connor shook his head. 'He's maintaining his airway. His breathing's just slowed along with his heart rate.'

Jessica's brain was racing. She was the paediatric consultant. This was her lead. But Harry was an extremely experienced anaesthetist. She wanted to be sure they were on the same page.

She turned to him. 'Warmed, humidified oxygen, contact rewarming with a warming unit, rewarmed IV fluids and temperature monitoring. Do you agree?'

He gave her a little smile over the top of his glasses. 'Sounds like a plan. I've paged one of my other anaesthetists to come down.' The nursing staff started to flurry around them, carrying out the instructions. Jessica felt nervous.

Hypothermia was more common in elderly patients than in children. Every year they had a few cases come through the doors of A and E, but she wasn't always on duty. And most of those kids were near-drownings—kids who'd been playing on frozen rivers or lakes and had slipped under the water.

Blake Connor, her registrar, looked up from Marcus's

arm. 'I've got the bloods.' He rattled off a whole host of tests he planned to run. 'Anything else?'

She shook her head. 'Right now, we're working on the assumption that he's unconscious due to his hypothermia. There's no sign of any head injury or further trauma. Keep a careful eye on him. I want to know as soon he regains consciousness. He'll probably be disorientated and confused. Most adults with a temperature at this stage start undressing. We might need to sedate him if he becomes agitated.' She scribbled in the notes then spoke to the nursing staff.

'We're aiming for a temperature gain of around one degree every fifteen minutes. Keep an eye on his blood pressure and watch for any atrial fibrillation. Is that clear?'

The nursing staff nodded and she looked around. 'Anyone seen Jackie? She was the one who brought Lily in. I need some more information.'

One of the paramedics touched her arm. 'She fell, coming back up the slope. We think she might have fractured her ankle. Once we'd dropped Lily here my technician took her along to Glasgow Cross.'

Jess felt a twinge of guilt. It was her fault Jackie had been on the scene. She'd wanted the expertise of the experienced nurse at the site. Now, because of her, Jackie was injured. It didn't seem fair.

'Lily's temperature is lower than Marcus's. It's twenty-eight degrees.' Harry had just finished sliding the oesophageal temperature monitor into place. He glanced at the monitor. 'She's borderline, Jess. What do you want to do?'

Jess pulled back the warming blankets to get a better look at her small body. Lily was right on the edge, hovering between severe and moderate hypothermia. It was a wonder she hadn't gone into cardiac arrest.

'How's her respiratory effort?'

Harry was sounding her chest. 'For a child who was submerged I'm not hearing any fluid in her lungs. Just a few crackles. She is breathing, but not enough to keep me happy.'

'Wait a minute, folks.' Jess held her hand up as the monitor flickered, going from a stable but slow heart rate to a run of ectopic beats. She shook her head.

Time was of the essence here. She needed to make a decision.

Lily was deathly pale. All her surface blood vessels had contracted as her little body was focusing its resources on keeping her vital organs warm.

Her lips and ears were tinged with blue, showing lack of oxygen perfusing through her body.

Her eyes fell on Lily's fingers and toes. Their colour was poor.

No. Their colour was worse than poor.

The blueness was worse.

The tinkle of the monitor indicated Lily had gone into cardiac arrest. Jessica leaned across the bed and automatically started cardiac massage with the heel of one hand.

It clarified things and made the decision easier.

'Harry, we're not going to wait. Call the team. Let's get her to Theatre and begin extracorporeal rewarming. Can you phone ahead? Let them know we are resuscitating.'

One of the nurses nodded and picked up the phone in the resus room. 'Paediatric ECMO in Theatre ASAP. Yes, it's one of the minibus victims. Four-year-old female, submerged, with a core temperature of twenty-eight degrees. She's arrested and currently being resuscitated. Dr Shaw has her intubated and they'll be bringing her along now.'

She replaced the receiver. 'Theatre one will be waiting for you.'

A wave of relief washed over Jessica. There was no drama. No struggling to find theatre time. It sounded as though the theatre staff was already prepared for the possibility of one of the hypothermic kids needing ECMO.

Extracorporeal membrane oxygenation worked with cardiopulmonary bypass to take over the function of the heart and provide extracorporeal circulation of the blood where it could be rewarmed and oxygenated. It had only been used in a few cases of hypothermia with cardiac arrest in the last few years, but had had extremely positive results with good outcomes for patients.

Lily was going to be one of those patients.

Jessica was absolutely determined.

Two porters appeared at either side of the trolley, ready for the move.

As they swept down the corridor towards the lifts she caught sight of Callum again, taking notes and talking to one of the nurses. He was still here?

She hadn't had a chance to think about him. She had been too busy concentrating her energies on keeping this little girl alive. She could feel the cold flesh under her hand as she pumped methodically, trying to push blood around Lily's body. Trying to get some oxygen circulating to her body and brain.

This was somebody's child. Somebody's pride and joy.

Their reason to get up in the morning and their reason to go home at night.

Any minute now some poor, frantic man and woman would turn up in A and E anxious to get news of their daughter.

Praying and pleading to hear the best possible news.

Trying not to think about the pictures their brains had been conjuring up ever since they'd heard about the minibus crash. Struggling to remember to breathe as they made the journey to the hospital.

A journey that probably seemed to take twice as long as it normally did.

Their 'normal' day had changed beyond all recognition. Had they kissed their daughter goodbye that morning before they'd dropped her at nursery? At the place they'd assumed she would be safe?

Had they spent a few brief seconds taking her in their arms and feeling the warmth and joy of cuddling a child before they'd left her that morning? Or had they given her the briefest kiss on the top of her head because they had been in a rush to get to work? Because they hadn't realised it could be the last time they kissed their child.

Would they spend the rest of their lives regretting signing a consent form to say their daughter could go on the nursery trip? The one that could have cost her life?

All these thoughts were crowding her brain. Any time she had to resuscitate a child she was invaded with *what-ifs*?

But the *what-ifs* were about her own life. She'd spent the last three years thinking about the *what-ifs*.

What if she'd been driving the car that night?

What if she hadn't been on call?

What if her husband hadn't stopped to buy her favourite chocolate on the way home?

The lift doors pinged and they swept the trolley out. She lifted her head. The theatre doors were open and waiting for them.

One of the perfusionists was standing by, already scrubbing at the sinks, preparing to insert the catheter lines that could save Lily's life.

This was why she did this job.

This was why after a year of darkness she hadn't walked away. She might not have been able to save her own child but she would do her damnedest to save *this* one.

Callum stared at his watch. It had been six hours since he'd last seen Jessica sweeping down the corridor, her thin scrub trousers clinging to her wet backside, her hand pumping the little girl's chest.

He'd felt physically sick at that sight.

Not because he wasn't used to dealing with casualties. Casualties of all ages and all descriptions were part and parcel of the job.

But seeing the expression on Jessica's face wasn't.

Everything about this situation was having the strangest effect on him. The sight of Jessica hadn't just been unexpected—it had been like a bolt out of the blue.

They'd been childhood sweethearts who'd broken up when life had moved on and they'd never moved in the same circles again. He hadn't even heard anything about Jessica over the last few years.

Her words on the steep embankment had intrigued him. *Things just didn't work out for me.*

It made his brain buzz. There was a whole world of possibilities in those words. But he didn't feel as if he could come right out and ask.

Particularly when the sick kids were the priority.

And his lasting memories right now were the way her body had felt next to his. The way they'd seemed to fit together so well again—just like they always had.

It was the first time in a long time that he'd felt a connection to a woman.

The first time in a long time he'd ever *wanted* to feel a connection to a woman.

Sure, he'd dated on a few rare occasions, but nothing had been serious. He'd never introduced anyone to Drew. It was almost as if he didn't want to let anyone into that part of his life.

Would he ever feel ready to change that?

The doors opened at the end of the corridor and Jessica walked through. She looked absolutely exhausted. There were black circles under her eyes and her skin was even paler than it had been earlier.

He was on his feet in an instant. 'Jess? How did it go?'

She reached out to touch his arm, her brown eyes fixed on his. 'The next few hours will be crucial. We've done everything we can. Lily's temperature is coming up gradually. Now it's just wait and see. I've just spoken to her parents.' Was that a tear in Jess's eye?

It was there—written all across her face—how much those words pained her. How much she hated it that things were out of her control. The only thing left to do was wait.

She flicked her head from side to side. 'I need to get a report on all of the other kids. I need to find out how they are all doing.'

'No.' He rested his hand on her shoulder. 'You need to take a break. Come and sit down. Have a coffee, have something to eat. You must be running on empty, you know that can't be good for you.'

He could see the struggle in her eyes. 'I just can't, Callum. There were twelve kids in that accident. I'm the consultant on call. They're my responsibility.'

Callum glanced at the notes in his hand. 'Four have

already been discharged. Another four have been admitted to the paediatric unit with mild hypothermia, a head injury, and some bumps and scrapes.'

Her eyes widened. 'How do you know all that?'

He gave her a little smile. 'It's part of the investigation after any major incident for the rope rescue crew. I always need to find out the outcomes for the victims. We need to look over everything that we did to make sure there were no mistakes.'

'And were there?'

He frowned. 'Apart from our doctor ending up in the Clyde? And your nurse fracturing her ankle?'

A little smile danced across her weary face. 'I don't think you have much control over tides and currents—no matter how much you want to. And Jackie? That's my responsibility. It was me who asked her to come on the rescue.'

He shook his head. He hadn't been able to shake the picture from his mind of Jessica falling into the icy river. It had made him feel sick to his stomach and would have to form part of his investigation.

'It's my job to make sure everyone is safe at the rescue site. It's my responsibility, not yours.'

Her shoulders relaxed a little. This was probably the first normal conversation she'd had all day. 'Do you want to fight me for it?'

'Will I win?' he quipped.

'Did you ever win?' she quipped back equally quickly.

He smiled. This was the Jess he'd once known.

He glanced at his notes. 'What about the other kids? I know about Marcus and Lily, but that still leaves another two.'

'One was Rosie, she was on the bus next to Marcus. The

other is a little girl called Kelly. Both have broken limbs and were taken to surgery by the orthopaedic surgeon.'

'I'll need to follow them up for the report.'

She paused for a second, as if trying to find words. 'It was nice to see you today, Callum, even though it wasn't the best of circumstances. I'm glad you're doing well.'

Something sparked in his brain. She was just about to say goodbye. And he didn't want her to. He didn't want this to be the last time he saw Jessica Rae for another thirteen years.

'But how are you doing, Jess?' The words were out before he had a chance to censor them. Should he really be asking her something like that?

Her eyes lowered, breaking contact with his. Had he offended her? He could see her taking a deep breath.

'If you need any assistance with the investigation, feel free to come back and talk to me.' It was a deliberate side-step. A deliberate attempt to move the conversation back to something more professional.

'I'll need a statement from you about the events.' He would. It wasn't a lie. Any event like this always needed information from all the professionals involved. Not least the one who had landed in the middle of the Clyde.

'That's fine, but can we do it some other time? I really want to check on the kids.'

What she needed to do was to rest. She looked as though a long night's sleep would do her the world of good. But he already knew that wasn't going to happen.

'Of course we can do it some other time. I need to follow up the adults at Glasgow Cross—I'll do that tomorrow. Then I'll come back here to see how the kids are doing.' He hesitated, just for a second. 'Will you be available at any point tomorrow?'

He was hopeful. He was more than hopeful. This might be work, but more than anything right now he'd like to see Jessica again. Any way he could.

She nodded. 'Leave it until later in the day. I'll be busy first thing in the morning with ward rounds and reviews.'

He gave her a little smile and he couldn't help the words that came out of his mouth. 'I'll see you then.'

There was a moment of hesitation, a flicker of something going through her eyes, and it struck straight at his heart. Was it panic? Was it fear?

Her shoulders had pulled back a little, moving away from him, and the urge to reach out and pull her back towards him raced through his mind.

Why would the simplest of words cause this reaction? Jessica had always been a fun-loving, gregarious young woman. And even though he hadn't seen her in thirteen years this seemed wrong to him. Out of character.

But did he even know Jess's character any more?

It took a few seconds, but Jess seemed to gather herself and gave him the slightest flash of her brown eyes. 'Tomorrow's fine, Callum. I'll see you then.'

She turned and walked down the corridor. He couldn't tear his eyes away from her.

Now, when she was wearing only thin green theatre scrubs, he could see that her weight loss was dramatic. He flinched, remembering having seen the outline of her ribs on the riverbank. Now he could see her legs and hips. Hips that had been pressing up against his earlier.

He'd reached the bottom of the corridor, near the nurses' station in A and E. He recognised one of the sisters— they'd gone to a few study days on some aspects of community safety.

He walked over to her. 'Hi, Miriam, how's things?'

The older woman looked up and shot him a friendly smile. 'Hi, Callum. I take it you were dealing with the kids in the minibus?'

He nodded. 'Not the best day of my life. One of your doctors was out helping us—Jessica Rae?'

Miriam looked confused for a second then waved her hand. 'Oh, you mean Jessica Faraday. I know she's reverted back to her maiden name but I can't get used to it. She's fabulous. One of the best consultants we've got. The kids were certainly in safe hands with her.'

Callum could feel himself furrowing his brow. 'Jessica Faraday? She was married?'

Miriam finished typing something on the computer. 'Yeah.' She was distracted, concentrating on the words in front of her.

'But she's not now?' Callum couldn't help but probe. Curiosity was killing him.

Miriam met his eyes. 'Sadly not.'

Things just didn't work out for me.

Jessica's words echoed in his brain. He still didn't know what they meant, and it just didn't seem right to be asking someone else. It didn't matter that Miriam was a colleague—one he'd spoken to on many occasions—he just didn't feel he could ask anything personal about Jess.

It was an invasion of her privacy. He had no right to ask anything about her. It didn't matter that his curiosity was currently burning so fiercely in his stomach it would probably cause an ulcer.

Suddenly he was conscious of what he'd just done. He'd been around hospitals long enough to know that even the simplest and vaguest questions could be entirely misinterpreted.

Miriam had gone back to her paperwork—not in the

least interested in why Callum was asking questions about Jessica. Thankfully, she had a hundred other things to worry about. The last thing he needed was rumours starting to spread in a hospital. He didn't want anyone to get the wrong impression.

What was the wrong impression?

He had no idea what he thought about all this.

All he knew for sure was that the haunted look in Jessica's eyes was going to stick in his brain for the rest of the day. And probably most of the night.

This was wrong. He shouldn't be thinking about her at all.

He had Drew to worry about. His little boy was his entire life and he didn't want anything to get in the way of that. He *wouldn't* let anything get in the way of that.

The custody battle had been fiercely fought, sapping all his energy and strength. And whilst he'd been on dates in the last year or so, no woman had really attracted his attention. No woman had ever been introduced to his son.

And that was way he intended to continue.

He should walk away.

He should run.

But somehow he knew that come tomorrow afternoon he would be right here.

Right here, waiting for Jessica.

CHAPTER FOUR

CALLUM STARED AT the clock and pulled out his cellphone again. *How is Drew?* he typed.

Drew had been clingy last night. Definitely not normal for him. He hadn't wanted to go to bed and had just said he didn't feel good.

After a day stuck in the freezing-cold Clyde, all Callum had wanted to do was hold him close. So he'd broken all his own rules and let Drew come into bed beside him.

There hadn't seemed to be anything obvious wrong with Drew. His temperature hadn't been raised. He hadn't had a rash. But he'd had a restless night and when he'd stirred his porridge around his plate that morning Callum had looked at the pale little face and had known he couldn't send him to school today.

Thank goodness for good friends. Julie and Blair were always willing to help out any way they could.

His phone buzzed.

Not eating and a little tired. But managing to watch the TV. Don't worry. Julie.

Don't worry. Fat chance.

The door next to him opened. Jess. He stood up straight away and walked over to her. 'How are you? Are you okay?' She looked a little better today. There was some colour in her cheeks, her caramel-coloured hair hung in waves around her shoulders and her pink woollen jumper gave the illusion of some curves.

There it was again. The little surge he'd felt yesterday when he'd seen her. That buzz of attraction. He hadn't imagined it. He hadn't imagined it at all.

She gestured down the corridor. 'I'm fine. Honestly. No ill effects.' She gave him a little smile. She was definitely a little more relaxed today but, then, Parkhill was her comfort zone.

'How are the kids?'

Her expression was still serious. 'We've still got two in ITU, both serious but stable. Four were allowed home yesterday, another four were kept for observation overnight but are being discharged today. The last two will be in for a few days, both have different kinds of fractures.'

He gave her a knowing smile. 'Busy day, then?'

She let out a little laugh. 'What? No way. We've only had another thirty admissions on top of the accident yesterday. It's practically been a walk in the park.'

'Thirty? Is there some kind of outbreak?'

She nodded. 'Yip.' She handed over a set of case notes to the secretary next to them. She folded her arms across her chest. 'It's called a Scottish winter.'

'What do you mean?'

She gave a little shrug. 'It's like this every year. Asthma and chest infections flare up and there's always an outbreak of norovirus somewhere. Public health had to recommend closing two nurseries yesterday.' She waved her hand. 'We've got a baby with chickenpox in ITU. Oh, and the usual slips, trips and falls. We're thinking of putting a sign on the door of ward 1C saying *Only people in fibreglass may pass these doors.*'

He couldn't help the smile dancing across his face. 'It's that bad?'

She gave a little sigh. 'It's just how things are. That, and all the parents that come to the desk and give it laldy.'

He smiled. 'Now, there's a word I haven't heard in a while.'

She rolled her eyes. 'It's the most accurate description. I said it the other day to one of the Spanish registrars and he was totally lost. Thing is, it's never the parents with the sickest kids who cause a scene, it's the ones who probably shouldn't even be in an A and E department and don't think they should be waiting.'

'We get our fair share in the fire service too. Last month it was a guy who called 999 every time his house fire alarm went off.'

'Did he have a fire?'

Callum shook his head. 'Nope. He just kept burning his toast and thought we should come out.'

'Thank goodness. I thought it was just us that got the crazies.'

He looked over at her. Although her outward appearance had improved since yesterday, he could still sense the tiredness in her body.

'Are you sure you want to do this today? We can do it some other time if it doesn't suit you.'

She shook her head. 'You're going to need the statement at some point and it's probably best I do it while it's all still fresh in my mind.'

'Have you got time for a coffee?'

She glanced at her watch. 'Actually, I've got a couple of hours.' She looked around her. 'Can we get out of here for a little while? I need to cover for someone tonight so I'll be here until tomorrow.'

He bit his tongue. From the look of her she'd already covered last night too. Did she really need to do it again? The thought of getting her out of this place was very appealing. Maybe some fresh air and a change of scene would lessen the tiredness in her eyes. There was no way he'd say no to her.

'Sure. As long as you don't mind travelling in a fire and rescue vehicle.'

Her eyes widened. 'You've got a fire engine sitting outside?' He could hear the edge of excitement in her voice. It was almost everyone's childhood dream to ride in a fire engine.

He laughed. 'No, I've got the four-by-four. But I'm on call and can be paged at any time, so I need to be ready to go.'

'Oh.' She looked a little disappointed. 'Does that mean you can't go anywhere?'

He shook his head, his heart clenching a little as he realised she'd looked a little sad at the prospect. 'Of course I can. But let's not go too far. That way, if I get paged I can drop you back here quickly. Is there somewhere local you'd prefer?'

She nodded. 'There's an Italian coffee shop that does great food and some killer carrot cake about five minutes' drive from here. Just let me grab my bag and coat.'

He stood for a few seconds until she reappeared at his side, wearing a thick purple wool coat and pink scarf. He smiled. 'I take it you came prepared today.'

'After yesterday? I've honestly never been so cold. The first thing I did last night was put on the fire, find the biggest, snuggliest pair of pyjamas I could and pull my duvet in front of the fire.'

The picture was conjured up in his head instantly. Snuggly pyjamas might not be the sexiest nightwear he would normally think of for a woman, but it still brought a smile to his face.

They walked outside into the cold air and she automatically moved a little closer to him, letting his body shield her from the biting wind. It was all he could do to stop his arm reaching out to wrap around her waist.

He felt on edge. He hadn't seen her in years. She had a whole other life he knew nothing about. Little things started to edge into the corners of his mind. Who did Jessica have to snuggle up to after a stressful day at work? Had she spent the night alone in front of the fire?

Curiosity was killing him. Particularly after the comment Miriam had made the previous day about Jessica reverting to her maiden name.

He had a burning sensation to find out why. It suddenly seemed really important—even though it shouldn't. Did Jessica feel the nervous edge that he did?

But Jess seemed relaxed around him. She shot him another smile as she climbed into the car. 'You would have been horrified. I even resorted to bedsocks last night!'

'Were they pink?' He started the car and pulled out of the car park.

'How did you guess?'

'Because some things don't change.' Pink had always been her favourite colour. The words had come out before he'd had time to think about them. Because nothing could be further from the truth. Things had changed, for both of them—probably more than they could ever have imagined.

Thirteen years was a long time.

There was silence for a few seconds, as if she was thinking the same kind of thoughts that he was.

She gestured to the side. 'This way.' She waited until

he changed lanes. 'I guess I always did like pink,' she said quietly. She touched the collar of her coat. 'I've even got a pink coat, I just didn't wear it today.'

Another little memory sparked into his brain. Jessica's wardrobe. She'd had the biggest array of clothes he'd ever seen. He shot her a smile. 'Knowing you, you've probably got a coat for every colour of the rainbow.'

She tilted her head to the side as if she was racking her brain. 'Emerald green.'

He raised his eyebrows.

'That's the colour I'm missing. I need to get an emerald-green raincoat and the rainbow will be complete.' She pointed in front of them. 'It's just over here. Pull in to the left.'

He halted just in front of the Italian-style coffee shop, walking around and opening the door for her.

The heat hit them as soon as they walked inside, along with a whole host of mouth-watering smells.

He pulled out a chair and helped her off with her coat, before sitting across from her and bringing out his array of paperwork. But his brain wasn't focusing on the paperwork.

Taking Jessica out of her own environment felt a little odd. It felt personal but this was business. A professional meeting. Nothing more, nothing less. No matter how casual it seemed.

No matter how *easy* it seemed.

Why did he have to keep reminding himself about that?

He pointed to the menu. 'What do you recommend?'

'Anything and everything. There won't be a single thing in here that you don't like.'

The waitress appeared at their side.

'Just a latte for me, please.'

'No.'

He couldn't help it. Her thin frame was too much for him. He was resisting the temptation to just order her some mushrooms, a portion of lasagne and some garlic bread. Things they used to eat together a long time ago and he knew that she liked.

He couldn't help but wonder who was looking out for Jess right now. Surely her friends had spoken to her quietly and told her she'd lost too much weight? It didn't matter that he hadn't seen her in years, he couldn't stand by and say nothing.

The waitress looked a little taken aback. Callum's eyes ran down the menu. 'You need more than just coffee. Order something else.'

He could see her take a deep breath, getting ready to argue with him. But he shook his head, the smallest of movements, then reached over and touched her hand. 'Don't.'

He kept his gaze steady. They'd been friends for such a long time. It didn't matter that he hadn't seen her in years. It didn't matter that fate had thrown them together. He had no idea what had happened in the last few years for Jess—and she might never tell him. But he could focus on what was in front of him.

The one thing he could do something about.

And she knew him. She knew him well.

She would know that he would never cause a scene, but she would also know that when he was determined, there was no way around him.

Her brown eyes were fixed on where his hand was touching hers. Was she annoyed? Did she think it inappropriate? Because he'd only done what had felt natural—and it didn't feel inappropriate to him.

He could see the long exhalation of breath, the relaxing of her shoulders, then she lifted her long dark eyelashes to meet his gaze.

The long dark eyelashes that used to tickle his cheeks.

The thought came out of nowhere, triggering a whole host of memories in his brain. Now, *they* could be inappropriate.

Jess's fingers moved under his. She looked at the waitress. 'What's the soup?'

'Minestrone or tomato and herb, both served with crusty bread.'

Jess pressed her lips together. 'I'll have the minestrone. Please.' She handed the menu over.

'I'll have the same—the soup and a latte.' Something fired in his brain and he remembered what she'd said in the car. 'And carrot cake—for both of us, please.' It wasn't what he would normally eat at this time. The paperwork was still in front of him. But right now it was the least of his concerns.

Would she tell him what had happened to her in the last few years? And, in return, would he be able to tell her about Drew?

He took the bull by the horns. 'You're thin, Jess. A lot thinner than you used to be. I'd rather have bought you a three-course meal than a plate of soup.'

'Who said I was letting you buy it?'

He smiled. There it was. The spark that had seemed missing at times. The spark that took him back thirteen years.

Every now and then it flared, reappearing out of nowhere. Then the thin veil would come back down and the Jessica that he had once known would disappear.

He leaned back in the chair. Sparring with Jess now

felt as natural as it had years ago. 'Oh, you're letting me. I can assure you of that.'

'Still a stubborn bossy boots, then, Callum?'

'I had a very good teacher,' was his automatic response. But it only took a second to know what he really should do. He stretched across the table and took both her hands in his. 'Actually, I'm still a concerned friend.'

He could sense her pull back a little. See her wariness at his actions.

'We haven't seen each other in years, Callum. We lost touch. You've no idea what's happened in my life and I've no idea what's happened in yours. If that accident hadn't happened yesterday, our paths might never have crossed again.'

'And that would have been a real shame.' He shook his head. 'I'm not glad the accident happened. I'm not glad those kids were injured. But I am glad our paths have crossed again. It's nice to see you.' His voice was low and the words said quietly. He hoped she could see the sincerity in his eyes.

She paused for a moment then said, 'It's nice to see you again too.' She gave him a little smile. 'You always were a pest when it came to food.' She had a glint in her eye, and he could see her visibly relaxing, sinking a little further into her chair and leaning her elbows on the desk so they were closer.

His reaction was entirely natural—he leaned forward too. 'Jessica Rae, I've no idea what you're talking about.'

She raised her eyebrows, her smile spreading across her face. She placed her head on her hands. 'What about the cookie incident, then?'

He stifled a laugh.

The memories came flooding back. A visit to the cinema with Jess asking him to hold her coffee and cookie that he'd bought her while she went and washed her hands. They'd been running late and the film had already started by the time they'd fumbled to their seats. It had taken Jess a few minutes to lift the napkin from her purchase and the scream she'd let out had caused the whole cinema to jump in shock.

'It was only a tiny nibble.' He shrugged his shoulders.

'It was a giant-size bite! And then you let me think that it was the boy behind the counter—you were going to let me go and complain.'

He couldn't stop laughing now, with the still indignant look on her face thirteen years later. 'Just as well the crumbs gave me away, then.'

Jess started to laugh too. Her shoulders shook as she bent forward and then threw her head back. Jess didn't have a delicate, polite laugh. It was loud and wholehearted, as if it came all the way from her toes.

There was something so nice about this. The way her skin glowed and her eyes sparkled when she laughed like that. The ease and familiarity of being with someone you felt comfortable around. Someone you shared a history with. Someone who made you feel as if you could look into their eyes and trust what they said.

Someone who wouldn't run out on you and your child.

Where had that thought come from?

The door to the café opened and a woman and her child bundled in out of the cold. The little boy's nose was glowing red underneath his woolly hat. He looked around the same age as Drew.

Callum pushed all thoughts of Drew's mother out of his head and leaned forward to pass a comment to Jess. But the expression on her face stopped him dead.

She'd gone from hearty laughter to deathly pale—almost as if she'd been caught unawares. He bit his tongue, stopping himself from asking what was wrong.

He had to give her time. He had to give her space. If Jess wanted to tell him something she would.

There was silence for a few seconds as he could see her gathering herself.

She nodded at his paperwork. 'This could take some time. Shouldn't we get started?'

The barriers were going up again. She was closing herself off from him. Going back to business as usual. 'What do you need from me?'

The waitress appeared and put down two bowls of steaming-hot minestrone and a basket of crusty bread. 'I need you to relax for a bit. I want to see you eat. Once you've finished we'll do my paperwork. I need a detailed statement from you.'

He didn't want the veil to come down. Because when it did Jess had the strangest look in her eyes, almost vacant, as if she was removing herself from the situation. It was obvious that she wasn't feeling any of the same strange sensations that he was. His brain was currently mush.

Being around Jess was flaring up too many memories in his mind. Sharing memories with Jess was both warming and setting off alarm bells in his head. He'd been awake most of the night, thinking about all the good times that they'd had together.

He hadn't even told her about Drew yet. And did he want to? He had no idea what he wanted to do about any of this. Could he be friends with Jessica or was it just a recipe for disaster? He'd just have to wait and see.

CHAPTER FIVE

It was the middle of the night. The snow had given way to sleet and was currently battering the windows in the old Glasgow hospital.

Whilst the ward was dark, most of the windows were adorned with festive lights. A Santa, a snowman and a reindeer stood out twinkling against the black night sky outside. A tree with multicoloured lights flickered at the end of the ward, and strings of icicles were hanging from most of the windows outside the ward bays.

A few little bodies shifted under the starched white hospital sheets and coloured blankets. Almost everyone was sleeping—unusual for a children's ward—with only a few little murmurs here and there. Alongside most of the beds were chairs and stools with an array of uncomfortable parents trying to catch a few hours' sleep as they watched over their children.

Jessica padded along the ward in her soft-soled shoes. She loved Christmas in the children's ward. Although most people in her circumstances would want to avoid this place, it was actually the one place at this time of year that gave her a little solace.

There were always people worse off than you.

Actually, no there weren't. No parent should outlive their child.

Here, in the ward, she felt safe. Everyone knew what had happened. No one asked awkward questions. If she needed a few moments on her own, she got them.

If she needed to be amongst people and in company, it was here.

If she needed to feel of value, there was no doubt she was needed here. There was always a little one to cuddle. There was always a parent to talk to in the quiet hours of night—to give some kind of explanation, to give some kind of comfort.

Mostly, she just liked to watch the kids sleeping.

There was nothing more comforting than watching a child sleep.

Tonight she was watching Grace Flynn, a seven-year-old with a rare form of aggressive bowel cancer. She'd had her tumours operated on twice.

Grace was a beautiful child. She wanted to be a ballerina, or an air hostess, or a teacher. She changed her mind every day. But she was becoming frailer and frailer with every visit. The chemotherapy and radiotherapy were having ravaging effects on her body. The surgeries were taking their toll. The battle was becoming harder and harder.

So tonight she was taking a little pleasure in watching Grace sleep. Watching the rise and fall of her little chest.

Moments like this always pained her. What was worse? Your child dying suddenly, with no chance to say goodbye, or dying slowly, painfully right before your eyes?

Her brain couldn't even begin to compare those issues. All she knew was that she would do everything in her power to help Grace and her parents.

Hopefully Grace would be able to be discharged home with her family tomorrow and get to spend Christmas at home.

She would love that. She might be the model patient but she always had a smile on her face when she was discharged home.

Jessica walked down the corridor, watching the twinkling lights on the windows and appreciating the stillness of the ward.

It wasn't always quiet in here. Some nights it went like a fair. Some nights she didn't even see the inside of her on-call room. Then there were other nights like tonight.

She sat down at the nurses' station and tapped a few keys on the computer, bringing up the file of one of the kids admitted earlier. She would never have been able to sleep anyway.

Images of Callum were currently swimming around in her brain.

It was the oddest of feelings.

Because she didn't know how she felt.

For the last few years she'd been sad. She'd worked hard to put one foot in front of the other and try and come out the other side. And now she finally felt as if she'd reached a plateau.

She didn't cry non-stop any more. She didn't spend every day wishing she didn't need to get out of bed. She wasn't insanely jealous of every woman pushing a stroller in the street.

Oh, she still had moments when things crept up on her and caught her unawares. When she needed a few minutes to gather herself or to wipe the stray tear that appeared on her face.

But things had eased. It was still the first thing she thought about every morning and the last thing she thought about at night. But it didn't fill her every waking moment of the day any more. She'd allowed herself to think about other things. To care a little about other things.

And work was her biggest comfort. It helped her tick along. It gave her a sense of purpose. A little confidence that she did have a life worth living.

Then something like this happened.

A blast from the past, totally unexpected. Totally unprepared for.

Callum was evoking a whole host of memories. Most of which were good. Some of which were distinctly edged with tinges of pink—the way all teenage first-love memories were.

It was a little unsettling. Not just seeing Callum but the whole host of *what-ifs* that had her flooded her mind afterwards—some of which had permeated her dreams.

What if she'd married Callum? What would her life have been like? Would they still have been together after all this time?

She tried to push the thoughts away. It felt disloyal. Disloyal to the memory of her husband, Daniel, and her little boy, Lewis.

Daniel had been the love of her life. She'd been blissfully happy. She'd thought they'd grow old together. She'd *expected* them to grow old together.

But as much as she'd loved Daniel, the loss of Lewis was even worse. As if someone had ripped her heart right out of her chest and squeezed it until every last drop of blood was gone.

The pain had almost killed her.

Maybe that was why her brain was drifting into unchartered territories. If she'd stayed with Callum, Daniel and Lewis would never have featured in her life.

She would never have suffered such torment and hurt

at their loss. She wouldn't have found herself wondering if she wanted to go on. To live a life without them.

Maybe Callum was a safe memory.

She opened her eyes, looking around to see if anyone had noticed her hunched over the keyboard. Two of the nurses were standing at the door of one of the rooms but they hadn't noticed a thing.

Her pager sounded and she was on her feet instantly. ITU. She had three kids in there right now. The baby with chickenpox and Marcus and Lily from the accident. She started saying silent prayers in her head as she walked swiftly down the corridor. She looked around. It was the dead of night and there was no one else about so she took off. Her soft running footsteps echoed up and down the passages of the long building until she reached the doors and squirted her hands with gel before entering.

The doors swung open. The steady whoosh-whoosh of the ventilators was the first thing that she heard whenever she stepped inside. In most instances it was a soothing sound, often not reflecting the serious condition of the patients inside. She took a quick look around the unit. It was brighter than the rest of the hospital, even though some of lights were dimmed.

She recognised a figure next to Lily's bed and walked over quickly. Pauline, the sister in ITU, was great. She'd been there for ten years, had a whole wealth of experience and, more importantly, good instincts. Jessica trusted her judgement, and she also valued her friendship. She'd been a pillar of strength for Jess in the last few years.

'What's up, Pauline?'

Pauline shook her head. 'She's gone from bradycardic and hypothermic to the opposite. Tachycardic and high temp. Isn't it amazing how kids go from one extreme to the other?'

Jessica cast her eyes over the monitor. Thirty-six hours ago Lily had had a heart rate of fifty and now it was one hundred and sixty. 'Darn it. The ECMO should be keeping her heart rate and temperature steady. She must have an infection somewhere. How's her suctioning been?'

Pauline's lips pressed together. She hated it as much as Jess did when kids got sicker. 'She's been suctioned every four hours and there's been no increase in her secretions.'

Jessica rolled her shoulders back, trying to relieve the tension in her neck and shoulders. Everyone knew that ECMO could have complications—bleeding, infections, neurological damage and kidney damage.

Jessica unwound the pink stethoscope from her neck. 'I'll have a little listen to her chest. It was clear earlier and her chest X-ray was fine, but you know how things can change.'

She placed her stethoscope on Lily's little chest and listened for a few seconds then frowned. 'I can hear crackles in her lungs. Can I have her chart? I'll get her started on IV antibiotics right away.' She scribbled on the chart handed to her. 'Are you okay to make these up or do you want me to do it?'

Most of the nurses in ITU had extended roles. The IV antibiotics could be sent up from the hospital pharmacy but that would take time. Time that Lily essentially didn't have. Pauline nodded her head. 'It's fine. I'll do it. It will only take a few minutes.'

Jessica continued to make a few notes. 'I'm asking for another chest X-ray. I want to see if there's any change from this morning. And I'll be about for the next few hours. Let me know if you have any concerns.'

'Not planning on having any sleep tonight, Jess? You know that's not good for you.' There was concern in Pauline's voice. And it was sincere—she always tried to look out for Jess.

Jess just gave her a little smile and kept writing. Sometimes she just liked to keep her head down.

'I meant to ask you, how do you know Callum?'

The question took her by surprise. She felt on guard, even with a woman she'd always trusted. But Pauline's face was open and friendly. 'Callum Kennedy?' she asked.

'Yeah, the fireman—the rope rescue guy. He was on the phone earlier, enquiring after the kids. He knows we can't give him any specific details. He just wanted to check everything was okay. Apparently he was in yesterday too. The staff say he's gorgeous.'

Callum was in here yesterday? Why hadn't she known that? 'What did he say?'

Pauline's eyebrows rose. 'He said you went way back—that you were old friends.'

She was obviously piquing Pauline's interest, and it made her wish she hadn't asked. Jessica felt the colour flare into her cheeks. What on earth was wrong with her? Callum was a good-looking guy and in a gossip hive like a hospital it was obvious people would comment.

Pauline was still talking as she adjusted the controls on Lily's monitors. 'Even David knows him. Says he's played five-a-side football against him. Apparently he's single.' She gave a little laugh. 'He also says the firefighter football team are a bunch of break-your-leg animals. He says he always volunteers to be goalie when they play against them.'

David. The solitary male staff nurse in ITU who was usually the butt of everyone's jokes. Just as well he was fit for it. He always gave as good as he got. And it was good to have a male in a predominantly female environment. Some babies responded better to a male voice—even seemed to be soothed by it.

And he always told any little boy who woke up scared and ventilated in ITU that the same thing had happened to him as a kid.

Some people were just destined to work with children.

Then again, David had just given her a vital piece of information. Callum was single. It seemed ridiculous. He was a gorgeous man, with a good job, and was fun to be around. Women would be beating a path to his door. Why on earth was he single? And, more importantly, why would she care?

'Jess? What's wrong?'

'Nothing. Nothing's wrong.' She could hardly look Pauline in the eye. Pauline was too perceptive by half. Her cheeks were practically bursting. She felt like some crazy teenager again.

'Jess, honey, no one would ever dare say these words to you. But I will because I care about you. Things are looking easier for you, Jess. Your mood has lifted, you don't have quite as many dark circles under your eyes. And once you start eating again…'

'What do you mean, Pauline?'

Pauline bit her lip. 'I mean that if you and Callum have history, *good history*, that might be a good thing.' She hesitated then continued, 'It might be something to embrace instead of run away from.'

'You think I run away from things?'

Pauline reached over and touched her arm. 'I think that you're ready. I think it might be time to start living your life again. I think it might be time to lift your head above the parapet and see what's out there. Whether that's Callum or someone else.' She gave Jess's arm a little squeeze. 'The next step will be hard, Jess. It might be easier if you took it with someone you used to know.'

She looked at Pauline's hand on her arm. The same place that Callum had touched her. The touch that had made every tiny hair on her arm stand on end and little unfamiliar sparks shoot up her arm. It had felt odd.

She wasn't sure how she felt about any of this. She'd spent a long time with one man and the thought of another—even one who was familiar—was alien to her. There was still that burning edge of disloyalty. Right now she couldn't even consider that Callum could be anything but a friend. No matter how her body reacted to him. It didn't help that her confidence was at an all-time low.

She caught a glimpse of her reflection in one of the windows in ITU. She hardly recognised herself these days. Even she was aware of how thin she was.

She'd once been proud of her figure. She'd liked the glow about her skin. But all that had been lost in the last three years. She barely even looked in a mirror any more. She got her hair cut when it took too long to dry in the mornings. She only put make-up on to stop people commenting on how pale she looked. What man could ever find her attractive now?

'It's only work, Pauline, nothing else.' The sadness in her voice surprised even her. Why were thoughts like this even entering her mind?

'But maybe it could be something else?' Pauline had raised her eyebrows and there was a hopeful tone in her voice.

Everything about this made her uncomfortable.

'If it hadn't been for the accident, our paths would never

have crossed again. It's just some crazy coincidence. Callum isn't interested in me.'

'Isn't he? Well, he apparently asked after you while he was in.'

'He did?' She hated the way her heart had given a little jolt at those words.

Pauline finished checking the controls on the ECMO machine and recorded them in the log. 'Yes. He did.' She stared at Jess. 'All I'm saying is there's a world of possibilities out there. Just leave yourself open to a few.' She hung the chart at the end of the bed and moved across to the next patient.

Jessica gazed at her reflection in the glass. A world of possibilities.

How on earth would she cope with those?

CHAPTER SIX

CALLUM WAS BORED. Bored rigid.

He usually liked coming to study days. There was always something new to learn in his job and some networking to be done. But this guy had been droning on for what seemed like hours. It felt like he was saying the same sentence over and over again. It didn't matter that the clock had only moved on ninety minutes, it felt like groundhog day.

The door at the back of the auditorium opened and he heard a little murmur around him, accompanied by the sound of over a hundred firefighters straightening up all at once. He turned sideways, trying to see what had caused that effect. Had the chief officer just come into the room?

No. It wasn't the chief officer. It was a woman with caramel-coloured hair and a sway to her step. His mouth fell open. Jess?

All of a sudden he was paying attention to what the man at the front of the room was saying. 'Ladies and gentlemen, I'd like you to welcome Dr Jessica Rae. She's a paediatrician at Parkhill, the children's hospital in Glasgow.'

Callum tore his eyes away from Jessica for a moment—something none of the other men in the room were doing—to look at his programme. It had someone else's name on it for the next lecture.

'Dr Rae is filling in for Dr Shepherd, who had an unexpected family emergency today. We're very grateful that she could find the time to step in for us. Dr Rae will be talking to us about paediatric smoke inhalation and immediate treatment.'

Callum watched as Jessica walked to the front of the room. Her hair was shining and resting in curls on her shoulders. And she was dressed cleverly in layers to hide how thin she was, and in bright colours to complement her skin tone.

'Hey, Callum, isn't that the lady doc from the minibus accident?' the firefighter sitting next to him whispered.

'Yes, it is.' He still hadn't taken his eyes from her. She was wearing a bright blue dress that was draped and gathered at the front. She looked good. She had more colour about her face today and was wearing bright lipstick.

'Wow. She looks gorgeous.' He turned and squinted at Callum, in the way only a friend could. 'Didn't you say you knew her from years gone by?'

Callum shifted uncomfortably in his seat. He knew exactly what was going on in Frank's head. 'Yeah. She's an old friend.'

Frank let out the lowest of whistles. 'Wish my old friends looked like that.'

The hackles at the back of Callum's neck immediately rose. Frank was only voicing what every appreciative man in the room was thinking. But that didn't mean that he liked it. He wanted to put a cocoon around Jess and protect her. Hide her away from the leering glances.

He hadn't seen her in more than a week and, boy, was she a sight for sore eyes. The fact that thought had sprung into his mind alarmed him. Why, all of a sudden, was he annoyed by the fact that other men found her attractive? What right did he have to feel like that?

More than once this week his hand had hovered over the phone, thinking of a reason to phone Jess again. Looking for any excuse just to speak to her.

But then his rational side had kicked in and brought him back into reality.

Too bad reality was looking kind of blurry right now.

Jess stood up at the podium and looked around the room. When her eyes rested on Callum he saw her give a little start, before she gave him a nervous smile.

'Hi, folks. I recognise some of the faces in here today because unfortunately, in our lines of business, our paths frequently cross.' She pressed a button and the presentation appeared on the wall behind her. 'I'm going to give you some up-to-date information on the best things you can do for a child with smoke inhalation.' She lifted her hand and gestured around the auditorium. 'I'm sure it's something you've all had to deal with.'

Jessica was confident at work. She was in control. That much was clearly evident. She could probably have done this presentation with her eyes shut. And it was nice to see her that way.

Her voice was steady and clear. 'We don't expect any of you to do anything more than the most basic first aid. I'm sure you're all aware that the paramedics and ambulances aren't always on scene immediately, so my job today is to give you enough information to feel confident in your first responses.'

She lifted her hand, pressed a button on the remote and the screen behind her changed. Then she turned back and gave the room a dazzling smile. 'Now, let's begin.'

* * *

It was officially the quickest thirty minutes of her life. She hadn't hesitated that morning when a colleague had asked her to cover for him. As a paediatric consultant at a teaching hospital she was often asked to give lectures to medical students and people in other disciplines. This was a walk in the park for her.

If only there wasn't a great big distraction right in the middle of the room.

Callum was definitely the proverbial elephant in the room today.

She spent the whole thirty minutes trying to avoid looking at him. She was sure that if she caught a glimpse of his green eyes she wouldn't be able to concentrate at all.

It was strange. She should have felt happy that there was a friend in the room, but instead she felt almost like a student undergoing an examination. It was just as well the firefighters went easy on her and there were only a few questions at the end. That was the beauty of talking just before the coffee break—no one wanted to hang around for long.

As soon as she'd finished the room emptied quickly. Her heart started to thud. Would Callum leave without speaking to her? Maybe he had to network with some of his colleagues and wouldn't have time.

'Hey, Jess. That was a nice surprise.' She started at his voice and turned around quickly as someone jostled him from behind and pushed them even closer together. It looked as if it was a stampede towards the strong smell of coffee.

Her hand went up automatically and rested on his chest. She could feel the heat of his body through his thin black shirt. 'Hey, you too. I didn't expect to be here. Just filling in for a friend.'

'What happened?'

'Mark Shepherd's wife has cancer. She had a bad reaction to her chemo, so he wanted to stay home with her.'

'I'm sorry to hear that. How are the kids from the accident doing?'

She raised her eyebrows. 'You mean you haven't already phoned today?'

He squirmed. 'Okay, I admit it. I'm a bit of a stalker.'

She laid her hand on his arm. 'But only in a good way. We've got four still in, but they're all improving. With kids we just take things one day at a time.'

Callum nodded slowly. He held his elbow out towards her. 'Have you time for some refreshments before you leave?'

'Hmm, firefighter coffee. Is it as bad as I think it will be?'

'Scandalous! We're very serious about our coffee, and we're even more serious about our cakes. I can guarantee you a fruit scone.'

'Something does smell pretty good around here.' She put her hand through his crooked elbow. 'Why do I get the impression that you're trying to fatten me up, Callum?'

He rolled his eyes and pressed his other hand to his chest. 'Tragedy, you've caught me out.' His face broke into a wide grin. 'Let's call it *looking out for a friend.*'

Her heart gave a little flutter. 'Friends? Is that what we are again, Callum?'

'I certainly hope so.' There was something so nice about the way he'd said those words. Not a moment's hesitation. He didn't even need to think about it for a second.

Friends. She liked that word. It felt safe.

They walked across the corridor to the coffee room. The queue had died down a little and she had a little time to peruse the cakes in the glass cabinet. The firefighters certainly did take their coffee seriously. This was an outlet of a popular coffee house, with all their famous tempting products on display.

He placed his arm on the counter and slid a tray in front of her. 'What can I tempt you with?'

Now, there was a question.

The thoughts that flooded her mind almost made her blush.

'I'll have a light caramel latte with two shots and a piece of the banana and nut loaf, please.' The words were automatic. She was used to ordering in one of these coffee shops—she didn't need to think twice.

He seemed pleased. Pleased that she didn't spend forever fretting over what to eat and drink. Patience had never been Callum's strong point.

They waited a few minutes while the barista made their coffee. 'How did you manage to wangle a franchise in here?' she said. 'I didn't think it would be allowed.'

He pointed to a sign near the door. 'Neither did we, but the coffee was getting worse and worse and tempers were fraying. They asked what we wanted and we told them. The profits from this franchise don't go back into the overall company. We have a ballot every year to decide which charity to support.'

He gave a little shrug. 'It works in our favour and in theirs. We get to support the charity of our choice, and they get to put us on their website talking about their contributions to charity. It's good publicity for them.' She smiled at the poster supporting research into Alzheimer's disease. 'Why did you pick that one?'

He picked up the tray and carried it over to a vacant table. 'We get lots of accidental house fires started by older people with memory problems—putting things in the oven or on the hob and forgetting about them. Some have early signs of Alzheimer's. We often go out and do community safety visits and fit fire alarms for anyone referred to us. It seemed a natural pick.' His voice lowered and she could sense the sadness in it. 'It caused us three fatalities last year.'

They sat down and Jess sipped her coffee. It was just as good as it was in every shop in the country. 'I think it's a great idea. I wonder if the hospital would consider it? The hospital kitchens are great, but the staff canteen is run by an outside firm. It's nowhere near as good as this.'

'I can give you some details if you want.'

'That would be perfect.' She leaned back in her chair. 'You could quickly make me the most popular woman in the hospital.'

'I'm sure you're that already.' His voice was low and he was looking up at her from over the top of his steaming cup of coffee.

She couldn't help the little upturn at the corners of her lips. When had the last time been that she'd had a man flatter her? It had been so long ago she couldn't remember.

Sure, there had been the odd unwanted leering comment, the kind that made your stomach turn—and not in a good way.

But this was different. It hadn't been invited. Or expected.

It was just—well, a nice comment. The kind that sent a little rosy glow all through you. Something she hadn't felt in a very long time.

It was kind of weird how she felt about all this. That first glimpse of Callum on the riverbank had been a total shock. And the way her body had reacted—her *natural* instinct—had been even more of a shock.

Because her natural instinctive response to Callum had been very physical. It hadn't helped that they'd been thrust together—in more ways than one—and parts of her body that had seemed dead had suddenly sparked into life.

It was taking time to get her head around all this.

And, to be frank, she was struggling.

In a way she wished she could be that naïve seventeen-year-old again, thinking that her heart was breaking as she left her first love behind.

If only she'd known then what she knew now.

That wasn't the thing that broke your heart. Not even close.

But all her memories of Callum were good. They were safe. Even if they came with a heavy dose of passion and teenage angst.

She didn't feel afraid around Callum. And she liked the way he was looking at her. It made her feel as if she was finally worth looking at again.

Pauline's words echoed around her head. *A world of possibilities.*

'Callum, I need to speak to you about something.'

The words jerked Jess out of her daydream. A well-stacked blonde was directly in her line of vision, her boobs inches from Callum's nose. Were those real?

'We need to talk about the meeting tomorrow at city headquarters. I need to give you a report to review before you go.'

Strange things were happening to Jess. The hackles had just gone up at the back of her neck and she felt an intense dislike for this extremely pretty and apparently efficient blonde. What on earth was wrong with her? She was never like this.

'Hi, Lynn. I'm actually in the middle of something right now.'

'What?' She glanced over at Jessica—whom she'd completely ignored—with renewed interest. 'Well, I'll let you finish up. But I'll need to see you in five.'

She turned to sweep away. Jess felt a smile sneak across her face as she realised Callum hadn't stared once at the boobs on display.

'Actually, I'll be a bit longer than that.' He gave a wave of his hand. 'I'll come and find you later.'

Lynn shot him a look of surprise, but Callum wasn't even looking at her any more. His attention was completely on Jessica.

Jess's heart gave a little flutter. She'd just recognised the sensation she'd felt a few seconds ago on Lynn's approach. Jealousy.

It was almost as if she'd landed in the middle of the icy-cold Clyde again, with the freezing water sweeping over her skin.

There was something very strange about all this. Being around Callum was making her feel again, something she thought would never happen. She'd been switched off for so long that she wasn't recognising everything straight away.

This was dangerous territory. She would have to take baby steps.

But all of a sudden it didn't seem quite so scary.

She gave Callum a little smile. 'So, tell me more about uni.'

She had to start somewhere and it was as good a place as any.

* * *

'Daddy, I don't feel good.'

Callum was sleeping but the little voice jerked him straight out of the weird dream that was circulating around his brain. Jessica dressed in a clown suit. Where did these things come from?

Yesterday had been fun. They'd spent most of the time together reminiscing. Talking about their past seemed to relax Jess. And he liked her like that.

He also liked the fact he was spending time with someone he trusted. Someone he didn't need to feel wary around. Somebody who wouldn't let him down.

But right now his paternal radar was instantly on alert. Drew was standing in the doorway, his eyes heavy with sleep and his hand rubbing his stomach. This was the second day he hadn't felt great. The second night Callum had put his dinner untouched into the bin.

Over the last two weeks Drew's symptoms seemed to flare up and then die down again.

He lifted up the corner of his duvet. 'Come over here so I can see you.'

Drew scuttled across the room and straight under the cover next to his dad. Callum pressed his hand to his head. He didn't feel warm—no obvious temperature. 'What's wrong, big guy? Do you feel sick?'

According to Drew's primary teacher half the class were off with a sickness bug. Maybe some of them had even ended up in Jessica's hospital. Rumours were circulating that it was norovirus.

Just what he needed. He still had the accident report to complete and there had been another incident at work today that would need to be followed up.

'Not sick, Daddy. Just a rumbly tummy.'

'Are you hungry? Is your tummy rumbling because you didn't eat any dinner?' He glanced at the clock. Two a.m. 'Do you want Dad to make you some toast?' It wasn't an ideal situation but if it settled Drew and got him back to sleep quickly, he could live with it.

Drew lay back against the pillows. 'No. Not hungry.' He moved a little closer. 'Just rub my tummy, Daddy, that will make it better.'

'You're sure? Do want a little drink of water?'

Drew shook his head and closed his heavy eyes.

Callum's hand automatically moved into position, very gently rubbing Drew's tummy in little circles. What could be wrong?

He hated to overreact. He hated to be an over-anxious father. But the truth was he had very few people he could bounce things like this off.

His friends Julie and Blair were the obvious choice but he wasn't going to call them at this time of night.

He glanced at the clock again. Maybe he would take Drew back to the GP in the morning. The trouble was, he hated going to the GP with a list of vague symptoms. A list of *not much but maybe it could be*.

It made him feel paranoid. It made him feel as if he wasn't coping. And that was the last thing he wanted anyone to think.

Did single mothers feel like this too?

Drew was the most precious thing in the world to him. He couldn't live with himself if he brushed something off and it turned out to be serious.

Maybe he should have asked Jessica yesterday. She was a paediatrician, she knew everything there was to know about kids.

But he hadn't thought about it and that made him feel

a little guilty. He hadn't even told her about Drew yet. Should he have? Theirs was a professional relationship. Nothing more, nothing less. But a tiny little part of his brain was nagging away at him, thinking that maybe it could be something else.

He still hadn't got to the bottom of her words. *Things just didn't work out for me.*

She'd been really careful today to keep steering the conversation back to him—or work, whenever he'd asked anything vaguely personal. She'd mentioned her mum and dad, a few old friends they'd known years ago. But nothing about herself.

Maybe he should wait until he found out what that meant before he gave it another thought.

He cuddled up with his little boy. Drew was his top priority right now.

The first person he looked at in the morning and the last person he looked at at night.

And that's the way it would stay.

CHAPTER SEVEN

THE WARD WAS quiet and he'd no idea where Jessica was. The nurse had just pointed down in this general direction.

He walked past a few windows, seeing children lying in beds with anxious parents next to them.

His heart clenched slightly. He would hate to be in that position. Thank goodness Drew usually kept in good health. He still hadn't got to the bottom of that stomach ache. The GP had basically fobbed him off and Callum didn't blame him because when they'd finally got an appointment, Drew had been full of beans and jumping around the place.

It was always the same with kids.

The ward sister he'd met a few times was standing next to one of the doors. 'Hi, Pauline.'

She gave him a knowing smile. 'Hi, there, Callum. And who might you be looking for?'

He sighed. He'd known from the first time he'd met her that Pauline could read everyone instantly. Why even pretend it was anything else? He still hadn't seen Jess, so this might work in his favour.

He leaned against the doorjamb and folded his arms. 'Let's just say I'm looking for our favourite doc.' He lifted his eyebrows. 'All work-related, of course.'

Pauline nodded. 'Of course.' But the smile was spreading further across her face. She lowered her voice. 'I think our mutual friend will be very pleased to see you.'

He felt something flare inside him. That acknowledgement—no matter how brief—reassured him. Pauline and Jess were good friends. If Jess was talking to anyone it would be Pauline. It gave him a little hope. It also gave him the courage to ask the question that had been gnawing away at him.

He hesitated for a second. 'Pauline—about Jess.'

She raised her eyebrows, as if he was about to say something she didn't want to hear. She was protective of Jess and that was nice.

'Jess told me that things didn't work out for her. And I know she's reverted to her maiden name.' He unfolded his arms and held out his hand towards her. 'I wonder if you could tell me what happened. I get the feeling I'm treading on difficult ground.'

Pauline bit her lip and glanced over her shoulder. Her eyes met his. 'You're right, Callum, it is difficult ground but I think that it's something Jess really needs to tell you herself.' Her eyes looked down, as if she was hesitant to say any more. 'Life hasn't turned out the way she expected. Jess should be married with a family to love and I'm hoping that's what she'll get. Just give her a little time.'

She pointed to the next set of doors. 'She's down there. Go and say hello.'

Was this better or worse?

His curiosity had just scaled up about ten notches.

He wanted to give Jess time to tell him—he really did. There was just that little edge of wariness. That lingering feeling left by a previous experience.

Jess was nothing like Kirsten, Drew's mother. They

weren't even in the same ballpark. But it didn't stop his slightest sense of unease as he walked down the corridor.

He pushed the feelings to one side. He'd already made up his mind about what he wanted to do next. He wanted to see how Jess would react. And he wouldn't know unless he tried.

Finally he caught sight of Jess's caramel-coloured hair. She was sitting talking to a little girl with curly hair with her leg in a bright pink fibreglass cast. It was Rosie, from the minibus accident.

He stuck his head around the door. 'Knock, knock.'

Jess looked surprised to see him. 'Callum, what are you doing here?'

'I phoned and left you a message. Didn't you get it?'

She shook her head then turned to the woman sitting next to her. 'Carol, this is Callum Ferguson. He's one of the fire rescue crew who were at the accident. He helped get Rosie out of the bus.'

'It's him, Mummy! It's him!' Having a cast on hadn't seemed to limit Rosie's movements. She wiggled over to the edge of the bed. 'The one I told you about.'

Rosie's mum stood up and held out her hand. 'Callum, my daughter has been talking about you non-stop. She seems to think you're a superhero. She saw you abseil down the side of the riverbank.'

Callum felt a little rush of blood to his cheeks. This was the last thing he had been expecting. He shook his head and knelt down beside the bed. 'You're much braver than me, Rosie. You tumbled down the bank in the minibus. That must have been really scary. The way I got down wasn't scary at all.'

Rosie held out her hands and reached round Callum's neck, giving him a big hug.

Jessica was watching. Watching—and trying to keep the smile from her face at his appearance. Callum seemed totally at ease, not in the least fazed by the little girl's action. Thank goodness. She had him on some sort of pedestal.

But it was kind of nice. Almost as if he was used to being in contact with kids.

Callum leaned back and tapped the pink cast. 'How is your leg? I love the colour of your cast.'

Rosie smiled. 'Thank you. Dr Rae and I have the same favourite colour. That's why I picked pink.'

'Well, I think it looks great. Your leg will be all better soon.'

Jess stood up and gave Carol and Rosie a smile. 'I'll leave you two. You can give me a call if you need me.' She nodded her head towards the door. 'Callum?'

She could smell his aftershave. It wasn't familiar. It was different from the one he'd used the day they'd abseiled back up the slope. It was more spicy, with richer tones. She liked it.

They walked along the corridor. Callum waved his hand, in which he had a big brown envelope. 'I've typed up the statement from the other day. I need you to read over it and sign it.'

She felt a flutter of disappointment. Business. Purely business. That's why Callum was here. Not for any other reason. A strange lump was forming in her throat. Once she'd signed the statement she would have no reason to ever see Callum again.

Her heart had leapt when he'd appeared. She hated it when it did that. She kept telling herself over and over again that this was nothing. This meant nothing. Just some wild, crazy coincidence that their paths had crossed again. This was work-related.

He turned to face her and she tried hard not to stare at his chest, which was instantly in her view.

She raised her eyes to meet his bright green ones. It was one of the first things she'd ever noticed about Callum, his startling green eyes.

'I can read the statement now, it will only take a couple of minutes.' There was no point turning this into something it wasn't. She saw him glancing at his watch, it was nearly six o'clock in the evening. He would be finished for the day—just the way she should be. Was he worried about being late? Did he have a date? Maybe that blonde from the fire station?

She hated the way that thought made her stomach curl.

'Have you finished for the day?'

'What?'

He'd moved a little closer and was towering over her, an impatient edge to his voice.

'I mean have you finished? You can't be on call again. I want you to come somewhere with me.'

She pulled back a little. There was something a little weird about him. Was he nervous?

She looked around her. The ward had quietened down. All patients had been seen, all prescriptions and instructions written. 'Yes, yes, I'm finished.' She was feeling a bit bewildered. A few seconds ago she had been sure everything was business as usual. He needed a signature to get the job finished so he could be on his way. And that had made her sad.

Now what?

A smile broke across Callum's face. 'Then get your coat.' She was turning towards her office when she heard him mutter something under his breath. 'You've pulled.'

She let out a burst of laughter and spun back around. 'Did you just say what I think you did?'

It had been a joke between them. A daft teenage saying that both had used years before. But it came totally out of the blue and instantly took her back thirteen years.

Callum's shoulders were shaking. 'Sorry, I couldn't resist it.'

Jessica stuck her hand around the office door and pulled out her woollen coat. There was a flash of bright pink. 'Think you can cope?' she asked as she wound her purple scarf around her neck and fastened the buttons on the bright coat.

He just nodded. 'You did warn me about the bright pink coat, and knowing you I wouldn't have expected anything less. Do you have gloves?'

She stuck her hands in the coat pocket and pulled out a pair of purple leather gloves. 'Sure. Why?'

'It's a nice night out there. Just a little dusting of snow. I'd like to walk instead of drive. Are you okay with that?'

She pulled out a woolly hat and stuck it on her head. 'I'm game if you are. But you've got me curious now. Where are we going?'

He gestured towards the door. 'Let's find out.'

They walked quickly through the lightly falling snow. It was pitch dark already—darkness fell quickly in winter in Scotland. The streetlights cast a bright orange glow across the wet pavements.

'So where are you taking me?'

Callum drew in a breath. He was still getting over the fact he'd asked her. It had been totally instinctive. He'd only made the decision once he'd set foot on the ward—particularly after what Pauline had said to him. The words had come out before he'd even had a chance to think about them. A signature would have meant he'd have no excuse to see Jesssica again. And he wasn't quite ready for that.

Drew was at mini-kicker football tonight. He went every week with Julie and Blair's son. One week Callum gave them dinner and took them, the next week Julie and Blair took them. Drew wouldn't be home until after eight o'clock.

'That would be a surprise.'

'Hmm…a surprise. How do you know I still like surprises?'

He gave her a little smile. 'It's an educated guess. Some things are just part of us—like our DNA. I'm working on the premise that the fundamentals haven't changed.'

They turned a corner and started walking along one of the main roads. It was busier now, the crowds jostling along all seeming to be headed in one direction.

The strains of Christmas music could be heard above the buzz of the crowds around them. Jess stopped a few times to look at the Christmas displays in some of the shop windows. Finally, he placed his hand in the small of her back as he guided her around the corner and into George Square.

'Oh.' He heard the little bit of shock in her voice as the recognition of where they were sank in. The square was bustling, packed with people here to see the annual switching on of the Christmas lights. A huge tree stood in the middle of the square, already decorated and just waiting for the lights to be lit. The Lord Provost already stood on the stage, talking into a microphone and trying to entertain the crowds.

'You brought me here? I can't believe you remembered.' Her voice had gone quiet, almost whispered.

This had been one of their first dates, coming to see the annual switching on of the Christmas lights in George Square. He hadn't planned this. He hadn't even thought about it. But as he'd driven to the hospital tonight he'd heard the announcement on the radio about the switch-on. It had almost seemed like a sign—a message. He'd had to ask her to come along. If only to try and take a little of the sadness out of her eyes.

'There's so many families,' she said as she looked around, dodging out of the way of a little girl with long blonde hair running straight for them.

'Yeah, there always are.' Lots of people brought their families to the turning on of the lights. It was entirely normal. But he couldn't help catch the little edge of something else in her voice.

'Over here.' Callum put his hand on her back again and guided her over to one of the street-vendor stalls. The smells of cloves, mulled wine and roasted chestnuts were all around them. Callum bought two cups and handed one over to her.

'Want to take a guess at what colour the tree lights will be this year?'

Jessica leaned against one of the barriers, sipping her mulled wine and watching the people around them. It was obvious that her brain was trying to take in their surroundings. 'They were purple the first year that we came here.'

'And they were silver the year after.' He kept his voice steady.

'And red the year after that.'

It was clear that they both remembered and for some reason it was really important to him that it was imprinted on Jess's brain just as much as it was on his. Half of him had been sure she would know why he'd brought her here, while the other half had been in a mad panic in case she'd turned around with a blank expression on her face.

'They were blue last year,' he murmured, not really thinking.

Jess spun round, the mulled wine sloshing wildly in her cup. 'You were here last year?'

Yes. He'd been here with Drew. But it had turned out Drew didn't really like the turning on of the lights. It was almost as if there was a little flare of panic in Jess's eyes. Did she think he'd been here with another woman?

Maybe this was it. Maybe this was time to tell her about Drew. It seemed natural. It was a reasonable explanation for what he'd just said. But the look in her eyes, that and the wistful tone in her voice when she'd remarked on the families, made him think twice.

'I was here with some friends.'

'Oh.' She seemed satisfied with that answer and rested her forearms back on the barrier.

The crowd thickened around them, pushing them a little closer together as people jostled to get a better place at the barrier. Callum wound his arm around her waist, holding her firmly against him, to stop anyone coming between them. The countdown around them started. Ten, nine...

It was the smallest of movements. Jess rested her head on his shoulder then a few seconds later he felt her relax a little more and felt some of the weight of her body lean against him.

A grin spread across his face. It wasn't like anyone could see it but it had been automatic and was plastered there for the world to see. Three, two, one.

'Woah!' The noise went around the crowd as the lights flickered on the tree, lighting up the square in a deluge of pink and silver.

'Pink! It's pink!' Jess yelped, as the wine sloshed out of the cup and she turned to face him. Her eyes were sparkling, her excitement evident. It was the first time since he'd seen her again that she looked totally carefree. Totally back to normal.

Her face was right in front of his, her brown eyes darker than ever before and their noses almost touching. He could see the steam from her breath in the cold night air. He placed his cup on the barrier and brought his hand to her hip, matching the hold of his other hand, and pulled her a little closer. He gave her a smile.

'My plan worked. I told them that pink was your favourite colour and that you'd be here.'

She let out a laugh and placed her hands on his shoulders. She didn't seem annoyed by him holding her. She didn't seem annoyed at all. In fact, if he wasn't mistaken, she was edging even closer.

Her dark eyes were still sparkling, reflecting the twinkling lights around them, 'Oh, you did, did you? I bet that took a bit of planning, especially as you didn't even know if I'd agree to come on a walk with you.'

He pulled her even closer. 'Oh, I knew. I was absolutely sure you'd come with me.'

He could turn back the clock. He could flick a little switch right now and this could be thirteen years ago. Standing almost in this exact spot.

She tilted her head to the side. 'Well, that was a bit presumptuous, wasn't it?'

He shook his head. 'I don't think so. But this might be.'

He bent forward. People around them were still cheering about the Christmas lights, breaking into song as the music got louder in the amplifiers next to them.

But Callum wasn't noticing any of that. The only thing he was focused on was Jess's lips.

And everything was just like he remembered. Almost as perfect.

The last time round Jess had tasted of strawberry lip gloss, and this time she tasted of mulled wine. He could sense the tiniest bit of hesitation as he kissed her, so he took it slowly, gently kissing her lips, teasing at the edges until she moved her hands from his shoulders and wrapped them around his neck, kissing him right back.

And then everything *was* perfect.

CHAPTER EIGHT

CALLUM LISTENED TO the NHS helpline music with growing impatience. It was funny how all rational thought flew out of the window when your child was in pain.

Drew was clutching his stomach again. He was pale and feverish, and he couldn't even tolerate fluids. But the pain was making him gasp and sob and Callum was feeling utterly helpless.

He glanced at his watch. It would be nearly midnight by the time the NHS helpline put him through to one of the nurses—and he told Drew's story *again*—then they would have to drive out to one of the GP centres. Who knew when his son would get some pain relief?

No. He couldn't wait that long.

As a member of one of the emergency services, he hated it when people used the services irresponsibly. But this didn't feel irresponsible. This did feel like an emergency. And he could explain later why he hadn't been prepared to wait for the helpline.

Jessica was on call tonight. Should he take Drew to Parkhill?

He hadn't even told her about Drew yet, and this would be a baptism of fire. But as Drew's father he couldn't think of anyone he would trust more with his son. He'd seen Jessica at work. He'd heard her colleagues talk about her.

She was undoubtedly a great doctor, who cared about her patients.

He was supposed to be taking Jessica out for dinner in a few nights' time. He'd been hoping to tell her about Drew then, and also to explain why evening dates could prove to be difficult. After a day of work he really didn't like to ask someone to babysit his son. He wanted to spend time with him. And he was hopeful that Jess would understand that. But now that would all have to wait.

Within minutes he had Drew bundled up into his booster seat, still in his pyjamas and wrapped in a fleecy blanket.

The roads were coated with snow and deadly quiet. Anyone with a half a brain was tucked up in bed. The only other traffic on the roads at this time of night was the gritters. He made it to the hospital in record time, parked in one of the emergency bays and carried Drew inside in his arms.

'I need to see Jessica Rae right away.'

The receptionist looked up, her face unfamiliar. 'Can you give me your details, please, sir?'

'Jessica Rae—I know she's on duty tonight. I want her to check over my son.'

The receptionist plastered a weary smile on her face. 'Give me your son's details. I'll get one of the doctors to see him.'

Callum felt his patience at an all-time low. 'Page Jessica Rae for me—*now*!'

One of the triage nurses appeared at his side and gave a knowing smile to the receptionist. They were probably used to frantic parents, but it didn't excuse his behaviour. 'Come with me, sir, and I'll start the assessment procedure for your son.' She reached over and brushed Drew's fringe out of his eyes, taking in his pale colour and the sheen on his skin. 'Let's get some obs.'

Callum felt himself take some deep breaths as he followed the nurse down the corridor. She was ruthlessly efficient, taking Drew's temperature, heart rate and blood pressure, then putting some cream on the inside of one elbow to numb the area and prepare it for a blood sample to be taken. As she scribbled down Drew's history, then held a sick bowl to let him retch into it, she gave Callum a tight smile.

'I know you asked for Dr Rae, but she's in surgery right now. She will see your son, but he needs some other tests done and some blood taken in the meantime. I'm going to ask one of the other doctors on duty to see Drew right now.'

There was something in the way she said the words. The quiet urgency in them. As if she suspected something but wasn't prepared to say it out loud. She had that look about her—the nurse who'd seen everything a dozen times and could probably out-diagnose most of the junior doctors.

'What do you think's wrong?'

She gave the slightest shake of her head. 'Let's leave that to the doctors, shall we?'

He tried his best not to erupt. To tell her that he didn't want his son to wait a second longer.

She glanced at him as she headed to the curtains. 'I'll get the other doctor now. The sooner Drew is seen, the better. Then we can get him some pain relief.'

He nodded automatically. Pain relief for his son. That's what he wanted more than anything. Anything to take the pain away from Drew.

'Dr Rae, there's a kid with an acute abdomen in A and E. Father is insisting you see him.'

Jessica pulled off her gown and gloves and dumped them in the disposal unit. 'Really? What's the name?'

'Kennedy. Drew Kennedy.'

She shrugged. She was the consultant on call. She'd see any kid with an acute abdomen anyway. 'I don't recognise the name, but tell them I'll be right there.'

She gave her hands a quick wash, trying to place the name. None of her friends had a son called Drew. And the surname? Well, there was only one Kennedy that she knew.

Her stomach gave a little sinking feeling as she rounded the corner into A and E. It couldn't be, could it?

No. Not a chance.

It couldn't be a nephew as Callum didn't have any brothers or sisters.

And Callum would have mentioned something as important as having a son. Wouldn't he?

But as she walked over to the curtains she recognised the frame hunched over the little figure straight away.

She froze.

She wanted to turn on her heel and run away. She wanted to disappear out of the hospital and take a minute to catch her breath. To try and get her head around the thousand thoughts currently spinning around in her brain.

But that was the second that Callum looked up. And his relief at seeing her was plastered all over his face.

She'd seen that look a hundred times. The parent worried out of their mind about their child. Hoping against hope that their worst fears weren't about to be realised.

Professional mode. No matter how she felt, or what her questions were, she had to move into professional mode right now. There was a sick little boy to be dealt with.

She kept her voice steady and calm. 'Callum? I didn't

expect to see you.' She picked up the chart, her eyes skimming over the notes and observations. 'Is this your son?'

Calm. Rational. That's how she was hoping she sounded.

Callum had the good grace to look embarrassed. 'Yes. This is Drew.' There was a shake to his voice. He really was scared for his son—he must be. He'd deliberately brought him here and asked for her, even though he'd known she would have questions. 'He's five and he's had a sore stomach on and off for the last two weeks. We've been back and forth to the GP with no diagnosis. But tonight he's much worse.' He lowered his voice. 'Sorry. I was going to tell you about Drew at dinner on Saturday.'

Her brain was still stuck on the 'five' part. She tried not to wince as she glanced at the date of birth. Drew was almost the same age as her son Lewis would have been.

She tried not to let the tight squeeze around her heart affect her. Everything was so unfair. Callum had the little boy she should still have. A little boy he hadn't even mentioned.

She took a deep breath and looked over at the little boy on the bed. The junior doctor had done everything he should, but he hadn't made any provisional diagnosis. Which meant he was stumped.

'Hi, there, Drew. I'm Dr Jessica. Do you mind if I have a look at your tummy?'

'No. Daddy, don't let them touch my tummy again.' She could hear the distress in the little boy's voice. The fear of someone touching a part of him that was already very painful.

She looked at the chart, making sure he'd been given some analgesia. 'Hasn't the medicine helped your sore tummy? It should have made it feel a little better.'

The little boy shook his head. 'It's still sore.'

'Can you tell me where it hurts if I promise not to touch?'

He nodded. His face was pale. 'It started in the middle but now it's over here.' He pointed to his left side.

She pointed to the IV in his arm. 'I'm going to put a little more medicine in here. It will work really quickly and help your tummy.' She nodded towards the nurse. 'Can I have point two milligrams of morphine, please?'

She waited a few minutes until the nurse returned with the syringe and ampule for her to check before administration. She prescribed the dose and signed the ledger before giving Drew the analgesic. She placed her hand on his forehead and bent down to whisper in his ear, 'It will start to work really quickly, I promise.'

Some doctors didn't agree with giving analgesia to paediatric patients before a diagnosis was made. They thought it could mask abdominal symptoms and delay a diagnosis. But Jessica had read a whole host of studies with evidence that analgesics reduced pain without interfering with diagnostic accuracy. Besides, Jessica could never leave a child in pain.

Right now, Drew was showing most of the signs and symptoms of appendicitis, but the pain for appendicitis was associated with radiating to the right, not the left.

She bent down and whispered in Drew's ear. 'Okay, I know I'm a lady doctor but I need to have a little check of your testicles. Do you know what they are?'

He shook his head.

She lifted her eyebrows. 'Your balls.'

He gave a little giggle.

She nodded. 'All I'm going to do is have a little feel to make sure they are where they're supposed to be. It will only take a few seconds, and it won't hurt, okay?'

He nodded and she checked quickly. It was important with boys to rule out a twisting of the testes, but everything seemed fine.

She did another few tests, one—the McBurney's—the classic indicator of appendicitis. But nothing was conclusive.

Drew's guarding was evident. Something was definitely going on.

The nurse appeared at her side. 'Drew's blood tests are back. They're on the system.'

Jessica gave a nod. No wonder the junior doctor had been puzzled. *She* was puzzled. 'Let's get an IV up on Drew and I'm going to order an abdominal ultrasound to see if we can get a better idea of what's going on.'

She walked over to the nearest computer and pulled up Drew's blood results. His white-cell count was up, just as expected in appendicitis. She gave a little nod of approval as she saw the junior doctor had grouped and crossmatched his blood too, in case surgery was needed at a later time.

She looked over at Drew again. He was curled up in a ball, guarding his stomach like a little old man. And the strangest feeling came over her.

She unhooked her pink stethoscope from her neck. 'Drew, I'm just going to have a listen to your chest. It will only take a few seconds.'

She placed her stethoscope on his chest, waited a few seconds then took a deep breath and repositioned it.

She looked sideways at Callum. 'Has Drew ever had a chest X-ray?'

He shook his head. 'I don't think so. He's never had any problems with his chest. Why? What's wrong?'

Jess signalled to the A and E nurse. 'Can you arrange a portable chest film for me—right away?'

The nurse nodded and disappeared for a few minutes. There was always a portable X-ray machine in the emergency department.

Callum walked over to her. 'What is it?'

She placed her hand on his chest. 'Give me a minute. I need to check something.' She wrinkled her nose. 'Have you ever had a chest X-ray?'

He rolled his eyes. 'Jess, I'm a fireman. I spent years working with a regular fire crew. Every time I came out of a burning building I had a chest X-ray.'

She nodded, it made sense, 'Right. So you did. And no one ever mentioned anything?'

He shook his head. 'Are you going to tell me what's going on? I'm going crazy here.'

She reached over and touched his hand. It didn't matter how upset she was right now. She'd even pushed aside the conversation she wanted to have with him right now. 'Callum, do you trust me?' Drew was the only thing that currently mattered.

His eyes flitted from side to side. Panic. Total panic. He ran his hand through his hair. 'Yes, of course I do, Jess. Why do you think I brought Drew here and asked to see you? There's nobody I trust more.'

The horrible reality right now was that she understood. She understood that horrible feeling of parental panic. That *out-of-control* sensation. She did. More than he would ever know.

She wrapped her other hand over his. 'Then just give me five minutes. Let me have a look at a chest X-ray for Drew. I promise, I'll explain everything.'

She saw his shoulders sag a little, saw the worried trust in his eyes.

She was telling herself that she would do this for any parent. That she *had* done this for any parent. But her conflicting emotions were telling her something else entirely.

The X-ray only took a few minutes and she pushed the film up onto the light box. It took her less than five seconds to confirm her diagnosis.

'Can you stay with Drew?' she asked the nurse.

'What is it?' The stricken look had reappeared in Callum's eyes, but she shook her head, pulled the chest X-ray down from the box and gestured with her head for him to follow her.

She opened the door to a nearby office and pushed the film back up on the light box inside. She flicked the switch and turned to face Callum.

'Drew has a condition called situs inversus.'

'What? What is that?'

She took a deep breath. 'It literally means that all his organs are reversed, or mirrored from their normal positions. Everything about Drew's symptoms today screamed appendicitis. Except for the positioning of the pain. Most people have their appendix on the right side. One of the true indicators of appendicitis is pain in the right iliac fossa.' She pointed to the position on her own abdomen to show him what she meant. 'But Drew's pain is on the other side—because his appendix is on the other side.'

'What does this mean? Is it dangerous? And how can you tell from a chest X-ray?'

She placed her hand on his shoulder. 'Slow down, Callum. One thing at a time.'

She pointed to the chest X-ray. 'Drew's heart is on the right side of his chest instead of the left. I can see that clearly in the chest X-ray.' She pointed at the lungs. 'I can also see that his left lung is tri-lobed and his right lung bi-lobed. That's the reverse of most people. This all gets a little complicated. It means that Drew's condition is known as situs inversus with dextrocardia, or situs inversus totalis.'

She tried to explain things as simply as she could. 'This is a congenital condition, Callum, it's just never been picked up. It could be that either you or his mother has this condition. It seems less likely for you as it would have been picked up in a routine chest X-ray.' She gave her head a little shake. 'It could be that neither of you has it. It's a recessive gene and you could both be carriers. Around one in ten thousand people have this condition.'

'Is it dangerous?'

She bit her bottom lip. 'It can be. Particularly in cases like this, when things can be misdiagnosed. But Drew's been lucky. Some people with this condition have congenital heart defects, but as Drew's been relatively unaffected that seems unlikely. It's likely if he had a congenital heart defect he would have had other symptoms that meant the condition would have been picked up much sooner. We'll do some further tests on him later. Right now we need to take him for surgery. His appendix needs to come out. How about we take care of that now, and discuss the rest of this later?'

He was watching her with his deep green eyes. She could see that he'd been holding his breath the whole time she'd been talking. He let it out in a little hiss. 'Will you do the surgery?'

The ethics of this question were already running through her mind. She had treated the children of friends on a number of occasions. It wasn't something she particularly liked to do—but in an emergency situation like this, the child's health came first.

'I'm the physician on call tonight. So it's up to me to perform the surgery. Would you like to find someone else to do it? That's always an option if you feel uncomfortable.'

He was on his feet instantly. 'No. Absolutely not. I want you to do it. I trust you to do it.' He looked her straight in the eye. 'There's no one else I would trust more.'

Things were still bubbling away inside her. It wasn't the time or the place, but she still had to say something.

'This isn't exactly ideal, Callum. And I'm not entirely comfortable about it. The surgery isn't a problem. There will be a registrar and an anaesthetist in Theatre with me. I'll need to go over the risks with you and get you to sign a consent form.'

She hesitated and let out a sigh. 'I kissed you a few days ago, Callum, so that complicates things for me. Obviously I didn't know about Drew...' she held up her hand as he tried to interrupt '...because you chose not to tell me. So, because I haven't met your son before, and don't have a relationship with him, that makes things a little easier.'

Her hands went to her hair and she automatically started twisting it in her hands, getting ready to clip it up for Theatre. She kept her voice steady. 'I'll perform your son's surgery and look after him for the next few days. I'll take the time to explain his condition and give you all the information that you need. After that? I have no idea.'

'Jess, please just let me explain.'

'No, Callum. Don't. Don't make this any more complicated than it already is. I've got more than enough to deal with right now.' She pointed back through the open door towards the curtains, where Drew was still lying on the trolley with a nurse monitoring him. 'Make yourself useful, go and sit with your son.' She walked out of the room, muttering under her breath, 'You don't know how lucky you are.'

Callum watched her retreating back and took her advice.

The nurse gave him a smile as he appeared back at Drew's side. 'You were lucky,' she said. 'Our Dr Rae is a fabulous paediatrician. Not everyone would have picked up that diagnosis.'

He gave a little nod. That didn't even bear thinking about. If he'd taken Drew elsewhere and some other physician had missed this...

It made him feel physically sick to his stomach.

He stroked his hand across Drew's forehead. His son was a little more settled, the morphine obviously helping to a certain extent. Drew was the most precious thing in the world to him. He couldn't stand it if something happened to his son.

It was obvious he'd hurt Jessica's feelings by not telling her about Drew. And he wished he could take that back.

But it was too late now.

He'd explain to her later—once this was all over. He really didn't tell women about Drew. Drew was precious. He was a part of his life he kept protected, tucked away. And he had intended to tell Jessica about him. He'd just wanted to wait a little longer until he was sure they might have some kind of a chance at a relationship.

A relationship? Where had that come from?

He hadn't had a real 'relationship' since he'd broken up with Drew's mother. But Jessica was different. She was Jessica. His Jess. Someone he'd known a lifetime ago. And someone he hoped he could trust around his son.

Someone he could introduce to his son without wondering about other motives. Whether they might only really be interested in him, and not his son. Whether they might only be interested in dating a firefighter. Or some other crazy reason.

There wouldn't be any of that with Jess.

Jessica was a paediatrician. She must love kids. Why else do this job?

And she'd been interested in him when he'd been a pre-university student with no idea about his potential career prospects. So he didn't need to worry about that.

Drew opened his eyes and stared at him. 'Where did the nice lady go?' he murmured.

'She'll be back soon. She's going to make your tummy better.'

'Is she? Oh, good.' His eyelids flickered shut again.

He'd make it up to Jess.

He would. And he'd try to get to the bottom of the haunted look in her eyes.

He just had to get his son through this first.

Jess pressed her head against the cool white tiles in the theatre changing room. It was no use. She couldn't take the burning sensation out of her skin.

Thank goodness this place was empty. As soon as she'd slammed the door behind her the tears had started to fall.

It was so unfair. Callum had a son the same age as Lewis. Or the age Lewis would have been if he'd survived. A little boy he got to cuddle every day. To read stories to.

What kind of conversations did a five-year-old have with their parent when they were lying in bed at night, talking about their day?

A little boy he'd got to dress in his school uniform and photograph on his first day of school.

All the memories that Jess wished she had.

All the memories she'd been cheated out of.

Just when she'd thought she was getting better.

Just when she'd thought she could finally take a few steps forward.

Of course she had friends who had children the same age as Lewis would have been. She hadn't cut them out of her life. She couldn't do that.

She was a paediatrician, for goodness' sake. She couldn't spend her life avoiding children of a certain age. That would be ridiculous.

But sometimes it was difficult. And they were good enough friends to sense that. To know when to hold her close. To know when to give her a little space. It was a difficult path, a careful balance.

But this was different.

This was Callum.

An old friend, who was evoking a whole host of memories.

First Callum had appeared in her life. Then he had kissed her.

He'd raised her hopes, given her a glimmer of expectation that there might be something else out there.

And now this.

She was hurt. She was upset.

Upset that Callum hadn't told her about his son.

But the horrible coiling feeling in her stomach was something else.

She was jealous.

Jealous that Callum had a son and she didn't.

It was horrible realisation.

She'd seen the interaction between them. The stress in Callum's face when he was worried sick about his son. The slight tremor in his hand after she'd explained the surgery and the possible complications and he'd signed the consent form. The trust in his little boy's eyes, for him, and, more worryingly, for her.

She gave herself a shake. Children looked at her like that all the time.

The doctor who could make them better. The doctor who could take their pain away.

So why was it different that this was Callum's son?

An appendectomy was routine to her. Even though Drew's appendix was on the opposite side of his body. It shouldn't complicate the procedure for her. It was just a little unusual.

Maybe it was something else?

Callum was trusting her. Trusting her with his son.

And although she was worthy of that trust, it terrified her.

Because she knew what it was like to lose a child.

Other people in this world had lost a child. Other parents in this hospital had lost—or would lose—a child. She'd had the horrible job of losing paediatric patients and dealing with the bereaved parents herself.

But this felt very different.

No one in her circle of friends had lost a child.

She wouldn't wish that on anyone. Ever.

No parent should outlive their child.

No parent should spend the rest of their life looking at the calendar and marking off all the milestones that their child had missed.

She started to open packs and change, putting on a fresh set of theatre scrubs and tucking her hair up into the pink theatre cap. She had to get her head away from those thoughts. She had to get her head back into surgeon mode.

She walked through to Theatre and nodded to the anaesthetist, who was poised ready to start scrubbing at the sink.

Her registrar appeared at her side. 'I was just looking at the chest X-ray of the little boy for the appendectomy. Fascinating, I've never seen a case of situs inversus before—have you?'

She shook her head. 'No, I haven't.'

Alex started scrubbing next to her.

He was staring ahead at the blank wall as he started automatically scrubbing his hands, nails and wrists. 'I'll probably never see one again in my career. This might be interesting to write up.' He turned sideways, 'Can't there be complications in these kids? Heart defects and other problems? Some kind of syndrome?'

He was starting to annoy her now. He was clinically excellent, but a little too removed from his patients for Jessica's liking. In her book caring was an essential component of being a paediatrician.

'Yes, there can be a syndrome—Kartagener syndrome. People with situs inversus may have an underlying condition called primary ciliary dyskinesia. If they have both they are said to have Kartagener syndrome.' She started scrubbing her nails with a little more ferocity. Just what she needed—a registrar who permanently thought the glass was half-empty.

She preferred the other approach—the glass half-full approach. Especially when it came to children.

'You know, Alex, I've got a really sick little boy out there. His dad only brought him to our A and E department because he's a friend of mine, and the GP has been fobbing off his son's symptoms for days.' She shook her hands to get rid of some of the water then started to dry them on a sterile towel.

'I'd like you to think about that before we start. I'd like you to stop thinking about this little boy as a case for a medical journal. Think about him as a little boy who loves playing football, watching cartoons and eating chocolate cereal for breakfast. Think about him as the light of someone's life. Because the patient comes before the disease in every set of circumstances.'

She pointed to the door.

'Out there we have a father who is worried sick about his little boy. And even though I've been clear with him and given him the rundown of the surgery and the complications, he's sitting out there right now, wondering if his little kid will have peritonitis, develop septicaemia or be the one in a million who will have a reaction to anaesthetic.'

The theatre nurse came over and held out her gown for her. She thrust her arms into the sleeves and snapped her gloves in place. 'So let's make sure that I don't have to go out there and give him any bad news.'

She glared at him and stalked over to the theatre table.

You could have heard a pin drop.

She knew she'd been harsh.

She never acted like that at work.

And the staff in here all knew her personal set of circumstances. They understood exactly where she was coming from.

Harry Shaw, the elderly anaesthetist—who stood in as Father Christmas every year with his grey hair and beard—gave her a smile.

His voice was low. 'You can do this, Jess.' He gave a little nod of his head. 'It'll be a walk in the park.'

She watched as the trolley was wheeled in. She could only pray it would be.

CHAPTER NINE

'WOW—JUST WOW.'

'What are you talking about, Pauline?'

The sister from ITU gave her a smile and pointed behind her at the delivery guy, who could barely be seen beneath the beautiful spray of pink, purple and orange gerberas. Jess was on her feet in an instant, reaching up and touching one of the petals. 'Aren't they gorgeous?'

Pauline was quicker, pulling the card from the top of the bouquet. She spun it around. 'Hmm… "For Dr Jessica Rae."' She held the card next to her chest as Jess reached over to snatch it. 'I wonder who these could be from?' She took a few steps away. 'I'm guessing Mr Tall, Dark and Very, Very Handsome. Otherwise known as Callum Kennedy.'

Jess felt her cheeks flush. 'Stop it!' She grabbed the card, putting it into her pocket without reading it.

Pauline tutted. 'I'm disappointed. He's a member of the emergency services, he should know better.'

'Know better about what?'

Pauline waved her hand. 'That we don't allow flowers in ITU.'

Jessica accepted the huge bunch of flowers and gave Pauline a smile. 'But these flowers aren't for ITU, these flowers are for me.' She pushed open the door to her office and placed them on her desk. 'Wow. Where on earth did he get these at this time of year?'

Pauline stood in the doorway and folded her arms over her chest. 'Must have paid a pretty penny for them.' She turned on her heel and walked away. 'It must be love.'

Jessica's stomach plunged. 'No, Pauline.' She pointed at the flowers. 'These are just a thank-you for looking after Drew.'

'Honey, a thank-you is a bunch of flowers from a supermarket. An enormous bouquet, delivered by a courier, that's a whole lot more.'

Jess sank down into the nearest chair. 'Oh.'

'Oh? That's all you can say? Just "Oh"?' She sat next to Jess.

'What did the card say?'

Jess bit her lip. Did she really want to get into this conversation? She dug into her pocket again and pulled the card out. Pauline was right, this wasn't just a thank-you. And she had a sneaking suspicion what it might be.

She read the message.

This was gigantic apology *and* a thank-you.

'What is it?' Pauline leaned forward and touched her hand.

'It's an apology.'

'An apology? What's Callum got to apologise for?' Her eyes narrowed, she was automatically moving into protective mode.

'It's…it's awkward.'

'What's awkward about it?'

Jess let out a sigh. 'He didn't tell me about Drew. The first time I found out was when he brought him in with appendicitis.'

Pauline's mouth fell open. 'How long have you known this guy?'

'Since I was a teenager. But I hadn't seen him in thirteen years. And I hadn't kept up with what was going on in his life.' Her voice dropped. 'Just like he hasn't kept up with what's happened in mine.'

'You haven't told him?' Pauline's voice was incredulous.

'It hasn't come up.'

'Just like his son didn't come up?'

Jess put her head in her hands and leaned on the desk. 'This is a mess.'

'Yes. It is.' Pauline never pulled her punches. It was one of the things that Jessica liked best about her.

She placed her hand at the side of her face. 'So, this guy—who you used to know thirteen years ago—and you only met again a few days ago, and brought his son to A and E, even though he hadn't told you about him?'

Jessica nodded.

'He brought his sick son to see *you*.' She emphasised the word strongly. 'Even though he knew that might make you mad. Even though he knew you might have a thousand questions. It was more important that he thought about the health of his child and—after seeing you in action— brought him to see a doctor he trusted with the health of his son. Doesn't that tell you what you need to know?'

Jessica flopped her head back into her hands. Someone else saying the words out loud made it all seem so much more straightforward. So much simpler.

She felt Pauline's hand on her back. 'Jess, what is it that you want?'

'What do you mean?'

'I mean, what are you ready for? I thought it was time for you—time to take some steps and move on. Callum seemed like a good idea. But maybe he's got as much baggage as you do.'

'And if he does?'

Pauline rolled her eyes. 'You need to think about this, Jessica. What do you want?' She pointed to the flowers. 'Are you ready to accept Callum's apology and whatever else that might mean?'

'I don't know. I mean I'm not sure. I was hurt that he didn't tell me about his son.'

'And what about Drew?'

'What do you mean?'

Pauline moved her hand to her shoulder. 'Look at me, Jess. I'm going to ask a hard question. How do you feel about having a relationship with someone who has a son?'

Jess's head landed back on the desk. 'I don't know. I mean, I *really* don't know. Drew's lovely. He's a great little boy. I've spent a little time with him on the surgical ward. He's made a good recovery and he's ready for discharge.'

'Is he ready for you?'

'What do you mean?'

'Do you and Callum actually talk to each other? Where's Drew's mother? She hasn't been to visit. She isn't named on the consent form.' Pauline dropped her voice and said almost hesitantly, 'Is she dead?'

'No. I don't think so. When I asked Callum to sign the consent he said something about Drew's mother being in America and him having full custody. I'm not really sure what happened there. I know she's been on the phone to the ward staff a few times every day.'

'Ah, so there's no other woman to get in the way?'

'Pauline!'

She smiled at Jessica. 'So what? I'm being a little mercenary. I have a friend to think about.'

Jessica's eyes drifted over to the flowers. They were beautiful and the irony of the blooms wasn't lost on her. Gerberas were her favourite flowers—had been for years. She was surprised that Callum had even remembered that, but there was something nice about the fact that he had.

She stood up quickly. 'I need to go for a few minutes.' She looked about the unit. 'Is everything okay in here? Do you need me to see anyone before I go?'

Pauline shook her head. 'Everything's fine and, don't worry, I'll look after your flowers for you.'

Jessica rolled her eyes and hurried down the corridor. She glanced at her watch. Although the hospital allowed parents to stay with their children at all times, most parents went away for an hour or so each day to freshen up and change their clothes.

The surgical ward had been a no-go area for the last few days. Callum was there constantly with his son. Just as she would have expected.

She'd had to review Drew a few times every day. His recovery was going well and it was likely she would discharge him today.

But every time she'd been anywhere in the vicinity Callum had tried to speak to her. She'd fobbed him off as best she could. The flowers were the biggest message yet that he was determined to apologise and pursue this.

She just wasn't sure how she felt.

Her stomach churned as she walked down the ward. It was ridiculous. She spent all day, every day in the presence of kids. Why on earth would this little boy be any different?

Because he was Callum's.

Because this could be something entirely different.

If only she could be ready for it.

Drew had a little DVD player on his lap and was watching the latest Disney movie. Although he had his clothes on, the curtains were pulled around his bed and lights in the room dimmed. Most children who'd undergone an anaesthetic took a few days to recover fully. A nap time in the afternoon was common—and when most of the parents took their chance to go home, shower and change.

'Hi, Drew.' Jessica took the opportunity to sit down next to his bed. 'What are you watching?'

He turned the screen around to show her. She nodded in approval.

'So, how are you feeling?'

'I'm good. When can I go back to mini-kickers?'

She wrinkled her nose. 'Is that some kind of football?'

He nodded. 'I go every week with my friend Joe. I love mini-kickers. It's my favourite.'

'Well, we can't have you missing your favourite for long. Lie back and let me have a little look at your tummy.'

His wound was healing well. The edges were sealed and there was no sign of infection.

'This is looking great, Drew. The stitches that I used will disappear on their own. But you also have some stitches inside your tummy and if you do too much, too quickly, then it can hurt.'

'Tomorrow?' He was serious. His little face was watching her closely.

So this was how a five-year-old boy thought. Couldn't see past the football. There was something so endearing about that.

She laughed. 'No. Not tomorrow. Maybe two weeks—if you're feeling okay. Do you like school? Because if you do, it will be all right to go back to school next week.'

He wrinkled his nose. 'School's okay. I like school dinner. Mrs Brown makes the best custard.' He leant forward and whispered in her ear. 'The custard here isn't nearly as good.'

'Really? I always thought the custard here was quite good.'

He shook his head and gave her a look of disgust. 'Oh, no. Mrs Brown's custard is *much* better.'

He was a lovely little boy, with Callum's searing green eyes and a real determined edge about him. They were so alike she could have picked him out from a room filled with a hundred kids.

'What's your favourite subject at school?'

It was something that preyed on her mind from time to time. She'd often wondered what her own son would have enjoyed most at school.

'Dinosaurs or volcanoes.' Drew was absolutely definite about what he liked. He tilted his head to one side. 'And I quite like the sticky tray.'

'The sticky tray? What's that?'

'For making things. I was making a Christmas card for my dad a few days ago at school. I've picked blue card and I was sticking a snowman on the front.'

'Ah.' Jess gave a smile. 'What were you using for the snowman? Was it some cotton wool—like the kind we have in here?'

'Yes. It got kind of messy. The glue stuck to my hands and then the cotton wool got all puffy.' His face was all screwed up, as if he was remembering the mess he'd made.

Jessica leaned across the bed. 'It doesn't matter if you made a mess. I'm sure your dad will love it.'

'But I'm not finished yet. I still need to put some glitter on. I want to put some stars in the sky.'

'And that will be gorgeous, Drew. Then it's my job to get you back to school so you can finish it.'

Drew shook his head. 'That one got a bit messy. Can't you help me make another one?'

Jess hesitated. Everything in her head was screaming no.

She was a hospital consultant. She had a hundred other things to be doing right now.

But for the strangest reason none of them seemed particularly important. Here was an opportunity to do something nice. To do the first real Christmassy thing she'd done in…goodness knew how long.

She hadn't even put her Christmas decorations up for the last three years. It had hardly seemed worthwhile when she wasn't really in the mood. They were lying stuffed in a box in her loft somewhere. Maybe she should think about pulling them out.

She smiled at Drew. Yes, she could go and ask one of the play advisors to come and help Drew make a card.

But he had a really hopeful look in those green eyes.

How could she possibly say no?

She walked over to one of the play cabinets and pulled out a drawer. The hospital's own kind of sticky tray. She lifted up the vast array of coloured card and fanned it out like a rainbow in her hand. 'What colour card would you like?'

Callum strode down the corridor. He hadn't meant to be so long. But three nights of sleeping in a hospital chair did strange things to your body.

He'd stepped out of the shower and had only meant to sit down for a few seconds at home. The next thing he knew he had a crick in his neck and was hopping about the place, trying to get dressed in the space of five seconds.

If he was lucky, today would be the day he got to take his son home. And as much as he liked going to the hospital and getting to see Jessica every day, he'd much rather have his son safe at home.

He'd promised Drew's mother that they could Skype tonight. She usually did it every week with Drew and had been annoyed that she hadn't been able to see him while he'd been unwell.

It was just as well children were so resilient. Drew had seemed to get over his mother's abandonment within a matter of weeks. Probably because he'd been surrounded by people who loved him. But Callum could never forget the impact it had had on his son. What kind of a woman did that?

He turned the corner, ready to head into Drew's room, and stopped dead.

It was a sight he'd never expected to see.

Drew looked nothing like the child he'd been a few days ago, pale-faced and in pain. Today he had colour in his cheeks and sparkle in his eyes.

Drew and Jessica. Paint was everywhere. Cotton wool was everywhere. Glitter was everywhere, including smudged all along Jessica's cheekbones. But most importantly Drew was smiling, Drew was laughing. His attention was totally focused on Jessica. And the way he was looking at her...

It tugged right at Callum's heartstrings. Kirsten, his ex-wife, had never been the most maternal woman in the world. And since she'd left Drew had never really had a female presence in his life, that female contact. Sure, there were his friends Julie and Blair, and Julie was fabulous with Drew. But he didn't see her every day—didn't have that kind of relationship with her.

This was the first time he'd realised what his son had been missing out on.

He felt a sharp pain in his stomach. He'd always felt as if introducing Drew to any of his girlfriends would have been confusing for a little boy. Taking things a step too far. He wanted to protect Drew from all of that. And to be truthful he'd never been that serious about any of them. He couldn't stand the thought of different women yo-yoing in and out of his son's life.

Then there was that lingering dread of introducing Drew to another woman, only for her to change her mind and speed off into the sunset, leaving him to pick up the pieces.

But maybe he had been wrong? Maybe he'd been cheating his son out of so much more.

Jess seemed so at ease with his son. But, then, she should, she was a paediatrician, she loved kids. It was the field she'd chosen to work in.

It made him even more curious. Why didn't Jess have kids of her own? It was obvious she would be a natural.

It almost seemed a shame to interrupt this happy scene, but he had to. He wanted to know if he could take his son home. He cleared his throat loudly. 'What's going on in here?'

Drew's eyes widened in shock. 'Hide them, Dr Rae! Hide them!' He cupped his hands over whatever it was he'd been making.

Jess jumped to her feet and stood in front of the table they were sitting at, opening up her coat to block his view. She gave Callum a wink then turned her head over her shoulder towards Drew. 'It's okay. He can't see a thing. Put them in the envelopes now.'

There was the loud sound of shuffling behind Jessica's back, along with little-boy squeals of excitement.

But Callum was kind of stuck in the view right in front of his eyes. Jess was wearing a red woollen dress, which clung to her every curve, leaving nothing to his imagination. He was kind of glad that her white coat normally covered this view. He didn't want everyone else seeing what he could.

Jess sparkled. Literally. Blue and silver glitter along her cheekbones.

He lifted his thumb up and touched her cheek. 'You got a little something on here.' He brushed along her cheekbone then his fingers rested under her chin. He half expected her to flinch and move away, but she didn't. She stood still, fixing him with her deep brown eyes.

A man could get lost in eyes like that.

If he wanted to.

He stared down at his thumb. 'Is this a bit of a giveaway?'

She shook her head and glanced over her shoulder again. 'How are you doing, Drew? Nearly done?'

Drew held up two giant white envelopes, looking ever so pleased with himself. 'Done!'

He stood up, but stayed behind Jessica, putting his hands on her hips and sticking his head around. 'Wait till you see what I've made you, Daddy.'

Callum knelt down. 'I can't wait. I'm hoping we can go home some time today. What do you think, Dr Rae?'

Jess brushed her hair back from her face, leaving traces of glitter everywhere, including shimmering in the air between them. 'Oh, wow! I guess we went all out with the glitter, then.'

'I guess you did.' She was still smiling at him. Not avoiding him. And not avoiding Drew. Did this mean she'd finally forgiven him? She might give them a chance at... something?

'What do you think, Doc? Is Drew ready for discharge?'

He could almost see the silent switch—the move back into doctor mode. 'Yes, I think he is. His wound is healing well. We've done a few other tests—an ECG and an ultrasound of his heart. There's been no sign of any problems.' Her face became serious and the smile disappeared for a few seconds.

'Right now I'm assuming that Drew's situs inversus in straightforward. But I understand you might want to talk to someone about it. So, even though I don't think Drew will need any kind of follow-up, I've asked for one of the other consultants who specialises in genetic conditions to give you an appointment so you can discuss any concerns that you have.'

Callum pulled back a little. 'But why? Can't I just talk to you?' The words she was saying made sense, but that didn't mean that he liked them.

She shook her head. 'I don't think that's a good idea. I performed Drew's emergency surgery, but I probably have a conflict of interest here.'

He raised his eyebrows. 'A conflict of interest, what does that mean?'

'You know what that means, Callum.'

'But you must have treated a friend's kid before?'

She nodded slowly and stepped a little closer, lowering her voice and glancing in the direction of Drew. He'd become bored by their chatting and was now doing a jigsaw at one of the nearby tables.

'Yes, I have treated children of friends before—but usually only in an emergency. I wouldn't willingly be the paediatrician for any of my friends' kids. It crosses too many boundaries—complicates things and leads to confusion all round.' She tilted her head to the side and gave him a little smile. 'I'm sure you understand.'

'Actually, I don't.' He folded his arms across his chest.

'What do you mean?'

'Friends. Is that what we are?'

'Of course.'

He didn't like it. He didn't like it at all. It didn't matter that the concept of only being friends with Jess had circulated in his mind for days.

In the cold hard light of day he didn't like that.

He wanted more.

He wanted to be more than friends.

The kiss had started something.

No. That was rubbish. Something had started more than thirteen years ago.

There was unfinished business between them.

'What if I don't want us to be friends?'

Her head shot up. 'What?' There was that fleeting look across her face again. She was hurt. But she wasn't getting his implication. She was thinking he didn't *even* want to be friends. Not that he wanted something more. It was time to put that right.

He stepped closer and placed his hand on her hip. 'What if I wanted us to be more than that?'

Her pupils widened and her tongue shot out and licked her lips. Her eyes darted to the side, obviously to see if anyone was watching. He pressed his fingers a little more firmly into her hip, pulling her closer to him.

Drew hadn't even noticed what they were doing, he was still engrossed in his jigsaw.

'I'm not entirely sure what you mean,' she murmured.

'Truth be told—neither am I.'

His other hand settled on her other hip, feeling the wool under his fingertips, along with the outline of her hip. He still had to find out what was going on with Jessica. He was no closer to that than he'd been a few weeks ago. She played her cards close to her chest.

But Drew was happy. He'd warmed easily to Jessica. He liked her. She made him smile. And after what he'd witnessed today he was willing to take some baby steps.

'But let's find out.'

She lifted her hand and touched the side of his face, her hand trembling. She bit her lip. 'What if I'm not sure?'

'Then we take it slowly. We find out together. Are you willing to try that?'

His heart was thumping against his chest wall. An answer had never seemed so important. He wasn't even entirely sure what he was asking. This was all new territory for him. New territory for them both.

He glanced over at Drew. 'How about a date? A family date?' He'd never done that before. It wasn't just a step for him—it was a leap. But maybe now was the time to find out.

He could see something fleeting pass through her eyes. A moment's hesitation. Did she want to say no? Did she want to walk away?

There it was again. Her tongue licking her dry lips. What kind of effect was he having on her?

'Let's embrace the time of year. I promised Drew I

would take him to see Santa at Cullen's Garden Centre in Largs on Saturday. They usually have a huge play park and real live reindeer for the kids to see. Do you want to come along?'

A nervous smile came across her face. 'A play park? Is that really a good idea after an appendectomy?'

He pulled her body next to his and gave a sexy smile. 'Oh, I think we'll be fine,' he whispered in her ear. 'We'll have medical supervision.'

The smile on her face seemed genuine now. 'I guess you will.'

CHAPTER TEN

HER BEDROOM WAS a mess.

No, her bedroom looked as if a tornado had swept through it.

Every jumper and pair of jeans she possessed was scattered across her bed. Along with every raincoat, woollen coat, hat, glove and scarf. It was a beautiful eruption of colour, but Jess was still standing in her bra and pants. No further forward than she'd been an hour ago.

She picked up the phone next to her bed and pressed the automatic dial. 'Pauline? Help.'

Her friend sounded as if she'd just woken up. 'What is it, Jess?' she groaned.

'What do I wear?'

'Tell me you're joking.'

'No. Why?'

'You phoned me at this time in the morning to ask me what to wear to meet Santa?'

Pauline already knew about the date. She just didn't appreciate the agonising Jessica was doing over her wardrobe.

Jess sagged down onto the bed. 'Please, Pauline. Tell me what to wear.' She sounded pathetic and she knew it. This was the behaviour of a teenage girl, not a grown woman with a responsible job.

But Pauline's voice came through loud and clear. 'I would have thought that would be obvious, Jess. You're going to meet Santa—you wear red. Wear your Christmas jumper—the one you wore on the ward last year. Drew will love it. And your skinny jeans and your big red boots. There. That's you sorted. Anything else, or can a girl get back to sleep?'

The picture was forming in Jessica's mind. She hadn't even considered her novelty knitted jumper with the great big Christmas pudding on it. It would be perfect. She stood on tiptoe and yanked it out of the back corner of her cupboard. 'Thanks, Pauline. I'll see you tomorrow.' She hung up the phone and held the jumper in front of her for a second before quickly pulling it over her head. Pauline obviously had better vision than she did. The jumper, along with her skinny jeans and red chunky boots, was perfect. She even had a red coat she could wear too.

She glanced at the clock again. She couldn't believe she was this nervous. It seemed ridiculous. This was a simple trip—a chance to get out of Glasgow and have a nice drive along the Ayrshire coast until they reached the garden centre outside Largs.

She should be calm about this. She should be relaxed. She fastened her red coat and wrapped her scarf around her neck. The forecast today said it would be cold—really cold—so she wanted to wrap up warmly.

Her make-up was already on. Even though she hadn't managed to choose her wardrobe, when she did wear make-up it was always the same—some light foundation, some mascara and a little bit of red lipstick. It seemed to give her the little bit of colour she always lacked.

There was a toot outside and her heart leapt into her mouth. Oh, no. They were here.

Why had she agreed to this?

What if Drew decided that he hated her?

What if she just found this all too hard?

She walked down the stairs and sat on the bottom step for a few seconds, taking a few deep breaths. She could do this. She had *chosen* to do this. And she had to remember that.

No one was forcing this on her—no one.

Callum had lit up something inside her that had been dead for a long time.

And no matter how much she tried to deny it, it had felt good.

Then there was Drew. He was a gorgeous little boy. Being in his company was easy. With his big green eyes and determined manner it was easy to like him.

The fears she'd had about constantly comparing him to Lewis weren't there. Lewis was a totally different little boy.

She took a sharp breath. That thought.

She did that frequently. Still thought about Lewis in the present tense—as if he was still there. Did all mothers do that? Did all parents who had lost a child still think of their child in the present tense?

Was that good or bad? She wasn't sure.

Things were changing. She was changing. Yesterday she'd even pulled the box out of the loft with her Christmas decorations and tree. It had been hard to look at them again, the pink and purple globes brought back so many memories of previous happy Christmases in this house. So last night when she'd been shopping in the supermarket she'd bought a whole host of new decorations—silver ones. It felt different. It felt right.

The pink and purple ones held too many memories. The

silver ones were new. With space available for memories of their own.

The car tooted again and she stood up, trying to ignore the fact her legs were shaking. She stared at herself in the mirror in the hall, taking in the look of absolute fear on her face.

She picked up the fake-fur-trimmed hat on the table in the hall and stuck it on her head. 'You can do this,' she told her reflection. She closed her eyes for a second.

Harry Shaw's face drifted into her mind. The expression on his face that day in Theatre when she'd just been about to operate on Drew. *You can do this, Jess. It'll be a walk in the park.* And he'd believed it. She had been able to tell by the expression on his face.

She opened her eyes and stared at her reflection again, adjusting her hat in the mirror. She looked herself in the eye and repeated the mantra, 'You can do this, Jess. It will be a walk in the park.'

She gave herself a little smile then headed out to the car, pulling the door closed behind her.

Now, if only she believed that.

Callum's fingers were drumming nervously on the steering wheel. Drew was happy. He was watching his favourite DVD in the back seat of the car, oblivious to his father's tension.

Callum squinted at the address again. This was definitely the right number. And he was definitely in the right street. He peered at the front door again. It was lovely, white with a stained-glass panel. He was sure he could see movement behind it. What was taking Jess so long?

He looked up and down the street. This was definitely one of the nicest areas of Glasgow. The street was filled with well-kept town houses with private drives and neat gardens. Wouldn't a town house be a little big for a single woman?

He shook that thought out of his head as the door opened and Jess came out. She was dressed in red today with a dark hat pulled over her ears.

There it was again. Even though he kept trying to ignore it. He was sure if they had him on one of those twenty-four-hour cardiac monitors his heart rate would shoot up every time he saw her. Jess was definitely wreaking havoc and adding to his chances of heart disease.

She gave him a little wave as she pulled the door closed behind her and started down the steps. Instead of walking around to the passenger side, she stopped and pulled open the rear door. 'Hi, Drew, how are you doing?'

Drew looked up from his DVD. 'Hi, Dr Jess. I'm good. Can I go to mini-kickers this week instead of next?'

She laughed. 'I can see five-year-old boys obviously have a one-track mind. I tell you what—let me think about it. Let's see how you do with Santa today.'

'Okay.' He pointed to the TV in the rear of the driver's seat. 'Do you wanna watch the dinosaurs too?'

She gave a little smile as she glanced at Callum. 'No, thanks. I'd better sit up front with your dad in case he gets lonely.'

'Aw, okay, then.' His eyes fixed on the screen again as she closed the door and walked around to the passenger side.

She slid in and started to unfasten the buttons on her coat. 'I was so worried about how cold it was going to be I totally forgot about the fact we'd be in the car for an hour.' She pulled her hat off her head, leaving her curls sticking up in all directions.

She seemed happy. She seemed relaxed and Callum felt himself heave a sigh of relief. He'd been so worried about this.

Worried that she'd change her mind.

Worried that she'd phone him and back out.

And although her face seemed relaxed, he'd noticed the way her hand was gripping her bag. Take things slowly. That's what they'd agreed.

He started the engine again and they pulled out onto the motorway, heading down towards Ayrshire. It was a bright day, with just a little nip in the air. Not quite cold enough to freeze yet and little chance of ice.

The road to Largs was always busy. It wound through various towns all haunted by a million sets of traffic lights, but the scenery made up for the slow-moving traffic.

'I didn't expect it to be so busy.' Jessica had leaned back in her seat and was changing radio stations for most of the journey. 'I thought people only went to Largs in the summer for the ice cream.'

He smiled. 'When was the last time you were in Largs?'

She frowned. 'I think I was a child. We were going to Millport for the weekend and had to get the ferry from Largs.'

'Did you get your picture taken on Crocodile Rock?'

She gave a little gasp. 'Hasn't every Scottish child got their picture taken on Crocodile Rock?'

He laughed. 'I've not taken Drew there yet. Maybe that's a trip for the summer.'

'What's Crocodile Rock?' came the little voice from the back of the car.

Jessica twisted round in her seat to talk to him. 'It's a rock that looks like a crocodile. Some people painted it red, white and black years ago and when I was a young girl everyone went to Millport in the summer and got their photo taken standing on Crocodile Rock.'

'But crocodiles are green!'

Callum tried not to laugh. Only a child's logic could say something like that. 'I'll show you some pictures of it later, Drew. I've got a photo taken standing on the rock. If you like it I'll take you over in the summer to see it.'

'Does it bite?'

'No, silly, it's a rock.'

Drew settled back into his chair. 'How far until we see Santa?'

Callum glanced at the road signs. 'About another ten minutes. We'll be there soon.'

'I'm hungry.'

'So am I,' Jess piped up. 'We'll get something to eat when we stop, okay?'

It was almost a relief to hear her say that. Even better was the sound of her stomach rumbling. It was like music to his ears.

She pressed her hand over it. 'Oops, sorry!'

It didn't take long to reach the garden-centre car park and Drew's DVD was instantly forgotten when he saw all the 'Santa's Grotto' signs. 'Look, Dad!' he shouted. 'They've got a sleigh and everything!'

He was out of the car like a shot and over at the painted barrier advertising Santa at the garden centre.

Jessica felt her stomach churn. He was so excited he was practically jumping up and down. It was so nice to see. So nice to experience. Lewis had been too little to really comprehend Christmas. Although he'd liked the presents, he'd still been a little scared of the man in the big red suit.

She felt Callum's arm around her waist. 'Everything okay?' Sometimes she felt as if he could almost read her mind. As if he knew when her thoughts were drifting off and taking her out of the present time and place.

She reached over and put her hand on his chest. 'I'm fine. I guess we'd better get in there before Drew bursts his stitches.'

They walked through the garden centre, past the blue-lit trees lining the driveway and fake snowmen and animals. Inside the garden centre they had a path to Santa's Grotto and another to meet the reindeer. Callum went to the nearby desk to buy tickets. It was already getting busy in the centre, with lots of families and children arriving all the time.

The entrance was gorgeous. It was filled with a huge variety of pre-lit trees, sparkling in a variety of different colours. There were shelves and shelves of lighted ornaments, coloured parcels, little nativity scenes, sequin-covered trees and models of little Christmas villages playing music. On the surrounding walls were thousands of tree decorations, all hanging in different colour schemes to make selections easier.

All around the place children were squealing with delight at seeing something new or squabbling over their favourite tree ornament.

Jessica felt a little hand slip into hers. She looked down and Drew was staring up at her with anxious eyes. She knelt down next to him. 'What's wrong? Don't you feel well?' She couldn't help it, she was immediately moving into doctor mode.

He shook his head. 'I couldn't see my daddy,' he whispered.

Jess smiled. From down here, in amongst the jostling throng of people, it was hard to make anyone out, particularly for a little boy who had been running to and fro between the attractions. But her bright red coat would be easily visible. When she stood up she could clearly see Callum's back at the ticket booth, but she wasn't a little boy.

She slipped her hand out of her red leather glove and grabbed Drew's hand again. The heat was rising in the garden centre so she unfastened the zip on his jacket. It was even nicer holding hands, skin to skin. Drew seemed relieved to have found her. His immediate trust in her was so apparent.

Callum appeared next to them and waved the tickets. 'All the visits are timed. We can't see Santa until eleven-thirty. Want to get something to eat and then we'll go and see the reindeer?'

They nodded and followed him into the busy café. 'Have a seat, you two, and I'll get us some food.'

Jessica and Drew sat down at one of the nearby wooden tables. The whole café was decorated for Christmas with tinsel, garlands and Christmas holly wreaths hanging all round the walls. There was a cup filled with crayons on every table along with ready-made Christmas colouring sheets. Drew wasted no time and started to colour in a picture of the North Pole. 'Have you given your daddy your card?'

He shook his head. 'We posted the other one to mum in America. Dad helped me write the envelope. But I hid his under his pillow this morning.' Drew giggled. 'He won't find it until we get home.'

Jess smiled, watching Callum's back as he pushed his tray along the rack, picking up food as he went. He hadn't even asked her what she wanted to eat. She had a sneaking suspicion he was trying to feed her up. And she didn't feel insulted or annoyed. It was kind of nice that someone wanted to look after her.

The tray landed on the table a few minutes later with a glass of milk and a bacon roll for Drew, some toast with scrambled egg for her, and a full breakfast for Callum. He lifted some other plates onto the table with some home-baked scones, along with a caramel latte for Jess.

He really did have the best memory in the world. All the things in the world she liked.

'Okay, everyone?' he sat down in the seat next to Drew and admired his crayoning. 'Let's eat and then we'll have a walk around the garden centre while we wait for our turn.'

Jessica looked around the room. It was full of families, all here either to buy a Christmas tree or pay a visit to Santa's Grotto. It had been such a long time since she'd been to a place like this.

She used to love visiting garden centres—especially around Christmas. She could easily have spent all her time off visiting one after the other, buying something in every place that she visited.

Something on one of the walls caught her eye. Little silver and red hearts, bunched together with bells to be hung from a Christmas tree. They were beautiful and just the sort of thing she would have picked in years gone by.

Callum followed her line of vision. 'Do you like them?'

She nodded slowly. A lump had appeared in her throat and she was too nervous to talk. She tried to clear her throat. 'I...I've changed my colour scheme. They would be perfect.'

He reached across the table and touched her hand. It was as if he knew. As if he'd just looked inside her head and saw that for a second she was struggling. 'Then we'll stop and get them before we leave. They look beautiful.' He took a sip of his coffee. 'Will your tree be red and silver this year?'

She shrugged. 'I bought some new silver decorations yesterday. I hadn't got much further than that.'

'Didn't you see the sparkly red ribbon near the door? It was on one of the trees.' Drew gave a little sigh. 'It was lovely.' Then he said quickly, 'But it's for a girl. It would be nice on your tree.'

'What colour scheme do you guys have?'

Callum choked on his coffee. 'You're joking, right? There's no colour scheme in our house. It's like a hotch-potch with every colour of the rainbow.' He smiled at Drew. 'Our colour scheme is whatever Drew's made at nursery or school that year. Right, son?'

Drew nodded and laughed. 'I've made lots of decorations. Daddy puts them all up on the tree.' He leaned forward and whispered in Jessica's ear, 'He says it doesn't matter if they're wonky.'

She felt a little tug at her heartstrings. She could just imagine their jumbled tree with haphazard decorations all made by a little boy. She wished hers could look like that.

Her silver and red decorations would seem drab in comparison. Suddenly the step she'd decided to take didn't seem nearly far enough. Not by a long shot.

She picked up a crayon and started to help Drew with his drawing. Callum's eyes were on her. He must have questions. But when could she tell him?

When could she tell him that there was a reason she wanted to take things slowly? It seemed almost deceitful when he'd invited her on a trip with his son.

He was still watching and smiling cautiously as he split the scones and put butter and strawberry jam on them. It was official. He was trying to feed her up. And he was doing a good job—it was the most she'd eaten in months.

But she didn't have the normal feelings she had around

food. Mostly she was uninterested or dissociated herself from it. These last few weeks she'd started to notice the beautiful aromas of food again—instead of just the smell of coffee. In the garden centre today food smells were abundant. From the freshly baked scones and other cakes to the smells of bubbling soup, bacon and toasted cheese. Today was probably the first time in a long time she'd felt truly hungry.

'Is it time to go and see Santa yet?' Drew could barely contain his excitement and it was so nice to see.

Jessica stood up and held out her hand towards him. 'Why don't we go and see the reindeer? Maybe your dad will be able to take a picture of them for you. How cool would it be to show your friends at school that you met one of Santa's reindeer?'

Drew jumped up like a shot. 'Oh, yes, Daddy! Could I take it in for show and tell?'

Callum was smiling again and stood up. He looked at his watch. 'We've still got half an hour to kill. I think we can take some pictures of the reindeer.'

Drew sped down the path ahead of them, giving Callum a few seconds to reach and grab Jessica's hand. It didn't feel strange. It didn't feel unnatural.

Just as holding Drew's hand earlier hadn't felt unnatural. In fact, it had felt entirely normal.

An older couple was walking down the path towards them and stood aside to let Drew barrel past them. The older man laughed. 'What a lovely family,' he remarked.

Jessica felt herself catch her breath. Her feet were still moving, still walking down the path, but she felt every muscle in her body stiffen.

That's what they must look like.

A family.

An ordinary family.

She felt Callum squeeze her hand. He could sense it. He could sense her unease again. It must be killing him that he didn't know what was going on.

She so wanted to tell him. She so wanted to tell him right now before she burst into tears in the middle of Santa's Grotto.

Guilt was crawling all over her skin. Was this a betrayal? A betrayal of the memory of Daniel and Lewis— the people she'd thought she would spend the rest of her life with?

She could feel that horrible tight feeling spreading across her chest. Her breath was catching in her lungs.

Callum's feet stopped moving and his hand slid out from hers, turning her round to face him and sliding his arms around her waist. She couldn't lift her head to look at him. It was too hard right now as she was struggling to breathe.

This was wrong. Wasn't this usually the stage that single men ran away? When they heard someone mention something about a family?

Instead, Callum was taking it all in his stride. He pulled her a little closer and whispered in her ear, 'Just breathe, Jess. I don't know what's wrong, but this is a good day.' His voice was steady and calm. 'Wherever you are, know that I'm right here. Breathe.'

His hand rubbed gently up and down her back. A few people wandered past. Drew had raced on ahead and was out of sight. To the rest of the world it must just look as if they were taking a few seconds for a sneaky cuddle. Only Jessica knew the demons she was currently fighting in her head.

Gradually, the feeling across her chest started to ease. Her muscles started to relax. Callum released his grasp and pulled back, stroking her hair from across her face. 'Okay?'

She nodded. She didn't know what to say right now. How on earth could she explain what had just happened? What had caused that reaction in her?

He took her hand again. 'Ready to see some reindeer?'

It was as if he knew better than to ask right now. But even though his gaze was kind she could see the questions in his eyes. There was no judgement, only wonder.

She squeezed his hand. 'I would love to see the reindeer.'

They walked down the path to the outside stall where the reindeer were. Drew was already standing agog. Of course none had a red nose, but the names of Santa's reindeer had been stencilled across the top of the stalls.

It was a wide paddock, with two members of staff—albeit dressed in elf costumes—on duty at all times. Jessica didn't know what she'd been expecting, but the reindeer seemed happy. They walked to the fence, and under the guidance of the staff allowed the children to stroke their coats and touch their antlers. They seemed healthy and in good condition.

Jessica had heard horror stories in the past about animals kept in children's play parks but it certainly wasn't the case here. In fact, the staff seemed enthusiastic, answering all the children's questions about the reindeer upkeep, with a few North Pole stories flung in for good measure.

'Can I get my picture with Comet, Dad?'

Callum nodded and knelt down as Drew posed next to the reindeer. Jessica waited until he'd finished then gave him a nudge. 'Go and stand next to Drew so I can take a picture of the two of you.' He obeyed and she snapped away happily. These would be great photos for Drew's show and tell at school.

'I want a picture with Dr Jess too!' shouted Drew.

Jess flushed. 'It's just Jess, Drew. You don't need to call me Dr Jess any more.'

Callum raised his eyebrows at her, obviously wondering if she would object to having her picture taken, but she swapped places with him and put her arm around Drew, letting Comet take pride of place in the background of the picture.

It was so easy to be around them. Drew had so much energy. No one would guess how sick he'd been a week ago. And Callum was every bit the doting dad that she'd expected him to be. It was so nice to see. And so easy to be a part of.

'Is it time yet, Dad?' Drew was bouncing up and down on the spot.

Callum looked at his watch. 'It's nearly eleven-thirty. Want to go down to the grotto?'

'Yippee!'

It was only a few minutes' walk. The path was lined with frost-covered decorations and houses. Christmas trees with green lights and gold stars lined the path, with red berry lights around the door of the grotto. Drew couldn't resist peering through the windows.

The garden staff had certainly gone all out to create a kids' paradise. They had staff dressed as elves, working away in a pretend workshop, piled high with sacks of toys. A little train ran around the outside of the whole complex with another elf driving it and children and parents in the carriages. 'Do we get to go on that too, Dad?'

Callum shrugged, 'I expect so.'

Jessica stood on tiptoe and whispered in his ear, 'I think

that's part of the way out. Probably to make sure you don't stay in here too long.'

The queue moved along quickly and Callum showed Drew's ticket. An elf hurried over. 'Drew Kennedy? Come over here until we check and see if your name's in the naughty or nice book.' She held out her hand towards Drew.

His eyes widened like saucers and he turned to Callum, who smiled. 'Go on,' he urged.

'They asked me his name when I bought the tickets,' he said. 'They also asked me to choose which one he'd like best from a list of toys.'

'Wow. They've really thought of everything here, haven't they?' She looked around. 'You know, I'd love to bring some of the kids from the hospital here. You know, the ones that spend half their life stuck in a ward? Things are so well organised here, it could be perfect.'

'Why don't you ask before we leave if there's any way you can arrange it?'

She gave a little nod then nudged Callum. 'Look!'

Drew gave a little gasp as the elf pretended to find his name on the Nice list. 'Fabulous!' she shouted. 'That means we can go in and see Santa.'

'Come on, Dad. Come on, Jess,' shouted Drew as he tugged at the elf's hand.

Santa's Grotto was beautiful, filled with lots of fake snow and an icy blast of cold air. Santa was bundled up in the most padded costume and thickest beard Jessica had ever seen. And he had the patience of a saint. He took each child in turn, never hurried, never concerned about what was going on around him, and sat him or her on his knee, asking lots of questions.

Drew was totally enthralled. 'Tell me everything you

want for Christmas,' Santa said with a wink towards Callum and Jessica.

Drew immediately reeled off a list of typical things a five-year-old boy wanted—a dinosaur, a racing car, a dress-up soldier's outfit. Then he stopped and pulled Santa down towards him, glancing towards his dad and whispering in Santa's ear.

Jess had a brief feeling of panic. Drew's eyes were on her the whole time he spoke to Santa. What was he asking for?

Santa smiled over at them both then spoke so quietly to Drew that neither of them could hear what he was saying. A few seconds later he handed Drew his present.

'Can I open it now, Santa?' he asked.

Santa nodded towards them. 'You'll need to ask.'

Drew jumped down. 'Can I, Dad? Can I?'

Callum swung Drew up into his arms. 'Say thank you to Santa and we'll go on the train. If you're good, you can open your present when we get to the car.'

'Yippee!' He squirmed around in Callum's arms. 'Thank you, Santa!'

They headed over to the train and Jessica laughed as Callum tried to squeeze his large frame into the carriage beside them. 'Budge up,' he said. 'It's a tight squeeze in here. This train is obviously designed for elves.'

The train ride was perfect. It started inside in the snow-covered landscape with snowmen and trees and wound its way outside to the garden centre, which was covered in a dusting of real snow and glistening in places with ice. The garden-centre staff had decorated huts to make them look as if they were still part of Santa's village.

After a few minutes the train came to a halt outside one of the buildings at the edge of the garden centre. It was a decorated barn. Jess and Callum looked at each other. They could hear the joyful squeals of children from inside. 'What on earth is in there?'

They waited as everyone alighted from the train, the elf standing at the front.

'Is there something else in there?'

The elf puffed out his already red cheeks. 'It's the winter wonderland—a children's playground.' He nodded his head at Drew. 'Your day's not over yet, pal.'

They walked inside and were hit with the wave of heat as soon as they crossed the threshold. The noise level was incredible. Every child who had visited Santa that morning had obviously ended up in here.

Around the edges of the playground were a variety of bedraggled parents sitting at tables, trying to make themselves heard above the noise.

Drew edged a little closer to his father. Jess knelt down next to him. The noise must be intimidating to a small child.

'Is there anything you'd like to go on?' she asked. Her eyes swept around the room and she put her hands on his shoulders. 'It's probably not a good idea to go on the trampoline or bouncy castle yet when you've had stitches in your tummy. But you could go over to the craft tables or into the games room if you wanted.'

Drew's hand slid into hers. 'Come into the games room with me.'

She nodded and gave Callum a smile as they made their way to the other side of the barn. He leaned over. 'This isn't like him. Normally he'd have made a beeline straight for the bouncy castle and dived straight on.'

Jess looked down at the little figure next to her. 'He's still in recovery mode. Being in hospital is a big thing for a kid. And having an anaesthetic takes a lot more out of them than you'd expect.' She rolled her eyes. 'Anyway, a bouncy castle or trampoline is the last thing he needs to be on right now.'

Callum gritted his teeth. 'Yeah, about that...'

'What?'

'I sort of bought Drew a trampoline for Christmas. He asked for it months ago and I bought it just the week before he was ill. It's sitting in the garage, waiting to be assembled. Am I going to have to say that Santa lost it?'

'What? No.' She shook her head. 'It's another few weeks yet. By then Drew should be fine. His stitches will be healed and he should be back to normal. But please tell me you've bought one of those big safety nets.' She waggled her finger at him. 'If you dare bring him into Casualty with a head injury because he's bounced off...'

He held up his hands. 'Whoa! No chance. With you on duty and knowing the abuse I would get, I can assure you the safety net is ready.' He slipped his arm back around her shoulders as they headed into the games room.

He bent his head lower. 'Anyway, I remember the days when you weren't quite so safety-conscious.'

'What do you mean?'

He started to laugh and pretended to fumble in his pocket. 'Wait until I get the list out. First, there was the day you decided we should all jump into the harbour. Then there was the time you thought it was good idea to try out that thirty-year-old sled...'

'That was a family heirloom!'

He raised his eyebrows. '*Was* being the operative word.'

She stifled a laugh. Callum brought back so many good memories. Things that she'd forgotten about for so long.

Things that she'd locked away inside the part of her mind that had stopped her from feeling joy any more.

It was so good to finally set it free again. It was so good to have someone to share this stuff with.

It was a bit quieter in the games room, with tables set with board games and a few electronic game machines. Drew didn't hesitate. He dropped Jessica's hand and raced off to watch the football game being played at the end of the room. Then he hesitated, turned round, took off his coat and hat and dumped them in her lap.

Callum pointed to one of the benches at the side. 'What do you say to another coffee? We could be in here for a while.'

'Sure. Thanks.'

The heat was building already. Jessica unfastened her coat and pulled off her hat and gloves. Callum disappeared to the coffee stand for a few moments and she leaned back against the wall.

Wow. So this was the stage Lewis would have been at. Her eyes drifted around the quieter games room and then to the noisy throng outside.

Which room would he have wanted to be in? Would he have been in the thick of things, wreaking havoc outside? Or would he have been in here, like Drew, plotting his fantasy football side?

She let out a little laugh. How on earth did five-year-old boys know how to do that?

It was so nice to sit in here and watch all the kids at their various ages and stages. And even though she was thinking about Lewis, she was thinking about Drew too.

She watched as there was a minor clash of heads outside on the bouncy castle, and for the first time she didn't go into doctor mode and run forward to intervene. It was minor—their parents could deal with it—and she didn't want to leave Drew unsupervised. Callum had trusted her to watch over his son, even if it was only for a few minutes, and strangely she was enjoying it.

She hadn't been asked to come with them as a doctor. She'd been asked as a…what? A friend? A girlfriend? A potential lover?

All the things she would have immediately shied away from a few months ago. But with Callum it all felt so easy. One look from those green eyes and she tingled right down to her toes. One brush of his hand and her whole body craved more.

It was taking her time to get used to these feelings again.

To *admit* to feeling them.

To let herself feel them without being overwhelmed by sensations of guilt and betrayal. Slowly but surely she was starting to let those feelings go.

She thought about the photo currently in her living room. A beautiful photo of Daniel and Lewis, caught wrestling on the floor together, laughing together with unbridled pleasure. It was the image that stayed in her head.

Right there, caught in that moment of happiness forever.

They would always be part of her life—a wonderful part of her life—but the shades of grey around that picture were moving.

She was starting to move.

Starting to see a life past that.

'Jessica.' Her head shot up. Drew was waving her over. 'Come and see my score. I'm the top striker!' He was jumping up and down on the spot, clearly delighted. She ran over and gave him a hug. 'Well done, Drew, that's fantastic!'

He hugged her back with the exuberance that only a five-year-old could show. It felt good. It felt natural. It felt right.

Baby steps, her brain whispered. Just keep taking baby steps.

Callum walked around the edge of the winter wonderland with the two coffees, trying not to let his 'health and safety at work' hat annoy him. The coffee area should be cordoned off to minimise the risk of scalds to all the hyperactive children who were racing around the place.

He froze at the edge of the games room. Jessica and Drew were hugging in front of the giant TV, Drew obviously excited about something.

But that wasn't what made him freeze.

It was the expressions on both their faces.

Drew's was one of pure innocence and pleasure. The joy of sharing his delight with a mother figure. The way he'd wrapped his hands around her neck and was talking nineteen to the dozen in her ear.

And the way Jessica was looking at Drew.

Like he was the best thing she'd ever seen.

It had the strangest effect on Callum. He should be happy. He should be glad that his little boy felt so comfortable around the woman he hoped would be his girlfriend.

He should be delighted that they obviously had a mutual admiration society going. So many of his other friends had told him tales of woe about new potential partners and children not getting on—this obviously wasn't the case here.

But there was the weirdest feeling in the pit of Callum's stomach.

He knew there was something else. He knew there were parts of herself that Jessica still had to reveal to him. And it didn't matter what his memories of Jessica were. It didn't matter what effects one look of those brown eyes had on his body. It didn't matter how much he kept trying to push any little nagging doubts aside.

The fact was he wanted more. More than she was currently giving.

He wanted everything. The whole package.

Whatever that might contain.

But until he knew exactly what that was, he had a little boy to put first. He couldn't risk Drew's feelings or emotions. He could see the trust in his son's eyes. He could see the way he was already forming pictures in his mind— pictures that included Jessica.

Those pictures were starting to form in Callum's mind too, but he had to be sure. He had to be certain about Jessica before things went any further. It didn't matter how much he wanted to kiss her. It didn't matter how much he wanted to hold her in his arms. After a few short weeks he knew exactly where he wanted this relationship to go.

Drew was reaching up, touching one of Jessica's curls and tucking it behind her ear as he talked to her. Jessica caught his hand in hers and planted a kiss on his palm.

That was what he wanted for his son. So much it made his stomach ache.

Jessica looked over and caught sight of him. She frowned, obviously seeing the expression on his face, and gave him a little wave. She ruffled Drew's hair and pointed back at the big screen before moving over towards Callum and taking the coffee from his hand. 'Thanks for that. What's up?'

'Nothing. Nothing's up.'

She tilted her head to one side. 'Are you sure? You looked unhappy.'

She was staring at him with those big brown eyes. *She was worrying about him.* The irony wasn't lost on him.

And she looked happier. She looked more relaxed than he'd seen her in a while. If he could forget the episode earlier, today would have been a perfect day.

There was a little sparkle about her, a little glow. Glimmers of the old Jess shining through.

She glanced over her shoulder to where Drew was engrossed again in his game. There was something different in her eyes, something playful.

She gave him a cheeky smile then grabbed his arm and pulled him round the corner, out of the line of sight of everyone. 'I wonder if I can make you feel better,' she whispered, then she leaned forward and wrapped her arms around his neck, rising up on tiptoe and kissing him gently on the mouth.

And at that precise moment all rational thought left the building.

CHAPTER ELEVEN

HER PAGER SOUNDED again. It was the fourth time in the last hour, but she'd been stuck in Theatre, performing surgery on a very sick baby with a necrotic bowel.

She pulled her theatre mask and cap off as the tiny baby was wheeled out of Theatre and off to ITU. She'd probably spend most of the night there, but she had to answer this page first.

She couldn't believe how tired she was. It was weird. For the last three years work had been her sanctuary. A place of focus. A place where she didn't have time to think about anything else.

And things here were good. Marcus and Lily, the two children with hypothermia, had both made a steady recovery and been allowed home. All the children from the accident had now been discharged and would be looking forward to Christmas with their families.

Christmas with a family. Something she hadn't even thought about for the last few years.

But the last few weeks had been different. Spending time with Callum and Drew had brought a whole new perspective to her life.

Life didn't just revolve around the hospital any more.

She didn't just wake up in the morning and stay there for as long as possible, only going home when the nurses eventually flung her out, then falling asleep straight away for the next day.

Work wasn't the first thing she thought about when she woke up in the morning. That was usually Callum and his green eyes—or Drew and whatever event he was looking forward to at school that day.

It was amazing how differently she felt about things.

In fact, tonight she'd been almost sorry that she was on call. She'd have preferred to spend more time with Callum and Drew.

For the first time in three years she was actually looking forward to Christmas. To spending it with people she loved. To have a Christmas when the focus wasn't just on being alone but sharing the time with others.

There was still the odd moment where she felt guilty. Usually in the depths of night when the feelings crept up on her unawares. When little voices in her head asked if she really deserved a second chance at happiness.

After all, she'd had her happy-ever-after. She'd been married to the love of her life and had had a beautiful son. Why should she get that chance again?

Was it fair?

Slowly but surely Callum and Drew were edging their way into her heart. Even just thinking about them brought a smile to her face.

It made her try to push the other voices away. Push them away into some dark place where she wouldn't hear them any more.

Her pager sounded again and she picked up the phone. The sister in A and E answered straight away.

'Bad news, Jessica. It's Grace Flynn. She's been admitted again. Her bloods have come back whilst we've been paging you—they're awful.'

Jessica's heart plummeted. Grace was a long-term patient. A seven-year-old with a rare form of invasive bowel tumours. She'd operated on another tumour only a few weeks ago and things hadn't looked good.

Children with cancer always had a wide team of staff looking after them at Parkhill. Grace had a paediatric consultant, a specialist oncologist, herself with her surgical skills and a whole host of specialist nurses. Even though doctors weren't supposed to have favourite patients, she'd been treating Grace for so long that she couldn't help but let the little girl have a special place in her heart.

'Have you sent her up to the ward or is she still in A and E?'

'The registrar's seen her and sent her up to the ward while we were waiting for her blood results and ultrasound. She knew her and thought she'd be more comfortable up there.'

Of course. Javier, the Spanish registrar, was familiar with the case. He'd dealt with Grace on a number of occasions over the last year. 'Ultrasound? Is there a chance her bowel is blocked again?'

She heard the sigh at the end of the phone. 'Put it this way, after a conversation with one of the other consultants he gave her a bolus of morphine and set up a continuous opioid infusion.'

Jessica sucked in her breath. News she didn't want to hear. Not for a child.

'I'll go straight up now,' she said. 'I can review the test results when I get there.'

Jessica replaced the phone and hurried up to the ward.

It didn't matter that she knew this was inevitable for Grace. It didn't matter that the doctors, family and nurses had already had discussions about future plans for Grace's care.

Her frail little body couldn't go through another round of surgery—or chemotherapy or radiotherapy. Her body had already taken all it could.

The best they could do for now was to keep her comfortable.

She pulled up the test results and her heart plunged when she saw them. Nothing was good. The blood results and ultrasound could only mean one thing. She read the notes that her registrar had written, the record of pain relief and a few further comments by one of the other consultants involved in her care and called in tonight.

There was nothing to disagree with. She would have done exactly the same things that they had done.

Grace's mum, dad and brother were sitting at her bedside, along with one of the other paediatric consultants involved in her care.

Jessica stood in the doorway for a second, trying to collect herself. She was trying to keep her professional face in place and doing her best not to cry.

Grace's mum looked up and rushed over, enveloping her in a huge, crushing hug. 'Oh, thank you for coming up to see her. I knew you'd come.'

This was breaking Jessica's heart. She had still had a tiny little glimmer of hope in her eyes—as if at any moment one of the doctors would suggest something different—something completely out of the blue that no one had thought of. But it just wasn't possible.

If there was any surgery in the world Jess could do right now to save this little girl she wouldn't hesitate. But it just wasn't to be.

Her eyes met Grace's dad's. They were strong, resolute. Resigned to their fate but determined to give his little girl as much as dignity as possible. He gave her the tiniest nod, but didn't move from his place, holding his little girl's hand.

Jess moved into the room and sat down in a chair in the corner. The lights in the room were dimmed and Grace's little chest was barely moving up and down.

Her heart was breaking. She was finding it difficult to think straight. The tension in the room was palpable. They all knew what was about to happen.

Parkhill was a children's hospital and the sad fact of life was that children did die. But it wasn't a common occurrence. None of the staff here were used to it. None of them wanted to be.

Every child's death impacted on every member of staff that worked here.

She felt a hand on her shoulder. Pauline. 'Sorry, Jess, but I need you in ITU for the baby.'

She nodded and stood up. She still had a job to do, no matter how difficult things were right now.

She walked over to the bed and stroked Grace's hair. There was a horrible pressing feeling in her stomach. She honestly couldn't do anything more for Grace, and there was a baby in ITU who needed her now.

But she couldn't just walk out of here and say nothing. This might be the last time she saw this little girl alive.

Then it came to her, the poem that she and Grace had made up one day Grace had decided she wanted to be a horse rider. It had been a wonderful daydreaming session, when Grace had decided the name and colour of her horse, where it would be stabled and how famous it would become.

Jessica bent down and whispered in her ear, 'Riding

across the fields, the wind is in your hair, holding onto Cupid's reins, as if you don't have a care. Racing through the grass, and tearing round the bend, all on a magical mission, to reach the rainbow's end.'

She felt tears forming in her eyes. In Grace's daydream that day she'd reached the end of the rainbow and found the mythical pot of gold. If only something like that came true.

She took one final look. One glimpse of the family that was about to be changed forever.

The walls were closing in around her. Suffocating her. She gave the family one final smile and left, her feet carrying her swiftly down the corridor before she unravelled any further.

Her phone beeped. Again.

She pulled it out of her pocket. *Drew and I are picking you up at nine a.m. to make sure you actually leave.*

She smiled. She was exhausted, both physically and mentally. The baby she'd performed surgery on had needed constant review throughout the night. It had been touch and go for a while. But finally, around six a.m., the little mite had seemed to turn a corner.

She rubbed her eyes. What time was it now? She looked around for the nearest window. Was it even daylight yet? Dark winter mornings were notorious in these parts. It was frequently still dark in the morning when kids were walking to school.

There was a smudge in the background of the window. The first few edges of a rising sun. She dug in the pocket of her scrub trousers to find her watch. Just before eight a.m. A feeling of dread crept over her. She knew where she had to go next.

Almost as if someone was reading her mind, the phone

next to her started to ring. One ring tone instead of two. An internal call.

Pauline picked up the phone swiftly. 'ITU Sister Jones. Yes, yes. I see. I'm really sorry.' Her eyes skittered towards Jessica, who felt her stomach tighten. 'I'll let her know. Have they? Okay, thanks for that.' She replaced the receiver and turned to face Jess, her face grave.

Jessica felt sobs rise up in her chest. Pauline's arm quickly came round her shoulders. 'Jess, it's been a big night. You were in surgery for hours, then with Grace's admission and the time you've had to spend in here…' Her voice tailed off.

'I should go back down. Back down and see the family.'

Pauline shook her head. 'They've gone home. Grace's brother was exhausted and Grace's parents decided they had to go home. They'll come back later today to make arrangements. John Carson, the other consultant, is meeting them then.'

It made sense. They would be exhausted. It would have been the worst night of their life. And John Carson had been sitting with them last night. He knew them inside out and had been involved in Grace's care from diagnosis.

Pauline placed both her hands on Jess's shoulder. 'Go home, Jess. That's what you need to do.' She glanced at the phone that was sitting on the desk. 'Go home with Drew and Callum. It's the best thing you could do right now. It's what you need right now.'

She nodded. She didn't even need to say the words.

This had probably been the second-hardest night of her life.

She'd felt herself unravel at some points. Felt as close to breaking point as she'd ever been. The only glimmer on the horizon had been the one in her heart.

Three years was a long time to nurse a broken heart. To go home to an empty house. To feel as if there wasn't much reason to get up in the morning. To wonder if anyone would miss you if you were gone.

Thank goodness she'd met Callum again. With his come-to-bed eyes and his sexy smile. The one that could stay in her thoughts for hours.

That tiny little black cloud that had still been hanging over her head needed to be banished forever. It was time to stop avoiding the subject and let him know why she found some things so hard.

She knew in her heart that he would understand. That he would support her. And that was all she could ever want. Spending time with Callum and Drew had become the most precious thing in the world to her. Something she didn't want to live without.

She gave Pauline a hug. 'Tell John I'll be available if he needs me.' She walked down the corridor and into the changing rooms. She didn't want to wait a minute longer.

If there was one thing she'd learned it was that life was too short. Life was for living.

There were only two faces in the world she wanted to see right now. And they both had a place in her heart.

Callum glanced at the clock. Two minutes to nine. Just as well this wasn't a school day. His fingers were tapping nervously on the steering wheel.

He couldn't work out why he was on edge. He just knew he was.

It was time. It was make or break.

He wanted this relationship to work. He wanted it to move on. But for that to happen there needed to be honesty between them.

He needed to know.

He needed to know what had happened in Jessica's life.

Drew had spent most of the night talking about Jessica. The glow in his eyes had told Callum everything he needed to know. His little boy had fallen just as hard as he had.

He watched the door of the hospital, willing Jess to appear, and finally she did.

She looked shattered. She obviously hadn't slept a wink last night.

Her coat was barely pulled around her shoulders and he could see her eyes searching the car park.

He gave the horn a beep and waved to her. Her face lit up and she hurried over. He expected her to jump straight in but she didn't. Instead, she opened the rear door, gave Drew a quick hug and dropped a kiss on top of his head.

'We've been waiting for you,' Drew said solemnly.

'And you've no idea how happy I am to see you,' she answered. Callum turned, watching as she enveloped Drew in another quick hug. She looked truly happy to see him—to see them both. He didn't know whether to leap for joy or let that little cautionary voice in his mind rear its ugly head.

She closed the rear door and opened the front passenger door, climbing in and sinking into the seat next to him.

'Hard night?' He could see the furrows in her brow, etching deep lines into her normally smooth forehead.

She gave a little sigh and a shake of her head, glancing across her shoulder at Drew. 'More than you can ever know.'

The words hung in the air between them. He could tell there was so much she wanted to say—but couldn't because Drew was in the car.

His little hand stretched over and touched Jessica's shoulder. 'Jess, are we going home now? Are you going to watch my movie with me? I've got my duvet on the couch for us. We can snuggle up.'

A wide smile spread across her face. Relief. Relief at the thought of getting away from the struggles of the hospital and spending the day with them. Stress free.

He felt his stomach clench a little more. Was he wrong to do this today? To ask her about her past and to put her on the spot about their future?

Part of him wanted to leave it, to stay in this happy limbo they were in. It felt like a safe place. But deep down he didn't want a safe place. He wanted much more. He wanted to be able to shout from the rooftops that he and Jessica were together. He wanted to make plans for a future for the three of them together, as a family.

He wanted to wake up every morning with Jessica by his side.

He wanted to be there to support her through whatever had happened.

He wanted to be a family.

And the only way to do that was to get rid of the elephant in the room.

He pulled out into the Glasgow traffic and started along the street. It was after nine so the morning rush was dying down. 'Want to go somewhere for breakfast before we get home?'

She shook her head. 'A duvet day with a film sounds perfect. I don't want to delay that for a second.' Her stomach gave a growl. 'But I'm starving. Do you have any bacon at home?'

'Daddy! Give her the chocolate we bought her!' Drew's voice echoed through the car. 'We bought you your favourite, Jess.'

Callum smiled and reached across her, opening the

glove box and pulling out the orange-flavoured chocolate. It had been her favourite years ago, and he expected it still was. He put the chocolate in her lap. 'That will keep you going until we get home. We stopped to pick it up on the way here.'

Silence. Absolute silence in the car.

He knew instantly that something was wrong.

Thank goodness Jess was sitting down because the colour drained instantly from her face and she looked as if she might pass out.

She swayed—even though she was sitting in the seat.

They were heading through the busiest part of town. There was nowhere to pull over and the traffic was a little heavier here so he needed to keep his eyes on the road.

'Jess? Jess? What's wrong?'

Was she sick? Maybe it was nothing. Maybe she was feeling faint because she'd been on her feet all night and hadn't had anything to eat. That would be just like Jess. Too busy to sit down for a few minutes and think of herself.

But he had the strangest feeling he wasn't even close.

'Stop the car.' Her voice was quiet, almost a whisper.

'What?'

'Stop the car!' This time she was definite.

He could see the flare of panic in her eyes. She absolutely meant it.

His head flicked from side to side, trying to see if there was anywhere to stop in the midst of the queued traffic. 'I can't, Jess. There's nowhere to go. You'll need to wait. What's wrong? Do you feel sick?'

'I'll get out here.' She flung open the door and jumped out of the car. Her bag was still sitting in the footwell of the car.

Callum was stunned. What on earth had just happened?

'Daddy? Where's Jess gone?'

'I don't know, Drew.' He looked frantically up and down the street in the direction she was walking, trying to find somewhere to pull over.

What on earth had gone wrong?

This was supposed to be a good day. How on earth could a chocolate bar cause a reaction like that?

All the nudging doubts he'd had about putting Jess on the spot vanished. Drew looked near to tears, sitting in the back of the car hugging his toy to his chest.

Something had upset Jess but she, in turn, had upset his son.

He couldn't have that. He couldn't have that at all.

This was crazy. And he couldn't let it go on a moment longer.

He'd been wrong. He'd been wrong not to sit her down and ask her right away what was going on in her life.

He'd been blindsided by her. She brought back a whole host of good memories and feelings. He loved being around her. She was beautiful—inside and out. He could see that. Even in the times she tried to hide it away.

He wanted things to work out between them.

His heart twisted as he watched the forlorn figure scurrying down the street and a whole new sensation swept over him.

He loved her. He loved Jess.

Just like he had years before.

Only this was different. This was a grown-up kind of love.

One that realised that nobody was perfect and everyone had history. And in his heart he knew she felt the same way—about him and about Drew.

So what on earth had gone wrong? He had no idea what had just happened.

But the one thing he knew for sure was that he needed to find out.

She was going to be sick. She was going to be sick everywhere.

She couldn't think or see straight.

Her hand reached out and grasped the wall, trying to steady herself.

A woman stared at her on the way past. She looked horrified. Did she think Jess was drunk at nine in the morning? Because that's the way she felt right now.

Her hand was gripping something tightly, her knuckles blanched white, her fingers growing numb.

Her hand was shaking. No, her whole body was shaking.

She leaned over and retched, trying to ignore the people walking past and looking at her in horror.

Unravelling.

She'd felt like that earlier on—in the middle of the night when she'd known Grace was about to die. She'd felt as if she hadn't had the strength to be there, hadn't had the strength to do the job she was supposed to be doing.

And now this.

Her whole world had just tilted on its axis.

In an instant. In a flash.

She stared at her hand, willing her fingers to open.

All this over a bar of orange-flavoured chocolate.

She heard the thud of feet running along the pavement. Felt a hand on her back. 'Jess. What is it? What's wrong?'

She could hear it all. The confusion in his voice. The concern.

She should have told him. She should have told him before.

Then he would have looked at her in pity and walked away. Then she wouldn't have dropped the walls around her heart and let him and his son in. Then she would have stayed safe. Locked in her own fortress where nothing could penetrate her heart and leave her exposed to hurt again.

She should have told him before.

But that would have made it all real.

Not the fact that it had happened. Not the fact that her husband and son had died. But the fact that she was telling him—telling him, as she prepared to move on with her life.

Because up until this point she hadn't really told anyone—she hadn't needed to. All her work colleagues already knew and bad news travelled fast, following you like a billowing black cloud. She was used to people whispering behind her then averting their eyes when caught.

Maybe this was what she deserved. Why should she get a chance at a happy ever after with a new family? Maybe she didn't deserve it.

All the doubts and feelings of guilt were rearing their ugly heads. How could she forget about her husband and son? How dared she?

Callum looked utterly confused. He bent down and picked up the bar of chocolate. 'You're retching over this?'

The look on his face said it all. He was at breaking point. She'd known for the last few weeks that Callum was holding back—stopping himself from saying what he wanted to.

She looked at the bar of chocolate in his hand. It must seem so pathetic, but it didn't feel that way to her.

'You don't understand—'

'You're right. I don't.' His voice was soft and he stepped closer to her, touching the side of her cheek. 'So tell me, Jess.' He glanced over at his car parked at the side of the road, where he'd left Drew on his own.

She couldn't bear to look. Couldn't bear to look at the little boy who'd won a place in her heart. Not while she felt so guilty. Frustration was building in her chest. She wanted to say so much but just couldn't find the words. They all seemed to get jammed in her throat. 'I lost them. I lost them this way.' She pointed to the bar of chocolate in his hand.

'Lost who? What way?' He looked totally confused. 'Jess, I want to understand. Really, I do. But I can't until you tell me. It's time, Jess. It's time there were no secrets between us.'

Her legs wobbled underneath her. They couldn't take her weight any more and she felt herself crumple. 'My husband. My son.' Sobs racked her body. The words were out. They were finally out there. For everyone in the world to hear. For Callum to hear.

'What?'

She couldn't stop. Now the tears had started they wouldn't stop.

She felt his strong arms on her shoulders. 'What do you mean, you lost your husband and son?'

He was crouching now, on the ground beside her. She looked up into his green eyes. He was totally thrown by all this. Probably knocked sideways.

Her voice was trembling. 'My husband Daniel and son Lewis were killed in a road accident.'

His shock was palpable. 'What? When?'

'Three years ago.' Her shoulders were shaking now.

He shook his head, his disbelief apparent. 'Why didn't

you tell me, Jess? Why didn't you tell me something like that?'

She was panicking now. People in the street were staring at them. 'I couldn't find the words. I didn't know how to tell you. I didn't know what to say.' Her breathing felt erratic, every breath a struggle. Her voice dropped, her eyes looking towards the horizon. 'It never felt the right time.'

Callum shook his head. 'How could you not tell me something as important as this?'

'How could you not tell me about your son?' The words shot out instantly. In blind panic.

He reeled back, looking as if he'd been stung.

She saw him take a deep breath and get to his feet, reaching over, putting his hands under her arms and pulling her up with him. He looked about him. 'This isn't something to discuss in the street, Jessica.'

People were staring. People had stopped what they were doing.

She looked over at the car. Drew's little face was pressed up against the window. He looked frantic and her heart went out to him. He had no idea what was happening. Just that something was wrong.

If she felt upset and confused, how must he feel?

The chocolate bar was on the ground at her feet. Tears welled in her eyes instantly. 'I can't do this,' she whispered.

'Can't do what?'

She put her hands out. 'This. Us.' She looked over at the car. 'Drew.'

She could see sadness mounting in Callum's eyes. He didn't understand. He didn't understand this wasn't about him and Drew. This was all about her.

She shook her head. 'You don't get it. You don't understand. Daniel and Lewis—they stopped to buy me my favourite bar of chocolate the night they died. They stopped at a shop just round the corner from our house.'

Her voice was breaking, trembling as she remembered, the memories rushing up so clearly and strongly, as if it had just happened a few hours ago. 'He sent me a text.' She let out a huge gasp of air. 'Daniel sent me a text saying they'd be five minutes late because they'd stopped to buy me chocolate.' She shook her head.

'The next thing I knew the sister from A and E came to find me. I was standing outside the hospital, waiting for them, wondering what was taking so long. She'd been phoned by Ambulance Control—the crew had radioed in once they knew who they were dealing with.'

Callum hadn't moved. He was still standing over her, his face unreadable. She must seem like a crazy woman, but everything seemed so clear in her head.

'What did she tell you?' His voice sounded a little wobbly too.

She looked up at him. She'd never seen his green eyes so full of conflict. She couldn't imagine how he must feel about all this. She'd never wanted to hurt him.

She'd never wanted to hurt Drew.

She took a deep breath, every part of the experience as painful now as it had been then. 'She told me Daniel had been taken to Glasgow Cross and Lewis was coming to Parkhill.' She looked off into the distance. It seemed easier to speak when she didn't have to look at him. 'That was normal after a RTA. The kids always came to us.'

'And then?'

He reached out and touched her hand, giving it a squeeze, willing her to have the strength to carry on. She could see tenderness written all over his face. She could almost reach out and touch the hurt he felt for her.

She'd been terrified to tell him. Terrified he would misunderstand.

She'd been right.

She looked at him. The tears were gone now. This was the worst part. This was the part that almost killed her.

'It was too late for them both. They were both dead on arrival. I never got to say goodbye, Callum. To my husband or my son.'

There was something so final about those words. So final, because she was saying them out loud. Her voice continued automatically—because she needed to get it all out. She'd held it in for so long. She'd wanted to tell him, but now it felt as if someone had released the dam and it had to all rush out.

'None of the staff knew what to do when Lewis arrived. It's so different when it's one of your own. Somebody else's child is just as important but you have an emotional detachment that allows you to do the job, not to think about the hopes, dreams and fears of that little person in front of you. And to a certain extent you need that. But when it's one of your own...' She met his gaze. 'The child of a friend, colleague or loved one. It's like the world stops turning. You can't function any more, autopilot just doesn't work.'

She wanted him to understand.

She needed him to understand. Because it related to why she couldn't find the words to tell him.

And he must understand it a little. He'd been the parent with the sick child.

How could she have performed surgery on Drew if she'd known him like she did now? How could she have got through that op?

He was watching her steadily. She could see the rise and fall of his chest. His words were hoarse. It was almost as if he was seeing the whole picture in his head. Feeling her pain. 'They didn't resuscitate?'

She shook her head. 'There was no point.' She couldn't hide the forlorn tone in her voice. 'I think both of them probably died at the scene. It was strange—I always thought if something like that happened I wouldn't be able to do that. That I would resuscitate for hours and hours, no matter how hopeless. But it was totally different. I didn't want my son disturbed. I didn't want people to touch him when I already knew it was pointless. I just wanted to hold him.'

She wrapped her arms around herself at the memory of it. 'Someone phoned Pauline and she came down from ITU. I held Lewis for hours. And Pauline held me.'

There was silence between them. She didn't need him to say anything—she didn't want him to say anything.

She couldn't imagine how he must be feeling.

Well, she could, but only in part.

She remembered exactly how she'd felt when she'd first heard about Drew. It had been a total bolt out of the blue. And this was much worse than that.

Callum looked deep in thought—as if a hundred different things were spinning through his mind at once.

He couldn't stop looking at his car, where Drew was. She wished she could read his mind. Know what he was thinking. He dug his hands deep into his pockets. 'So, what's changed, Jessica? You may not have told me this before but it was still there. Still circling in your head every day.'

She felt a single tear slip down her cheek. It was so hard to put this into words. She looked at the little face staring out of the car window towards her and it made her heart ache. She so wanted to hold him. She so wanted to take him in her arms and give him comfort. Because she loved him. She loved that little boy—just as much as she loved his father.

Callum's face looked more than confused—he looked numb. As if he was trying to work out where his place in all this was. She'd done this to him. It had been her.

It was all her fault.

She was hurting people that she loved. Again.

'You don't get it.'

'No, Jess. I don't get it.' He reached over and pulled her towards him. For a second they stood in the street, their heads bowed, their foreheads touching.

If she could, she would stay this way forever. With Callum holding her as if he could take all her cares and worries away.

Because this was killing her. She hated herself right now. She hated hurting those that she loved.

'It was my fault, Callum. Don't you see? It was my fault that Daniel and Lewis died. If they hadn't gone to get me that chocolate, they wouldn't have been on the road at that time. They wouldn't have had that accident.' She reached over and grabbed his hand from his pocket. 'Just like you did today. You and Drew.' She shook her head as fiercely as she could. 'I can't have that. I can't have that on my conscience. Something happening to the people I love because of me.'

He lifted his head from hers and reached up and touched her cheek. His hand was freezing. They'd been standing out in the cold for far too long. Trying to dissect their lives in the middle of the street.

She knew this was ridiculous. Everything about it was so wrong.

She'd been hurt before. She was desperate.

How could this compare to losing her husband and son? It couldn't. And yet it was hurting every bit as much.

She'd started down that road. The one that was going to lead her to a new life. She'd started to feel again.

She'd started to trust.

She'd started to love.

And there would never be anyone as perfect for her as Callum and Drew. She could never feel as much as she did now.

And it was disintegrating all around her. Slipping through her fingers like grains of sand.

Callum shifted on his feet. He looked over towards the car again and something must have clicked in his head.

'What age was Lewis, Jessica?' His voice was sharp, abrupt.

'He was two. He was just two.' She was confused. It was a natural question. But it didn't seem quite right.

His eyes darted to the car. 'So he'd have been the same age as Drew is now?' There was something in the way he said it. As if he was having a different conversation from her.

Her heart squeezed. The whole host of thoughts that she'd had at first about Drew came flooding into her mind. The comparisons with her own son, which had all faded as the weeks had progressed and she'd got to know this other little boy.

'Yes. Yes, he would.' Why was her voice shaking? Why did she feel as if she'd just sealed their fate?

'Oh, Jess.'

It was the little gasp in his voice. The way the words came out. As if his world had just crumbled in on itself.

He shook his head, very slowly. Were those tears in his eyes?

His voice was trembling. 'This was never about us, was it, Jess? This was never about me and Drew. This was about you—looking for a replacement family.'

'What? No.' She shook her head. 'Not at all.'

But Callum had switched off. It was almost as if he'd detached himself. 'You don't love me and Drew, Jess. You love the *idea* of us.' He was shaking his head again. 'I should have known.'

She couldn't believe this. She couldn't believe his brain was thinking this way. But she was so undone she couldn't think straight.

'I need you to love me, Jess. *Me*. And I need you to love Drew. For who *he* is. Not just the thought of a replacement for your own little boy. My little boy's already had a mother who walked away from him. I can't expose him to that again. I need you to love Drew with your whole heart. Love every inch of him—and every inch of me.' He was shaking his head again. 'You've broken my heart, Jess—truly you have.'

'But I do love you, Callum. I do. And I love Drew too.' Even as she said the words they sounded desperate. Like the last-ditch attempt to save something that was already slipping through her fingers.

This was over. This was finished.

It didn't matter that she'd been the one telling him she couldn't do this any more.

Part of her had still wanted him to tell her they could make it. That they could still have a chance of something.

But it wasn't to be. This was all too much for him. He hadn't signed up for this. That much was evident.

Her heart was breaking all over again.

She couldn't look at him. It was just too hard.

'We've both made a mistake here, Jess. I wanted you to

be something that you just weren't ready to be. And you wanted us to replace something that you've lost.' He bit his lip. She'd never seen him look so shattered. So resigned to their fate. 'Neither of us can do that.'

His voice was tired. 'Get in the car and I'll drop you home. It seems we both have a lot to think about.' He took a deep breath and touched her cheek one more time. 'I'm sorry about your husband and son, Jess. I really am. I'm sorry that things just haven't worked out for us.' He pointed over his shoulder. 'But right now I have to put the needs of my son first.'

He shifted slightly, blocking her view of the car. 'I want you to say something—anything—to placate Drew until we drop you off. Can you do that for me and for Drew?'

'Of course,' she whispered. 'I would never do anything to hurt Drew.'

'Too late,' he whispered as he turned towards the car and walked away.

CHAPTER TWELVE

THE DOOR OPENED and Callum jumped about a foot in the air. Drew and his little friend walked through the door, football boots in hand.

'You're back already?' He rubbed his eyes. Hadn't he just sat down?

He couldn't believe it was that time already. Julie and Blair walked into the room behind the boys and Julie folded her arms across her chest.

'Boys, go up to Drew's room for ten minutes and play. I want to talk to Drew's dad.'

Blair gave a shake of his head as he crossed the room. 'Why don't I just start running the bath and put them both in it?' He glanced at Callum on his way past. 'You're in for it, mate.'

Callum straightened up instantly. Julie and Blair were two of his closest friends. He'd never had any problems with either of them. They'd been fabulous, helping him with Drew. But even though they had a good relationship, Callum knew that Julie wasn't a woman to be messed with.

He stood up and walked towards her. 'Is something wrong?'

She waited a second, tilting her head to listen for the sound of the boys' footsteps going up the stairs and out of earshot.

'You...' She pushed her sharp finger into the middle of his chest. 'You're what's wrong. Kitchen. Now.' She turned on her heel and walked through to his kitchen.

'Ouch.' Callum rubbed the middle of his chest and started to follow her. He had a sinking feeling Blair had known exactly what he was doing when he disappeared with the boys.

Julie knew her way around the house. The coffee machine—which was only used on special occasions—was sitting on the counter and filled with water. She switched it on and turned to face him, folding her arms across her chest again.

'Right. Spill.'

Callum sat down on one of the breakfast bar stools. 'Spill what?'

She threw her hands up. 'You're the one sitting in a dark living room, staring at Christmas-tree lights. Tell me, how long were you there for? One hour? Two?'

Yeah, the Christmas-tree lights. The hotch-potch of decorations, along with the new silver and red ones that Drew and Jessica had picked out at the garden centre. Another reminder of Jessica. Along with the picture of the three of them Drew had drawn at school that was currently stuck to the fridge. Or the photo Drew had put on his bedside cabinet of him sitting on Jessica's knee at the winter wonderland.

Or the fact she was haunting his dreams. Every. Single. Night.

Julie was waiting. Waiting with her steely glare for an answer.

'I've had a hard few days at work. It's been chaos.'

'Pull the other one, Callum, it's got bells on.' She hadn't

moved. The coffee machine was starting to bubble next to her.

'I don't know what you mean.'

She shook her head and started clattering around, pulling cups from cupboards and thumping them down on his worktop. 'I'm the one who's been in the company of your little boy. Your little boy who's missing Jess. She's all he'll talk about, Callum—well, that and some promise Santa made him.'

'Drew said something?'

She nodded as she put the coffee in the machine. 'Oh, Drew said a whole lot. All about some fight and how he wanted to see Jess and you won't let him.'

Callum put his elbows on the worktop and his head in his hands. 'It's difficult, Julie. I found out something about Jessica—and it's made me rethink everything.' He shook his head. 'But Drew's hardly said a thing. He's asked a few times if she's coming round, but that's it.'

Julie pulled the chair out on the other side of the breakfast bar and sat down directly opposite him. She counted off on her fingers, 'Apparently on Monday he asked if she would be coming for dinner, on Tuesday he asked if she could go to the pictures with you both. On Wednesday he asked if she would be here after his Christmas party.' She let out a sigh. 'Whether you like it or not, Callum, this is affecting your little boy.' Her face was deadly serious. 'What did you find out?'

He hesitated. He hadn't spoken to anyone about this. It felt like a betrayal. His stomach was churning at the thought of Drew remembering every day that he'd asked after Jess. Protecting him seemed more important than ever. 'She wasn't truthful with me. She didn't tell me something really important.'

'Like you didn't tell her about Drew until you had to?'

He cringed. It felt like a low blow. And it was just what Jess had said. But from Julie's mouth it had been a lot more sarcastic. He nodded and held up his hands. 'I know, I know, but that was different.'

'Different how?'

Blair hadn't been kidding. He was in trouble.

He shook his head and waved his hands. 'Her husband and son died in a car crash three years ago. She didn't mention them at all. She just told me things hadn't worked out for her.'

Julie's hand had shot up to her mouth. He could see her take a deep breath. 'So, how did you find out if she didn't tell you?'

Trust Julie to cut straight to the chase. 'Well, she did tell me. But it was out of the blue. After she reacted badly to something and said she couldn't do this any more.'

Julie screwed up her face. 'Are you trying to talk in riddles?'

'I told you—it's complicated.'

There came the sound of shouts and splashes from upstairs. She shrugged. 'I've got time.'

Drew felt wary. The things that had been circulating through his brain for the last few days were all on the tip of his tongue. The things that had given him a pounding headache and kept him awake every night jumbled around in his head.

'It was all over a chocolate bar.'

'What?'

He couldn't keep his exasperation in check. He stood up, almost knocking his stool over, walking over to the counter and pushing some pods into the machine and propping the cups underneath.

Julie stayed silent. It must be killing her, not breaking the silence. But he knew exactly why she was doing it. She was forcing him to say all this out loud.

He placed the coffees on the breakfast bar and sat down again. 'I bought Jessica her favourite chocolate bar and I gave her it when we picked her up. After a few minutes she freaked out and jumped out of the car before I even had a chance to pull over. She said she couldn't do it. She couldn't have a relationship with me and Drew.'

Julie raised her eyebrow. 'Over a chocolate bar?'

Total disbelief was in her voice. She was waiting for the rest.

Callum sucked in a deep breath. 'Apparently her husband and son had stopped to buy her chocolate the night they had the accident. If they hadn't...' His voice tailed off.

'If they hadn't—what?'

'If they hadn't stopped she thinks they wouldn't have been killed. They wouldn't have been on that part of the road at that time of night. She thinks the accident was her fault.'

Julie sat for a few moments, biting her lip. She looked up from the coffee cup she had continued to stir. 'No. She doesn't.'

'What?' It was not what he'd expected her to say.

Julie sighed. 'Oh, Callum. This is much bigger than I ever expected. Tell me what else she said.'

He racked his brain. Did he really want to share everything Jessica had said? He'd been mulling over this for days. Going over and over things in his head. Maybe it would be useful to get another perspective.

He looked at the picture pinned to the fridge. 'It's all about Drew, Julie. This all comes down to Drew.'

'Why do you think that?'

'Her little boy—her son was the same age as Drew. If he'd lived he would be five too.' This was the hardest part. The part he hated most. 'She's looking for a replacement, Julie. She's looking for a replacement for her son—and maybe her husband.'

Julie looked shocked. She stood up sharply. 'Tell me everything. Did she say anything else to you that day? Anything at all?'

He winced. 'She told me that she loved me. She loved me and Drew and she couldn't put us in the same position her family were in. She didn't want to hurt us.'

'She told you she loved you?' Julie's voice rose.

He nodded and stared down at his coffee. He couldn't even bear to take a sip.

'She told you she loved you?' This time she was practically shouting.

'Yes. But it doesn't make a difference. She didn't mean it. It's not us that she loves. It's just the idea of us.'

Julie walked straight over to him, barely inches from his face. She looked furious. 'And what did you do then, Callum? What did you do when she told you that she loved you both?'

A horrible, cold sensation swept over his skin. Every hair on his arms stood on end. His actions had seemed perfectly reasonable at the time. He'd been so upset for her. And so upset for them too. He didn't want to be replacement for what Jess had lost. He wanted Jess to love him and Drew the way that they loved her—with their whole hearts.

'I told her to get in the car and say something to placate Drew. I told her I'd drop her off.'

'Oh, Callum.' Julie turned away. She put her arms up to her face and stood still for a few moments.

'What? I have to protect my son, Julie. Drew's the most

important thing in the world to me. I won't let anyone hurt him. Not even her.' The words came spilling out. Why did he feel as if he had to defend himself?

'Drew's been through all this before. He had a mother who treated him as if he wasn't good enough. Who walked away from him. How can I put my wee boy through something like that again?' He shook his head. 'I can't. I won't.'

Julie touched his arm. 'But Jessica isn't Kirsten, Callum. Not by a long shot. From all the stuff that you've told me about her, they couldn't compare. Surely you know that?' Her voice was wavering.

And his heart started to pound in his chest. He knew what she was saying was true. He had just needed someone else to say it out loud for him. Jess was nothing like Kirsten. He knew in his heart of hearts that Jessica would never have walked out on her son. A thought like that would never even have occurred to Jess. She was made in a totally different way.

Julie spun back round and there were tears in her eyes. She pointed to the stool. 'Sit down.'

It was *that* voice again. Do or die.

He sat down numbly. Julie should be on his side. So why did he feel as if she wasn't?

'Callum Kennedy, you've been my friend for four years. You know I love you. But sometimes you are a complete git.'

'What?'

'When you're wrong, Callum, you're *so* wrong it's scary.'

He was starting to feel sick now. Sick to his stomach. She had that horrible female intuition thing, didn't she?

'What do you mean?'

She started pacing around the kitchen, her arms flailing

around her. 'This wasn't about a bar of chocolate, Callum. This was *never* about a bar of chocolate. This was about a woman learning to let go and love again. She's scared, Callum—she's terrified. And with your reaction—frankly—who can blame her?'

'What do you mean, she's scared?'

'You and Drew—you're not a replacement family for her.' Julie looked at him in disgust. 'You could *never* replace her family, Callum.' She pressed her hand to her chest. 'They will always be with her—in here—forever. This is something totally different. Don't you see?'

He was starting to feel panicked. The last sensation in the world he ever felt. Not even in the middle of a fraught rescue. But he was feeling it now. His mouth felt bone dry. The lump in his throat was as big as a tennis ball. He shook his head. 'No. I don't see. Tell me.'

Julie reached her hands across the breakfast bar and clasped his. She looked at the drawing on the fridge. 'Callum, we both know how your son feels about Jessica. It's written all over his face. But how do *you* feel about her?' She pointed her finger to his chest again, this time a lot more gently. 'How do you feel in here?'

The million-dollar question. The thing that kept his stomach constantly churning because no matter what he did the feeling wouldn't go away. The words he didn't want to say out loud. Because then he would have to admit to a whole host of things.

Her pointed finger felt like a laser burning a hole straight through to his heart.

He looked up. 'I love her.' He could feel his voice breaking. But he didn't want it to. He took a deep breath and tried again. 'I love her, Julie.' This time the words were stronger—more determined.

It felt like a weight had been lifted off his shoulders. The acknowledgement of saying the words out loud. Admitting to himself and his friend how he felt.

Julie sagged back down into the stool opposite him. She put her elbow on the breakfast bar and put her head on her hand. 'Then what you going to do about it, dummy?'

CHAPTER THIRTEEN

THE CANDLES FLICKERED around her.

They were beautiful, spilling yellow and orange tones along the pale cream walls in her house.

The Christmas decorations had been closing in around her. A permanent reminder of another Christmas alone. Sitting in the kitchen was different. The orange and pomegranate spice of the candles was soothing. She'd been trying some deep-breathing exercises. Anything to try and take her thoughts away from the constants on her mind.

Callum and Drew.

The door rattled then the doorbell started ringing and didn't stop.

'Jess? Jess, are you in?' The door rattled again.

Her heart started to race instantly. She recognised the voice. She'd recognise it anywhere. Something must be wrong. Drew. Something must be wrong with Drew.

She ran down the hall and yanked the door open. 'What is it? Is it Drew? Has something happened?'

Callum was stuck with his hand still in mid-air—frozen to the spot. It was almost as if he hadn't expected her to answer.

She looked down at the car parked at the side of the road. Drew wasn't in it. His car seat was empty.

Callum shook his head. 'No. No, it's not Drew. He's fine.' Then he paused. 'Well, actually, he's not fine.'

'What is it?' Her stomach was clenched. Was he in hospital? Had there been an accident?

Callum stepped forward, closing the gap between them. She could smell him. His distinctive aftershave was immediately invading her senses, bringing a whole host of memories. Bringing a whole heap of regrets.

He reached up and touched her cheek. 'He misses you. *We* miss you. That's what's wrong with Drew...' He paused. 'And with me.'

It was the last thing she'd expected to hear. She couldn't breathe. All her muscles contracted.

He put his hand on her shoulder. 'Jess, please. Can we talk?'

Her brain started to race. She was confused. She'd thought he hated her. The last time she'd seen him she hadn't been able to read the look on his face. Had it been confusion? Or resignation?

She felt overwhelming relief. Drew was fine. There hadn't been an accident. She couldn't help the way her brain worked. But, then, any parent would be the same—their first thought in a moment of panic would be for their child.

Parent. The word that had popped straight into her mind.

Her reactions to Drew were those of a parent. And her thoughts about Callum? She loved him so much it hurt to even be in the same space as him.

So, if this wasn't about Drew, why was Callum here?

She tried to focus. The messages between her brain and her mouth were getting muddled. There was so much jumbling around in there.

'Jess, can I come in?'

Her feet moved backwards automatically, creating space for him to come through.

He walked into the hall and glanced in the direction of the darkened living room. He took her hand and led her inside, bending down to switch on the lights of her Christmas tree.

Christmas lights. The ones she'd been trying to avoid. The new twinkling red berries and silver stars lit up the room. They had been her fresh start. But the chance to build new memories had been destroyed. All the tiny little hopes that had started to form. All the baby steps towards some new memories—like buying the new decorations with Drew—had been wiped out.

She was trying hard to focus. Trying to make sense of it all. Part of her was angry. This was the man she'd hoped for a future with. She might not have been truthful with him, but his reaction had still hurt.

'What are you doing here, Callum?' The tone of her words revealed the exhaustion she was feeling. Every bone in her body ached. She hadn't slept for days. She couldn't eat. The truth was she just couldn't go on like this.

His hands went to her waist and she gasped. His fingers were icy cold. It was only then she realised he wasn't wearing gloves or a jacket. Why on earth was he out on a freezing night like this with no jacket? Had he been in that much of a rush?

'I came here to apologise.' His voice was deep and husky. Was he being sincere? 'I came here to apologise for how I reacted the other day when you told me about your husband and son. I'm not proud of myself, Jess. I didn't understand.'

He was apologising. She felt shocked. Then she noticed

the lines around his eyes and on his forehead. It was like a mirror image of her own face. Maybe Callum had had problems sleeping too. She shook her head. 'How could you understand? I would never wish something like that on you.'

'No. That's not what I meant.' He was babbling. 'Of course I don't know what it's like to lose a wife and child. But I didn't understand how you were feeling about us. Us—me and Drew. I got confused. I thought you were looking for a replacement. I thought you were using me and Drew as a replacement for your family.'

She pulled back. How could he think that? A million different things flew about her brain. 'But why? Why would you think that?'

Things started to drop into place. The questions. The expressions on his face. The age. This was all about Drew's age.

'Is this because Lewis and Drew would have been the same age?' For a second it felt as if someone had just dropped her back into the icy River Clyde. 'You think I would try and replace my little boy with another?'

No. It didn't even bear thinking about. How could anyone think that? She tried to keep calm. Sure, a few comparisons had swept through her brain. She'd even been a tiny bit jealous of Callum when she'd first found out about Drew. But to think she would try and do something like that?

She ran her tongue across her dry lips.

Wow. Maybe it wasn't such a leap in the dark. If the shoe had been on the other foot, might that have occurred to her? If she was the one with a child and Callum had lost his wife and child, would she wonder if he was trying to replace them?

Maybe. Just maybe. Even if it was only for a few seconds.

He pulled her closer, his chest pressing against hers. 'Jess?' He could see she was lost in her thoughts. He stared at her with his dark green eyes and she could see the sincerity on his face. 'I don't think that. I don't think that now. I was shocked. I never expected something like that had happened to you. I couldn't make sense of it in my head.'

It was easy. It was easy to feel his arms around her. It felt so good to sense him touch her skin again. But there was so much more to say. She couldn't expose her heart to this kind of hurt again. She wouldn't survive.

'Is that what you came to say?' She was trying to distance herself from all this. She could accept his apology—if that's what he wanted to offer. She could accept it, and then walk away. No matter how good it felt to be in his arms.

'No. That's not what I came to say.' He reached up and brushed her curls behind her ear. 'I came to tell you that I'm sorry. I'm sorry and I love you. Drew and I love you. I know I made a mess of this, Jess, but please don't give up on us. We want you to be part of our lives.'

'But—'

'Shh.' He put his finger against her lips then traced it over her cheekbones and eyelids. The feel of his light touch on her skin was magical. She could forget about everything else that had happened and just let this touch lull her into a false sense of security that everything would be fine.

She opened her eyes and took a deep breath.

'Don't say no. Please, don't say no, Jess. I can't be apart from you. *We* can't be apart from you.'

'But why, Callum, why now?'

'Look at me, Jess. I haven't slept in days. Neither have

you—I can tell. This…' he waved his arms in the air '…is driving me crazy. I didn't mean to walk away. I just wanted to protect Drew. I needed to know that you were there because you loved *us*, not just the idea of us.'

'But how could you ever doubt that?'

He tapped his finger on the side of his head. 'Because I wasn't thinking straight. When you told me about your husband and son, I went into defence mode—protecting my son, protecting my family.' His hand cupped the side of her face. 'But you're part of my family now, Jess. You, me and Drew. I love you. I don't want to do this without you.'

She felt herself start to shake. From one extreme to the other. Callum was looking into her eyes and telling her that he loved her. Telling her that he and Drew loved her, Jessica Rae.

She wanted to believe him. She really did.

But ten minutes ago she had been wondering just how to get through one night. And even that had seemed too much for her. Even that had been taking candles and deep breathing.

'I…I…I don't know, Callum.'

He pressed his hand to her chest. 'How do you feel? How do you feel when you see me and Drew?'

There was no doubt. No doubt for her at all. It was the one thing that was crystal clear. 'I love you. I love you both.' But even as she said the words she felt fear and she instinctively made to pull away.

Callum lowered his head so it was level with hers—so he could look straight into her eyes. 'I know you're scared. I get that now. I can deal with that. *We* can deal with that together—as a family.'

She lowered her gaze. 'But how, Callum? When I saw that bar of chocolate it brought so many memories back.

What if something happened to you and Drew? I can't go through that again.'

He gave her a smile. 'I know you're scared. But it's a big old scary world out there, Jess. You and I work in it every day. And what makes it all right is the people around us.' He took her hand and placed it on his chest. She could feel his heart beating under her palm. Thump, thump. Thump, thump.

'I can't promise you that everything will be perfect. I can't promise you that nothing will ever happen to any of us. I can't promise you that I'll never stop to buy you a bar of chocolate again. There are some things in this life we have no control over.' His other hand wound through her hair. 'What I can promise you is that I'll love you faithfully for every second that I'm here. I'll do my best to keep you and Drew safe. And if you have fears, talk to me about them. I'm here for you, Jess. I've waited thirteen years to get the woman of my dreams. I'm not about to let you escape now.'

Thirteen years. It seemed like a whole lifetime.

It had been a whole lifetime—for both of them.

'Can you give me a chance, Jessica? Can you give us a chance?'

He knew. He knew she'd been scared. He knew it had all felt too much for her and she'd needed some space.

But the love that she'd felt for Callum and his son had never faltered—not even for a second. Instead, it was growing, every single day.

'I'd like that, Callum,' she breathed. 'I'd like that very much.'

She could see the sparkle appear in his eyes. 'Then wait here.'

He turned and vanished, leaving her standing in the living room with only the red and silver twinkling tree lights.

She heard her front door open and some muffled voices then a little giggle. A little boy's giggle.

Callum appeared at the doorway with Drew standing in front of him, clutching something in a Christmas box.

'Drew!' She couldn't help herself, she rushed over and hugged him as tightly as she could. 'I've missed you. Have you been a good boy?'

Drew was bouncing on his toes. 'Watch out, Jess. You'll squash your present. I made it specially.'

She turned to Callum, shaking her head in wonder. 'But how? The car was empty. Where was he?'

It was then she noticed. Under his thick jacket and hat Drew was wearing his pyjamas and slippers. Callum wasn't the only one who'd left the house in a hurry.

Callum gave her a nod. 'I have some good friends—they helped me out, in more ways than one.'

His finger brushed her cheek again and he knelt down on one knee opposite in front of her. Drew sat on his knee and held out the box. 'This might not be the most traditional way of doing things, but it probably suits us best.' Callum smiled at his son. Drew had a huge smile plastered to his face. 'We want you to marry us, Jess, and stay with us forever. We promise to love you, for now and for always. Will you marry us, Jess?'

Drew's little hands were shaking with excitement. She reached out and took the little red box, pulling off the lid and looking inside. Her hands were trembling. A few hours ago she had been feeling helpless and miserable, expecting to spend another Christmas alone, just wishing for it all to be over.

This was the best present she could ever have hoped for.

Her eyes squeezed shut for a tiny second.

She opened them again. Yes, they were still there. She wasn't imagining this. It was really happening.

She looked inside the box. There was one of the tiny Christmas decorations that she and Drew had bought together. A tiny little red heart. Except this one had been twisted on to some tin foil to make a ring. There was a little piece of folded paper next to it.

'I made it. Jess. Do you like it?'

She looked into their smiling faces. This was hers. This was her family. For now and for always.

'I love it.' She lifted the makeshift ring out of the box and put it on her finger, watching as it gleamed in the twinkling tree lights. 'It's perfect.' She gave Drew a kiss.

He pressed the little bit of paper into her hand. 'This is the real one we've picked for you. Daddy says it's a pink diamond because pink's your favourite colour.' He looked a little sad. 'But we couldn't get it tonight.'

Jessica looked at the printout. It was beautiful. It was breathtaking. 'It's perfect.' She smiled and looked at the little red heart. 'But every Christmas I want to wear this ring, because you made it for me.'

She put her hands around Callum's neck to meet his mouth with a kiss. She couldn't have wished for anything more. A family, not just for Christmas but forever.

Drew was standing at the fireplace staring at the chimney. 'Can I write a thank-you letter for Santa?'

Callum frowned. 'But it's not Christmas yet. You've not had your presents yet.'

Drew gave him a little knowing smile. 'Oh, yes, I have. Santa and I made a deal. He's just delivered his present early.'

Jessica linked her arm around Callum's waist. 'It seems

our son has been making deals without telling us. What else do you think he asked Santa for?'

She could see the gleam in his eye. 'Let's hope it's a little brother or sister,' he whispered as he bent to kiss her.

* * * * *

HER MISTLETOE
WISH

LUCY CLARK

Lucy Clark loves movies. She loves binge watching box-sets of TV shows. She loves reading and she loves to bake. Writing is such an integral part of Lucy's inner being that she often dreams in technicolour, frantically waking up in the morning to try and write down as much as she can remember. You can find Lucy on Facebook and Twitter. Stop by and say 'G'day'!

CHAPTER ONE

REGGIE SMITH RACED into the outpatient clinic, smiling and waving to the patients who were awaiting her attention. The clinic was decorated with tinsel and baubles and a sad-looking branch from a gum tree had been potted in the corner, dressed with twinkle lights in an effort to add a bit of festive cheer to the people waiting to see the doctor.

Christmas was Reggie's favourite time of year because it always brought hope and she was a big believer in hope. Plus, in the weeks leading up to Christmas, everyone seemed to be in a happier mood, calling a quick 'Have a great Christmas' or 'Merry Christmas' or 'Happy holidays'. Of course, Sunshine General Hospital was also abuzz with the annual hospital auction to be held ten days before Christmas and as Reggie was part of the organising committee, there was still much to do.

'Four weeks until Christmas and I haven't even started my shopping,' one of her closest friends, Mackenzie, had said to her only yesterday as they'd finalised the venue for the hospital auction.

'I'm almost done.' Reggie had grinned widely.

'Show-off,' Mackenzie had returned.

Even thinking about it made Reggie smile as she

screeched to a halt at the outpatient clinic desk. 'Sorry, sorry,' she called brightly. 'I was held up in A and E. Sorry, sorry.' Her words were genuine as she honestly didn't like to keep people waiting but sometimes, especially where she was concerned, time seemed to have a habit of disappearing.

'It's just like you, Reggie.' Clara, the clerk, smiled as she pointed to a bundle of case notes, indicating they were Reggie's patients for the morning. 'Luckily, the new general surgeon covering Geetha's maternity leave has already started the clinic so you shouldn't be too far behind.'

'I didn't think Geetha was leaving for another week,' Reggie said as she hefted the notes into her arms.

'Handover period,' Clara offered. 'Don't you ever read your emails?'

Reggie's answer was to grin and shrug. 'You know me!' She looked at the top name on the case notes in her arms. 'Er...Mr Searle. Would you like to come on through?'

She waited while Mr Searle, an elderly man in his sixties, stood and started walking towards her, barely leaning on the walking stick in his right hand.

'You're walking really well,' she said, clearly impressed as the two of them walked slowly down the corridor towards her consulting room. 'I spoke to Mackenzie, your orthopaedic surgeon, the other day and she told me how pleased she was with your progress. After today's check-up, you might be able to get a break from this place for a while.'

'I'm looking forward to it,' Mr Searle replied as he headed through into her consulting room. 'No offence intended,' he added.

'None taken,' she remarked, waving her hand in the air with a dramatic flourish. 'I love it when my patients are well enough to get back to living their normal lives.' Her eyes were alive with delight, her voice filled with happiness, but as she turned to close her consulting-room door, the door directly opposite hers opened.

The smile slowly slid from Reggie's face, her eyes widened in shock, and her jaw dropped open in disbelief as Flynn Jamieson—*the Flynn Jamieson*—stood opposite her. He was dressed in a pair of navy trousers, a crisp white shirt and striped university tie. His hands were on his hips as he stared at her with his piercing blue eyes.

'Do you have to be so noisy, Reg?'

At the use of the familiar name, especially as he was the only person she'd ever allowed to call her that, Reggie's eyes flashed with fire as annoyance replaced surprise. 'Please don't call me that. Excuse me.' With that, she closed her consulting-room door, effectively shutting out the sight of him.

She leaned against the door and closed her eyes for a moment, unable to ignore the repressed pulsing desire, the one only Flynn could evoke, and the way her entire body seemed to be trembling just from the sight of him. What on earth was Flynn Jamieson doing here? In Australia? In Queensland? In Maroochydore? In Sunshine General Hospital—*her* hospital?

No sooner had the questions started running around in her head than the answer materialised like magic. 'Surgeon covering Geetha's maternity leave,' she whispered. Why, oh, why hadn't she read her emails? The head of the surgery department was a great communicator, always keeping the surgical staff informed with the latest happenings, but it was Reggie who was the bad receiver of these communications, which meant she really had no one else to blame but herself for being shocked at Flynn's appearance.

'Reggie?' Mr Searle's voice brought her attention back to the present and she quickly opened her eyes and pasted on a smile, forcing herself to push all thoughts of the disturbing Flynn Jamieson to the back of her mind. So what if he was here? So what if she would be required to work with him? She'd worked with him before and they'd made a good professional team. The fact that he'd broken her heart six years ago meant nothing to her now. *He* meant nothing to her now. Nothing at all.

'Sorry, Mr Searle.' Reggie dragged in a breath and placed the pile of case notes on the desk, taking Mr Searle's from the top and opening them up as she sat down in the chair. 'Let's get your examination underway.'

For the rest of the Monday morning outpatient clinic Reggie did her utmost to avoid any and all contact with Flynn, forcing herself to focus on being her usual bright and cheerful self for the sake of her patients. They deserved nothing less but once her last patient for the morning had exited her consulting room, Reggie immediately picked up the receiver of the internal hospital phone and called Mackenzie.

'It's Reggie,' she stated before Mackenzie could even squeeze out a 'hello'. 'We have to meet. Are you free? Coffee shop across the road from the hospital in ten minutes?'

'I think I can do that. What's wrong, Reggie?'

'The worst thing possible.'

'What?'

Reggie could hear the worry in Mackenzie's voice but it was nothing compared to the utter panic and devastation in her own. 'It's Flynn. He's *here!*'

'This is an emergency,' Reggie told her friends fifteen minutes later as they all sat round a table, sipping coffee.

'I cannot believe Flynn is back,' Sunainah said, her sparkling new wedding rings gleaming brightly on her left hand. Reggie tried not to look at them, or Bergan's, or Mackenzie's. During the past eighteen months, all three of her closest friends had found their true loves and were now happily married. She had tried not to let it bother her, had tried to remain as happy and as optimistic as she'd always been, but deep down inside, late at night when she was all alone in her apartment, she had curled into a tight little ball and cried, feeling incredibly lonely.

And now, to top everything off, Flynn Jamieson was back in her life. He was the only man she had ever truly given her heart to, the only man she had ever truly loved, and yet he was the only man who had ever truly crushed her beyond despair.

'What are you going to do?' Bergan asked.

'What do you mean, what am I going to do? I'm going to yell and scream and bellyache and do my best not to fall apart in front of him. I mean…' She spread her arms wide as she slumped back in her chair. 'It's *Flynn.*' Reggie closed her eyes. '*My* Flynn,' she whispered, as Mackenzie put her arms around Reggie and hugged her close.

'How did he look?' Bergan asked.

Reggie sighed and shook her head as though she were a completely lost cause. 'Good. *Really* good.'

'But he is not married anymore, is that correct?' Sunainah asked.

Reggie sighed and looked at her friends. 'Not as far as I know, but then, I stopped reading the latest society gossip of the rich and famous after I saw the picture of him and his blonde, buxom bride splashed across the front pages. A man does not break off an engagement with one woman and then marry another in under a fortnight.' She glared at her untouched coffee, her voice as dark as the beverage.

Less than twenty-four hours after Flynn had taken her out to a romantic restaurant, given her red roses, plied her with the finest champagne and then strolled with her along the beach at sunset, stopping momentarily to go down on bended knee to not only confess his love for her but profess that it was *she* he wanted to spend the rest of his life with—he'd come round to her apartment and called the whole thing off, telling her it had been a mistake.

'Stupid romance. Stupid rich people. Stupid Flynn,' she grumbled, her frown deepening. 'And I thought I was going to have a good Christmas this year. Fat chance of that happening now.' She sighed, trying to figure out how she was supposed to deal with working alongside him every day until Geetha returned from maternity leave, which could be anywhere from six to twelve months from now.

Lifting her gaze from scowling at her coffee, it was then Reggie noticed that her three friends were giving each other very worried looks. They'd all known each other so well, for so many years, having been through so much together, that sometimes there was no need for words to communicate exactly what they were thinking.

They'd met at medical school, all of them having come from very different backgrounds, but their past adversities had been the one thing that had ended up binding them together. None of them had had an easy ride throughout their life but in looking out for each other and offering constant support, they'd formed their own family unit. So Reggie could easily read their expressions and she shook her head.

'I'm not going to fall for him again. I can tell that's what you're all thinking, aren't you,' she stated rhetorically.

'Well…' Sunainah shrugged.

'You've always said he was your one true love,' Mackenzie added.

'I'm more worried about you turning into a crazy nutter again,' Bergan added, her words matter-of-fact but filled with love. 'I mean, after you broke up you not only removed every single trace of Flynn from your life, destroying and disposing of all the very expensive gifts he'd given you, but you cut your hair super-short, coloured it purple and threw yourself into matchmaking your friends.'

'Well, I can't do the last bit anymore,' Reggie pointed out, indicating the wedding rings her friends were wearing, then added thoughtfully, 'I could possibly colour my hair again. I've always wanted to go green. What do you think? Green streaks?'

Before her friends could answer, Bergan's and Mackenzie's phones rang. They quickly answered them and while they spoke, Sunainah reached across the table and took Reggie's hand in hers.

'Just…pause, Reggie. Stop and take a breath.' Sunainah's phone started buzzing with a reminder and she shook her head. 'I am sorry, Reggie. My clinic will be starting in five minutes. I need to—'

'Go.' Reggie waved her hands towards her friends, shooing them away. 'Thanks for giving me probably the only fifteen minutes you had spare. I do appreciate it.'

'Sorry,' Mackenzie said, as she and Bergan stood.

'Emergency,' Bergan added.

'My afternoon theatre list will be starting late so call me if I'm needed to help out,' Reggie told Bergan.

'Will do,' her friend replied.

Reggie picked up her coffee, sipping it as she watched her friends finish their drinks quickly and head back to the hospital. She prided herself on always being happy, always having a bright smile on her face, a genuine smile, one that would bring happiness to others. Forever optimistic—that's what her friends had called her, yet now she wanted to wallow in her despondency, blaming Flynn Jamieson for making her feel this way.

'Definitely green hair,' she mumbled to herself a few minutes later, unable to lift herself out of her grumpy mood.

'I think it would look great,' a deep male voice said from behind her, a voice she instantly recognised and one that set her entire body alight with sparks of joy and excitement. Reggie turned round to look over her shoulder but didn't see him. Had she imagined it? Was she going insane, thinking every deep male voice belonged to Flynn?

She turned her attention back to her drink and almost jumped with fright when she saw Flynn lowering his six-foot-four-inch frame into the chair opposite her. She quickly put her coffee back onto the table before she spilled it. 'Don't do that, Flynn. You know I don't like being scared.'

He nodded. 'I do. Sorry. Couldn't resist.'

'Try.' She glared at him suspiciously. 'How long have you been lurking around here?' She indicated the immediate vicinity around her table. Had he overheard them all talking?

'I came in as your friends were leaving. I received a very cool look from…Bergan, is it?'

'Yes.' She frowned. 'How did you know that?'

'You showed me quite a few pictures of all your friends during our time together in the Caribbean. Don't you remember?'

Reggie sat up straighter in her chair, squaring her shoulders. 'I can't remember a lot of things about the Caribbean. It was so long ago.' She tried to inflect a touch of nonchalance into her tone but could tell from the disbelieving look on his face that he wasn't really buying it.

Flynn nodded slowly then just sat there, staring at her as though he was drinking in the sight of her. 'How have you been, Reg?'

She gritted her teeth at his familiarity, not wanting to give him the satisfaction again of seeing how the intimate name flustered her. 'I'm…fine.'

'Freaked out? Insecure? Neurotic and emotional?' he checked, and she shook her head in annoyance.

'Don't be cute, Flynn.'

He spread his arms wide and leaned back in his chair. 'I don't know how to be any other way.' His smile was big, his eyebrows were raised and his twinkling eyes were clearly teasing her.

'I see your arrogance is still in check.'

He surprised her by chuckling and she instantly wished he hadn't, the warm, inviting sound washing over her like a comfortable blanket. She'd always loved his laugh, always loved making him laugh, but not like this, not through silly barbs and jibes.

Reggie bit her tongue, needing to get her ridiculous hormones under control, to remain cool, calm and collected. 'What are you doing here?

'In the coffee shop?'

She levelled him with a glare. 'Flynn.' There was warning in her tone.

'Oh. At Sunshine General? I'm covering Geetha's maternity leave.'

'So I gathered but…er…' How did she ask this without sounding self-important? 'Did you know I was working at Sunshine General?'

Flynn didn't answer her but instead checked his watch. 'We're going to be late for afternoon theatre if we don't get a move on.'

'I don't care,' she continued to grump as Flynn stood. He obviously hadn't been told the morning elective theatre lists had run overtime. She watched as he shoved his hands into the pockets of his trousers and stared down at her with that crazy little smile touching the corners of his lips. It was a smile that had never failed to set her heart racing and now was no exception.

'You're sounding like Scrooge, Reggie.'

'Bah, humbug,' she muttered as she finished her now-cold coffee and stood. She didn't really want to walk back to the hospital with Flynn because even being this close to him was already causing her body to react with all the hallmarks of years gone past. Her heart was beating wildly, her mouth was dry, her knees were shaking and she momentarily leaned on the table for support.

'How can *you* not be in the Christmas spirit? You, who always wanted it to be Christmas all year round? The woman who loved wishing everyone happy holidays as she walked around the hospital or went to the shops or the gym or, in fact, anywhere.' Flynn pressed a finger to his lips in thought.

'In fact, I remember you animatedly and jovially wishing the Prince of the Netherlands the happiest Christmas one year. Then the next day you gave a homeless man the same greeting in exactly the same way.' He shook his head in bemusement. 'That's one thing I always liked about you, Reggie. You treated everyone, prince or pauper, the same. You afford everyone the same courtesy.'

Reggie glared at Flynn, her anger beginning to rise. 'Don't compliment me.'

'Why not?'

Her mind tried to think of a reason because she could hardly tell him that his words had warmed her heart. She didn't want her heart to be warmed by Flynn. Not now. Not ever. But he was still standing there, waiting for her reply. 'Just…because.' She shook her head and walked out of the café, waving her thanks to the owner and managing to muster a half-hearted smile. She hated herself for feeling this way, for not spreading joy and happiness, as was her wont, but seeing Flynn again, even walking alongside him as he fell into step beside her was throwing her completely off balance.

'Just because? What kind of answer is that?'

'The only one you're going to get.' She pressed the button at the pedestrian crossing with great impatience, wanting the light to turn green instantly so she could walk away from the man who had hurt her so bitterly. Still, she wasn't the same woman she'd been six years ago. Once more in her life she'd been forced to pick herself up and keep moving forward. His rejection of her had only served to make her stronger and because of that she could and would stand up to him.

Drawing in a deep breath, she turned to face him, to give him a piece of her mind, to tell him to leave her alone, but it was only then she became aware of other people coming to join them at the traffic lights, waiting to cross the road. She was forced to step closer to him, to rise on her toes so she could direct her words closer to his ear.

'Whatever happened between us happened a long time ago, Flynn.'

'It wasn't that long ago,' Flynn pointed out, stepping closer to her, dipping his head and heightening the repressed awareness she was experiencing. She closed her eyes, desperate to remain in control of the situation and not be swayed by the cologne he was wearing, the same scent she'd introduced him to all those years ago, assuring him the subtle spicy scent suited him much better than the woodsy one he'd been wearing. She couldn't believe he was still wearing the hypnotic, alluring scent.

The lights turned green, the beeping sound from the pedestrian crossing startling her slightly. She opened her eyes and belatedly realised that while everyone else had moved off, she and Flynn were just standing there, close—too close—looking at each other. She swallowed over her dry throat, desperate to ignore the tingles and sparkles and butterflies and all the other sensations this man had the habit of creating deep within her.

'It was another lifetime ago,' she eventually retorted, before turning and walking across the road, having to run the last little way as the flashing pedestrian sign had already turned red.

'It was a good lifetime, though.' His voice came from behind her and she glanced over her shoulder, not realising he'd crossed the road behind her. 'We had a good time together.'

'I don't want to talk about it.' She stopped walking for a moment and turned to glare at him. 'Why are you here? Why now? Why—?' She broke off, her voice cracking on the words. She looked away from him and shook her head, unable to believe her body and mind were betraying her by reacting to his enigmatic presence and becoming so emotional.

Swallowing, she shook her head and turned away from him, knowing it was better to beat a hasty retreat than say something she would regret. While Flynn may have broken her heart, it wasn't in her nature to be mean or malicious.

She didn't want to look behind her, didn't want to know whether or not Flynn was following her. She didn't want to know his whereabouts, she didn't want to work alongside him in the clinic and she didn't want to deal with him during operating lists. She wanted him to go, to leave the hospital and Maroochydore—in fact, leave Australia…and leave her alone.

So why, after the way he'd been smiling at her in the coffee shop, did she get the feeling that wasn't about to happen?

CHAPTER TWO

REGGIE WAS GLAD she had a busy theatre list to focus her thoughts. It was easier to push the reappearance of Flynn Jamieson in her life to the back of her mind and instead be calm and controlled as she removed Mr Philmott's gallbladder, relieved young Cynthia Schroder of her inflamed appendix and performed a hernia repair on Mrs Grant.

Between cases, she did her best not to run into Flynn, knowing he was operating in the next theatre. At one point, she was in the doctor's tearoom, just finishing a much-needed cup of coffee, when she thought she heard his voice out in the corridor. Panic filled her insides and as she glanced wildly around the room she realised there really was no place for her to hide.

Quickly washing her cup, she headed to the door, intent on slipping out of the room as he came in. Never had she been more grateful to Ingrid Brown, one of the general surgical registrars who had been assigned to assist Flynn in Theatre, because as they came into the tearoom Ingrid was intent on keeping Flynn's attention firmly on her.

'Reg?' Flynn interrupted Ingrid the instant he saw

Reggie standing by the door. 'How's everything going in Theatre?'

'Great,' she offered, and quickly left the room, trying to ignore the spate of tingles that seemed to flood right through her body from the quick glance she'd received from Flynn. Why was it that even after six years, after breaking her heart and making her feel as though she was worthless, he could still create such havoc with her senses?

And that was the way things went for the next week, with Reggie doing her best to quickly slip out of a room the instant he walked in. Keeping a nice, uncomplicated distance between them was helping her to focus on her patients, on the planning for the hospital Christmas auction and on keeping her paperwork up to date. The fact that she was as jumpy as a long-tailed cat in a roomful of rocking chairs every time a nearby door opened or she heard male voices in the corridor meant nothing.

Self-preservation was of paramount importance in situations such as this, but even through all her efforts of avoidance she was having difficulty sleeping because the instant she lay in her bed and closed her eyes, memories of her past encounters with Flynn flooded her mind.

So many memories yet such a short time together. For the first two weeks in the Caribbean, she'd kept her distance from him, trying to figure out whether he was like all the other wealthy people she knew or whether he was, in fact, a normal person. Reggie had had very good reasons for distrusting the wealthy, but thankfully he'd turned out to be the latter…or so she'd thought.

Having been raised in an exclusive and snobbish Melbourne suburb, born to incredibly wealthy parents, Reggie had instantly recognised the name of Flynn Jamieson when he'd arrived at the understaffed Caribbean hospital for his six-week contract. Their fathers had been involved in some sort of business venture together and their elite community had been small, to say the least.

Of course, Flynn hadn't had a clue of her own true identity and after she'd realised he really was interested in providing medical treatment to people in need, not just working there because it had been a good opportunity to advance his career, she'd started to thaw towards him.

She'd allowed herself to be affected by his gorgeous, sexy smile, his bright, twinkling eyes, his smooth, hypnotic voice. And once she'd fallen for him, hook, line and sinker, he'd revealed his true colours, discarding her feelings and dismissing her out of hand.

And yet somehow, all these years later, he still managed to make her knees go weak with one of those smiles, make her heart pound wildly against her chest with a simple wink and make her melt in a boneless mass at the sound of his voice. It was wrong. Wrong that he still had such a hold over her emotions, and she resented him for it.

The following Monday, after she'd managed to avoid him once more during the general surgical elective theatres list, Reggie had stopped by her small office in the surgical block to finish writing up some notes and collect her computer and cellphone. It was late in the day and she was thankful the rest of the administrative staff had already left for the day because the last thing she felt like was talking to people.

'So unlike you,' she murmured, as she hunted around

for her house keys, having already forgotten them twice in the past few days. She blamed Flynn's presence for her lack of joviality and general absent-mindedness and once more wished he hadn't chosen to come to Sunshine General and inadvertently torture her just by being around.

She heard a sound outside in the corridor and instantly she was alert, listening for evidence of Flynn. Deciding to forget the search for her keys, knowing her neighbour, Melva, had the spare set, Reggie quietly locked her office door and all but sprinted out of the department.

Whether or not it had been Flynn she'd heard or one of the cleaners, she didn't care. Bumping into Flynn was too exhausting as it not only set her body into a trembling mass of uncontrollable tingles but also taxed her mind as she tried to fight the urge to throw herself into his arms and press her lips to his. She knew it was wrong to want to do that but sometimes it was difficult to deny the urge.

Reggie headed to the front of the hospital, looking forward to getting home, having a quick bite of dinner and then running a long, luxurious bath where she would soak until her skin was all wrinkled and pruney, washing away the cares of her day…and the acceptance that she was just as much attracted to Flynn as she'd ever been.

She stood at the taxi rank and looked up and down the road, unable to believe that at just after seven o'clock in the evening, on a Monday night, there were no taxis parked and waiting outside the hospital.

'There are always taxis here,' she murmured, spreading her arms wide.

'Not tonight, from the look of things,' Flynn's deep voice said from beside her, the sound causing her heart to flip-flop with delight before a ripple of awareness washed over her. Reggie closed her eyes, trying to pull some sort of shield around herself, but she'd had a busy and emotionally exhausting day and wasn't sure she had the energy for yet another run-in with Flynn.

Dragging in a deep breath, she opened her eyes and turned to look at him, deciding it was easier to face the situation than to make it worse by pretending to ignore him. 'Do you think you might not continue to creep up on me?' she asked, trying to keep her tone polite and impersonal but failing miserably.

'Only if you stop dashing from a room every time I walk in,' he countered, his clever eyes telling her he'd been aware of her avoidance tactics.

She looked down at her feet then cleared her throat. 'Er…how was Theatre this afternoon?'

Flynn stared at her for a split second before nodding. 'Good.' He paused and she noted a small smile twitching at the corners of his lips. 'No patients died.'

'Always a good thing,' she replied instantly, before she could stop herself. It was a private joke between the two of them, extending back to his first operating session in the Caribbean. The equipment at the hospital hadn't been as up to date as that in the hospitals in Australia and afterwards she'd asked him that same question.

'How did things go in Theatre, Flynn?'

'Good,' he'd replied, pulling off his cap and gown. 'No patients died.'

Reggie's laughter had filled the air at his words and it had been at that exact moment that she'd realised

Flynn Jamieson was indeed a good man and she would
be wrong not to give him a chance. She, herself, was
proof that people shouldn't be judged by who their parents were so she shouldn't do the same to Flynn. 'Always a good thing,' she'd replied as he'd joined in with
her laughter. From that day onwards, the two of them
had been almost inseparable.

Reggie pushed the memory aside and glanced up
and down the street as though willing a taxi to mirac-
ulously appear. She shifted her laptop bag to her other
shoulder, wishing she hadn't added a few hefty manila
folders filled with paperwork to it.

'You remembered,' he said softly, reaching out to
take her bag from her.

'It's OK. I've got it,' she told him, grasping the strap
and doing her best to ignore his comment. She didn't
want to stand here and reminisce about the past.

'Of course.' He dropped his hand back to his side.
'Habit. I always used to carry your bag for you when
we were together.'

'But we're not together anymore, Flynn, and I'm a
big girl now and can do it all by myself.' Her polite
smile was starting to slip and not only was her exhaustion shining through, so was her lack of patience.
'Look, Flynn, do you mind if we don't do the trip down
memory lane? I've had a hectic day and I just want to
get back to my apartment, eat and have a—'

'Relaxing soak in the tub,' he finished for her, his
words indicating just how well he did know her. 'Of
course you do.' He took a step away. 'I'll leave you
alone.' With that, he turned and walked away without
another word, leaving Reggie standing at the front of

the hospital, beneath the bright lights, with other people milling around, both patients and staff.

She frowned at his quick retreat. It wasn't that Flynn was leaving her all alone, deserted in the wilderness. He was merely doing as she'd asked. She should be grateful for that, so why was it she felt guilty for sending him away?

'No taxis?' an elderly man asked as he came to stand beside her, looking up and down the street.

'There's an international sporting match being played at the stadium,' another person offered as she came to stand on the other side of Reggie.

'Ah, all the taxis have taken their chances there.' Reggie smiled and nodded, pulling her cellphone from her pocket. 'I'd best ring for one. Would you like me to book one for both of you as well?' she offered, feeling her natural joviality return. The others agreed and within minutes Reggie had ordered taxis for them. 'They said it would be about another ten minutes.'

'Thank you, dear,' the man said. 'I might go and sit down to wait.'

'I'll join you.' But no sooner were the words out of her mouth than a white car pulled up into the taxi rank. Reggie did a double take as Flynn exited the car and came round to her side, taking her bag from her shoulder and holding open the passenger door.

'Your taxi awaits, Dr Smith.'

The others who were waiting with her all laughed and clapped, drawing more attention.

'I've called for a taxi,' she spluttered as Flynn put a gentle hand beneath her elbow and guided her towards his car.

'It won't go to waste,' the elderly man said, indicating a few other people who had come to the front of the hospital, hoping to find a swag of taxis.

'So that's settled,' Flynn remarked, as a stunned Reggie sat in the passenger seat. He closed the door then turned to the other people standing there. 'I apologise for not being able to be your personal taxi but I do wish you all the merriest of Christmases and a prosperous New Year.' Then, with a small bow, he came round to the driver's side, slipped behind the wheel, buckled his seat belt and the car merged seamlessly with the flowing evening traffic.

'What…what are you doing?' she asked, the shock slowly starting to wear off.

'I'm giving you a lift home. I thought that was obvious.' Flynn snapped his fingers at her. 'Keep up, Reg.'

'Don't call me that.'

'Why not? I've always called you Reg. In fact, if memory serves me correctly, I was the only one you *allowed* to call you that.' Flynn's smile was wide and bright. 'It made me feel special.'

'That's why I want you to stop.'

'I'm not special to you anymore?'

'Flynn, can we just stop this charade?' she said abruptly, her exhausted temper getting the better of her.

'Which way do I go?'

'You go back to wherever it was you came from, get out of my life and leave me alone.'

'No. I meant to your house. I don't know where you live.'

Sighing with exasperation and deciding it was far better to work with him rather than against him as that would facilitate her arriving home sooner and thus escaping his presence, she said, 'Turn right at the next set of traffic lights. Down two blocks then right, left, right, right.'

'Right,' he said, with a small chuckle.

Reggie rolled her eyes and stared out the window, determined not to say anything else. She'd been kidnapped and she was grumpy. Why was it Flynn seemed to bring out the worst in her?

'You always used to say I brought out the best in you,' he offered, and it was only then that Reggie realised she'd spoken out loud.

'That was before.' She shifted in her seat and stared at him. 'I know I shouldn't aggravate the designated driver but as you've basically kidnapped me, I just might.' She dragged in a breath. 'What we had all those years ago, Flynn, is over. I can learn to accept the fact that you'll be here while Geetha's on maternity leave—'

'The next six months,' he offered.

'And I can even learn to work alongside you as a professional colleague, but at no point in the scenario of the two of us working at the same hospital does it mean we're going to rekindle the relationship we had before.' She shook her finger at him to emphasise her words. 'You didn't choose me, Flynn. You broke off our engagement and within less than a fortnight were married to another woman.' Reggie crossed her arms over her chest and refused to say another word.

'Reg.' He turned right and started to slow the car.

'I told you not to call me that. I can't believe you thought you could just waltz back into my life and be so…so…familiar. We are not friends, Flynn. Far from it.'

'Reg.'

'All we are is colleagues. Nothing more. There will

be no cute looks from you, no flirting, no "Do you remember when?", no—'

'Reg.' He slowed the car to a crawl, peering through the windscreen.

'No "no patients died" type of thing. OK? We are not a couple and we never will be,' she huffed.

'Regina! Shut. Up.' He brought the car to a stop and pointed to the front windscreen. It was then she did as he'd suggested and what she saw made her eyes go wide with horror.

'That's my apartment building. My building…it's on *fire*!'

Reggie opened the door and was out of the car like a shot. 'Reg! Wait!' She heard Flynn's voice in the distance but couldn't wait. Her building was on fire. Her apartment. Her neighbours' apartments. Her neighbours.

'Melva! Melva!' she called, as she ran down the street. There were police, flashing lights and people everywhere. The firefighters were doing their job, working hard to take control of the angry orange flames that were engulfing the home where she'd managed to carve out a new life for herself.

In a state of shock she continued to call out Melva's name. Her elderly neighbour would have been getting ready for bed. What if she hadn't been able to escape? What if she was still in there!

'Whoa! Reg!' Flynn was right beside her, grabbing her arms as she barrelled headlong towards the area the police had cordoned off. 'You can't go in there.'

'But she needs me.' Reggie tried to shake loose from Flynn's grasp but he was hanging onto her with a firm grip. 'Melva!' she called again.

'Stop.' A policewoman came across and stood in Reggie's path, effectively blocking her. 'That is a burning building.'

'That's *my* building,' Reggie begged. 'Please? Melva. My neighbour—' Reggie broke off as she saw a fireman coming out of the building with a woman over his shoulder. 'Melva!' She choked on the word and it was only then she felt the soothing and strong presence of Flynn right next to her, his arm around her shoulders, not only holding her back from rushing headlong into a burning building but also providing her with strength and comfort.

'We're both qualified surgeons at Sunshine General.' His words carried authority as he spoke to the policewoman. 'As the ambulances are…' he paused for a second and listened, the sirens easily heard in the distance '…still on their way, and you have a woman there who needs medical assistance, why don't you let us help out?' As he spoke, he pulled out his hospital identification, proving he wasn't lying. The policewoman checked it thoroughly and nodded.

'What about her?' She gestured towards Reggie, who was watching the fireman gently place Melva on the ground a safe distance from the burning building. His fellow firemen were already calling for his return to the building.

'Let her treat her neighbour and she'll be fine,' Flynn said.

The policewoman seemed to dither for a second but when Flynn smiled reassuringly at her she nodded. 'All right. We're already short-staffed. Medical kits are over there next to the police cars,' she said, pointing. The policewoman's partner was already kneeling by Melva's side, pressing his fingers to her carotid pulse then shaking his head.

At her words, Flynn removed his arm from Reggie's shoulders and like a racing horse bursting from the barriers Reggie was at Melva's side like a shot.

'Melva. Melva, it's Reggie. Can you hear me?'

'You know her?' the policeman asked, moving back before Reggie could shove him out of the way. Her hands were busy, checking Melva's pulse, leaning down to see if she was still breathing.

'She's my neighbour.' Now that Reggie was actually able to be doing something, she was much calmer, just as Flynn had predicted. She glanced up to find Flynn returning with the medical kit and oxygen mask, as she continued her attempts to get a response from Melva.

'You live here?'

'Lived. Past tense.' Reggie couldn't even think about everything in her apartment that was in the process of burning. All she cared about was Melva. She kept calling to her, willing her to open her eyes. Her breathing was definitely restricted. Reggie didn't like it.

'Quick. The oxygen,' she said, holding out her hands towards Flynn.

'What about your other neighbours?' the officer asked. Reggie just wanted him to keep quiet but she also knew that he had a job to do.

'The family in number two, upstairs, are interstate. The young couple in the other upstairs apartment should still be at work.' She reached into her pocket and pulled out her cellphone, tossing it at the officer and telling him the names of her neighbours. 'Search through my directory and find their information.' Reggie turned her attention to Flynn. 'Melva's pulse is faint. Her breathing is definitely restricted. We may need to intubate. No patient response.'

No sooner had the words left her lips than Melva stopped breathing.

'She's stopped,' Flynn reported. He opened the medical kit and reached for a face shield and gloves. In another instant he had checked Melva's mouth was clear and had her head tipped back, ready to perform expired air resuscitation.

'Come on, Melva. Breathe.' Reggie's words came through gritted teeth as she counted out the breaths, readying herself in position for cardiopulmonary resuscitation. She kept counting, Flynn kept checking for a pulse.

'Come on, Melva. This is getting beyond a joke, and I'll tell you right now,' she said in time with her movements, 'you are not dying tonight. Not if I have anything to do with it.' Her words were clear and determined and filled with promise.

Flynn did another two breaths then checked for a pulse. 'It's there.' He looked over at Reggie, noting the look of relief cross her face.

'Atta girl, Melva.' She rested back on her heels for a second before helping Flynn to secure the oxygen mask over Melva's mouth and nose. The ambulance sirens had drawn closer and in another moment they were silenced, but the blue and red flashing lights filled the darkness of the night as whoever was driving came up the kerb and onto the grass, getting as close as possible to where they were treating Melva.

'I'll speak to them,' Flynn said, standing up and striding purposefully towards the paramedics.

'She has a few burns to her arms and legs,' Reggie

pointed out, and reached for the medical kit. 'Melva,' she called again, still watching the rise and fall of the other woman's chest. 'We're going to take good care of you,' she said, as the paramedics came over to give them a hand. They wrapped wet towels around the burns on Melva's arms and legs, Reggie very happy when Flynn reported that her breathing was improving.

'Do you know if she has any allergies?' Flynn asked.

'Not that I know of.'

'OK.' He spoke to one of the paramedics. 'Can you get me some midazolam so we can get Melva here ready for transfer?' He returned his attention to Melva as she started to cough a little more.

Reggie quickly hooked a stethoscope into her ears and listened to Melva's breathing. 'Still rasping. Let's give her some salbutamol via nebuliser just to open those lungs.'

'Yes, Doctor,' the paramedic replied.

'Reggie?' As Melva said her name she coughed and Reggie immediately took the other woman's hand in hers.

'Yes, it's me. I'm here. You're going to be fine.'

'So much smoke. Couldn't see.' Melva's words came out broken but there was also a hint of panic in her voice and the last thing they needed right now was for Melva's anxiety to rise.

'It's OK now. Shh. I'm here. I'll take care of you.'

'But the apartments...'

'I'll take care of it. You just relax and leave everything to me.

Flynn looked across at her. 'Reggie, if you need any help—'

'I said I'd take care of it,' Reggie returned, her words a little crisp.

'Of course.'

She frowned for a moment. Flynn? Backing down? Not insisting on being the big, strong hero, coming to the rescue of the damsel in distress? She met his gaze for a split second and saw nothing there but reassurance. Perhaps he had changed. Perhaps he was different from the way he'd been six years ago. There was truth in his eyes, as though he was desperate to let her know that he meant what he said.

Could she really trust him again? Reggie couldn't deny she was relieved he was with her, somehow empowering her with the strength and professionalism she needed to help her elderly neighbour.

Reggie pressed her fingers to Melva's pulse and was pleased to find it a little stronger than before. 'You're doing just fine, Melva.' Reggie held the other woman's hand and kissed it. 'You have an oxygen mask on so just lie still. I'm looking after you.'

'Good. Means I'll be OK.' Melva managed a weak smile beneath the mask, her eyes opening only for a second before she closed them again then started coughing.

'Relax. Breathe easy,' Reggie encouraged, and looked up to see just where Flynn was with getting that salbutamol organised. 'Flynn?' she called.

'Right here, Reg.' He was walking towards her, carrying the portable nebuliser. Soon they had Melva settled, with the salbutamol easing the pressure in her lungs as the paramedics transferred her to the stretcher.

'You'll come with me?' Melva asked, her voice still a little raspy.

'Try to keep me away,' Reggie said with a smile

as Melva was settled into the ambulance. She stopped for a moment then turned and looked at their building. Smoke was billowing out but thankfully the firefighters had managed to contain the raging flames, protecting the properties on either side. People were everywhere, being kept at a distance, more police had arrived to assist with crowd control and another fire engine was just pulling up so the men and women who had already been battling the blaze for quite some time could rest and recuperate.

She knew the drill. She'd been involved in many a rescue situation over the years but now, as she continued to watch the place she'd called home become nothing more than a wreck, she couldn't help an overwhelming sense of helplessness engulf her.

Her eyes filled with tears and although she tried to blink them away, knowing she needed to remain strong, to be there for Melva, she couldn't shift them. Sniffing, she raised a shaking hand to her lips as the scene before her blurred into a watery mess. As a tear dropped from her lashes and rolled down her cheek, she almost jumped when Flynn's warm and comforting arms drew her close.

She knew she should resist. She knew she should push him away, keep her distance from the man who had broken her heart beyond repair, but she couldn't. She wanted his comfort, needed his strength, and for the first time in years Reggie gave in to the vulnerabilities she'd successfully kept at bay for far too long.

'Oh, Flynn,' she murmured against his chest, hating herself for loving the comfort he offered. 'What am I going to do now?'

'Shh,' he crooned, resting his chin on her head and tightening his hold on her. 'We'll figure it out.'

'We?' The word was barely a whisper as she snuggled in a little closer to him, her ear pressed to his chest, and there she could hear that his heart was beating a lot faster than it should. 'We?' she asked again, a little louder, and as she edged back just a touch, lifting her head so she could look at his face, she saw in his eyes determination mixed with a healthy dose of repressed desire.

'We,' he confirmed with a definitive nod.

CHAPTER THREE

'REGGIE?'

She felt a hand on her shoulder rousing her from her light doze. Someone was gently shaking her awake, their deep voice tender and soothing.

'Reg?'

She breathed in deeply, recognising the sound of Flynn's voice. Oh, Flynn. How she'd missed him. The way he'd always held her close, supporting her, listening to her, comforting her. She'd loved the way he'd called her 'Reg', the one syllable sounding so special and unique and perfect from his lips. She sighed with happiness, letting the dream of his presence wash over her.

She remembered the first time he'd kissed her, *really* kissed her, not just a quick peck on the cheek. She'd all but melted into his arms and kissed him back with equal abandonment. Until that moment she'd never known kissing someone could feel so real, so right, so romantic.

They'd known each other for only two weeks and she'd been astounded at how his thoughts had been so aligned with hers. 'I just knew it would be perfect between us,' he'd whispered against her mouth when they'd finally come up for air. As though by unspoken mutual consent, from that moment onwards they'd been a couple. They'd strolled hand in hand along the beach at sunset, worked side by side at the hospital, gazed longingly into each other's eyes. She had accepted his words, his touch, his love, and she'd thought it would last forever.

Sadness crept into her soul and she started to rouse from the dream, wishing she had the chance to go back and rewrite her past. Oh, Flynn. Why? Why? She shifted, trying to shake off the tender hand on her shoulder…the one that was trying to wake her.

'Reg?' She heard his voice, more clearly now. She felt his breath fan her face and slowly her mind lifted itself from the fuzziness of that state between dreams and reality. Reggie opened her eyes and looked around, taking a moment to remember exactly where she was.

She was in the female ward, sitting in a chair by Melva's bedside. She'd obviously fallen asleep, the exhaustion of the day having finally caught up with her. A busy day at the hospital and then…and then the fire. The fire that had burned her apartment and all her belongings to the ground and had almost taken Melva's life. She looked at Flynn, realising he was crouched down beside her chair, his lips curved in a small smile.

'Hi, there.'

'Was I snoring?' she asked, and was delighted when his smile increased.

'Not that I can report. I'll have to check with Ayana, though,' he said, indicating where the night sister was seated at the nurses' station, writing up some paperwork.

Reggie looked back at Melva, pleased to see her friend sleeping soundly. The echo-cardiograph was still monitoring Melva's heart rate and from what Reggie

could see, everything looked to be within normal pa-
rameters.

'She's doing well,' Flynn confirmed, and stood when
Reggie eased herself out of the chair, wanting to read
Melva's latest set of observations. Feeling stiff from
sitting too long, Reggie stretched her arms up over her
head, shifting slightly from side to side as she worked
out the kinks in her back. As she lowered her arms she
glanced at Flynn, surprised to find him watching her
every move. She blushed and straightened the hem of
her knit top, which had ridden up a little.

'Er...' She cleared her throat as she tried to focus
on the information on the monitor. Come on, Reggie.
Pull yourself together. It's not as though Flynn hasn't
admired your body before. Good heavens, she used to
go swimming with him in the sea wearing a bikini.
But that had been then, when they'd been together as a
couple. This was now, when he was nothing more than
a colleague...and possibly a friend?

He had stated he was going to help her out and he'd
held her so tenderly, so carefully, so...lovingly? She
pushed the thought away and gave her thoughts a mental shake.

'All her vitals are steady,' Flynn continued. 'Her
heart is strong, the burns on her arms and legs are ban-
daged and will eventually heal,' he continued.

'And on top of all this she now has the emotional
trauma of dealing with losing her life-long possessions,
reminders of her husband and family and all those trin-
kets she's collected over the years. She shouldn't be
forced to start again, not at her age.' Reggie reached
for Melva's hand and held it in hers. 'She has been such
a good friend to me since I moved into the apartment

block. I need to do whatever I can for her…and for the other tenants.'

'The fire wasn't your fault, Reggie,' he pointed out. 'Preliminary findings show there was a fault with the wiring.'

'Then I should have been more diligent, forcing the landlord to check these things out more thoroughly.' She pressed a kiss to Melva's hand before she turned and walked to the end of the bed. 'I feel as though I've failed her. What sort of Christmas is she supposed to have now?'

Flynn put both hands on her shoulders then turned her to face him. When she didn't immediately look at him he placed his fingers gently beneath her chin and lifted it so their gazes could meet. 'It's not your fault.' His words were earnest and intent.

'But—'

'It's not your fault.' He spoke with carefulness, as though he was desperate to get the words to sink in.

'Still, there has to have been something I could have done to prev—'

He silenced her by pressing his index finger tenderly to her lips, knowing the touch would effectively silence her. He leaned in closer, bringing his mouth closer to her ear so she could hear him when he whispered clearly, *'It's not your fault.'* Then he gathered her into his arms and held her tightly. 'You're not going to do yourself any favours by playing the what-if game, Reg.'

She closed her eyes as his message finally began to penetrate through her thick skull. 'I know you want to rewind time, to do anything you can to spare Melva the emotional upheaval she's going to go through, but you can't.' His words were barely above a whisper as she once more allowed herself to rest within his arms.

How she'd missed this. Having someone with big strong arms hold her, comfort her, support her in times of need. How she'd missed Flynn. She felt so comfortable and secure in his arms that a moment later, she yawned, a big, long yawn.

'You're exhausted,' she heard him murmur, but now that she'd mentally accepted there was nothing she could have done to alter tonight's outcome of the fire, it was as though her entire body was starting to shut down.

Plus, Flynn was making it very comfortable for her to stand there, leaning into him, knowing his big, strong arms would support her and keep her safe. At this particular moment it didn't matter one jot what had happened between them all those years ago. What mattered was that Flynn was offering comfort and she was going to be selfish and accept it.

The memories from her past, the memories she'd tried so hard to push away, to ignore, to never think about again, were returning with a vengeance as she continued to lean against him. She knew he wouldn't let her fall, that he would support her, and for a wild moment she desperately wanted to go back in time. Back to when Flynn had professed his love for her. Back to a moment when her life, for the very first time, had felt…complete.

'Go back,' she mumbled into his chest, her words incoherent.

'Reggie?' Flynn eased away just slightly to look down at her, but she only seemed to snuggle in closer. Who was he to argue? He closed his eyes, allowing himself to absorb the sensation of once again having his Reg in his arms. It was clear the attraction they'd felt for each other all those years ago was still alive and well…at least, it was on his side. Could she feel it, too?

'Reggie?' He tried again and when the only answer he received was her steady and even breathing, he realised that the day had definitely taken its toll on her. Not only had she been watching over Melva for the past few hours but she'd also answered a barrage of questions from the police, providing them with whatever information she could. Thankfully, both her other neighbours had been contacted and although they were devastated at the loss of their belongings, at least none of them had lost their lives. Therefore, he wasn't the least bit surprised at Reggie being so completely wiped out that she was literally asleep on her feet.

'Come on, Reg,' he murmured, shifting her slightly in his arms so he could guide her as they walked quietly out of the ward.

'Where are we going?' she asked, half roused. He couldn't help but smile down at the gorgeous sight of her, her short, black hair sticking out a little at the sides and her eyelids half-closed.

'You need sleep,' he replied.

'Good idea. Residential wing will have a bed free.'

'Goodnight, Ayana,' Flynn called quietly as he waved to the night nurse. 'If there's any change in Melva's condition—'

'I'll call you and Reggie immediately,' Ayana promised. 'Get her to a bed, and soon, Flynn. She really is asleep on her feet, isn't she?' Ayana smiled as Reggie continued to lean against Flynn. It would be far easier for him to scoop her into his arms and carry her through the hospital but he was already mindful of the looks they were receiving with her snuggled so closely against him. The last thing he wanted was for Reggie to have to deal with a barrage of gossip on top of everything else that had happened to her.

They headed out of the ward towards the lift, Reggie more than content to let him guide her. That way she didn't have to think about anything. She couldn't remember being this exhausted since she'd been an intern, trying to cope with the all-nighters followed by a full day shift. Perhaps the trauma of losing all her possessions, of the impending frustration and stress of dealing with the insurance company, of having to go out in the morning and buy new clothes and shoes and... She didn't even own a toothbrush. Not anymore.

'And all the Christmas presents,' she groaned, her words muffled as she spoke into Flynn's chest, another layer of stress falling on her shoulders.

'What?' Flynn bent his head so he could hear her more clearly.

'I'd finished my Christmas shopping. Now it's all gone.' She wanted to cry, she wanted to scream and bellyache and wail, but she was just too exhausted.

'We'll sort it out,' Flynn promised her as they headed out into the humid December night.

'Thank you, Flynn. You always were so reliable... except, you know, when you broke my heart.'

'You're mumbling, Reg. Can't understand a word,' he told her. 'And you're starting to trip over your own feet,' she heard him say, and the next instant she felt as light as a feather, floating along in the breeze. She looped her arms around Flynn's neck and rested her head against his shoulder, only belatedly realising he'd scooped her off her feet and was carrying her, striding purposefully towards the residential wing like the gallant hero she'd always thought him to be.

'Flynn,' she sighed as her head was finally placed onto a soft pillow. She had no idea just how much time had passed and could have sworn she'd been strapped into a car at one point. Perhaps Flynn had decided to drive around to the residential wing rather than carry her the entire way.

At any rate, she was simply glad to finally be in a bed, a sheet being pulled over her, the ceiling fan whirring gently above to keep her cool throughout the night. Someone was removing her shoes and once that was done she drew her knees up and snuggled into the inviting world of dreams.

'Sleep sweet, Reg.'

Flynn's glorious deep words washed over her and then she dreamed he'd placed a kiss on her forehead. 'Mmm, Flynn. I've missed you,' she whispered.

He straightened up and stared down at the woman sleeping in his spare room. She'd missed him? Really? Was that just the exhaustion talking? Did she mean 'miss' as in she'd wanted to see him again? Because from the moment he'd seen her at the hospital the impression he'd gained had definitely been the opposite, especially as she'd spent the better part of the last week avoiding him.

With her breathing settling into an even rhythm, letting him know she was definitely sound asleep, Flynn knew he should leave yet he couldn't seem to move. Watching Reggie sleep made his heart contract with pain and pleasure as his mind was flooded with a round of what-if's.

She was the woman he'd once loved with all his heart, the woman he'd planned to marry and spend the rest of his life with, the woman who had managed to show him he was a person of worth, to accept him for exactly who he was…and then everything had exploded. He'd been weak, had allowed himself to be manipulated, and it had brought him nothing but pain and mortification.

'Not anymore.' He shook his head and exhaled heavily. When he'd accepted the job at Sunshine General, he hadn't known Reggie was working there, not until a few days before his starting date, when he'd had a meeting with Geetha to fill in the remaining paperwork.

'The staff here are very friendly, especially Reggie,' Geetha had told him after they'd finished dealing with the red tape. Flynn had literally frozen at the name.

'Reggie?' It might not be the same person, he'd rationalised, astonished to find his heartbeat had increased. The name 'Reggie' might actually be referring to a man named Reginald, not a dynamic woman called Regina who had the biggest blue eyes, fringed with dark lashes and the most encompassing laugh he'd ever heard.

'Reggie Smith, she's one of our general surgeons.' Geetha had shaken her head. 'Incredibly talented, should have been head of department years ago but instead she prefers to work as a functioning member of the team, at least that's what she tells me.'

'Reggie Smith.' Flynn had settled back in his chair, his heart racing at the thought that soon he'd see Reggie again. Was that a good thing? He'd thought about her constantly over the past six years, especially when his marriage had broken up. He'd been tempted time and time again to find her, to track her down, but what would he say to her when they met again? *I'm sorry I broke your heart. Can we try again, please, because I can't seem to get you out of my mind?*

He'd also presumed she would be happily married with a couple of children, that she'd moved on with her life…her life without him. Thoughts like that had stopped him from trying to find her. Reggie deserved the world of happiness, especially after the abominable way he'd treated her, and if she'd found that happiness with some other man, he did not want to know about it.

Now, though, not only had he been granted the opportunity to see her but to also work alongside her. She wasn't married, didn't have children, and if the way she'd just whispered his name into the pillow was any indication, perhaps there was a small spark of hope. It was clear, on his part, that the attraction he'd felt all those years ago certainly hadn't diminished. The question was, could Reggie forgive him for his past behaviour? If she couldn't, there was no hope of them moving forward together.

His phone started to ring and he quickly left the room, wondering who would be calling him at this hour of the night. Another emergency? He hoped not. He didn't want to leave Reggie alone in his town house, concerned she'd wake up and not know where she was.

He checked the caller ID and saw it was Violet. He quickly answered the call. 'Hey, Vi. Everything OK?'

'It's Ian,' she told him. 'He has a temperature. I don't know what to do. You know I fall to pieces when he gets sick.'

'What are his symptoms?' Flynn walked through to the lounge and slumped down into a comfortable chair as he listened to Violet describe five-year-old Ian's symptoms. 'It does sound like it's just a tummy bug, especially as you haven't been feeling well. You've given him paracetamol?'

'No. No. Good idea. I'll do that. Hold on. Don't hang up.'

Flynn closed his eyes, feeling strange receiving a phone call from Violet while Reggie was asleep in the next room. It was as though the two different parts of his life, family and the separate life he was trying to build, were once more colliding. He'd been given a second chance with Reggie and he wasn't going to blow this one. If she knew he was still in contact with Violet, that might jeopardise everything, and the fact that she'd just been murmuring his name in her sleep was a good sign that things *were* progressing the way he was hoping.

However, he also knew he'd have to tell her about Violet…at some point. Right now, though, he was going to do his best to keep his two very different worlds as far apart as possible. He didn't want anything jeopardising the chance that he and Reggie might be able to pick up where they'd left off six years ago. Now, that certainly would be something to dream about.

Reggie opened her eyes, stretching her arms above her head. She'd had a wonderful sleep but a moment later, as her mind began to wake up, she remembered the events of yesterday evening. Her apartment had burned down.

'Melva!' She sat bolt upright in the bed, thinking fast. She'd get out of bed and go check on Melva, then start figuring out what to do next. No doubt she'd have to go shopping as the clothes on her back were literally the only clothes she had. She could borrow some from Mackenzie and…

She frowned, looking around the room, taking in her surroundings. This wasn't a tiny room in the residential wing. 'Where am I?' As she continued to inspect the room, she realised she was in Sunainah's spare room… or what had previously been Sunainah's spare room. Her friend had moved out of this town house when she'd married Elliot. The town house had been vacant since then and listed on the hospital's bulletin board. Her eyes widened as realisation dawned. 'Oh, no!'

Reggie flicked back the covers and checked the floor for her shoes, quickly slipping her feet into them as she tried to piece together what she could remember of last night's events *after* the fire.

She'd been at Melva's bedside. Sunainah, Mackenzie and Bergan had all come to find her once they'd heard the news—her friends were always there when she needed their support. Then, being the stubborn woman she was, she'd refused to leave Melva's side until her neighbour had been settled in the ward. She could remember sitting by Melva's bed…then…she'd fallen asleep. Someone had woken her up and—

'Flynn!'

Reggie shot to her feet and opened the spare-room door, pushing her hands through her hair as she walked through the lower part of the town house towards the kitchen—Flynn's kitchen. She was in Flynn Jamieson's town house and by the scents of coffee and pancakes wafting from the kitchen it appeared he was making breakfast.

Sure enough, she found him standing at the stove,

expertly flipping pancakes in the air and catching them in the frying pan. 'Flynn?'

'Ah.' He turned and looked at her over his shoulder, his smile bright and welcoming. 'Good morning, Reggie.' He indicated the table, which was set with plates, knives and forks, a glass of juice and a bottle of maple syrup in the middle. 'Take a seat and I'll bring you your breakfast.'

'You know how to cook now?' Still trying to wrap her head around this surreal moment, of having Flynn cook breakfast for her, she moved towards the table and dropped down into the chair, glad of its support. 'Back in the Caribbean you weren't sure how to boil water.'

He grinned at her. 'I wasn't *that* bad but, yes, during my time there I realised a lot of things about myself and how I needed to become more self-sufficient.' He checked the pancake again. 'Almost done.'

'You always were full of surprises,' Reggie murmured, her tone indicating that some of those 'surprises' hadn't always been good ones.

Flynn's answer was to wink at her, and her insides instantly flooded with a tingling warmth. Why, oh, why couldn't she be immune to his charm? She immediately looked away from him and stared at the empty plate in front of her, trying to get her thought processes jump-started.

'I've called the hospital,' Flynn said a moment later, 'and been informed that Melva has slept peacefully throughout the night and was sitting up, drinking a cup of tea.'

Reggie lifted her head and sighed with relief. 'That's great news. Thanks for the update.'

'You're welcome. Coffee?'

'Uh…most definitely, please.' She frowned as she watched him pour her a cup of coffee, not adding any milk or sugar before placing it on the table before her.

'You still take it black, right? No sugar?'

'Correct.'

'That's because you're sweet enough.' He smiled brightly. 'Isn't that what you always used to say?'

'Flynn, stop it.'

'Stop what?'

'Trying to take us down memory lane.' She spread her arms wide. 'What are you doing here?'

He stared at her as though she'd gone completely loopy. 'Did you hit your head last night? Are you feeling all right?'

'Flynn,' she growled, her teeth gritted, her tone filled with warning. He had the audacity to laugh.

'Reg, I'm not exactly sure what you mean.'

'Here. In *this* particular town house.'

'It was listed on the bulletin—'

'I know. I know it was listed but why did *you*, of all people, have to move in?'

'I don't follow.'

'Sunainah used to live here and Richard lived here before her and before that Richard's parents and before that…I don't have a clue, but the point is, you're living slap bang in the middle of my three closest friends.'

'And the problem with that is…?' he asked, carrying the frying pan towards her and placing a perfectly round, perfectly cooked pancake onto her plate.

'Thank you,' she said politely. 'It's just odd that *you*, the man I was once going to marry, is living *here*. Among my friends. In the town house they wanted me to move into. Joining the cul-de-sac crew.'

'There's a crew?' His eyes were alive with delight at this news. 'Do they get together for movie nights and dinners?'

'Flynn, be serious.'

'I am. Do you know how much I've always wanted to be accepted as just part of a crew, part of a team?'

That stopped her. 'You have?' She was surprised at his words and stared at him for a moment, realising there was still so much she didn't know about him.

'Anyway, you were saying your friends wanted you to move in here?'

'Yes, but I was more than happy where I…was.' Reggie sighed as the weight of the previous evening's events fell on her shoulders like a tonne of bricks. She slumped forward and buried her head in her hands, not even the delicious scent of the pancakes able to help in this situation.

Flynn put the frying pan back on the stove top, adding more mixture before coming over, placing his hands on her shoulders and gently starting to massage them. 'I'm sorry your place burnt down, Reg.' His words were simple, effective, perfect.

'So am I,' she said, leaning back a little to grant him more access to her neck, her eyes closing at the touch of his hands. How did he still manage to know exactly what she needed? Straightforward words and a bit of support. No flowery sentiments, no immediate solutions to problems. Just support. That was all she needed at this moment and he was offering it in a caring and gentle manner.

'You still have magic hands,' she sighed after a few minutes. 'And thank you for the pancakes. They're my favourite.'

'I remember.'

'They do make me happy, Flynn, I just can't…'

'You can't show it the way you usually do. The ever optimistic, happy and bubbly Reggie. I get it.'

'Get what?'

'With me, everything's different. You think there's too much water under the bridge between us. That it would be impossible for things to move forward between us.' He nodded. 'I understand.'

'Do you?' Did he really understand just how much he'd hurt her all those years ago?

'I might even be so bold as to declare that I understand *you*, Reggie.'

She laughed without humour. 'I've changed.' She shifted a little in her chair, acutely aware of the way he was making her feel with his hands on her shoulders, massaging gently. The air between them seemed to be charged with unspoken conversations, things they should have said but hadn't…things they shouldn't have said but had.

'Everyone changes, Reg, but hopefully not in essentials,' he offered, releasing her shoulders. 'I think you're still the same Reggie, wanting to help others, smiling, laughing, spreading sunshine wherever possible. I watched you do that when we were together in Sint Maarten, amazed and in awe of your ability and—' He dropped his hands and quickly pulled out the chair next to her and sat down, facing her, his expression determined. 'I'd like to help, Reggie. I'd like to take a leaf out of your book and spread a little sunshine.'

'Wha—? Flynn?' She closed her eyes and shook her head for a moment. 'I don't understand.'

'I want to help you and your friends. I can help by

relocating Melva and your other neighbours.' His words were intense and earnest. 'And…' he held up a hand '…before you say I'm doing what all wealthy people do and throwing money at the problem, I want you to know that's not entirely true. My intentions are pure and honourable. Even if these people weren't your friends, even if they were complete strangers, if I'd heard about their hardship, I would still have wanted to help.'

Reggie thought on his words for a moment, seeing the truth in his eyes. He seemed so completely animated at the idea, his eyes twinkling with anticipatory delight. She wished he wouldn't look at her that way because right now he was far too handsome for his own good and that simply made it all the more difficult for her to keep her distance. Besides, who was she to stop him from helping others? 'I think that would be a nice thing to do, Flynn. Thank you.'

'So you'll accept my help?'

'Yes. I think my neighbours and I would be very grateful for your help, especially if you can help with relocation. Trying to find a new place to live this close to Christmas? It really *would* take a Christmas miracle to pull it off.'

'Then be prepared for a miracle.' He stood and returned to the stove, expertly flipping the pancake. 'Because I already have a plan with regard to temporary accommodation for you and your neighbours.'

'You do?'

'Yes. I've had a look online and there's a small apartment complex, near shops and public transport, with three partially furnished vacant apartments.'

'Three?'

'Yes. One for Melva, once she's ready to leave hospital, and the other two for your other neighbours.'

'What about me?' she asked, her tone a little indignant.

'Ah. Now, for you I have the perfect place. It's not going to be too far from Melva and the others, it's close to the hospital, it's furnished and the landlord has said you can move in today.'

'Today? It sounds like a miracle. Where is this place?'

Flynn winked at her and spread his arms wide. 'It's here. You're going to live with me!'

CHAPTER FOUR

'WHAT?'

Reggie stared at him as though he'd grown another head but Flynn either didn't notice or didn't care. '*Live*... with you?' Her heart was pounding wildly in her chest at the mere thought of living with Flynn, of sharing the same intimate space as him, of seeing him last thing at night and first thing in the morning. She was glad she was sitting down as her entire body had turned into a trembling mass of jelly.

'Why not? It makes perfect sense. I have a spare room and you'll have sole use of the bathroom. I can use the *en suite* and we work at the same hospital.' He shrugged one shoulder. 'It makes perfect sense.'

'And you're sure this other place you've found only has three free apartments?'

He smiled and nodded as though humouring an indulgent child. 'Yes, Reg.'

Could he hear the hysteria in her voice, see the panic in her eyes? She was positive he could from the way he was still trying to sell her on the idea. 'So what do you say, new roomie? Let's start the day with a healthy...' he stopped and looked down at the pancakes '...or sort of healthy breakfast.'

Reggie continued to gape at him, her mouth hanging open as he plated up his pancake and carried it to the table. Before he sat down, he removed bowls of fresh strawberries and whipped cream from the fridge, placing them on the table next to the maple syrup. As far as he was concerned, this was a done deal. She had no say in it and anger started to replace her earlier incredulity.

'I am not moving in here.' She enunciated each word crisply.

He considered her words for a moment then asked logically, 'So where will you go?' He added strawberries, cream and syrup to his pancake, behaving as though this was just another ordinary breakfast conversation.

'I'll go to a hotel for a while.'

'And waste your money when there's a perfectly good room—free of charge—here for you? Until the insurance money comes in, you're better off using your funds to buy clothes and shampoo and other essentials you'll need, rather than having to pay for accommodation.' His words were matter-of-fact and logical and she hated him for them.

She sighed again, her frustration clear. Didn't he realise that with what had happened between them, with the way he'd taken her to the highest of highs when he'd confessed his love and proposed to her then plummeted her to the lowest of lows less than twenty-four hours later when he'd broken her heart by cancelling their engagement, that there was no way she could move in with him?

'Mmm, smells good.' He pointed to her plate. 'Come on, Reg. Eat up. We're due at the hospital in an hour's time.'

'What?' She blinked at him in astonishment. 'You're not even going to suggest I take the day off? That given the circumstances of my recent emotional trauma, of losing practically everything I own, except for my laptop, my phone and the clothes on my back, I shouldn't stay in bed and rest?'

'I know you, remember.' He leaned over and spooned some strawberries onto her pancake. 'Regardless of what may or may not be happening in your life, the last thing you would ever do is let your patients down. You're not about to cancel a fully booked outpatient clinic because of personal reasons. You and I both know that being with your patients, helping them out and making their lives just that little bit easier, is going to be the best medicine to take your mind off things…at least, for a little while.'

She frowned at him. He did know her, at least on some levels. On other levels…she'd kept a lot hidden from him, previously rationalising that they had a lifetime together to discover all there was to know about each other.

'True. Working will help me to process everything that's happened,' she rationalised, including Flynn's offer for her to stay with him. 'Working will keep my mind focused.' She would go to work, see her patients, help people out, spread a little sunshine, as Flynn had termed it, and then, she was sure, life would seem a little clearer. At least, so she hoped. She looked down at her pancakes and breathed in appreciatively. 'These do smell good.'

'They taste good, too.' He ate another mouthful and winked at her, the action causing Reggie's insides to start fluttering. Why was it that one simple look from him, whether it was a wink or a smile or one of his long stares across a crowded room, made her feel so… special, so unique, so feminine? Flynn had always had been able to turn her insides to mush, to make her want to fan her face because her cheeks were tinged with heat from excited embarrassment. Now was no exception and it was far easier to concentrate on eating than trying to avoid his hypnotic gaze.

She really had no intention of permanently staying here with him because even the thought of living under the same roof as Flynn set her entire body on fire. The man was too dangerous at the best of times but to be around him both at work and at home, no doubt dreaming about him whilst she slept, would make it nigh on impossible for her to keep her emotions in check.

Still, his offer did solve her immediate problem so for the moment she would just let everything roll. She would have breakfast and a shower, mentally and figuratively washing the grime of yesterday away before popping over to Mackenzie's to borrow some clean clothes. She was glad he'd mentioned that he'd use the en suite because even thinking about standing naked beneath Flynn's shower, with him in the same house, made her feel all flushed with self-consciousness. Perhaps it would be better to just go to Mackenzie's and shower there.

After eating half of her pancake and enjoying her coffee, she was about to tell him of her plans when he beat her to it.

'I need to dash to the shops before we head to the hospital so why don't you make free use of the place? Wash away all the bad things that happened yesterday and reconnect with your usual optimistic self?' He smiled encouragingly as he said the words. 'Oh, and I contacted Mackenzie last night and she's brought over some clothes for you. They're in the drawers and the cupboard in the spare room—or *your* room as it now is.'

'You…contacted Macken—' She stopped and shook her head, unable to believe how thoughtful he'd been. 'It would have been very late.'

'Your friends love you, Reg.' He spoke softly and with sincerity. 'They don't care what time of day or night it is, they're there for you. That type of friendship is rare and incredibly special.' He looked down at his plate for a moment before meeting her gaze once more. 'Only a fool would throw away such a thing.'

His words were slightly pointed and she wondered whether he was calling himself a fool. Was he admitting that he'd made a mistake all those years ago? Was he saying he wanted to reinstate himself into her friendship circle? Was he a friend who…loved her?

Reggie found it difficult to look away. There, seated opposite her, was the man who had always been in perfect control. He'd been immaculately groomed and dressed from the first day they'd met in Sint Maarten. Being raised in a wealthy, controlled environment where most decisions had been pre-set for him had been something he hadn't even thought of rebelling against until he'd met her. He'd told her she'd liberated him, shown him a different side to life, and that his love was hers forever. And she'd stupidly believed him. She should be wary not to make the same mistakes twice.

She tried to swallow but found her throat exceedingly dry. Reaching for her orange juice, she was surprised to find her hand trembling a little. Still, drinking the cool, refreshing liquid helped to break the intense moment.

'Had enough?' he asked, pointing to her plate and breaking the moment. She nodded quickly, not trusting her voice to work. Flynn stood and quickly cleared the table. She watched him for a few minutes as he moved comfortably around the kitchen. He had such swift and defined movements, those broad shoulders of his looking firm and in control, the material from his crisp, white shirt pulling tautly across his triceps.

Reggie breathed out slowly, her gaze hungrily taking in every nuance of the man. She swallowed and cleared her throat, and when he looked her way, she realised she quickly looked away. 'Er…' She racked her sluggish mind for something to say. 'Breakfast was delicious. Whoever taught you to cook did a good job.'

'That would have been my cooking teacher at the community centre.' His tone dipped a little as he spoke, his eyebrows raised in silent question, his eyes letting her know he'd been well aware of her visual caresses.

Reggie frowned and looked away. 'Not your wife?'

'My ex-wife,' he replied pointedly, then shook his head. 'She had no idea how to cook either. One of my patients put me onto the class and the next thing I knew I was learning how to make a beef Wellington.'

'You can do a beef Wellington? I can't even do that.'

He grinned. 'Then I shall have to make you one.' He gave the countertops a final wipe. 'Perhaps there are quite a few things you don't realise about me.' Like how he was determined to show her he'd changed, that he was willing to make amends for the way he'd treated her all those years ago, like how he was almost desperate for her forgiveness.

'Perhaps,' she said, surprised at the huskiness in her voice. What was it about this man that set her alight so instantly? They'd met, they'd worked together, they'd tried to fight the natural attraction that had sprung up between them but had failed. Flynn had confessed that perhaps it was a good thing, perhaps the mutual chemistry they felt for each other was one of those rare gifts that shouldn't be ignored, so they hadn't bothered to try ignoring it at all and thus had begun the happiest, most wonderful weeks of Reggie's life. Flynn holding her. Flynn laughing with her. Flynn kissing her.

Six weeks. They'd known each other for just six weeks. Friendly colleagues for two weeks, dating for two more and then falling in love for two blissful weeks. So fast, so quick, so incredibly perfect.

As he stared back at her from the other side of the kitchen, she really felt powerless to look away, as though the past and the present were colliding and both of them could sense it. When her cellphone rang, she almost jumped out of her skin. Flynn chuckled before reaching across to the bench where he'd obviously put it last night. He'd even plugged it in to recharge the battery. How thoughtful. She frowned for a moment. Had he been this thoughtful six years ago?

'Mackenzie,' he remarked, looking at the picture of her friend that had come up on the display.

'Oh…uh…thanks.' Reggie rose from her chair and accepted the phone, taking it into the spare room so she could have some privacy. 'Mackenzie?'

'How are you doing this morning?'

'I'm at Flynn's place!' She leaned back against the door, ensuring it was closed. 'I must have been so tired he brought me home with him and put me to bed!' Her words were half whispered, half squeaked as she spoke at the speed of light.

'I know.' Mackenzie chuckled.

'Oh, of course you do. You came over and helped him by delivering some clothes! Why didn't you wake me up?'

'Not on your life, Reggie. You needed sleep.' Mackenzie said in her best motherly voice. 'Flynn sent me, Bergan and Sunainah a text message telling us you were staying with him. I think it's a great idea.'

'But he doesn't just want me to stay for last night, he wants me to *move in with him*.'

'I know.'

'Do you know everything? Does everyone else know what's going on in my life except me?'

'It's not like that, Reggie.'

'And I'll bet you all think this is a good idea? Are you insane? This is *Flynn* we're talking about. The man who broke my heart into tiny little pieces and scattered them to the wind.'

'I remember.'

'I cried on your shoulder, I ate too much ice cream, I went over and over everything he'd ever said to me, trying to figure out what I'd done wrong to chase him away.'

'I remember.'

'I talked about him ad nauseam, I drove you insane. I told you time and time again that I was over him but I was just kidding myself and then, when I finally *did* get over him and moved on with my life, he swaggers back in and *takes over*.'

'He's not taking over. He's only trying to be nice and helpful, especially as since it's Christmas the majority of hotels are already booked up. Add to that the fact that Bergan doesn't have room because Richard's parents are coming home for Christmas, Sunainah's place is full because she married into a ready-made family and I have one of John's sisters and her family arriving the day after tomorrow.'

Reggie slid down the door, crumpling into a heap on the carpet, realising the truth of what Mackenzie was saying. 'I'd forgotten all that.'

'Not surprising. Look, honey, I'm not trying to make light of you losing everything in the fire, it's completely devastating and it will take a while for you to process things, both with the mounds of insurance paperwork and on an emotional level, but staying at Flynn's keeps you close to us, to *your* family, and right now you need to be surrounded by family. We're all here for you and we'll do whatever we can to help—and so will Flynn,' she added. 'He's a good guy, Reggie, and no matter what happened between the two of you all those years ago, you know, deep down inside, that it's true.'

'It's not a question of whether he's good or not, Mackenzie, it's a question of whether or not I can resist him,' Reggie blurted.

'Oh.' Mackenzie said the word slowly as though realisation was just dawning. 'Ah. Yes. I hadn't thought of things from that angle, just the logistics of your present predicament.'

'Well, start thinking that way. I can't stay here with Flynn. I can't stop staring at him, remembering how it felt to be held by him, to be kissed by him, to be in love with him.' She closed her eyes, the pain from her past beginning to return. 'He hurt me, Mackenzie, and, yes, it's all in the past, but what if I allow myself to get close to him and he hurts me *again*?'

'What if he doesn't? Reggie, the one thing I remember you telling me a few years after you'd broken up was that you thought Flynn had never really opened up to you, that the attraction between you two had happened so fast—'

'And the break-up even faster,' Reggie put in.

'That at times you wondered if you ever really knew him. Plus,' Mackenzie continued before Reggie could say another word, 'there was also a lot about your past that you never told him.'

Reggie opened her eyes and looked at the blank mushroom-coloured wall opposite her. 'True.'

'Maybe this is the chance to rectify that.'

'What point is there in opening up to him now? Rehashing the wounds of my past?'

'Call it finishing unfinished business. You always wondered how Flynn would react once he learned who you really were. Now is your chance. Who knows? It might be cathartic. Once he knows the truth of your past, if he reacts the way you always thought he would—'

'By rejecting me, like everyone else from that world,' she interrupted again.

'Then it might help you get him out of your system once and for all. Then you can really move forward with your life.'

'I have moved forward,' Reggie declared, not wanting to open the box she'd hidden in the back of her mind, the one she'd marked 'Do Not Open'. 'I've changed a lot. I'm happier than I used to be. I've put myself out there. I've dated other men and—'

'And secretly used Flynn as your yardstick the entire time. No man was ever good enough. Or, on the flip side, you'd end up solving your date's problems and helping them get back together with their old girlfriends.' It was Mackenzie's turn to interrupt. 'Think about it, Reggie. You and Flynn have unfinished business. Talk to him. You might be surprised at what you discover.'

Reggie pondered Mackenzie's words for a moment, realising there was a hint of common sense in them. 'I didn't know he could cook and those pancakes were delicious.'

'There you go, then. Plus, if you think about it, with the way Christmas tends to get hectic in surgical theatres, you'll probably be spending most of your time at the hospital, rather than catching up on sleep at Flynn's place.'

'It does get busy.'

'Then after Christmas you'll have plenty of time to look around and find somewhere to live that suits your needs, and once the insurance money comes in, I'll gladly volunteer to go furniture shopping with you.'

'Yeah.' Reggie sat up a little straighter, her confidence beginning to return. 'I don't need to stay here forever, just the next few weeks.' She thought it through rationally. 'And I do spend a lot of time at the hospital over Christmas. I really wouldn't be here all that much.'

'See?'

'And it was very nice of him to offer.'

'He's a nice man and, if you let yourself admit it, I think you'll see he's also a good friend.'

'Friend?' She tilted her head to the side and considered the word. 'I guess I've never really thought about Flynn that way, as a friend. It was so powerful and intense between us we didn't really have the opportunity to truly become friends.'

'So you'll stay?'

'You know…' Reggie levered herself up off the floor '…I think I will.'

'Yay! A temporary member of the cul-de-sac crew.'

Reggie laughed at Mackenzie's words, feeling a return of her usual optimistic self. 'I can already hear your thoughts, Kenz. Dinner parties, games nights and Christmas parties.'

'You know me too well, Reggie.' Mackenzie laughed along with her friend. 'Feel better?'

'I do. I really do, which, given I've lost practically everything, is not a bad feeling to be having.'

'Good. Oh. I've gotta go. Ruthie's just woken up.'

'Right-oh. I'll talk to you later.'

'You know it, cul-de-sac crew member!'

Reggie was still smiling as she entered the bathroom, finding a set of towels waiting there for her along with a fresh bar of soap. 'How thoughtful.' And he really was, she realised. Taking care of her last night, making her breakfast this morning and offering to help relocate her neighbours. 'Friends,' she repeated to herself as she stepped beneath the soothing spray of the shower. 'I can be friends with Flynn.' She was proud of the conviction in her words.

By the time he returned from wherever he'd had to go, Reggie was showered and dressed in the borrowed clothes.

'Wow.' Flynn's eyebrows shot up as he saw her standing there dressed in a navy skirt, white shirt and navy jacket. Her short feathered black hair was still drying and her face was clear and fresh and devoid of make-up…and she looked incredibly beautiful. 'You look—'

'Like Mackenzie?' Reggie shook her head and looked

down at the demure clothes in disgust. 'No colour. No vibrance. No pizazz.' She snapped her fingers as she spoke, which only made Flynn laugh as he carried the shopping bags through to the kitchen. He dumped them on the table before turning to look at her once more.

'I mean, I love her and everything and I really do appreciate the loan of the clothes but we have absolutely nothing in common as far as how we dress,' she continued as she followed him.

'It's true that you prefer to wear bright colours, sometimes even mixing and matching different print materials that ordinarily should *never* go together but somehow look completely perfect on you.'

Perfect? She brushed the thought aside. 'You're a textile expert, eh? Now, *that* I definitely didn't know. Please, continue, oh, wise fashionista.'

Flynn's eyes flashed with repressed humour and, while keeping a straight face, he slowly walked around her, murmuring and nodding as though deep in thought. 'Yes. Yes. I can see what you mean. It *is* rather conservative for the likes of Ms Regina Smith, General Surgeon Extraordinaire, but I think I can solve the dilemma quite easily.'

'You can?' She couldn't help the way she felt so incredibly self-conscious with him walking around her, looking her up and down, and although she knew they were only pretending, somehow his visual inspection had become more of an intimate caress. She fought against the sensation, determined not to spoil this lighthearted moment. They'd always been able to joke together, to tease each other in a good-natured way, and now that it was happening again she started to realise just how much she'd missed him.

'Oh, yes, indeedy I can.' He crossed to the bags he'd placed on the table and reached inside, pulling out a small white box. He held it out to her.

'What's this?' she asked.

'Open it.'

Dropping all pretence, Reggie accepted the gift box with surprise. It wasn't tied or secured in any way and after she gently eased the lid off she saw white tissue paper. She glanced at Flynn, who only nodded with encouragement. She moved the folded tissue paper aside to reveal a bright and beautiful Christmas-patterned silk scarf.

'Oh!' She stared at it in astonishment for a moment before carefully pulling it from the box. Flynn instantly took the box from her hands as she ran the silken threads through her fingers. 'Flynn. It's...' she met his gaze '...lovely.' To her astonishment, she felt tears begin to gather behind her eyes and she quickly looked away, desperate to pull herself together and gain some sort of control over her emotions. Always difficult when Flynn was so close.

'I thought you might need a bit of colour in your life, particularly this morning, and I couldn't go past the bright Christmas theme.'

'It's perfect. Thank you.' Reggie continued to sift the scarf through her fingers as she tried to ignore the lump in her throat. Then, out of nowhere, logical thought seemed to click in and she looked at him, angling her head to the side, a slight frown marring her brow. 'Wait a moment. It's not even eight o'clock in the morning. How did you manage to buy this when the shops aren't even open?'

Flynn shrugged. 'I know a guy.'

'Of course you do.' Reggie shook her head, remembering how easily things came to wealthy people. It annoyed her that the knowledge put a dampener on what was yet another thoughtful gesture from Flynn. He'd gone out of his way to do something nice for her and she shouldn't care about the logistics. Deciding to ignore it, she tied the scarf around her neck, the bright reds and greens instantly bringing more colour to her outfit.

'Definitely perfect.' Flynn stepped forward and fixed the back of her collar before bringing his fingers to his lips and blowing a kiss into the air. 'Very festive. The fashionista has done it again.' He raised one arm in the air with a flourish.

Reggie's previous annoyance instantly fled in light of his antics and she laughed. She'd always believed that if a person didn't want to be in a bad mood, they could simply decide not to be, that they had the power over their own emotions to change the way they were feeling, and that was exactly what she was going to do right now. She wasn't going to dwell on the fact that Flynn came from money, that he'd lived a pampered life, that his family's wealth had been one of the reasons for him breaking their engagement.

No. She was going to step forth into her new life. The life where she was Flynn's housemate for the next few weeks. The life where she had the opportunity to buy new things, to start afresh. The life where that fresh new start might even include Flynn.

CHAPTER FIVE

REGGIE TOLD HERSELF she didn't feel self-conscious driving to work with her new housemate, that she didn't care if people saw them pull into the doctors' car park together or that they walked side by side into the hospital and onto the ward for the early morning round. She and Flynn were friends and colleagues and it wasn't uncommon for friends and colleagues to carpool. So many people working here did it. Being with Flynn, constantly, was nothing to be remarked on.

'Whoa, Reggie,' Ingrid, the general surgical registrar, commented quietly as they waited in the nurses' station for the rest of the ward-round participants to arrive. 'Did I just see you arriving at work with Dr Gorgeous Legs?'

Reggie couldn't help but grin widely at the nickname. 'Dr Gorgeous Legs?' she asked with a hint of incredulity.

'Sure. Nice long legs that lead up to a firm torso and a perfectly handsome face.' Ingrid eyed Flynn as she spoke.

'You're almost licking your lips.'

'Who could blame me?' Ingrid sighed then looked

pointedly at Reggie. 'So give. How did you score a lift with him?'

'My car's still being fixed at the garage, you know, after those joyriders smashed into it the other week.' She shook her head innocently, hoping to change the subject. 'There it was. Legally parked on the side of the road while I did my grocery shopping and, wham— the next minute it was destroyed as they smashed fair into it. Still, at least it can be repaired. After the fire and all last night, the last thing I would have wanted was to have to buy a new c—'

'Yes, yes. I'm sorry about your car and your apartment.' Ingrid impatiently waved her words away. 'That doesn't explain how Gorgeous Legs gave you a lift.'

'Oh. That's easy. Flynn and I are old friends.' Reggie said the words as matter-of-factly as possible, picking up a pen and pretending to study that day's ward-round sheet with great interest. Ingrid wasn't being sidetracked or fooled by Reggie's faked nonchalance.

Ingrid's eye brows almost hit her hairline. 'Really?' There was an insinuation in Ingrid's very interested tone and Reggie was sorely tempted to spin her a yarn, to say that they were actually a long-lost brother and sister, separated at birth. Or that Flynn had saved her life by donating a kidney. Flippant and funny. Anything to hide her true self behind a mask of bright happiness, but as she looked over to where Flynn was chatting with a heavily pregnant Geetha, who was doing her final ward round before handing over her patients to Flynn, Reggie realised that he deserved better.

'We worked together during our final year of general surgical training.'

'Oh.' Ingrid was clearly disappointed with her answer and as Geetha was calling the ward round to order, there was no time for the registrar to say anything else. Throughout the round Reggie frequently found herself standing beside Flynn, remembering past ward rounds they'd conducted together in that small Caribbean hospital.

'Do you remember the first time we did a ward round together?' he asked her as they walked towards the cafeteria to grab a quick coffee before their clinic started.

Reggie smiled. 'You were dressed in a three-piece suit.'

'You wore a bright yellow sundress.'

'We were working in the Caribbean, Flynn. It's hot there.'

'It was practically see-through, Reg. Gave my heart a mighty big flutter.'

She grinned at his words, hearing the teasing note. 'Really?'

'I'd been working in the UK, where it had been freezing cold and raining, before catching my flight. I literally got off the plane in the Caribbean, raced to the hospital and arrived three minutes before the ward round started. You were the first person I saw and you were…a vision of loveliness.'

'Oh.' She could feel her cheeks beginning to suffuse with colour at his sweet words.

'For a moment I thought I was hallucinating.'

'Really? You looked very uncomfortable.' She laughed nervously, trying to disguise the fact that his words had affected her. He'd really been that instantly attracted to her? She couldn't remember him telling her that. She gazed up at him, their eyes locking, silently communicating. The moment between them was starting to stretch, starting to change, starting to become more intense than she was ready for. She needed to lighten the mood somehow.

'I was.'

'But you were determined not to show it.'

'I was exceedingly stubborn back then.'

'Yes. Yes, you were.' As they stood in the cafeteria line, she smiled up at him. 'And very stiff and rigid.' She picked up his arm and gave it a shake. 'You're much more loosey-goosey now.'

'Loosey-goosey?' Flynn chuckled as he reached out with his free hand and straightened the bright Christmas scarf around her neck. He exhaled slowly as Reggie released his arm, their fingers brushing lightly, almost caressing. The smile started to disappear from his mouth as he continued to gently tug and pull the scarf, smoothing it with his fingers.

'All fixed, Mr Fashionista?'

It was the sound of her voice, a little softer, a little huskier than normal, that made him shift his gaze to encompass her. 'Yes,' he replied softly. 'Perfect. As usual.'

'Perfect?' There was that word again and Reggie cleared her throat, desperate to try and keep their previous light-hearted banter in her words.

'As usual,' he repeated, his intense gaze penetrating deeply into her soul.

'You thought I was perfect?' The words were barely a whisper and for a moment she wasn't even sure she'd spoken until he nodded, the movement small but definite.

'Always.'

'Oh.'

'Are you two moving forward in the line or do you

mind if I cut in front of you?' the impatient male nurse said from behind them.

'Er…' Reggie blinked, looking away from Flynn, unable to believe she'd been standing in the busy hospital cafeteria line just staring at him. Her only saving grace was that he'd been staring back at her. Flynn stepped aside and gestured for the nurse to precede them.

'We're not in as much of a rush as you. Please,' he offered politely. The nurse rolled his eyes before walking between them and advancing before them in the line.

'You really are more…I don't know.' Reggie shrugged her shoulders and gave him a quirky smile. 'Relaxed, I guess, is the best word to describe you.'

'Plus, I'm not wearing a three-piece suit.'

'True,' she said, indicating his navy trousers, white shirt and tie, which had a parachuting Santa Claus on it. 'Very loosey-goosey.'

'And…' he remarked, picking up the end of his tie and pressing it.

A moment later Reggie heard 'Jingle Bells' playing in an electronic, tinny way. It lasted for a whole ten seconds and she couldn't help but giggle.

'Your tie plays "Jingle Bells"?' She was amused but also pleasantly surprised. When they'd first met all those years ago he would never have worn anything like this.

'Yes.'

'Your tie plays "Jingle Bells" and you're only showing me this *now*.'

Flynn grinned widely as they edged forward in the line. 'I knew if I'd shown you before ward round you would have wanted to play it for every patient and ward round would have taken way too long.'

'That's exactly what I would have wanted to do.' She pushed a hand through her hair and shook her head in stunned amazement.

'I know you, Reggie.'

'So you keep reminding me.'

As she said the words she felt the smile begin to slip because there was still so much he *didn't* know. How would Flynn react when he found out about her past, about what had happened to her, what she'd lived through? She'd managed to hide it from him before but would it make any difference now to their burgeoning relationship?

After the way they'd just openly stared at each other, it was clear the attraction was alive and well and yet she had no real idea what she felt for him, apart from enjoying his company, and right at this moment she wasn't sure she was ready for that to end. Flynn made her feel special and pretty and feminine and no other man had ever been able to achieve all three…and most certainly not with a simple lift of an eyebrow.

They ordered their coffees, Flynn paying for them before she could pull her money from her pocket, and after thanking him, something she seemed to be doing a lot of lately, they headed to Outpatients.

'Now you're both late?' Clara said as they walked in together. She pointed to the different piles of case notes waiting for them both. They grinned at the outpatient clerk. 'One day I'd love it if clinic could actually start on time,' Clara said pointedly.

'We'll try and make it a Christmas miracle,' Reggie promised as she scooped up the notes, ensuring she didn't spill her coffee in the process.

'I'll believe it when I see it,' Clara joked, smiling and shaking her head in bemusement.

Today Reggie was in no hurry to avoid Flynn. Instead, she was delighted every time they met in the corridor or headed out to call in a patient at the same time. It was as they were almost finished with clinic that she received a call from Bergan in Accident and Emergency.

'Reggie? I need you.'

'OK. Can you give me fifteen minutes or—?'

'Now,' Bergan interrupted, and before she rang off she added as an afterthought, 'And bring Flynn. I need him, too.'

'OK.' Reggie hung up and headed out into the corridor. Instead of calling in her last patient, she knocked on Flynn's consulting-room door. They'd have to leave it to Ingrid to finish up with the clinic list but, thankfully, there were only two or three patients left to go.

'Yes?' he called, and when she entered it was to find him and one of the clinic nurses helping their elderly female patient to her feet, the nurse ensuring the woman's walking frame was stable. 'Ah, Dr Smith. Good timing. Could you hold the door for Mrs Baladucci, please?'

'Certainly.' Reggie held the door as the nurse and Mrs Baladucci exited the consulting room, then she turned to face Flynn, who was quickly writing up the case notes before closing them and adding them to the 'completed' pile.

'Let me guess. Emergency?' Flynn asked.

'How did you know?' She stared at him for a moment before shaking her head in astonishment.

'You have a…certain look in your eyes and around the corners of your mouth whenever there's an unknown medical problem.'

'I do?' Reggie touched her fingers to the corners of her mouth, feeling a little self-conscious.

'I know you.'

'Oh, will you stop saying that? Please?' She spread her arms wide. 'There's actually quite a lot you don't know about me, Flynn. Yes, you knew me six years ago and, yes, we were very close and, no, I may not have changed in essentials, but will you stop constantly pointing out that you know me because, in reality, you don't.' The words tumbled out of her mouth before she could stop them.

Flynn stared at her in surprise. 'I didn't realise it upset you so much.'

'Well, it does.' Reggie gritted her teeth for a moment. 'I don't know what you want from me, Flynn. I don't know if the offer to help relocate my neighbours or having me stay at your place comes with any sort of strings attached but I just can't deal with too much more right now.'

'There are no strings attached,' he said quickly. 'And what I want from you, Reg, is quite simple.' He stood and looked her directly in the eyes. 'I want your forgiveness.'

'Forgi—' She stopped, too stunned to speak. She couldn't remember anyone ever asking her for her forgiveness before, especially someone who had hurt her so badly.

'So...we're needed in A and E?' he asked, breaking the moment and tidying the desk.

'Y-yes.' Reggie blinked, working hard to compartmentalise her thoughts. Flynn wanted her forgiveness. Bergan needed her in A and E. Patients. Trauma. Expertise. That's what she needed to focus on right now and, dragging in a breath, she pushed her personal thoughts aside. 'Retrieval team.'

'I'm part of the retrieval team? I don't remember—'

'Bergan said she needed you.' Reggie threw her arms in the air in complete exasperation. 'That's all I know.' Then she turned and headed out, wanting to get down to A and E as soon as possible so she could concentrate on something other than the way Flynn was constantly spinning her first one way then the other. She wished he'd stop because the motion was starting to make her feel ill.

In A and E, several of the retrieval team had already changed into the blue and yellow jumpsuits that stated they were part of the medical team at Sunshine General. Reggie headed over to where Bergan was gathering everyone together in the nurses' station, feeling rather than knowing that Flynn was directly behind her.

She tried hard to switch off her awareness of him and focus on whatever Bergan had called them down to assist with. Professional. She needed to be professional. After all, she'd worked alongside Flynn before; in fact, they'd worked exceptionally well together in the Caribbean...and that had been part of the problem. Too good, too close, too quickly.

Bergan cleared her throat and everyone around fell silent, waiting for her to speak. 'The key players are here. We're just waiting for Mackenzie but she's just getting out of Theatre so we'll begin without her.' Bergan pointed to the computer monitor, which was revealing a picture of the main beach in Maroochydore. 'We've had a report from the surf lifeguards that a shark has been sighted on the beach. They've closed the area but have just spotted a person, out to sea, floating. One male, approximately in late fifties to sixties. They're sending out a boat now and request immediate assistance.'

She turned to Flynn and Reggie. 'You two, go in the chopper. You both have the relevant experience when it comes to shark attacks, having treated and operated on victims before. I want you at the scene, stat. The instant they have that body out of the water, you need to be standing by.'

'Is there just the one victim?' Reggie asked, her mind going through the different injury scenarios they might be facing.

'That's the report at this time. Go and change. Get to that chopper.' With that, Bergan turned her gaze to the rest of the team. 'Everyone else, listen for your posts.'

'Change rooms are this way,' Reggie said, before Flynn could ask. They walked quickly along the corridor, down the side of A and E towards the changing rooms. 'Retrieval suits will be just inside the door. Once you're changed, we'll meet back in the corridor, grab the retrieval gear and head up to the chopper.'

'I guess all that experience in the Caribbean has come in handy. I hope I can remember what we need to do,' Flynn remarked as they hurried along. 'I've been working very much inland for the past few years.'

Reggie smiled at him reassuringly as they reached the changing room doors. 'You'll be fine and if you forget, just ask me.'

'I'll do that,' he promised, as he punched in the code for the male changing rooms at the same time she tapped in the code for the female changing rooms. 'See you in five minutes.'

'Or less,' she remarked, pushing open the door.

Ten minutes later, they were both changed, seated in the chopper with their medical retrieval backpacks and ready for take-off.

'Any word from the surf lifeguards?' Reggie asked their pilot through the headset.

'I'll patch you through to Bergan,' he replied.

'What's the latest?' Reggie asked a moment later as they headed out towards the sea.

'They've got the man in the boat. Left arm is partially detached, incision bites to left side of abdomen,' came Bergan's clear words. 'There is also a report of a second victim. Young girl, twelve years of age. Lacerations to right side, unconscious, right foot missing.'

Reggie closed her eyes as Bergan spoke, knowing full well that Flynn could hear every word through his own headset. She tried to picture the victims' wounds, tried to keep her mind focused, imagining herself moving through the motions of treatment. At times like these they couldn't afford to think about the personal, about those poor people who had suffered such horror. In order to remain professional, they needed to remain detached.

'The boat should be on the beach in two minutes.'

'What's our ETA?' Flynn asked the pilot, watching Reggie closely, whose eyes were tightly shut. He knew she was trying to think things through, to imagine the wounds and the treatment they'd require. He could also remember the first time she'd been like this. Their very first retrieval together.

They'd been sitting in an ambulance, being driven from the hospital on Sint Maarten, towards a luxury hotel where several guests had been crippled with a gastro bug. As they'd been the only surgical residents at the hospital, it had fallen to them to treat the patients. Flynn had met Reggie only the day before and while he'd been instantly attracted to her, he hadn't been at all sure how she performed under pressure.

'She's far too happy for her own good and although she did well in ward round, I have to wonder if she's got what it takes to cope in emergency situations,' he'd told Violet when he'd spoken to her on the phone after his first day.

'I'm sure she'll be fine, Flynn,' Violet had responded. The two had known each other since they'd been toddlers, their mothers the best of friends, and Violet had been the closest thing he'd had to a sister. Their mothers had always said that one day the two of them were destined to marry, but both he and Violet had laughed it off, preferring to remain just good friends. 'If she's a qualified doctor and doing the same surgical training you are, then she must have some smarts,' Violet had wisely pointed out.

Flynn had frowned, unable to believe the instant attraction he'd felt towards his new colleague. Perhaps doubting her abilities was his way of dealing with that unwanted attraction? At any rate, he'd hoped she was good because he hadn't really fancied having to carry the weight of running the surgical team on Sint Maarten on his own for the next six weeks. 'I'm still not convinced.'

'Anyway,' Violet had continued, 'Tell me about the more relaxed pace of life. Nice and slow? Sunshine all the time? I hope so because seriously I thought your parents were going to pressure you into a coronary if you hadn't left.'

'You're exaggerating, Violet,' he'd returned.

'Six weeks of sun, surf and drinks with little umbrellas in them. Utter bliss.'

'Sunburn, sand stuck everywhere and incompetent colleagues.'

Violet laughed at him, not taking his words seriously. 'She must be pretty if you're already labelling her as incompetent. You always do that, Flynn. It's a protective measure. Any time you feel out of your depth, you look for the negative.'

'I do?'

'Look, Flynn, just promise me you'll stop burning the candle at both ends and try to enjoy yourself. Get to know this colleague of yours. What did you say her name was?'

'Regina Smith. Although she's already informed me that she hates being called Regina, that she much prefers Reggie—like she's some sort of trucker. Then she throws her arms around me in one of those uncomfortable friendship-hug things, telling me what a wonderful time we'll have working together. Far too happy for her own good.'

Violet wasn't able to stop laughter from flowing down the telephone line. 'She sounds fantastic, Flynn, and perhaps just what you need for the next few weeks. A little holiday romance, eh?'

'Bite your tongue. You know I'm not interested in any sort of relationship. Not with the pressure our parents are putting on us.'

'It'll never happen, Flynn. You and I are destined to be best friends. Nothing more. Now go. I have a feeling that this Reggie Smith may just surprise you.'

And she did. As they travelled in the ambulance,

heading towards that luxury hotel, Reggie's eyes were closed as though she was trying to catch up on her sleep.

'Conserving your energy?' he asked.

'No.' She spoke the single word before opening one eye to look at him, the corners of her lips turning upwards. 'Concentrating.' She closed her eye and lapsed back into silence.

'Er...OK. Well, would you like to talk about what sort of scenarios we might encounter and how you envisage us handling the situation to ensure an effective and prompt outcome?'

'That's what I'm doing,' she replied. 'I like to close my eyes and picture the situation, visualise myself treating the patient. That way I know exactly what equipment I need and the best way to handle things.'

'You...*picture* yourself doing this?'

'Yes. Try it.' She opened one eye again and looked directly at him. 'Close your eyes.'

'I don't think—'

'We have another five minutes before arrival. Just try it at least.' She closed her eyes again and, feeling utterly stupid and knowing he probably looked ridiculous, Flynn eventually closed his eyes.

'Let's say the patient complains of right-sided abdominal pain with localised tenderness in the middle. I see myself palpating their abdomen, ensuring it isn't appendicitis or hernia. Although there's an outbreak of a gastro bug, it doesn't mean that one of our patients isn't suffering from that but is rather suffering from something far more serious. Not that I'm trying to imply that gastroenteritis isn't a serious condition but simply pointing out that we need to be on top of things.' She paused to take a breath but before she could start again he jumped in.

'You're a talker,' he stated, opening his eyes, feeling mildly silly for agreeing to do things her way but impressed she'd actually managed to get him to comply.

Reggie's grin was bright and wide, like her gorgeous blue eyes as she opened them to look at him. She leaned forward in her seat, as far as the seat belt would allow and looked directly into his eyes. 'I've been told the only way to shut me up is to kiss me.' She waggled her eyebrows up and down suggestively and then sat back in her seat and openly laughed at the stunned look on his face. 'Relax, Flynn. I don't bite.' She winked at him. 'Not unless you want me to.'

The old cliché somehow sounded fresh coming from Reggie's lips and it was only then he realised he'd been staring at her mouth, as though his thoughts were more than willing to follow her lead.

And indeed, the first time he had kissed her had been to shut her up. He couldn't remember what she'd been talking about but he did remember not hearing a word of what she'd been saying, more fascinated by the way her lips moved, wanting desperately to kiss them, to show her just how desirable she was.

Now, many years later, with so much water having flowed rapidly under the bridge between them, Flynn wanted nothing more than to lean forward and kiss those incredibly perfect lips of hers...lips that fitted so snugly against his own. How he'd yearned for them over the years. How he wanted to pick up where they'd left off. How he wished he'd been stronger back then and had stood up for what he'd really wanted out of life.

'Preparing for descent,' the chopper pilot said.

'Copy that,' Reggie returned, and opened her eyes. She looked directly at Flynn. 'Ready?'

'Yeah.' He nodded his head for emphasis and cleared his throat, unsure whether she'd heard him properly through her headphones. He needed to pull it together. To be professional. He knew Reggie—and their patients—were counting on him but sometimes it was difficult to be around her, especially when there were so many memories of their time together intruding into his thoughts.

As the chopper landed and they disembarked, Flynn tried not to notice the way even the blue and yellow overalls made Reggie look sexy. Carrying their gear, they headed over to where the surf lifeguards' boat was being pulled up onto the sand. Reggie was taking the lead on this one and he'd learned, that first day, as they'd treated over thirty patients at the hotel for various complaints, that she was indeed an exceptional doctor.

Bright, talented and absolutely gorgeous. A lethal combination and one he was far from being immune to.

CHAPTER SIX

ON THE BEACH, the surf lifeguards had set up a shield to give them some privacy while the man, whose name was only given as Kev, was carried from the lifeboat to where Flynn and Reggie were opening their emergency backpacks, ready to get to work.

'Establish IV line, get that plasma up and going, stat,' she stated, and Flynn nodded.

'Agreed.' Although they both knew what they were doing, it was important to communicate effectively and clearly exactly what procedures they were undertaking.

As soon as Kev was placed in front of them, they both had their gloves on. As Kev was wearing a wetsuit, Flynn took out the heavy-duty scissors and immediately began cutting away the neoprene fabric so they could better see what they were dealing with. After peeling away the section from his chest, most of which was covered in blood, Reggie hooked her stethoscope into her ears to check Kev's heart rate while Flynn grabbed a large bandage and applied pressure to Kev's left arm, ensuring it was as secure as possible to assist with stemming the bleeding.

'Hi, Kev,' she said to the man, who was semiconscious. 'I'm Dr Reggie Smith with Sunshine Gen-

eral. This is Dr Flynn Jamieson. We're here to help you.'
She smiled at him as she unhooked the stethoscope.
With the paramedics on the scene, one of them came
over and was able to hold Kev's head stable until they
could get a neck brace onto him.

'The girl.' Kev spoke the words through gritted teeth
as Flynn picked up a penlight torch from his medical
kit and performed Kev's neurological observations. As
they worked, both Flynn and Reggie called their findings to each other.

'Heart rate is elevated.'

'Pupils equal and reacting to light. Best to put the
line in his foot,' Flynn remarked, before looking down
at Kev. 'The girl's been found. The surf lifeguards are
bringing her in now.'

'She was…being taken farther…out to sea. Had…
to save her.' His words were disjointed but understand-
able, which showed his cognitive function was clearly
working.

'You did great, Kev. Now I need you to try and relax.
We're here to help you.' Reggie was taking the tubing
she required from the sterile packaging. She checked
both feet for pulses and reported they were both there.
She also asked Kev to wiggle all his toes for her and
although it hurt, he was able to do as she asked. 'You'll
feel just a little scratch,' she told him as she prepared
to insert the cannula into his foot.

'I've felt more…than that today,' he retorted. 'What…
what are you doing?'

'You've lost a lot of blood, Kev,' Flynn told him. 'We
need to replace those fluids as soon as possible. Once
we have some fluids into you, we can give you some-

thing for the pain. Can you wiggle the fingers on your right hand for me?'

'I'm not important,' Kev told them.

'I beg to differ,' Reggie replied, as one of the other paramedics came over to help. She left him to finish off inserting the drip and turned her attention to Kev's abdomen. 'I just need to have a little look around, see what the damage is, and then we can give you something for the pain,' she told him.

'The girl. The girl…is all that's important,' he said, his teeth gritted in pain. 'Need to save the girl.'

'You did save her,' Flynn reassured him.

'I did?' At this news, Kev seemed to relax a bit. He closed his eyes. 'Couldn't save my own girl but…this is good.'

Reggie and Flynn briefly looked at each other, wondering what on earth Kev could be talking about. The bite marks on Kev's abdomen were clear but deep. Flynn had already packed one of the puncture wounds with gauze and Reggie grabbed another bandage from her kit and applied pressure to one area on Kev's lower left abdomen.

'Hold this,' she instructed the paramedic, who had now finished setting up the drip. 'I think it's time we gave you something for the pain,' she told Kev. 'Are you allergic to anything?'

'No. No, but had a heart attack…six years ago now… but good since,' Kev replied, unable to shake his head as the paramedic was now attaching a neck brace to keep Kev's head as still as possible.

'And you're not taking anything? No fish oil?'

'Vegan now,' he told her. 'Flaxseed oil.'

'Good. That's all fine.' Reggie reached into her medical kit for the syringe that had already been drawn up with the medication and clearly labelled. 'Check ten milligrams of morphine,' she said.

Flynn glanced over, checked and confirmed the medication she was about to give Kev, before replying, 'Check.'

'There you go, Kev,' she told him as she administered the medication via the butterfly cannula. A few moments later Kev's features began to relax.

Now that Kev was out of pain, Flynn was able to increase his investigation of the abdomen. 'Not sure if the patient has voided, given the wetsuit, but possible bladder and kidney rupture, large and small intestinal damage but both lungs appear fine. Suspected fracture to left neck of femur and probable pelvic bone damage.'

'And the arm?' Reggie asked, after she'd rechecked Kev's heart rate. She took the stethoscope out of her ears and met Flynn's gaze. He didn't need to say anything—the look in his eyes told her that the arm didn't look at all good and the chances of Kev keeping it were minimal.

'Took the brunt of the attack.' Kev's words were barely audible. She nodded, indicating she understood exactly what he was not saying. The salty sea wind was whipping around them and she was glad of the screens the paramedics had erected. The lifeguards on the beach were keeping the onlookers at bay as best they could. When a shark alarm was raised, it tended to send a thread of panic through everyone who was around, whether they'd been in the water nor not.

'The boat? The boat?' Kev asked, still concerned, even though the morphine was definitely working. 'Is it in? Where's the girl?'

'The sea's a bit choppy,' one of the paramedics reported. 'They've got her in the boat. They're on their way,' he reassured their patient. Still, Kev seemed slightly agitated again. Something was clearly bothering him.

'Wasn't supposed to…turn out like this,' he mumbled, and Flynn frowned.

'Let's get him back to the hospital so he can be prepared for surgery. With the sounds of sirens in the distance, it appears the cavalry is on the way so we can leave the girl to Bergan and her team.'

'Good thinking.' Reggie pulled her walkie-talkie from the medical kit and contacted the helicopter pilot. 'You ready to head back?'

'Got a patient for me?' he asked.

'Copy that. Name is Kev—that's all I have at the moment. We'll stretcher him now. ETA six minutes.'

Now that the transfer was organised, Reggie did a final check of Kev's vitals, pleased to see he was responding well to the fluids and pain medication, and yet he still seemed uneasy. Then again, he'd just been bitten by a shark but her intuition told her it was more than that.

'Good news, Kev,' she said brightly. 'We're getting you off the beach.' She checked the bandages they'd applied, pleased with his situation. They'd managed to get to Kev as quickly as possible and even though he was in his late fifties, it was clear that he was the type of man who looked after his health.

'Wait. Wait.' Kev's eyes snapped open, the look in them as wild as the sea. 'The girl. Is she OK? I need to know. Please? Please?'

'They're still coming in, Kev, but the other staff from

Sunshine General have arrived. They're brilliant and know what they're doing. They'll take good care of her.'

'We need to get you back, Kev. Your abdominal injuries need further treatment and surgical interven—' Flynn started.

'I need to give you…a message,' Kev interrupted, his tone forceful.

'For whom?' Reggie asked, trying to use her calming voice to placate him a little. They needed him transferred as soon as possible but she didn't want to risk agitating him further by not giving him the respect he deserved.

'Write it down.'

'It's all right. We can do this back at the hospital. You're nice and stable now and we'd like to keep it that way,' she told him.

'Please? I need to give you a message…for my wife.'

'You're going to be fine, Kev. You can tell her yourself when you see her.'

'No. No. She hates me.' He closed his eyes at the words. 'Write it down.'

Reggie looked across at Flynn, who shrugged one shoulder. 'He's the patient. It's his call.' She nodded and pulled off her bloodied gloves before reaching into the medical kit, finding a pen but no paper.

'Wait a moment,' one of the paramedics said, unzipping his overalls and digging into his trouser pocket before pulling out a clean napkin. 'Use this.'

'Thanks.' Reggie accepted it from him then looked at Kev. 'What do you want me write?'

'I hope saving this girl…makes up for not saving ours.' Kev closed his eyes as he spoke and for a moment Reggie's throat closed over, an immediate lump forming there, which was difficult to swallow over. Kev had lost his daughter? 'Did you get that?'

'Uh…' She quickly scribbled down his words. 'Yes.'

'Also, tell her to remember…remember Coffs Harbour at New Year's…and the dingo dance.'

'Dingo dance?' Reggie raised her eyebrows as she looked at Kev. 'Sounds interesting.'

'You got that?' he asked again, and she nodded.

'All written down,' Reggie reassured him, before tucking the pen and paper into a pocket in her retrieval suit. 'What's your wife's name?' she asked.

'Michaela.'

'OK. That's all done. Now, I really think it's time we get you onto that chopper and back to the hospital.' Reggie smiled down at him.

Once again Kev seemed to relax a bit more but he looked determinedly at her and asked, 'You'll let me know about the girl?'

'As soon as we know anything, we'll let you know,' she told him. With the assistance of the paramedics they transferred Kev to a stretcher. 'Take him over to the chopper. I'll just quickly debrief Bergan and Mackenzie,' she told Flynn, who nodded. She watched for a moment as the screens were lowered and the lifeguards did their best to stop onlookers from taking photographs on their cellphones. The police were there as well, a few of them clearing the way for Kev to be carried to the helicopter.

As she started to walk away, a police officer came running up to her.

'Is it all right to talk to the patient now? We need to try and piece together what happened.'

'He's been given morphine and Penthrane so he

might be a little vague on details but give it a go,' she encouraged. 'We need to have wheels up in five minutes.'

'Understood,' the police officer said, and headed off after Flynn and the paramedics who were carrying Kev's stretcher towards the chopper.

Reggie quickly trudged her way through the sand towards Bergan, the wind still whipping at her hair. It was at times like these she was glad she'd cut her hair short. Reggie looked around at all the beachgoers, some packing their things up and leaving, others standing behind the area the police had cordoned off, teenagers taking photographs with their cameras and cellphones.

Emergency personnel were doing their jobs, working together like a well-oiled machine. Reggie hadn't even been aware of the police arriving but without them who knew how many people would have tried to sneak a look around those screens while she and Flynn had been treating Kev.

'We are a curious species,' she murmured to herself as Bergan walked over to her, the two meeting out of earshot of onlookers. 'Hey, there.'

'Your patient all ready for transfer?' Bergan asked.

'Yes. Left arm almost completely torn off. Amputation is a definite consideration but I'll get John to consult when we get back to the hospital.' Reggie pointed to where the surf lifesaving boat, after battling high waves brought on by an oncoming storm, was finally reaching the beach. 'You and Mackenzie OK to take care of the girl?'

'Yes. You'll probably be in Theatres by the time we return but I'll keep you informed.'

'Kev—my patient—was really concerned about the girl so I'd appreciate that.'

'No problem.'

Reggie turned and jogged towards the chopper, looking back to see them lifting the young girl from the boat and carrying her to a second screened-off area, away from prying eyes. She certainly hoped the girl was strong enough to make it through.

'Excuse me!' a woman called from behind the police tape, and when Reggie looked at her, the woman quickly ducked beneath the tape and ran towards her. 'I'm looking for Kev.'

'I'm sorry,' Reggie said, her tone filled with apology. 'You'll need to wait behind the tape.'

'I'm his…er…wife. Michaela.'

Reggie nodded. 'Yes. He's told me about you. Come with me. You can ride in the chopper with us.'

Michaela face turned pale. 'So he really has been attacked. I thought it was a bad joke.'

'We need to go now,' Reggie urged, breaking into a jog and urging Michaela along. 'Kev needs immediate surgery.'

Michaela shook her head. 'I never come to the beach. I can't stand it but he loves it.'

'Never mind about that now.'

'But you don't understand. I only came down so he could sign the divorce papers. I've been pressuring him to do it for months but he kept refusing.'

They'd reached the chopper and Reggie's heart went out to the woman as she read guilt and remorse in Michaela's eyes. She placed her hand on Michaela's shoulder, her words warm. 'Focus on being brave for Kev.

It doesn't matter what's happened in the past, he needs you now. Can you do that?'

Michaela seemed to consider that for a moment before she nodded. 'Yes.'

'Good. Let's get you into the chopper.'

'Why does everything bad happen at Christmas?' Michaela muttered as she climbed into the chopper, sitting down and allowing herself to be strapped in by the pilot. Reggie introduced her to Flynn, who had just finished doing Kev's observations.

'Can he hear me?' Michaela asked, as the rotors of the helicopter started to whirr above them.

'He's been given pain relief to make transport easier,' Reggie said apologetically as she strapped herself in and donned her headphones.

'Six minutes and we'll be at the hospital,' the pilot announced, then the chopper lifted smoothly upwards.

'Call through to the hospital and have John Watson standing by,' Reggie instructed.

'Copy that,' the pilot returned.

'Is that Mackenzie's husband?' Flynn asked, and Reggie nodded.

'Excellent orthopaedic surgeon,' she told him as both she and Flynn kept a close eye on Kev's condition. Thankfully, the trip was non-eventful and John was there waiting for them when the pilot landed the helicopter safely on the roof above the A and E department. A short lift ride down and they were wheeling Kev's bed through to the treatment room. After transferring him to a hospital bed, Reggie and Flynn performed observations again, Michaela standing in the corner out of the way, watching and listening in disbelief as Reggie spoke clearly, giving details of Kev's condition to the A and E staff, as well as John.

'I can't believe it. I just can't believe it,' Michaela kept repeating. Kev was still drowsy from the analgesics and it was clear he needed to go to Theatre as soon as possible. Reggie took Michaela out of the treatment room, down the corridor to a small waiting room, where she started to explain the operation to her.

'Michaela, we need you to sign the consent forms as you are his next of kin.'

'But we're supposed to be getting divorced. I have the papers here for him to sign and then that's it.'

'However…' Reggie tried to remain calm, to get her point across in the most straightforward way because the longer they had to delay taking Kev to Theatre, the worse the outcome would be for him. 'In the eyes of the law you are still listed as his next of kin.' Reggie looked into Michaela's eyes. 'I know all of this has come as a shock but he really does need surgery and we can't progress until—'

'Dr Reggie Smith. Dr Reggie Smith,' came the call over the A and E intercom. 'Code Blue, TR One.'

'What?' Reggie was on her feet and racing back towards trauma room one, her mind going faster than her body as she thought through a thousand different scenarios in the thirty seconds it took her to return. 'What happened?' she asked as she pulled on a pair of gloves and a protective disposable gown.

One of the A and E nurses was performing cardiac massage on Kev.

'Blood pressure dropped. We lost output. He went into defib,' Flynn announced, as he prepared to push fluids, John readying the crash cart. 'Vitals dropped suddenly.'

Reggie was checking Kev's pupils. 'Come on, Kev. Stay with me. You can do it.' She shook her head. 'Not reacting to light.'

'Give me one of adrenaline,' Flynn ordered, as the nurse continued cardiac massage, another of the nurses bagging Kev to pump air into his lungs.

Reggie checked for a pulse and when she couldn't find one Flynn put his stethoscope into his ears and listened for a heartbeat.

'Nothing.' Flynn shook his head and glanced at Reggie. She nodded encouragingly, her eyes eager. 'Push fluids. Get ready to shock him.' Flynn looked at John, who nodded.

'Come on, Kev. Come on. You've come too far. You're a hero, Kev. An absolute hero,' she told him, as she watched Flynn administer the fluids. She closed her eyes for a second, wishing for a miracle, but even she knew the situation was bad. Kev had lost too much blood and even though they were continuing to do everything they possibly could to revive him, there was no guarantee he'd make it through surgery.

'Charging,' John said.

'Clear!' Flynn called, and everyone stepped back from the patient. 'No output.'

'Shock him again,' Reggie instructed, and again John charged the machine.

'Clear!' Flynn called once more, and after the shock had been administered, Reggie pressed her fingers to Kev's carotid pulse.

'Again,' she instructed.

'Reggie—' Flynn began.

'Again!' There was desperation in her words.

'Charging,' John called.

'Clear!' Flynn said, but after the third time there was still no output. 'I'm calling it.'

Flynn met Reggie's gaze, holding it for what seemed an eternity. She knew it was the right thing to do, that Kev had already been through so much, that he simply hadn't been able to fight any longer. He'd done his bit. He'd saved a twelve-year-old girl's life and he was a hero.

Flynn walked round to where she stood and put both hands on her shoulders, looking intently into her eyes. 'I'm sorry, Reg.'

'We did our job.'

'Do you want me to talk to his wife?'

'No.' She patted the pockets of her retrieval suit, looking for the napkin on which she'd written Kev's last words. 'I'll do it.'

'I'll go with you. Support is always good at a time like this.'

Reggie nodded and walked on wooden legs down towards the small room where she'd left Michaela not that long ago. Flynn's nearness really was comforting and she momentarily wondered whether he hadn't been offering support for *her* rather than for Kev's wife.

With the bright and cheerful Christmas music playing softly through the hospital's system, they entered the waiting room and just the forlorn look on Reggie's face must have adequately conveyed the situation to Michaela as the other woman instantly burst into tears.

'We did everything we could,' Reggie said, the words sounding hollow and inadequate as Michaela crumpled into a chair. Reggie put her hand on the other woman's shoulder, wanting to offer her support. 'His heart couldn't handle the stress of the attack. He passed away a few minutes ago.'

'No. No. This isn't the way it was supposed to happen.'

Reggie swallowed and looked up at Flynn, who nodded encouragingly for her to continue. She held the napkin between her fingers and looked down at the words she'd scribbled there not that long ago. 'He did leave a message he wanted me to pass on to you.' Reggie paused for a moment, not sure she could get the words past her lips but knowing she had to. 'He said he hoped saving the little girl today made up for not saving yours.'

At that, Michaela let loose with a fresh round of tears and Flynn quickly offered her some more tissues. It was incredibly difficult in these circumstances to know what to do or say and although they'd been trained in how to handle these sorts of situations, having the theoretical knowledge and watching someone's heart break into pieces because a loved one had passed away were two very different things.

'He said for you to remember Coffs Harbour at New Year's and the dingo dance.'

Michaela raised her head, hiccupping as she spoke. 'Why on earth would he say that?' she asked, blowing her nose amidst the tears.

Reggie shrugged, unsure what the relevance was. She was about to say she didn't know when Flynn spoke.

'Perhaps he wanted your last memory of him to be a happy one,' Flynn said, his voice deep and soft and filled with compassion.

Surprise lit Michaela's eyes. 'Oh.' Then she nodded.

'The dingo dance.' A small smile touched her quivering lips. 'He was so funny that night.'

'Is there someone we can call to come and be with you?'

Michaela took her phone from her handbag and nodded. 'I can do it.'

'OK. I'll get one of the nurses to come and bring you a drink. We'll be back as soon as possible.'

'Yes. Of course. You must be busy.' Michaela nodded and dabbed at her eyes with a fresh tissue. 'I don't know how you do it, how you cope.'

The lump was back in Reggie's throat and after they exited the room she quickly walked down one of the side corridors of A and E, needing to have a moment or two to herself. Bergan's office was down this secluded corridor and she quickly dug around in her pocket for her hospital pass card, but her fingers seemed to have turned into sausages. She needed the escape, to slip into Bergan's room, to cry and let the pain out, but the tears were already beginning to flow.

'Just let them go,' Flynn's voice said from behind her, and she jumped a little, not having heard him follow her. She turned and in the next instant she was in his arms, their firm warmth providing her with a protective shelter from the stormy emotions pounding at her heart.

'I've got you, Reg. I've got you,' he murmured softly near her ear, but as he spoke, Reggie could hear the thickness in his tone and as she buried her face into his chest, her body racked with sobs, she realised that Flynn was also shedding a few tears.

She was touched at this deeply personal, deeply sensitive side to him that she couldn't remember seeing before. They'd worked together on patients before, they'd lost patients before, but in all the time she'd spent with him he'd always managed to keep a close rein on his most intimate emotions.

Now he was sharing them with her and she couldn't help but feel…quite privileged.

CHAPTER SEVEN

REGGIE WASN'T SURE how long they stood there, their arms wrapped around each other, supporting each other. The job they did wasn't easy. It was bad enough when they were in Theatre and things didn't go their way, the patient dying during surgery, but to have gone out to the beach, to have spent time with Kev, having him confide in her, giving her the message to pass onto Michaela… and then to lose him.

Yes, it hurt, but it also felt incredibly good to have Flynn's strong arms about her. The pain was there but the fact that it was shared really did provide a level of comfort. It had been so long since anyone had just held her, without a hidden agenda, without wanting anything from her. Flynn was offering her comfort and she hoped in some way she was giving him back just the same.

She had no idea how long they stood there and a part of her never wanted it to end but she knew it must. It was their job to pull themselves together, to head back into the fray, as it were, and to help someone else who was still alive and who needed their expertise.

Slowly Reggie's tears started to subside but she was more than happy to stay where she was, at least for the moment. The memory of having Flynn's arms around her…of the way he would sometimes rub his thumbs in small circles in her lower back, giving her a gentle and sensual massage. Would he do that now? Did he want to do that?

Before the emergency, he'd asked for her forgiveness. The fact that he'd done that and also the way he'd been so incredibly thoughtful and helpful and wonderful and supportive was making it far too easy for her to fall in love with him all over again.

She knew he was here at Sunshine General covering Geetha's maternity leave but then what? What were his plans once Geetha returned in six months' time? There were just too many questions. Too many emotions. Too much…Flynn. She knew she needed to pull back, to try and find some sort of perspective where he was concerned, although how she was going to do that she had no clue.

Feeling a little better, Reggie started shifting slowly in his arms. She was becoming far too aware of how perfect his torso was, how he smelled of that deep, earthy spice that had always been intoxicating to her senses, and how she wanted nothing more than to ease back, lift her head and have him press his lips to hers.

He'd done it time and time again in the past and as his arms loosened, allowing her to shift a little more, she couldn't help but look up at him. His gaze automatically dipped to take in the contours of her mouth, the atmosphere between them changing from one of supportive colleagues to one of experienced familiarity.

She looked into his gorgeous eyes, hooded by those gorgeous long lashes, his straight nose, his cleft chin and his slightly parted lips. His arms were no longer protective and supportive but instead were bands of warmth, heating her up all over. Didn't the man have any idea just how powerful his hold was over her? She wanted him to kiss her, to follow through on the urge that seemed to be so tangible between them you could have cut it with a knife.

'Reg.' Even the way he spoke her name was filled with repressed desire. 'I really want to kiss you.'

At his words she gasped, her lips parting and her eyes widening at the bold but honest statement. Her hands were still halfway around his back from holding him close while she'd wept but now she brought them around to the front, to rest against his chest as she continued to look at him.

She really wasn't sure what to say or do because although she was longing to have his mouth pressed to hers once again, knowing she would be able to experience those thrilling sensations only Flynn had ever been able to evoke, she also remembered the pain he'd put her through when he'd broken her heart. She could forgive him. She knew that but could she trust him with her heart again? Was his desire to kiss her simply born from the moment they were sharing or was it something deeper?

He lifted his hand to run his fingers through her short dark hair. 'I like this colour. When we met it was longer and a honey brown and you were the most effervescent and wild and crazy and most wonderful person I'd ever met, and even then I had trouble keeping my lips from yours. It appears, all these years later, that the urge is as strong now as it was then.'

He cupped her chin with his hand and brushed his thumb over her parted lips. If she'd thought she'd been on fire before, his sweet and gentle caress had only enhanced the power surging between them.

'I know I'm being selfish, Reg,' he continued a moment later when she hadn't spoken. 'Especially after the way I treated you all those years ago, and I really need to tell you how sorry I am. I was arrogant and rude and didn't take into consideration that your feelings were much deeper than I'd originally thought.'

'You asked me to marry you, Flynn!' Reggie shook her head and twisted from his embrace. Flynn instantly released her, dropping his arms back to his sides. 'You proposed marriage and I accepted. Then, the next day, you turn up at my room and tell me you need to call it all off. Just like that. No explanation, just that you'd made a mistake and that you were no longer…free to pursue a relationship with me. Less than two weeks later I read—in the society columns—that Flynn Jamieson, of the well-known wealthy Jamieson family and heir to the Jamieson Corporation, had wed his childhood sweetheart, Violet Fleming, a young philanthropic socialite who was on the board of so many charity organisations it was almost impossible for the newspaper to list them.'

'Reg…I—'

'What, Flynn? Please tell me what happened back then because I've spent the past six years trying to figure things out. What did I do wrong? Was I too enthusiastic? Did everything just happen too fast? Sure, I may be spontaneous and, yes, in my life, once I make a decision, things tend to move really fast and I'm off like a rocket, but what a lot of people don't realise is that I think about things far more deeply than anyone would ever guess, and when you proposed to me I didn't take it lightly or as some sort of flippant twenty-four-hour whimsy.' She shook her head and spread her arms wide.

'I'm just not sure how you could have misconstrued my true feelings for you, especially as when you proposed I threw my arms around your neck and smothered your face in kisses while saying "Yes, yes and yes" over and over again! Don't you think that during the time we were together I hadn't dreamed of you asking me that question? That I didn't feel that strong and abiding connection that—stupid me—I thought you'd felt, too…or at least I believed you when you said you did.'

'Reg!'

'What?' Reggie leaned her head against Bergan's office door, wishing she had her pass key on her so they could at least enter and have a bit of privacy. She was tired and edgy after the retrieval, and then having her patient pass away…it was all becoming too much. Now they were just waiting for the young girl to arrive in A and E, in case she required surgery.

It definitely wasn't the time for them to be having *this* discussion, the one she'd wanted to have with him ever since he'd come back into her life—to ask him why he'd really called off their engagement. Apparently time just wasn't on her side at the moment.

'Will you let me get a word in edgeways?'

'Go for it.' She turned and leaned her back against the door, closing her eyes and waiting for him to speak.

He was quiet for a moment before saying softly, 'It was a mistake.'

Reggie was glad she hadn't been looking at him when he'd spoken those words because the pain that instantly pierced her heart, she knew, would have been clearly reflected in her gaze. She tried to focus on the

Christmas music playing through the speaker above, hoping that her days really would be merry and bright, but how could they possibly ever be that way again when Flynn had just confirmed that proposing to her had been a mistake?

'Thanks for confirming that,' she returned, realising she needed to get away from him. In some ways it was the last thing she'd expected him to say, to admit that what they'd had in Sint Maarten had been a mistake, but he'd said it to her back then and he was only confirming it now, all these years later.

The sounds of ambulance sirens nearing the hospital could be heard over the Christmas music and the next instant both her and Flynn's pagers started to beep. She dragged in a deep breath, pushed her personal thoughts aside and stepped away from the door.

Raising her gaze to hover just near the top of retrieval suit, focusing on his Adam's apple, she mumbled, 'Looks like we're needed again.'

With that, she edged past him, ignoring the way her body burst with excitement as her arm brushed against his. Retrieval suit or not, the slightest touch from Flynn would no doubt always set her on fire and it was probably something she should simply learn to accept, rather than fight. She was attracted to Flynn. Fact. He thought the two of them together was a mistake. Fact. All of this made it highly plausible that she would no doubt die from a broken heart.

'Clamp,' she instructed the theatre nurse, Susan, as they entered their fourth hour of surgery. The young girl, Lola, had a perforated bladder and kidney and her bowel was in a bit of a state. 'Nothing we can't fix,' she and Flynn had reassured Lola's poor parents.

Working in conjunction with the urological surgical team, as well as Mackenzie and John for Lola's ortho-paedic injuries of an amputated right foot, Flynn and Reggie were determined that this young girl would live. Kev had given his life for her and there was no way any of the team was going to do anything but their best for Lola, no matter how tired they might be.

Lola would need to be on dialysis while her kid-ney healed and then there was the inevitable right-foot prosthesis she would require, but for the moment both Reggie and Flynn were concentrating on performing an ileostomy, having already successfully completed a resection on the large intestine. They'd had to make a large cut down the centre of Lola's belly in order to gain access to the area. Usually the procedure was per-formed laparoscopically but in Lola's case that hadn't been an option.

Between the dialysis and the prosthesis, Lola would also have to deal with the temporary stoma they'd been forced to insert—where they attached her small intes-tine to the outer wall of her body. Her stools would need to go through the stoma into a drainage bag outside her body. All of that was a lot for a twelve-year-old to cope with, especially as it would all be combined with the emotional trauma of being swept out with the ocean current into dangerous waters until Kev had come to her rescue.

As Reggie pulled off her gloves quite some time later, handing Lola's care over to Mackenzie and John, who were the next surgeons to treat Lola's plethora of injuries, she was physically and emotionally drained.

'That poor kid,' Flynn murmured, as he de-gowned in the anteroom next to Reggie.

'Her whole life has just changed,' she replied, removing her mask and cap before running her fingers through her hair, fluffing it up.

'It'll never be the same again.' Flynn continued to watch her, both of them now dressed in their scrubs. Bits of Reggie's dark hair stuck out at all angles, making her look cuter than ever. A lopsided smile slowly tugged at the corners of his mouth and, unable to resist the chance to touch her, he stepped forward and brushed his fingers through the locks so they didn't look so wild and unruly. 'Lovely,' he said.

'Tired,' she returned, unable to put her shields up. After what Flynn had said to her before Lola's surgery Reggie had most definitely wanted to put a bit more distance between them but right now all she really wanted was to find a nice, comfortable bed, curl up and go to sleep.

The feel of his fingers in her hair, his hand cupping her cheek, the way he looked down into her upturned face, the way he looked into her eyes for a brief moment before nodding, as though reading her thoughts, was lovely. To have him here, have him near, have him caring for her. It was something she'd dreamed about for such a very long time that when he put his arms around her shoulders and led her out of the anteroom, she was more than happy to let him.

'Get changed. I'll write up the notes and meet you back here in ten minutes. OK?'

'Sounds good,' she murmured, and headed into the female changing rooms. She was at that stage of exhaustion where she had so many thoughts running through her head that none of them made any sense. One thought blurred into another and they all continued to tumble until she was unable to process anything. So much had happened today and as she slowly changed out of her clothes, almost falling over once or twice, feeling light-headed as though she was drunk, all she could think about was getting to that nice, comfortable bed.

'You're starting to make a habit of this,' Flynn murmured not too much later as they headed to his car. There was a light smattering of rain outside but the air was still rather sticky and humid. She knew he was referring to the exhaustion she'd felt last night.... Had it only been last night? She liked it when her days were full, when time didn't drag, but the past few days had been filled with far too many conflicting emotions, even for her.

'I'm sorry if I'm being a nuisance,' Reggie remarked, the balmy weather having woken her up a little, but Flynn instantly dismissed her words.

'You're not. You've been through a lot, Reggie, and your mind needs time to process everything. At least I don't need to carry you to the car tonight.'

Reggie frowned at him. 'Stop talking about me as though you're the authority on me,' she protested as he unlocked his car and opened the door for her. She stepped forward and only realised a split second later that they were standing facing each other with only the car door between them. She lifted her chin, annoyance making her brave.

'Why not?'

'Because you don't know me, Flynn. Because you've admitted to me that you and I were a mistake, one that should never have happened, that you regret—'

'What?' He frowned as he interrupted her. 'I never said that.'

'Yes, you did. Just before Lola's surgery. We were outside Bergan's office and you admitted it was a mistake to—' She stopped talking again but only because Flynn had put his finger across her lips, startling her and causing her body to be flooded with a mass of tingles at the feather-light touch.

'You once told me the only way to effectively shut you up was to kiss you and I'm very close to doing that, Reg.' He breathed out a calming breath but she could see his eyes flashing with a mixture of desire and frustration. 'What I said to you before Lola's surgery was that it was a mistake to have treated you the way I did. It was a mistake to allow myself to be persuaded by my family. It was a mistake to turn and walk away from you.'

Reggie stared at him then blinked one long blink as though she was desperately trying to process his words. 'A mistake to…'

'Walk away from you. I have many regrets, Reg, and…' He cupped her face, the frustration leaving him as he gazed into her eyes as though she really was the most important and precious person in the world to him. Her legs started to quiver, to turn to jelly, and she quickly put out a hand, clutching the edge of the car door in order to steady herself. 'You are perhaps my biggest regret of all.'

'I am?'

His smile was instant and gorgeous and his eyes were twinkling with mild amusement. 'Yes.' Flynn indicated to the car. 'Get in, Reggie. I think it's time we talked.'

She did as he suggested, trying not to fumble with her seat belt as his words reverberated around her head.

Time they talked? Talked about what? About the past? About how he'd left? About how she'd been utterly devastated and heartbroken? Because if they did that, then that discussion would lead to the present and she wasn't at all sure she was ready to reveal to Flynn just how incredible he made her feel.

She loved being near him, spending time with him, laughing with him, and it was also what she wanted more than anything in the world…but…had too much already passed between them? Was it possible she could forgive him for hurting her all those years ago? For breaking her heart and leaving her feeling as though she'd been living a lie ever since?

'You must talk about this,' she could well remember Sunainah saying a few months after she had returned from the Caribbean. 'Talk about your love for this man, this Flynn. It is important for you to do.'

'No, it isn't.'

'It is not healthy, Reggie. If you keep it all bottled up inside, then a day will come when you are unable to contain it any longer. It will bubble up and burst everywhere, making an awful mess,' Sunainah had persisted.

'I can cope with this, Sunainah. I've coped with worse. You know about my past. You know the betrayals I've coped with. Flynn's betrayal is just another one to add to the pile.' She'd shrugged then shaken her head.

'It's my own fault, really. I, in all my romantic stupidity, thought Flynn was different. That he was a man who truly cared about me, who meant it when he said he loved me. Turns out he didn't. He's no different from any other rich man. Only out for what he can get.' Even as she'd spoken the words her heart had been pierced with pain, her voice breaking on the last words.

Sunainah had hugged her close and a fresh bout of tears had fallen on her friend's shoulder. 'What will you do?'

'What I always do.' Reggie had sniffed and dabbed at her eyes with a tissue before blowing her nose. 'I'll cry and then box everything up in my mind and shove it into a dark corner. Then I'll pick myself up and rely on my awesome friends to be there for me.'

'We are pretty awesome.' Sunainah had chuckled.

'And I will be as bright and cheerful as I know how. If I fold a facade around me, one I can control, letting people believe I am forever the happy-go-lucky girl, I'll be able to cope.'

'I hope you are correct.'

Reggie had hugged Sunainah close before standing up to pace around the room. 'I will be happy. I'll lock my love for Flynn away and never think about it again.'

'That is impossible.'

'Probably.' She'd stared at a photograph of the two of them together, standing on the beach at sunset, holding big, colourful drinks with little umbrellas in them. 'Goodbye, Flynn,' she'd whispered, then kissed the photograph and handed it to Sunainah. 'Hide this somewhere for me.'

'Are you sure?' Sunainah had asked.

Reggie had closed her eyes, a single tear falling from her lashes before she'd taken a deep, cleansing breath and slowly released it. Then she'd opened her eyes, forced a smile onto her lips and laughed. 'Positive.'

'Is that the answer to my question or your projected attitude?'

'Both.'

And Reggie had done her best to be that happy-go-lucky girl for the past six years, doing her best to redirect her thoughts whenever she'd accidentally caught herself thinking about Flynn, wanting to know what he was up to, where he was working, whether or not he had children with his stunningly gorgeous wife. She'd stopped reading the social pages, turning off the television or radio at any mention of the Jamieson Corporation. She hadn't wanted to know.

She'd focused on her work, an ever-present smile on her face, her bright and cheerful attitude becoming less forced and more of who she really was. And whenever she had slipped for a minute and indulged herself by wondering what the heir to the Jamieson Corporation was doing with his life, she would force herself to go out on a date. There was no shortage of handsome men working at the hospital but none of them had ever been able to break through the walls she'd erected so firmly about her heart.

Then Flynn had appeared, standing across the corridor from her clinic room, and everything had started to crumble. Now he wanted to talk? Now he wanted to set the record straight? He *hadn't* thought the two of them together was a mistake? Was this a world she wanted to enter again? Surely a leopard didn't change its spots. Surely, given that Flynn had hurt her once, he would do it again.

He switched the radio on as they drove through the quiet streets of Maroochydore but where Reggie had wanted nothing more than to sleep before, Flynn's words had been like a shot of adrenaline and she was now very much awake.

He wanted to talk. That could mean anything, so what on earth was he going to say...and was she going to like it?

CHAPTER EIGHT

'ANOTHER LONG DAY,' she murmured as they walked into his town house. She didn't know if she could face this 'talk' with Flynn on top of the day they'd had. Maybe she should just go straight to her room and hide there for as long as she could.

'I'll put the kettle on,' he said. 'Why don't you sit in the lounge and I'll join you in a moment?'

'Actually, Flynn, if you don't mind…' Reggie eased her way through the kitchen, aiming towards the downstairs bedroom. 'Can we talk later?'

'No.'

'But I'm exhausted.'

Flynn looked at her for a long moment before shaking his head. 'No.'

'No?' she questioned, feeling her annoyance beginning to rise. 'You can't make me sit down and talk about something I'm not sure I want to talk—'

Without a word, he moved quickly, gently scooping her into his arms and pressing his mouth to hers in one swift motion, effectively shutting her up, just as he'd warned her earlier. Reggie barely had time to register his movements before a flood of delight and excitement zinged around her body like an out-of-control pinball.

He knew how to move his mouth against hers in order to garner a response of pleasure and it appeared he wasn't above using this knowledge and skill right now.

At first, though, he didn't move his mouth, just pressed his lips to hers as though needing to reacquaint himself with her gloriousness, but after breathing her in, after closing his eyes and allowing the drug that was Reggie to once more flow through his system, Flynn eased back ever so marginally and deepened the kiss.

Slowly, slowly, slowly. As though inflicting the most exquisite torture on their senses, he coaxed her lips to part gently, the taste of her fuelling his desire. She was all sweetness and light and sunshine, bringing her unique brand of pleasure back into his life. It was what she'd done all those years ago, breaking down his barriers, wanting him, needing him, teaching him how to lighten up, not to take things so seriously, to be free from repression.

'You're too stuffy,' she'd once told him, and he'd been impressed with the way she'd teased and laughed at him, so unlike any of the other women he'd met throughout his life. Most of them had only wanted one thing—access to his family's fortune.

'Women aren't interested in *you*, son, and they never will be,' his father had told him time and time again. 'All they want are clothes and shoes and jewellery and anything else your money can buy them. Sure, they might show a smidgen of affection for you in the beginning but it'll wane. It always does.'

'So…you and Mum?' Flynn had questioned him. 'What? Mum only married you for your money?'

'Your mother had money of her own, son. That's the point. Marry someone who already has money and you know they don't want you *just* for your money.' His father had dragged heavily on his expensive Cuban cigar, then coughed. 'Even then, they're happy to take whatever you give them. Everyone has their price.'

And yet, when Flynn had met Reggie, he'd had the distinct impression that she really *didn't* have a price at all. All she'd wanted out of life had been to be happy and to spread that happiness to others. She was a clever, caring and charismatic woman who had completely turned his head.

They'd both been staying in the short-term accommodation apartments owned by the hospital to house the doctors who spent time working in Sint Maarten, so they'd bumped into each other quite frequently. Then one night, in the apartment complex's large, almost empty dining room, when Flynn had been sitting alone at a table, Reggie had pulled out the chair opposite him and sat down.

'Well, it seems completely ridiculous for the two of us to be eating by ourselves, especially as you're new here,' she'd offered by way of explanation. Before he'd been able to say a word, the waitress had brought over their meals and he'd found himself eating—and enjoying—dinner with Reggie Smith.

The more time he'd spent with her, the more intrigued he'd become. She was so carefree, crazy and challenging, making him re-evaluate some of his ideals. Soon he'd been unable to stop himself from kissing her and before his time in Sint Maarten had ended, he'd found himself proposing to the most wonderful and exhilarating woman he'd ever known.

Now Flynn gathered her as close as he could, unable to believe he was permitted to hold her once again, to tenderly caress her back, to continue to absorb her delightful response to the kisses he was pressing to her lips. Didn't she have any idea just how perfect she was for him? How he'd wished he hadn't been so spineless all those years ago and had stood up for what *he'd* wanted instead of continuing to allow his overbearing father to dictate his life?

But that was then and this was now. He'd made the break, he'd taken control over his own life and somehow he'd found his way back to the one place he'd always felt like he belonged—with Reggie's arms wrapped around him, her mouth responding enthusiastically to his.

'Flynn.' She whispered his name as she reluctantly broke her mouth from his, her breathing erratic and uneven. She put both hands on his shoulders and eased back. 'We can't do this again.' She tried to shake her head but instead found her lips once more captured by his. She moaned with delight, wanting his glorious torture to continue forever as well as wanting it to finish as soon as possible so she didn't end up revealing just how much she still cared for him.

She knew she should push him away, to break the contact. Self-preservation was usually high on her list of priorities but this was Flynn and where he was concerned she'd never been able to think straight. When they'd first met he'd turned her mind to mush. When they'd argued he'd turned her mind to mush. When he'd smiled at her, hugged her, kissed her, he'd turned her mind to mush.

At first, in Sint Maarten, she'd done her best to keep their relationship strictly professional, wanting to deny the uncharacteristic desire she'd felt towards him. She hadn't dated wealthy men. That had been her one rule and even though Flynn hadn't told her about his excessively rich family, from the moment she'd met him she'd known exactly who he was.

She'd appreciated his skills as a doctor, she'd liked the way they'd seemed to work together so seamlessly, enjoying the inventive ways and solutions he'd devised for dealing with a variety of situations. What she hadn't expected was to find herself wanting to spend more time with him, to talk to him, to tease him, to laugh with him outside working hours.

And then he'd broken her heart, he'd rejected her love and he'd left her. Even though she wanted to see where this frightening natural chemistry that still existed between them might lead, she wasn't sure her heart was strong enough to endure another rejection from him. As the pain from her past, the pain she'd locked away so tightly, started to bubble up and over, she felt a surge of power course through her and pushed her hands against his shoulders.

'No!' She broke from his embrace and took a step away, bumping into the wall and almost tripping over. Flynn instinctively reached out a hand towards her, wanting to help her, but she shifted farther away.

'Reggie?'

As she looked at him, she was pleased to see he was equally as out of breath, as shaken up with repressed desire as she was. It was nice to know she wasn't the only one affected by the raw, animalistic power that still existed between them.

'I can't do this, Flynn.'

'Do...what?'

'This!' She indicated the distance between them,

the thick, heavy attraction that was surrounding them, wanting to draw them closer.

'Why? What is it that's stopping you?'

She stared at him with incredulity. 'Er…how about the fact that you broke my heart?' She turned to walk away, not wanting to relive the pain and mortification he'd inflicted on her. She'd been very disciplined *not* to think about it and she wasn't about to start now, especially *not* in front of him.

Flynn nodded. 'If it's any consolation, I broke mine as well.'

That stopped her. Frowning, she turned to face him. 'What?'

'As I said before at the car, walking away from you that night was not only the hardest thing I've ever done but also the stupidest.'

'Stupidest?'

Flynn raked a hand through his hair, his agitation quite evident. 'I was a fool, Reggie, and for years I've wanted to humbly beg your forgiveness. Now that you're here, in front of me, willing to listen to me, that's exactly what I'm doing.' He looked into her eyes. 'Will you? Can you…forgive me?'

Reggie stared at him in utter astonishment. 'But… wait a second. If breaking up with me broke your heart as well, why did you do it?' She spread her arms wide, her eyes revealing just how perplexed she was with what he was saying.

'My parents.' He shook his head. 'Pressure from my father, emotional blackmail from my mother.' He raked a hand through his hair. 'All my life I'd been told that women would never be interested in *me* for *me*. That when they looked at me all they would see was a walking chequebook. Money would always win out against love, or so I'd been led to believe. But the other fact was that my mother was very ill back then, and there was some controversy as to whether I should even go to the Caribbean in the first place. Although I haven't necessarily seen eye to eye with my parents over the years, they're still my parents and I'm honour bound to them.'

Reggie snorted at his words. '"Honour bound". Ha. What honour? The world of the wealthy. It has its own way to bully and oppress.'

'Er...yes.' He seemed astonished she understood.

'I take it her health improved as you did indeed come to the Caribbean.'

'Yes, and while I was there, while I was with *you*, I started to see the world differently. *You* helped me to see it differently and I started to realise the world I'd been raised in had certain...flaws.'

'One being that it was OK to think for yourself?'

'Yes.' Again he was surprised at her insight.

'And the marriage you entered into the instant you left me?'

'It was my mother's final wish.'

'Let me guess. Your mother was good friends with Violet's mother?'

'The best of friends, yes.'

Reggie shrugged and turned away from him, walking into the lounge room and slumping down into a chair, closing her eyes.

'As ridiculous and as old-fashioned as it might sound, our mothers had always talked of Violet and I marrying, all our lives. We were to have children who would bind our two families together forever.'

'And how did you and Violet feel about this?'

Flynn shrugged. 'Violet was more like a sister to me. Neither of us have siblings. As far as the arranged marriage went, I guess as I'd always been told that was what was expected of me, I didn't think about it much. Until…until I met you.'

'You were OK with having an arranged marriage?'

'Back then, I guess I was…but as I've said, then I met you and everything changed.'

'But the wealthy are supposed to marry the wealthy.' She shook her head, looking at him through her lashes. 'It's snobbish and elitist and not to mention outdated.'

'And yet it's still happening even today.' Flynn sat down on the lounge next to her, facing her, needing her to understand. 'My mother's health deteriorated while I was in Sint Maarten but I didn't know that as I hadn't been answering their calls. I'd wanted to shut out my life, ignore the pressures waiting for me once I returned to Melbourne. I wanted to live in the world you and I had created for ourselves, to stay happy in our bubble.'

'And when you finally reconnected with that world?'

'I was told my mother had been admitted to hospital only a few hours before. Guilt swamped me, especially when my father continued to lecture me about my ir- responsible behaviour of not staying in contact. And there I was, calling them to tell them the good news, to let them know that I'd found the woman of my dreams and that I was engaged.

'When I told my father that I'd most certainly come home but that I was bringing my new fiancée with me, he told me I might as well stick a scalpel directly into my mother's heart and kill her instantly. He blustered about how the wedding to Violet was set. That it was my mother's final wish to see Violet and I married and that was what was going to happen.

'He talked to me long and hard about my duty, my honour, my need to step up and do the right thing. He convinced me that there was no way any woman— *you*—could ever feel anything deep and abiding for me, nothing that would stand the test of time.'

Flynn closed his eyes and shook his head. 'He'd sent his private jet to the airport for me and I was to be on it the following afternoon. Alone. I was so eaten up with guilt. My mother had been ill and I'd been selfish enough to shut her out simply because I'd been with you.

'I paced around, thinking things through, trying to rationalise whether or not you truly loved me, and yet somehow...my thinking changed. I did find it difficult to believe that you could really love me for me, that you must know about my family's money and that was the only reason you'd even given me the time of day.'

'You were angry with me.' Reggie's statement was soft but clear. 'I could see it in your eyes.'

He closed his eyes for a moment as though recalling that horrible scene in her room when he'd called off their engagement. 'I was, but only because I'd convinced myself you couldn't possibly love *me*,' he admitted honestly. 'It was easier for me to break it off with you if I believed you'd only been interested in me for my family fortune.'

'The wealthy can behave however they like and nine times out of ten they do. A law unto themselves.'

Flynn looked at her with a hint of surprise. 'I disagree with that statement, at least as far as I'm concerned.'

'Perhaps now, but not back then. Your father dictated

your path and you just let him. You let his voice get into your head and control you, just as it always had.'

'I know, but…' Flynn shifted in his seat, defence at her attack on his father grating on him, even though he knew what she was saying was absolutely true. 'My mother was ill. *Gravely* ill. She passed away five days after the wedding.'

'And was she happy?'

'Seeing me married to Violet? Yes, she was. It was what happened after that which I didn't appreciate.'

'Being stuck in an arranged marriage?' she guessed.

'Well, there was that, but, more importantly, not three days after my mother's funeral my father threw a large wedding reception, inviting everyone who *should* have been invited to what he termed was "the society wedding of the year".' Flynn waved his hand in the air as though he was announcing a headline.

'Did you know about it?'

'Of course.'

'And you couldn't stop it?'

'I wanted to but everyone kept saying it was what Mum had wanted, that she'd helped to plan it and that if it didn't go ahead, we were dishonouring her memory.'

'And there's more guilt piled on.'

'Exactly.' Flynn reached over and took Reggie's hand in his. 'I was also highly conscious of you. I kept wondering what you must be thinking.' He looked down at her fingers, stroking them lightly. 'I knew you probably hated me and I wouldn't have blamed you for the atrocious way I'd behaved. You didn't know that because of my social status, because of my family's wealth, my picture would be splashed around on every glossy magazine in Australia.'

'Actually...' she nodded '...I did know about your wealth.'

He angled his head to the side, frowning a little. 'You mean after I left the Caribbean?'

'No. I knew exactly who you were from the moment we met.'

'What?'

'I knew you were the heir apparent to the Jamieson Corporation.'

'You did?' He looked down at her hand again, before meeting her eyes. 'That wasn't why you...?'

He trailed off, feeling stupid for even voicing the thought, but suddenly he recalled his father's bitter words, the doubts that he had placed in Flynn's head once upon a time. Caught up in the grief of losing his mother, breaking things off with Reggie and being pressured to marry a woman who was more a sister than a wife, Flynn's temper had exploded when his father had refused to back down about the wedding reception.

'If you go ahead with this, I will not attend,' he'd told his father.

'Don't be ridiculous, Flynn. Of course you'll be there.'

'No. I've only just buried my mother and I want time to grieve before we go splashing our fake happiness around the society pages.'

'Fake happiness! Violet is a fine woman and she'll make you a fine wife. She's perfect for you, Flynn. She always has been.'

'I think Violet might have something to say about that.'

'Violet does whatever she's told. She doesn't have an

original thought in her head. She's been told her whole life that she's going to marry you and she's accepted it.'

'Then she's wrong.' Flynn had shaken his head. 'I love someone else, Dad.' There. The words had finally been spoken and where Flynn had somehow thought they would make a difference, his father had flicked the statement aside with a wave of his hand as though he had been shooing away a pesky fly.

'What do you know about love? Some gold-digging nurse you met in the Caribbean? A holiday romance? That's not serious, Flynn. All women see when they look at you is dollar signs. They want your money, not you. That's where Violet is different. She comes from money.'

'And the fact that you and her father are merging your businesses has nothing at all to do with this.'

His father had spread his hands wide as though indicating he had nothing to hide. 'Just seizing an opportunity, son.'

'Sure.' Flynn had stalked to the window and looked out at the extensive grounds. So green when everywhere else in the country had been brown due to drought. 'She wasn't a nurse and she wasn't a gold-digger.' He'd spoken the words more to himself than to his father, needing to reassure himself of the real reasons Reggie had admitted to loving him.

'You think that, if it helps you sleep at night but, rest assured, if she knew you had money, that would be the only reason she latched onto you.' His father had tapped his own chest. 'I've just saved the company tens of thousands of dollars in settlement fees, not to mention protecting us from having our private affairs splashed all over the papers.'

'Oh, but splashing this wedding reception all over the papers is fine?'

'It's controlled. Now, go and find Violet and thank your lucky stars you had a mother who was looking out for your best interests by finding you the right wife.'

Flynn exhaled slowly as he ran his fingers over Reggie's hand once more, marvelling at her soft, silky skin. These were the hands that had performed intricate surgery on twelve-year-old Lola, the hands that had held his as they'd walked along the beach, the hands that had caressed his face before she'd whispered the words 'I love you' near his lips.

'Are you trying to ask me if I fell in love with you because of your *money*?' She all but spat the word at him.

'Er…um…'

'You don't sound too sure about that, Flynn.' Reggie pulled her hand from his and stood from the lounge, pacing up and down. 'Do you know, it was *because* I knew you came from money that I tried to keep my distance, tried to keep the relationship between us strictly professional.'

'You hugged me on my first day as a way of greeting. That wasn't keeping a distance, Reg,' he stated.

Reggie shrugged. 'That's how I greeted everyone. I didn't want to call attention to the fact that I knew who you were by doing anything different.'

'So you didn't love me?' Flynn felt compelled to asked as he watched her. It was difficult not to stand and drag her back into his arms because when Reggie got fired up like this, she was more dynamic, more beautiful, more alluring than ever.

'Well, of course I loved you…back then. I did agree to marry you and, contrary to how *you* may do things, when I accept a marriage proposal, it's because I'm in love with the man who's asking.' She glared at him, almost daring him to comment.

'I was in love with you back then, too,' he said. 'But I'd been raised to do my duty to my family and... No.' He shook his head again before standing and walking towards her, his hands open, palms up, indicating he had nothing to hide. She stopped pacing for a moment and looked at him. 'No. No more excuses. I hurt you, Reggie and for that I apologise.'

She gave him a brief nod, showing she accepted his words, and while part of her wanted nothing more than to throw herself into his arms and press her mouth to his, the other part was still simmering with repressed anger. Flynn came from money, from a wealthy and prestigious family, and she knew, firsthand, that those types of people couldn't be trusted. Had he changed? Well, he was divorced from his pretty socialite wife, or so the tabloids had reported a while back, but who was to say that was actually true?

She angled her head, needing to check. 'You *are* divorced from Violet, aren't you?'

'Yes.'

Reggie clenched her jaw and crossed her arms over her chest. 'But you still want to be sure that I didn't chase after you for your money, don't you? You'll always be wondering, right?' When he didn't immediately answer she rolled her eyes and started to pace again.

'Well, you'll be pleased to hear, Flynn, that I have *never* been interested in one single penny of your precious Jamieson Corporation millions. Not then and most definitely not now. Even accepting your help with relocating my neighbours, knowing the big corporation was footing the bill and no doubt using it as a tax dodge, was a big hurdle for me to personally overcome.'

'I didn't offer the corporation's money to help those people, Reg,' he quickly interjected. 'I'm offering my own. The wealth, as you term it, that I have now has nothing to do with my father's corporation. The money I have came to me after my mother's death. My inheritance. I was cut out of my father's will and, therefore, any claim to the corporation the moment I signed the divorce papers.'

That stopped her pacing. She stared at him in surprise. 'You...you've walked away from your father?'

'From his blackmail, from his controlling presence, from his world? Yes.'

'Oh.' She dropped her arms back to her sides. 'I didn't realise.'

'It's been three years now.'

'You've been divorced for three years?'

'Officially, yes.'

'Oh,' she said again, the anger starting to dissipate. 'And you didn't...?' She stopped. How could she possibly ask him if he'd thought of her during that time? Whether he'd tried to find her? Had he even really cared about her amidst all his other family politics?

'Didn't what?' he prompted, but she shook her head and thankfully he dropped the subject. Flynn took a tentative step towards her and when she didn't back away he tried another and another until he was standing before her. 'It was a mistake for me to marry Violet.'

'Yes.'

'It was a mistake for me to treat you so badly.'

'Yes.'

Flynn reached out and brushed his fingers through

her gorgeous black locks. 'Do you think we can try again?'

'Try again…as in…what? What does that mean?'

'It means…' he reached down and linked his free hand with hers '…that we see if, after everything we've been through, whether we're still…compatible.' His tone was soft, smooth and inviting. Reggie could feel herself beginning to crumble, could feel the walls she so desperately wanted to keep in place begin to weaken, and when he bent his head and brushed a soft and tantalising kiss across her cheek, her eyelids fluttered closed and she breathed in the scent of him.

Good heavens. The man smelled fantastic. How did he do that after such a busy and stressful day?

'I don't…' She stopped and swallowed over the dryness of her throat. 'I don't know, Flynn.'

'Why? Because I hurt you before?' He brushed a kiss to her other cheek, lingering a little longer.

'Mmm-hmm,' she sighed, parting her lips to allow the pent-up air to escape.

'Do you think you can trust me again?' He whispered the words near her mouth, keeping such a marginal distance that she started to yearn for his lips to be on hers once more. From their very first kiss to their very last, his mouth had always fitted hers perfectly, as though they'd been made for each other. 'Do you?'

'I don't know.' The whispered words were barely audible and Flynn drew back slightly. He cupped her face with one hand and brushed his thumb over her parted lips. She gasped with surprised delight, opening her eyes to stare into his. 'The attraction is clearly alive and well.'

'Yes.'

'And I know you trust me as far as work is concerned.'

'Yes.'

'And you know I'd never force you to do anything you didn't want to so I can safely say that you can trust me with your honour.'

'Yes.'

'So what is it, Reggie? What is it that is holding you back from giving me…giving *us* another chance?'

Reggie bit her lip, the intrusive thoughts from her past bursting forth into her mind at his question. Why couldn't she give him another chance? 'Because you're wealthy and I don't trust wealthy people.'

'What?' He eased back, dropping his hand to her shoulder. 'I don't understand.'

'Wealth corrupts. Even the nicest, strongest people. It corrupts them.'

'And you know this how? Because of me being unable to stand up to my father all those years ago?'

'No. This has nothing to do with you, Flynn. It does, however, have everything to do with me.'

'You? You've been hurt by wealthy people before?'

Reggie couldn't believe the way her repressed memories, ones she'd carefully locked away in a mental box with 'Do Not Touch' written all over it, continued to flood her mind. Her anxiety and agitation started to increase and she turned away from Flynn, needing distance, needing space. She sucked in a breath and then another one, trying not to hyperventilate while she desperately searched for her self-control. She breathed out, unable to believe the fear rising within her, making her throat go dry, almost choking her. Flynn frowned, noting the paleness of her complexion.

'Reg?' She could hear the concern in his voice.

She closed her eyes and shook her head, knowing she needed to say these words to Flynn. It was true that she would love to have another chance with him and where all those years ago she'd been unable to talk about her past, unable to open up to him and tell him the disgusting things that had happened to her, she knew if there was ever any hope of any sort of future for herself and Flynn, she had to tell him the truth.

'I can't say it.' The words were a whisper and when he crossed to her and put his hands on her shoulders, coaxing her to look at him, all she could do was close her eyes and shake her head vehemently.

'It's all right, Reggie. Whatever you have to say, I'm here.' He'd never seen her like this before, so small and childlike. The Reggie he'd always known had been larger than life, vibrant, funny, with the most infectious laugh. 'You're starting to really worry me,' he said, and it was then, when she heard the tremor in his voice, that she knew she had to do this.

She swallowed again and opened her eyes. As she lifted her chin so she could meet Flynn's gaze, her heart was pounding furiously in her chest.

'Easy. Gently. It's all right, Reg. I'm here. Right here. Nothing you can say will change that.'

'You haven't heard what it is I have to say.'

'Trust me, Reg.' He brushed a feather-light kiss across her lips, not to break the mood or for any romantic reason but rather to give her courage. 'Please?'

Reggie breathed out again and nodded, his hands on her shoulders helping to calm her anxious brain. 'OK.' She breathed out, unable to believe she was really going to open that hateful box and expose herself, her inner self, to Flynn.

'All those years ago, when we first met, I knew who you were because I was raised in Melbourne, not far from where you lived.'

'What?' It had clearly been the last thing he'd expected her to say.

'I hate wealthy people because…my parents were wealthy. In fact, my father knew your father.'

'What?' She'd clearly stunned him.

'When I turned eighteen I changed my name by deed poll to Regina Smith.'

'Why?' Flynn was starting to get a bad feeling in his stomach at what she was saying. 'What name were you christened with?'

She forced calmness into her words as she spoke. 'My name was…Regina Anne Catherine Elizabeth Fox-Wallington.'

'Fox-Wallington?' He whispered the surname with incredulity and disbelief.

'I see you remember my family well.'

'You're *that* Regina? The young girl who was abused by her parents?'

She forced herself to keep her chin up, to keep looking into his eyes, seeing his own disbelief at what she was saying. 'Yes,' she confirmed. 'I'm *that* Regina.'

CHAPTER NINE

'OH, REG.' FLYNN shook his head, anguish in his voice. 'I remember. It was in the papers, on the news. They'd been abusing you for years. Physically as well as emotionally.'

Strangely enough, now that she'd come this far, now that she'd confessed the secret of her real identity to Flynn, the pressure of the anxiety started to dissipate. She cleared her throat, amazed at how normal her voice sounded when she spoke. 'For years my parents made sure their private physician looked after me, treating my wounds, isolating me when they took longer to heal than expected.'

'What?'

'Wealth corrupts. That doctor had no problem with being paid off and when the truth finally came out, he had the gall to state that he would often suggest they send me to another boarding school in order to save me from their wrath. I was nothing but a punching bag to my father and my mother would slap me around and then put her cigarettes out on me. The physician was struck off the register and is doing gaol time.'

'Oh, Reg.' Tears came into Flynn's eyes as she recounted the events with little to no emotion. It was a defence mechanism, he knew that, but, still, the traumas she must have endured. 'How did you finally managed to bring it all to light?'

'The last school they sent me to, when I was sixteen, was rife with bullies and, quite frankly, by then I'd had enough of being everyone's punching bag. I'd tried to talk to my teachers at school, to counsellors, but no one would ever believe that the great and powerful Walter Fox-Wallington would ever hit his own child.

'As I was treated by their private doctor, there were no medical records of my injuries, of my broken bones, of my extensive bruising—no *proof*—so why *would* anyone believe me? As far as the teachers and counsellors were concerned, I was a spoiled and wealthy brat who was clearly troubled and who loved to make up stories about her parents.

'Besides, if they actually did find the courage to question my parents, which a few of them did, my father would pull his financial support from the school or slap a law suit on anyone who dared question his word.' Reggie shrugged both her shoulders, Flynn's hands rising and falling with the action. 'You can do anything with money. At least, that was my father's motto and one he used to spit at me every time he "donated" enormous sums of money in order to keep people quiet.'

'But surely someone knew he was corrupt?'

'I'm sure plenty of people did but blackmail, self-preservation and the power of wealth go a long way to buying silence. Besides, he'd simply smile brightly and tell people I was a delusional teenager, a spoiled brat with a grudge against her parents.'

'So…how did you…escape that life?' He was agog at what she was saying.

'I ran away from boarding school. I stowed away on a goods train and ended up in Sydney. There, I found a drop-in centre and a solicitor, Elika, who wasn't afraid to take the case on. Pro bono, of course.'

Flynn was still stunned as he stared down into her face. She'd been through so much and his heart ached for her. No wonder she hated people with money. She had good reason to. 'I remember the story breaking.' His words were soft. 'I remember my father doing everything he could to distance himself from the Fox-Wallington fiasco, as he termed it. He also pulled any and all investments he had in your father's companies.'

'So he wasn't as much concerned with what had happened but rather with protecting himself.'

Flynn shrugged. 'Everything was business to him. Even my mother and myself, although my mother knew what sort of life she was signing up for when she married him.'

'The wealthy have their own set of rules and heaven help anyone who dares to stand up to them or go against them.'

'Ain't that the truth.' His words were filled with heartfelt honesty and as Reggie looked into his eyes she saw that perhaps, just perhaps, there was a possibility that Flynn really understood what it was she was trying to say.

'So where are your parents now? I can't remember what happened.'

'They're dead.' The words were said with no emotion, no relief, no bitterness, no pain. 'When my father realised he couldn't buy off the solicitor, he and my mother left the country for Spain.'

Flynn rolled his eyes. 'No extradition.'

'Exactly. They lived there for almost two years, in perfect luxury, before dying in a boating accident.' She frowned, her voice dropping just a little. 'I wasn't sad when I was told of their deaths. Instead, I demanded to see the bodies—just to make sure.'

'You did? It wasn't…traumatic?'

'I'd just started medical school, so I'd seen my fair share of cadavers. Besides, I'm not meaning to sound callous but I needed to know if it was true. To help me come to terms with the horrific things they did to me, I needed to see their cold, dead bodies on that slab.' She looked away from him. 'I'm sorry if that sounds harsh but—'

'I understand, Reg. Those people weren't your parents, they were the monsters who had made your life a misery.'

Reggie jerked her head up in surprise. 'Yes. Exactly.'

'You had to be sure it was really over.'

'And it was. I identified their bodies and with Elika's help organised for their cremations. There was no funeral, no wake, no chance for people to "honour" those monsters.'

Flynn rubbed his hands along her shoulders, knowing he shouldn't be at all surprised at the inner strength this woman possessed. He gazed down into her eyes. 'You are incredible, Reg. So strong and always so happy and bubbly and yet you've been through so much pain. How did you cope?'

'Well, for a start, I found some wonderful friends at medical school. Sunainah, Bergan and Mackenzie have all been through their own pain and anguish and somehow, although the four of us are incredibly different, we bonded because we all understood what it was like to be a victim.'

'And it's a friendship that's as strong and as true over twenty years later.'

'Yes.' She smiled, thinking of the way she and her friends had stuck together through thick and thin…and how they'd all managed to find the man of their dreams, that one special person they could always rely on, no matter what. The smile started to slide from her lips as she gazed up at Flynn. Was *he* her one special person? The one she could rely on, no matter what?

She'd thought so once before but he'd let her down. Was it possible she could take a chance again? Put her heart out there? Would Flynn hurt her again, especially now that he knew the truth about her past? He was looking at her as though she was the most wonderful, most special and most precious person in the world to him. Was that real?

He'd mentioned the attraction between them being still as strong…possibly stronger than before and he'd been right. When he put his arms around her, she felt as though she'd come home. When he kissed her, she felt as though her entire world was filled with sparkles and rainbows and pure happiness. When he gazed down into her eyes, as he was doing right now, her heart constricted and her breathing became shallow, wanting him to look at her that way always, to support her always, to love her always.

Could they try again?

'Reg, you are special to me. I hope you believe that.'

'I want to,' she whispered.

'Then do it.' He cupped her face and smiled at her before dipping his head to brush his lips lightly across hers. Reggie closed her eyes, wanting to absorb every sensation he was evoking within her, wanting to lose herself in the pleasure and happiness only Flynn could give her. They'd been so good together all those years ago. Perhaps now they could be better. She parted her lips to deepen the kiss but Flynn edged back. 'Reggie?'

'Mmm?' she sighed, her eyes still closed.

'There's just one thing I need to know.' There was a tentativeness in his tone and she immediately looked at him, worry piercing her.

'What?' She searched his beautiful blue eyes and instinctively realised what it was he was still confused about. 'The money?'

'Yes. Your father, from what I can recall, was worth a lot of money.'

'He was. He left it all to my mother, expecting her to outlive him. She, however, hadn't made a will and as their daughter I inherited it all.'

'You did?'

'I did.'

'So...you're wealthy?'

She shook her head. 'No. I didn't want a penny. I signed the entire fortune over to Elika, the solicitor who helped me, the one person who I knew was unlikely to be corrupted. Then I changed my name. My past was gone. Erased. I had a clean slate and I could start again.'

'Wait.' He eased back and held up one hand. 'Let me get this straight. You gave the *entire* Fox-Wallington fortune away?'

'Yes.'

'But that would have been...billions.'

'Wealth corrupts.' She tried to edge away from him

but he immediately put both his hands on her shoulders again.

'But what about medical school?'

'What about it? I did what normal people do. I accepted government funding to pay my university fees, found a cheap place to live and worked all sorts of jobs in order to have enough money to eat.'

'And this solicitor, Elika, what has she done with all that money?'

'Ever heard of the Moffat Drop-in Centres?'

'For teens and abused children?'

'Yes, as well as children and teenagers living on the street, or those who are having a hard time. There's a centre here in Maroochydore that Bergan and Richard do a lot of work with.'

'That's you?'

'No. That's Elika, the solicitor. Well, she's more of a businesswoman nowadays and well into her sixties, but she's still making a difference and the drop-in centres are just the tip of the iceberg. She works with various organisations both in Australia and overseas to help people in need.'

'You just gave all that money away?'

'Why wouldn't I? As far as I was concerned, it was blood money and, besides, it had never brought me happiness. All I've ever wanted was to be normal. A normal girl, doing a normal job, living a normal life.'

'Wow.' He shook his head in wonderment.

'What?'

'You're…so strong.'

'It took me years to piece myself back together, to figure out who I wanted to be as an adult, and with the help of my friends I think I've done a pretty good job.'

'Why didn't you tell me any of this all those years ago?'

'Because it's also taken me years to learn who to trust. It's not an easy thing for me to do and, for the record, I had planned to tell you everything the day after we became engaged, but—'

'But I broke it off.' He closed his eyes, unable to believe how ridiculously stupid he'd been back then. 'And I turned out to be yet another wealthy person you couldn't trust.'

'That's how I saw it.'

'But, for the record, Reggie—and I'm not trying to defend my actions back then or justify my behaviour— I wasn't corrupted by money. I was corrupted by guilt. I didn't marry Violet because my father threatened to cut me off without a cent. I did it because my mother was dying and it was the one thing that would make her happy, to see her son happily settled.'

Reggie looked up into his eyes and for the first time since they'd been talking reached up and brushed her fingers across his cheek. 'You loved your mother.' It was a statement because she could see clearly in his eyes, hear it in his voice.

'I did. Very much.'

'You wanted to make her happy in her last days.'

'Yes, but I let myself get pressured into doing something I should never have done. I resent that now.'

'But you're not that man anymore. I can tell. You're stronger now. You're more...*you*.' She shook her head. 'I'm not explaining that well.'

'No. You're right. I am different.' He gave her a cute, lopsided smile. 'Perhaps these six years apart haven't been a total waste of time.'

'Perhaps we both needed to do some more growing up.'

'Exactly. I've found the courage to change, not because anyone's told me to but because I needed to, for myself. I needed to find out who I was, without my parents, without Violet and without any other pressure.'

'And have you?'

The smile on his lips increased as he shifted towards her, his arms coming about her waist to draw her near. 'Yes. It took me a while to realise it, that I needed to change my life because I wasn't happy.'

'It can be the most difficult thing in the world to do, to take a stand and follow your heart, to do what you know is right.'

'Yes.' He smiled at her. 'And now I need to do what I know is right, to follow my heart and kiss you once more, Reg.'

Reggie loved hearing those words from his mouth and as she sighed against him she couldn't help but raise one teasing eyebrow. 'Only once more?'

His grin widened as he settled her into his arms. 'I like the way you're thinking.' And with that he lowered his head and claimed her mouth in a kiss filled with passion and promise. Exactly what those promises might be she had no idea, but for now she was more than happy just to go with the fact that she'd managed to work up the courage to tell Flynn about her past... and he hadn't rejected her. He'd understood. He'd supported her. He'd accepted.

He was also doing the most wonderful and delectable things to her mouth, tantalising and teasing her senses. The love she knew had never died welled up in her heart, bursting forth with delight throughout her entire body. She loved Flynn. She always had but she knew of old that to love someone didn't necessarily mean there would be a happy ending.

Still, he knew just how to hold her, just how to kiss her, just how to drive her completely crazy with longing. He knew that rubbing small circles at the base of her spine caused tingles to explode within her. He knew that pressing sweet butterfly kisses along her cheek, towards her ear and then down to her neck made goosebumps break out over her entire body.

He knew that whispering words of delight, telling her just how attractive he found her, how he was drawn to her, how he couldn't get enough of her, all drove her almost to distraction.

Soon she was light-headed and swooning, leaning against him for support as her knees started to give way. Within another second Flynn had scooped her up into his arms and carried her to the lounge. He sat down, settling her in his lap, his arms shifting to hold her tightly, his mouth not leaving hers for an instant.

Reggie sighed against him, unable to believe she was finally back here again, back in his arms, back where she'd yearned to be for so very long. Flynn was here. *Her* Flynn, and he was kissing her exactly as he had during all her dreams about him.

'Mmm,' she moaned as he continued to wreak havoc with her senses. She could feel his restraint, feel he was trying to keep things soft and steady, not wanting to scare her away, but didn't he realise that she didn't scare easily? She wanted him. Couldn't he feel that?

The fact that he was taking things slowly was only making her desire for him increase and when he eased his mouth from hers to trace her lips tantalisingly with his tongue, knowing how the action drove her crazy, his breath mingling and blending with hers, Reggie thought her heart would burst.

'Flynn,' she breathed. 'I want you.'

'I know.' He kissed her cheek.

'This can't be wrong. Not a second time.'

'No.' He kissed her other cheek.

'Shouldn't we go…somewhere a little more comfortable?' The words were a husky whisper as he continued to kiss her neck, Reggie tilting her head to the side to grant him all the access he desired.

'No.'

Reggie's eyes flew open, his one-word answer like a stylus scratching its way across a record. 'No?'

'No,' he repeated, his voice thick with repressed desire.

She shifted so she could look at him better and as she did so he seemed to take it as a sign to remove her from his lap and to settle her next to him on the lounge. 'Flynn?' She swallowed over the confusion even she could hear in her voice.

'Reg, I don't want to rush things.' He bent and kissed her lips as though needing her to know he was still very much on board with what was happening between them. 'This time we need to take things slowly.'

'Because we didn't take things slowly last time?'

'Exactly. And…' he brushed the backs of his fingers across her cheek and then pushed some of her dark, spiky locks behind her ear '…you deserve better. With everything you've confessed to me, plus with everything that's happened in the past few days, I think we're definitely starting to move way too fast again. Don't you?'

Reggie stared at him, unable to believe the words

were coming out of his mouth. How was it possible he could be even more wonderful, more considerate, more chivalrous than she remembered? He cared about her. He *really* cared about her and he was willing to prove that by slowing things down. She opened her mouth to agree with him but found the words were stuck behind the bubble of emotion, so she nodded instead.

'I was wondering, just this morning, how you were able to deal with your home burning down so easily, how you could just accept the fact and not wallow and cry and scream, as you most certainly have every right to do, but now...' Flynn brushed his thumb over her lips before bending and mimicking the same action with his lips '...with everything you've been through, you've built up an amazing resilience to things beyond your control. That, my beautiful Reg, is an amazing quality and you have it in spades. You just pick yourself up and keep on moving forward and I want you to know just how much I admire you.'

'Oh, Flynn.' She couldn't believe he was saying such nice things to her and quickly fanned her face with her hand, needing to lighten the atmosphere around them with a touch of humour. It worked because he smiled warmly in response. 'You say the sweetest things.'

'I meant every word.'

She dropped the pretence for a moment and nodded. 'I don't doubt it.'

'Good, because I think the next thing we should discuss is getting some sleep—me upstairs, you downstairs and, no, that isn't a euphemism or meant as a *double entendre*.'

Reggie laughed; the sound lighter and freer than she could ever remember hearing before. Flynn removed his arm from around her shoulders, then stood and pulled her to her feet. He held her hand as he walked her to her room. 'Make free use of the bathroom. I'll use the en suite.'

'OK.' She stood at the door to her room and looked up at him. She smiled then stood on tiptoe and kissed him. 'Who said chivalry was dead?' she asked rhetorically.

'Taking things slower is a good thing.'

'Yes.'

'We deserve the time to really get to know each other again.'

'Yes.'

Flynn smiled and took her hand in his, raising it to his lips. 'Sleep sweet, Reg.' Then he bowed from the waist and headed up the stairs, blowing her one last kiss from the top. Reggie couldn't help but giggle as she entered the room, sighing romantically.

'Oh, Flynn, you really do know how to make a girl feel special,' she whispered, and it was so true. She could trust him. He was showing her that by not rushing into things. He cared about her and it was still a little difficult for her to get her head around that realisation. Was it possible that this time they'd be able to really move forward with their life together? A normal life together? After all, wasn't Flynn the most perfect man for her?

Surely, with everything they'd discussed tonight, there was no way he'd ever hurt her again. Right?

CHAPTER TEN

FROM THE NEXT morning, even though they hadn't specifically discussed it, they appeared to be back together. When Reggie had come into the kitchen for breakfast, Flynn once more having already made the coffee and toast, he'd crossed to her side, given her a hug and brushed a light kiss across her lips.

'Good morning,' he'd said, smiling warmly at her.

'Morning,' she'd returned, before hugging him back, unable to believe how wonderful it felt to be so familiar with him again. He drove them to the hospital but still kept his distance in front of their colleagues, which she was happy about because she wasn't ready for everyone to be staring and gawking at them when she was still trying to figure things out.

He took her shopping for clothes and shoes and all the other little things she needed, not appearing bored by any of the shops they visited or insisting she shop at the most expensive places. She modelled clothes for him, twirling and laughing and smiling and trying to remember when she'd last been this happy. Her car was returned from the garage and he insisted she leave it in his garage, parking his own car in the driveway.

The little girl, Lola, who had been attacked by the

shark, was starting to make progress with her recovery and while it would indeed be a long journey, all the surgeons involved in her care were happy with the way her body was coping with the trauma.

Things were also building up for the hospital's Christmas auction and Reggie and Mackenzie spent quite a bit of time finalising the details.

'One of the outpatient ward clerks signed me up for the bachelor auction that very first morning I was in Outpatients,' Flynn told Reggie when she noticed his name on the sign-up sheet.

'But you're not a bachelor anymore,' she felt compelled to point out.

'Well, technically I am as I'm not married.'

'But we are in a…relationship…' She looked at him with concern. 'Aren't we?'

Or did he just think their time together was a fling? Something to keep him occupied during his six months at the hospital? Had she grasped the wrong end of the stick again? Did she feel more for him than he felt—

'Stop,' he commanded, and when she looked at him, her eyes wide with concern and worry, she noticed he was smiling at her, slowly shaking his head from side to side. 'I can hear your thoughts from here, Reg.' He cupped her face and brought his lips down to warm hers. 'Of course we're in a relationship. Together. Both of us. Mutually exclusive. But apart from our closest friends, no one at the hospital knows that. To pull out of the auction now would raise suspicion.'

'And you don't want to do that?'

Flynn tugged her into his arms, nuzzling her neck once more. 'I like having you all to myself, Reg. I like not having people gossip about us as we walk by. During our lives, and for different reasons, we've both been the topic of discussion and while I know it will happen one day, that the cat will be out of the proverbial bag, I just want a bit longer to have you all to myself.' He pressed his mouth to hers, making her swoon with delight from his glorious kisses.

'I guess it is for a good cause,' she rationalised.

'And I'm absolutely positive that there's a very special woman who's going to ensure she wins the auction.' He glared pointedly at her.

'Really? Which woman is that?' Reggie giggled but pretended to ponder the question. 'Ingrid Brown? She's very interested in you.'

He wrinkled his nose. 'A great surgical registrar but not my type.'

'Clara from Outpatients? Or perhaps—' Her words were cut off as Flynn kissed her into silence.

'You are going to win that auction, Reg,' he whispered in her ear after tantalising her with a thread of butterfly kisses, a spate of delighted goose-bumps flooding her skin. 'Even if I have to give you every last cent.' He lifted his head and looked into her eyes. 'I don't want to be with any other woman—except you.'

Reggie sighed into him as his wonderful words penetrated her heart, accepting the way his mouth continued to create havoc with her equilibrium.

She was still walking on feathers, on pillows, on air when she met Bergan, Mackenzie and Sunainah for coffee. Christmas wasn't that far away and everywhere she went there were people collecting for charity, Santa Clauses in every store, tinsel, carollers and a generally festive atmosphere that was difficult to ignore.

'So…you and Flynn? Still super-happy?' Mackenzie asked.

'Do you even need to ask? Just look at her,' Bergan pointed out. 'It's as plain as the nose on your face,' she remarked, before sipping her coffee.

'You are even happier than usual,' Sunainah added.

'And this time,' Mackenzie remarked as she grinned widely at her friend, 'the happiness you're shining out at the world isn't forced—it's real.'

Reggie giggled, nodding her head at the three of them. 'It's so wonderful and exciting and new and scary and—'

'We've all been there.' Bergan's tone was matter-of-fact. 'A mixture of emotions that keeps your insides churning with angst and delight. You don't need to go on about it.' She wasn't usually one for gushy sentimentality but she reached over and pressed a kiss to her friend's cheek. 'And I couldn't be happier for you,' she said softly, and all of them laughed.

'So are there any plans for a wed—?'

'Stop!' Reggie held up her hand, cutting off Mackenzie's sentence. 'There has been no discussion about anything except that last time we rushed into things far too quickly and this time, well, Flynn wants to take his time.'

'Are you two sharing…a room?' Bergan asked coyly.

'No. Again, he wants to take it slowly.'

'But you have told him about your past? He knows who your parents were?' Sunainah asked quietly.

'Yes.'

'Then it is good he is wanting to take it slowly.' Sunainah nodded in approval. 'I am liking this Flynn Jamieson more and more.'

'But it would be great if we could get to know him better,' Mackenzie pointed out.

'Uh-oh.' Bergan rolled her eyes. 'I'd know that organising look anywhere. Warning. Warning. Cul-de-sac crew gathering imminent.'

Reggie laughed. 'I think it would be great for Flynn to get to know the rest of you much better, too.'

'No doubt Elliot, Richard and John will want to take him under their wing, teach him the dos and don'ts of dealing with the four of us?' Mackenzie clapped her hands. 'Oh, it's just the way I've always wanted it. The four of us, living near each other, helping each other, being a family together.'

Reggie wanted to point out again that nothing was permanently fixed between herself and Flynn but one look at Mackenzie's brightly smiling face and Reggie swallowed the words. For now she could keep her concerns to herself. Like Flynn, she wanted to take things slowly, make sure that they were both on the same page, that they wanted the same things out of life.

For example, she had no idea whether he planned to live in the Sunshine Coast once his contract at the hospital had ended. Did he want to have children in the future? Did he want to travel? How did he see their working relationship? Did he want to work at a different hospital from her? When would he be ready to take their relationship to the next level? Was he still in contact with his father? Did he want her to meet his father? What had really happened between himself and Violet, his ex-wife?

When they'd been together in the Caribbean, he'd occasionally spoken of Violet and his family. 'I'm an only child and so is she,' he'd once told Reggie as they'd walked hand in hand along the beach, admiring the breathtaking sunset.

'Our mothers are the closest of friends and although Violet is a few years younger than me, the two of us have sort of been raised together. We went to the same schools. I was told to look out for her. We played together when we were young. We celebrated birthdays and Christmases with each other's families.'

'So she's just a friend?' Reggie had asked, slightly jealous of the wonderful life he was describing.

'Yes. Nothing more than a friend,' he'd confirmed.

And yet not too long after they'd had that conversation he'd been married to Violet. Now that he'd told her the true circumstances surrounding that union, Reggie still had questions. Was he still friendly with Violet? If so, *how* friendly? Or had their forced marriage been the undoing of a lifetime of friendship? Was that why he didn't talk about her much?

That evening, as they sat watching an old movie together, Reggie really wanted to ask him about Violet, find out some of the answers to the questions that were spinning around in her head, but every time she opened her mouth to speak, she found the words simply wouldn't come out. Surely if he was still in close contact with Violet he would have said something. Wouldn't he? Perhaps the fact that he hadn't spoken much about her indicated their marriage had indeed wrecked the friendship and now the two of them were estranged.

'What am I supposed to do?' she asked Mackenzie as the two of them put the final touches on the ballroom, ready for tomorrow night's Christmas auction. They'd worked closely with the event co-ordinator and she had to admit that the room did indeed look incredibly festive, with green and red tinsel around the place, twinkle lights and a large Christmas tree in the corner. Still, they were responsible for the table decorations and as they'd spent the last few weeks making them, as well as getting people to donate things for the auction. But no matter how many great items were up for bidding, the bachelor auction was most definitely the highlight of the night.

'You're supposed to talk to him,' Mackenzie told her. 'If you want to know about Violet, just ask him. He'll tell you.'

'It's not that I don't trust him,' Reggie began, and Mackenzie raised one eyebrow in question. 'OK.' She spread her arms wide. 'So perhaps I do have a few trust issues. I just want to be sure, this time, that he's not going to up and leave me again. I won't be able to live through the pain a second time. I just won't survive.'

'And you think he's still in touch with Violet?'

'He has to be. Their families are connected and yet he's said nothing about seeing his father at Christmas, or—'

'OK. OK,' Mackenzie interrupted, and put her hands on Reggie's shoulders. 'The only way for you to get rid of this stress and anxiety you're heaping on yourself is to talk to him.' Mackenzie's phone rang and she stared at Reggie for a moment longer before answering it.

'You're right. You're right. I know you're right,' Reggie said, more to herself than to her friend. 'I'll talk to him about it tonight. He'd be open to the discussion…' She bit her lip. 'I hope.'

Mackenzie finished her call. 'That was John.'

'Emergency?'

Mackenzie grinned. 'Yes, but not of the medical

kind. Ruthie's having a sleepover at a friend's house and my husband *needs* me.' She waggled her eyebrows up and down and Reggie couldn't help but laugh.

'Then you'd better get out of here.'

'I can stay and help you finish up here and—'

'Just go. You're lucky enough to have a husband who is crazy about you, so don't go keeping him waiting.'

Mackenzie hugged her friend close. 'Thanks, Reggie.'

Reggie sighed as Mackenzie went, going through the motions of setting up the rest of the table centrepieces before standing back and surveying the room. It looked fantastic. The auction night would be wonderful. They were going to raise a lot of money and she was prepared to pay top dollar for Flynn. No way in the world was she letting Ingrid Brown or any other woman secure the auction prize of a dinner date with the man she loved.

'I'm looking forward to winning you at the auction,' she'd told him the previous night. 'Then I'll have my very own slave.'

'Hey, that's not the terms of the contract. Whoever wins the auction gets to have dinner with me. That's it.' He'd shaken his head and waggled his finger at her. 'No one said anything about slave duties.'

Reggie had playfully slid one hand up his arm and then walked the fingers of her other hand up his chest, and Flynn's grin had widened. 'That depends on what you classify as *slave duties*.'

'Hmm.' He'd accepted the kiss she'd placed on his lips. 'I guess it does.'

After that, they didn't talked much for a while, the two of them completely absorbed in each other, but when things started to get a little heated, Flynn was the one to put on the brakes. 'You make it very difficult to take our time and to go slowly with this relationship,' he murmured against her lips. 'Especially when you are so incredibly delectable and addictive,' he continued, pressing kisses to her neck.

'Likewise,' she returned, plunging her fingers into his hair and bringing his head back so their lips could meet once more. 'It's difficult, Flynn. I want you so much.'

'I know.' He pressed his mouth to hers, slowing things down before lying next to her on the soft rug on the living-room floor. He continued to hold her in his arms, the two of them just lying there. 'I like just... being with you. There's no stress or tension or pressure to be something I'm not. I can be myself with you and you can be yourself with me, and all of that means more to me than anything, Reg.'

He levered himself up onto one elbow and looked down into her beautiful face. 'I don't want you to think I take you for granted. I know what we have between us is rare and unique and incredibly special and I just don't want to mess it up.'

Reggie grinned. 'Slow it is, then.'

'It's the right thing for both of us,' he remarked, before looking past her and frowning.

'What's wrong?' she asked, a frisson of concern churning within her belly.

'Huh?'

'You're frowning. Is there anything I can help you with?'

The frown cleared at her words. 'Nothing's wrong.'

'Really?' Reggie shifted her head so she could see him better. 'Is it your father?'

Flynn shrugged one shoulder. 'I haven't seen or spoken to him in over three years and most of the time I'm fine with that but...'

'Christmas can highlight the fact that families are estranged.'

'Exactly.'

'What did you used to do at Christmas?'

'He'll hire caterers, hold a huge, lavish affair at his house with lots of people he doesn't know, as well as all the people who work in his companies. They'll all get drunk, make mistakes by sleeping with the person they like least and wake up the day after with a multitude of regrets.'

'Sounds like a riot,' she remarked blandly, rubbing her fingertips over the frown lines on his forehead, wanting to do whatever she could to ease them. 'Do you want to see your father?'

'No.' The answer was immediate. 'I've tried in the past to make contact with him and he hasn't appreciated it one little bit. As far as he's concerned, he has no son.'

'Oh, Flynn.'

He swallowed and she knew if she pressed him on the issue he might clam up. She knew what it was like to be disowned by people who were supposed to love you. The wealthy really did have their own set of rules. It was sad that they lived by them. 'So this year,' he said after a moment, 'I am definitely looking forward to starting a new Christmas tradition.'

'Really?'

'With you.'

'Yes.' She kissed him.

'And no doubt the cul-de-sac crew have their big parties and present-giving? Mackenzie and Bergan are already swamped with family. I met Richard's parents yesterday.'

And so they discussed plans for Christmas Day, Reggie more than pleased that it appeared he wanted to spend the day with her. She wanted to ask about Violet. About whether he'd wanted to see her, but she didn't. And now, looking at the festive ballroom, looking perfect for the hospital's Christmas party, she wanted to push aside that one niggling fear of doubt that kept telling her that things seemed too perfect.

'Good things don't happen to me,' she whispered to herself as she headed out into the late-afternoon sunshine. It was such an odd feeling. She had good friends around her. She had a place to stay while all the insurance claims on her apartment were settled. Her neighbours were more than comfortable in the temporary housing Flynn had been generous enough to not only find for them but pay for them. He'd also insisted on remaining anonymous, telling Reggie he didn't need people to be beholden to him.

And above all, she had Flynn back in her life, back wanting to be with her, back wanting a future with her? Hopefully that was the case. Why else would he be insisting they take things slowly? Why else would he be insisting they start their own traditions together?

As she headed down the street towards the hospital, which was only two blocks away, Reggie wondered whether she should tell Flynn that she loved him. Would her declaration change things? Was it what he was waiting to hear before they took their relationship to the next level?

'Oh, why aren't these things as easy as a hernia repair?' she mumbled, as she stopped at the pedestrian lights and pressed the button. She looked down the side street, seeing a family—a mother, a father and little boy—chatting together. A family. A normal family. It was something she'd longed for all her life. The man had his back to her but the woman, with her long blonde hair falling slightly over her face, was folding the stroller and putting it into the boot of her fancy car. The boy was clinging to his father, clearly a little sleepy and more than content to relax in the big, trusty arms that held him.

Reggie sighed, instinctively knowing that Flynn would make a wonderful father. Wouldn't it be nice if that were them? Having spent a lovely day out together, looking forward to heading home and relaxing. Normal people. Normal lives.

The woman closed the boot then held her hands out for the boy. As the man turned to hand the child over, Reggie saw his face. His smiling face—the face smiling at the blonde-haired woman.

'Flynn.' The whispered word left her lips in utter disbelief. The pedestrian lights turned green. Reggie didn't move. Couldn't move as she watched the woman say something to Flynn, both of them laughing brightly. Flynn kissed the little boy and the boy kissed him back, both of them clearly comfortable with each other.

Part of Reggie's mind was racing, panicking, trying to figure out what it was she was seeing, while the other part of her mind was stuck, standing still in stunned shock. Who was the woman? Who was she? Reggie thought back to all those years ago, of the times when she'd read the glossy society mags…and then she remembered where she'd seen that blonde woman. She'd seen her dressed as a bride, she'd seen her looking lovingly up at Flynn as he'd stood beside her—the groom.

The woman was Violet. His ex-wife. After Violet had put the little boy into the car, she'd turned, hugged Flynn close and then pressed a warm kiss to his lips.

Reggie's heart was breaking. It was breaking again. *Flynn* was breaking her heart all over again...and yet it was impossible for her to move. Misery and despair flooded her as the pedestrian lights turned red. Stop. Don't walk. Don't move. Your life is over.

She waited, knowing the inevitable was about to happen, and her heart started pounding out a scared tattooed rhythm against her chest as he began to turn in her direction. In another moment he would see her standing there...watching him.

She shook her head. She didn't want to see him. Didn't want him to see her. Run and hide. *Flee!* Her mind was starting to scream commands at her body but her legs didn't seem able to follow their lead as she remained exactly where she was.

He waved goodbye to the boy in the car, the boy who looked just like him, the boy who was definitely old enough to be his son. If Flynn had a son, why on earth hadn't he told her about him? Was it a condition of his freedom from his father? To hand over access to his son? Was Violet supposed to be in contact with him?

She knew her mind was going into overdrive, clutching at straws to try and make some sort of sense from what she was seeing. The traffic around her was starting to slow again and she became peripherally aware of other people joining her at the pedestrian lights, pressing the button and waiting beside her.

Could they hear the wild pounding of her heart?

Could they feel her pain? Her terror? The one man she'd loved with all her heart had hurt her, not once but twice!

He was turning in her direction, taking a few steps up the street as he continued to wave to the car as Violet indicated and pulled out from the kerb. Reggie couldn't breathe. It was impossible to drag air into her lungs because within a split second he would see her...standing there...watching him betray her.

The moment their gazes met, it was as though the world seemed to stop spinning. Flynn looked confused, then shocked, his eyes widening. His step faltered for a split second, as though he was deciding what it was he should do. He'd just been caught kissing his ex-wife! What would he do?

The next instant he increased his speed, walking with purpose, a determined look in his eyes.

Reggie shook her head and took a step back, even though he was still quite a way away from her. The traffic around her slowed and then the pedestrian lights turned green. The people around her started walking across the street. She looked from the lights back to Flynn and shook her head. Now that she'd actually moved, her body seemed capable of more reaction. Her eyes immediately flooded with tears and her lower lip began to quiver.

'Reggie!'

She shook her head, panic rising within her. She couldn't face him. She didn't want to hear his reasoning, his excuses. All her life people had reasoned with her, provided excuses for the terrible things that had happened to her, and now the one man in the world she'd started to trust, the one man who had captured her heart, was going to break it once again.

'Reg! Wait. I can explain!' His words reached her ears but she brought her hands up, covering them, blocking out his words as she turned and raced across the road just in time. In another instant the traffic started up again, leaving Flynn on one side of the road and Reggie on the other.

Worlds apart, or so it seemed. Flynn had told her she could trust him, that he was different from all the others, but it appeared he'd been lying to her.

Brushing the tears from her eyes so she didn't trip over, Reggie made her way down the street, almost running towards the hospital as though it was her one and only lifeline. The instant she rounded the door, she headed down the stairs, needing to hide herself away, needing to find a place where she could expel the pain from her heart, where she could drag in a cleansing breath, where she could start to make a plan to regroup.

Could she recover from a broken heart yet again? She didn't think so.

CHAPTER ELEVEN

'REGGIE?' BERGAN'S VOICE came over the phone when Reggie had answered the call. 'Where are you?' She'd already rejected several calls from Flynn's cellphone. He was the last person she felt like talking to. How could he? How could he do this to her? She'd opened up her heart, her soul. She'd bared her pain, her horror to him and this was how he thought it was OK to behave? To betray her? No. No. No. The pain in her heart intensified and she choked on another sob.

'Reggie?' Bergan spoke again and it was only the evident concern in her friend's voice that prompted Reggie to answer.

'What?' There was no disguising the tears and pain in her voice as she sniffed and snuffled.

'Where are you? What's happened?' Bergan's tone was insistent and filled with that protective love Reggie had relied on more than once throughout the course of their friendship.

'I... Flynn...' Reggie tried to get the words out but it appeared it was impossible. She'd only just managed to calm herself down, thinking she might be ready to call one of her friends to come and get her, but now that she actually had to put into words what she'd seen,

Reggie found the wave of anguish was washing over her once more.

'He was here in A and E, looking for you, and was quite frankly beside himself with worry. What's happened?'

'Is…is he still th—?' She couldn't finish the sentence, the panic that he might be listening in to this conversation making Reggie skittish again.

'No. I sent him away.'

'Good.' She sighed with relief. 'Good.'

'Where are you?' There was more insistence, more concern in Bergan's words than before.

'When things go belly up, go down, down, down and get as far away as possible.'

'Ah…taking a leaf out of Sunainah's book, eh? Hiding in the basement beneath the stairs. It's a good place, I have to admit. OK. Stay put. I'll be there soon.'

'Don't tell him.' The words were out before she could stop them. 'I don't want to see him. I don't want to speak to him. *Ever.*'

'Relax, Reggie. I've got your back.' With that Bergan disconnected the call and Reggie sat beneath the stairwell in the hospital basement, hugging her knees to her chest.

It was the same place she'd found Sunainah, so long ago now, when Sunainah's life had looked as though there was no possibility for a happy ending. Now her friend was happily married to Elliot, the two of them enjoying being parents to Elliot's wonderful children and even talking about having some of their own. Things had worked out for Sunainah but Reggie couldn't see any possibility of things working out for her and Flynn, not now that he'd betrayed her.

Honesty. That was the main thing she needed out of any relationship. Pure and open honesty, and stupidly she'd thought Flynn had thought the same way. Cover-ups, lies and deceit played no part in her life. Hadn't he understood that?

So why on earth had he been warmly kissing his ex-wife?

He'd been holding a little boy who looked just like him and who he appeared to love very much. Reggie had been able to see that clearly in his eyes. Did Flynn have a son? If so, why hadn't he told her about him? Why had he felt the need to keep secrets from her? Not to trust her? To hurt her by betraying her yet again?

She'd been a fool to think that things were looking up for her, that finally she might be able to find the elusive happiness she'd been searching for all her life. Over and over again people came into her life and they let her down. If it weren't for Mackenzie, Sunainah and Bergan showing her it was indeed possible to trust, Reggie would have given up long ago and allowed the spirit of pessimism and depression to invade her heart.

She searched her pockets for a tissue and eventually found one, dabbing her eyes and blowing her nose, knowing she could well play the part of Santa's lead reindeer with her red face.

'Reggie?'

Finally she heard Bergan's voice echo down the stairwell and held her breath, her eyes wide as she listened to the footfalls on the stairs. Were there two people coming down? Had Flynn been lurking in the shadows? Watching Bergan? Following Bergan, knowing she would lead him to where she was hiding?

'Reggie? I'm alone,' Bergan said, as though answering her unspoken question.

'Are you sure?'

'Yes.' There was absolute certainty in Bergan's words and Reggie breathed out a sigh of relief as she wriggled out from her hiding spot and brushed herself off. The instant Bergan stood before her, Reggie threw herself into her friend's arms, fresh tears spilling forth. Bergan placated her, stroking her back as the gut-wrenching sobs started all over again.

'Here's a fresh pack of tissues,' Bergan eventually offered after a minute or two. Reggie eased back, knowing she must look a sight and immediately wiped her eyes and blew her nose. 'Flynn told me what happened.' Bergan spoke softly. 'He says it's not what you think.'

'How would he know what I think?' Reggie asked, a fresh bout of tears stinging in her eyes. 'He lied to me, Bergan. He kept asking me to trust him and I did and I told him all about my past and how people have constantly let me down—all my life—and now he's done it to me. Not once, but *twice*!' Her words were scattered, broken up between sobs and hiccups, her voice high and bordering on hysteria. *'Twice!'* She held up two fingers as though to confirm it. 'Why am I so stupid? Why do I let him do this to me?'

Bergan shrugged. 'I don't know, Reggie, but first things first. We need to get you out of here. I've left Richard in charge of A and E and I'm taking you—'

'Not to the cul-de-sac.' Her words were instant, her eyes flashing with insistent fire. 'You have people staying with you and so does Mackenzie and I don't want to be near Flynn. I just need space. I need to be able to breathe and to think things through and—'

'I understand and I know the perfect place for you to go. Somewhere safe.' Bergan held out her hand to her friend.

'You do?'

'Come on.' Reggie allowed herself to be led away by Bergan, but couldn't help the need to constantly look over her shoulder just in case Flynn was lurking around the corner. 'Relax. Flynn's gone. He left the hospital over half an hour ago. He said he had some things to organise.'

Reggie sighed with relief at knowing Flynn really wasn't on the hospital grounds and when she was safe in Bergan's car she rested her head back against the seat and closed her eyes, her head starting to pound. All she could see, all she could think about was the image of Violet and Flynn, kissing each other. It was as though it was burned into her memory and would remain there forever. At least the last time he'd broken her heart there had only been him telling her it was over—not the vision of him lip-smacked with his ex-wife! How could he have done that to her?

When Bergan stopped the car, Reggie found herself outside the new apartment block where Melva and her other neighbours were staying. The apartments Flynn had organised.

'Melva's place?' There was a hint of hope in Reggie's tone.

'What do you think?'

'This is perfect,' Reggie remarked, nodding. 'I haven't found the time to come and visit my neighbours since the fire and...' She looked at Bergan. 'This *is* just what I need. Some Melva therapy.'

'An escape,' Bergan remarked, smiling at her friend.

'Yes.'

'Go and spend time with Melva. I'm sure the evening nurse who comes to change the dressings on Melva's burns would love the night off, knowing you're going to be staying here for the night.'

'Of course I'll change Melva's dressings. That woman has always been there for me, from the first moment we met.'

'I know.'

'And it's all right with Melva?' Reggie checked as she undid her seat belt and alighted from the car. Her answer was to have her neighbour open the front door and come out to her, walking frame in front in order to steady her.

'Oh, Reggie. What a wonderful surprise. I was delighted when your young man called and said you were coming to stay.'

'My young…man?' Alarm bells instantly began to ring in Reggie's ears as she looked quickly at Bergan, whose answer was to simply shrug one shoulder and sigh.

'I can't take credit for thinking to bring you to Melva's. It was Flynn's idea. He said if you needed space then he would give you space.'

'Flynn organised all of this?' Reggie wasn't sure whether to feel betrayed by Bergan or happy that Flynn had realised she needed space. Darn him for being his usual thoughtful self. It made it even more difficult for her to remember the pain he was causing her. 'That is so like him,' she growled between gritted teeth. 'Why does he have to do something nice when he's hurt me so badly?'

'Perhaps he's trying to show you how much he cares.'

'Then he should care by *not* kissing his ex-wife.'

'Listen,' Bergan said, hugging her friend close and whispering in Reggie's ear. 'I think the man is crazy about you. Even Richard agrees. Flynn is head over heels in love with you.'

'Ha!' Reggie snorted. 'He's got a funny way of showing it. By lying to me. By not telling me about…' She stopped, closing her eyes on the memory that was once more flashing before her eyes. 'You know what? It doesn't matter. *I* want to see Melva. *I* want to spend time with her, so that's what *I'm* going to do.'

'Good for you,' Bergan replied. 'Rest and relax. Get rid of your anxious mind. Enjoy your day off tomorrow. Sleep in. Watch TV. I'll see you at the hospital auction tomorrow night.'

Reggie grimaced at these words. 'I don't know if I want to go. I don't know if I want to see Flynn. It's too soon, especially if he's trying to control my life from afar.'

'Reggie.' Bergan smiled at her friend. 'He's not controlling anything. You are in complete control of all your faculties. Just relax and think about tomorrow when tomorrow comes.'

'Are you coming in for a cuppa, Bergan?' Melva asked from the doorway. 'I've just bought some nice new cups. They're very flash, bone china, and I spent a bit more on them then I should have but then I decided that after everything that's happened, I deserved a treat. Did you know,' Melva continued, 'that apparently we get paid a recovery allowance to help us buy new things while we're waiting for the insurance money to come through? I thought I'd be out of pocket for weeks but at the moment I seem to have more money than I know how to deal with.'

Reggie closed her eyes for a moment, delighted with the beaming smile on her neighbour's face, knowing instinctively that Flynn was the one who had provided that allowance. Insurance companies didn't settle up that quickly. He was using his wealth for the good of others and her heart warmed at the thought.

Perhaps he *was* different from the other people who had allowed money and position to corrupt them. Deep down inside she knew Flynn wasn't like that. He didn't use people and lie to them. So why hadn't he told her about Violet? About the boy? Why hadn't he been able to trust her?

'No, thanks, Melva,' Bergan replied, her words snapping Reggie's attention back to the present. 'Just dropping Reggie off. I need to get back to the hospital.' She hugged her friend again and looked pointedly at her. 'Call me later if you want to talk.'

'No need to worry about that,' Melva said. 'Reggie and I are going to have a great ol' chin-wag, aren't we, love? Now, come on in. Ooh, look. Here's a delivery van pulling up. Good heavens, it's like Grand Central Station out here at the moment.'

Sure enough, the driver of the delivery van was soon walking towards them, a parcel in his hands.

'I'm looking for Reggie Smith?'

Reggie's eyes widened at that, then she frowned in confusion. 'Uh…that's me.'

'OK. If you could sign here.' He waited until she'd done as he'd asked, then handed over the parcel. 'You ladies have a lovely evening,' he said with a polite smile and just as quickly as he'd arrived, he disappeared.

'What is it?' Melva asked, and a stunned Reggie gave it a quick shake.

'I don't know.'

'Then come inside and we'll open it.' Melva turned to Bergan. 'Bye-bye, deary. Thanks for dropping her off. I'll take it from here.' Melva pointedly winked at Bergan, not being very subtle, but Reggie decided to let it go for now.

After waving goodbye to Bergan, Melva and Reggie headed inside to see what exactly was in the package. 'There's no return address, except for a local department store.' Reggie closed the door and walked into the comfortable lounge room, remembering to admire the décor of the apartment.

'Ooh. A mystery.' Melva found a pair of scissors and handed them to Reggie so she could open it.

'Hmm.' Reggie looked slyly at the elderly woman. 'Is it really?'

Melva giggled as Reggie cut open the top of the parcel, then pulled out a toothbrush, a tube of toothpaste, a pair of soft satin pyjamas and a hairbrush and clean, new underwear that was scarlet.

'Now, *those* are far more expensive than my tea cups,' Melva remarked, before whistling, the noise making Reggie blush. 'Is there a note?'

'No, but I think we both know exactly who they're from.'

'They're from the same person who's found this furnished apartment, who's paying my allowance and who rang me, not half an hour ago and asked if it was all right for you to come and visit for the night.'

'What did he say?' Reggie asked softly.

'He said you'd had a shock and he wanted you to

have some space and time to process everything. He thought spending some time with me, the closest person you have to a mother, might be good for you. I told him I was more like your grandmother but I knew what he meant.'

A lump formed in Reggie's throat as Melva recounted what Flynn had said to her. 'You know who he is, don't you,' she stated quietly.

'Of course, dear. I lived in Melbourne for many years. I used to do private hairdressing for the likes of those people.'

Reggie's eyes widened at this news. 'So...do you know who I—?'

'Yes, dear.' Melva eased herself down into a comfortable high-backed armchair. 'I've known from the first moment I clapped eyes on you.'

'And yet you never said anything?' A lump welled in Reggie's throat.

'Why? What was the point in dredging up pain?' She shook her head. 'A person's past is their past. There's nothing they can do to change it. They can only learn from it and move forward into a better version of their future. If you get stuck in quicksand you either stay there, not caring that you can't get out, or you do something about it.' Melva looked at Reggie and nodded, pride in her voice. 'You were one of the strong ones. You were able to leave your past behind you, go to medical school, make something of your life, but sometimes...like with your young man...well, it just takes a little bit longer for people to figure things out. He had to get out of the quicksand and he could only do it for the right reasons.'

'Do you think *I'm* involved with those reasons?'

Melva chuckled. 'What do you think, ya silly goose?'

Reggie frowned, listening carefully to what Melva was saying. She knew the wise woman was right, even though the last thing Reggie wanted was to be rational about all this. Her emotions were mixing again, tumbling over each other in a mass of confusion.

It was true there was no way she could change what had happened in either her past or the one she'd shared with Flynn. The past was the past. She knew deep down inside he was a good man and while they'd both made mistakes—him for leaving her and her for letting him—it didn't change the fact that he'd hurt her.

Logically, she knew time and a bit of distance was necessary for her to sort her thoughts out but emotionally she wanted to be mad at him, she wanted to hold on to her anger. She wanted to continue being annoyed with him, especially as he really did seem to know her very well. He'd realised that her spending time with Melva, away from him, away from Mackenzie, Bergan and Sunainah—being with someone who was completely impartial to all that had gone before—was exactly what Reggie would need.

'Hmm,' she growled softly, the frown still marring her forehead.

'Don't overthink things, Reggie. Sometimes you just need to go with the flow.' Melva waved her hands in the air.

Reggie sighed and turned her attention back to Melva, the frown immediately disappearing. 'How did you get to be so wise?' she asked.

Melva chuckled. 'I'm eighty-two years old, darling, that's how. I've picked up a thing or two about this whole game-of-life thing.' She sighed. 'Now, are you going to make us a cup of tea in my new fancy cups and start enjoying yourself or do I have to get cross with you?'

Reggie instantly smiled as she stood to her feet. 'Tea it is.'

Even though she'd had a lovely time with Melva, Reggie didn't sleep all that well. Her mind was constantly churning with everything she knew about Flynn, trying to piece together exactly what sort of man he was. Before yesterday she would have said he wasn't the type of man to cheat on a woman but she'd seen the way money could corrupt even the most saintly of men.

If that little boy was his son, then it was something she would have to deal with if there was any hope of a future with Flynn. Did she want a future with Flynn? Her heart was saying yes, yes, yes, but her mind was saying no, no, no.

Then what of Bergan? Her strong, determined friend, who would stand like a guard with swords crossed to staunchly protect her from any enemy, had crumbled and gone along with the plan Flynn had put into place. She knew that happiness came from within and that she couldn't rely on someone else, couldn't hold them responsible for her own happiness, but she also accepted that to go through the rest of her life with Flynn by her side would, indeed, go a long way to making her happy.

She'd tried living without him before and it had been difficult. If things really weren't as they seemed, if she'd somehow grabbed the wrong end of the stick then perhaps…maybe…would she really be foolish enough to employ some small level of hope?

'Oh, Flynn,' she whispered over her cup of early-morning coffee as she stood looking out of Melva's kitchen window as the sun rose, shining its glorious light all around. The darkest little cracks and crevices changed from a dull grey to vibrant colour. The yellows, pinks, purples and blues. Slowly but surely it was as though the world was waking up, coming to life, wanting to celebrate the new day.

Wasn't that how she'd been since Flynn had returned to her life? Filled with colour? Wanting to celebrate life? She'd forced herself to become a bright and bubbly person, always seeing the glass as half-full rather than half-empty, always wanting to look on the bright side of things, always wanting to surround herself with happiness, but now she knew as an absolute certainty that without Flynn in her life, that's all her life would ever be—forced happiness.

'Good morning, dear,' Melva said as she shuffled into the kitchen, the walking frame supporting her. 'Oh, good. You've already made the coffee.'

'I was going to bring you a cup but I confess to being sidetracked by the glorious sunrise.'

Melva nodded as Reggie quickly fixed her a cup. 'Let's go out onto the balcony and watch it together.' This they did and once they were seated, Melva asked her, 'So what have you decided?'

Reggie's quirky smile was instant. 'You know me too well.'

Melva chuckled but waited patiently for Reggie's answer.

'I think that I at least…I need to hear what he has to say before I can make any other decision.'

Melva snorted at this. 'Really? I think you've decided more than that.'

'What do you mean?'

'This isn't just about listening to the man, Regina.'

'It's not?'

'No.' Melva shook her head. 'What is wrong with you young people these days?' She put her coffee cup down on the table. 'I think it's great you want to listen to him, darling, but this is also crunch time.'

'Crunch time?' It was Reggie's turn to shake her head. 'I don't—'

'Do you love him?'

'Er…I…'

'It's a simple question, Reggie. Yes or no?'

Reggie swallowed. 'Yes.'

'So no matter what he might say to you, you're willing to face the consequences? Fight for him? Move heaven and earth to ensure the two of you stay together this time?'

Reggie's heart fluttered with excited fear. What if Flynn told her that the little boy was his son? Would she be able to accept that? Was she willing to be a part of his son's life? What if Flynn still had a lot of wealthy friends? Would she be able to spend time with them? Melva was right. Was she willing to fight for Flynn? To make sure that his life and her life were intertwined together—forever?

'Yes,' she replied again. 'I am.'

Melva's grin was wide as she nodded her head, as though encouraging Reggie to continue.

'I need Flynn in my life.' Reggie said the words more to herself than to Melva. 'I know I can survive without him, I've done it for the past six years, but I'm not sure if I want to just survive anymore. I've been doing that for most of my life—surviving. I want to be happy,

Melva.' Her chin wobbled as she spoke the words and tears immediately sprang to her eyes. 'I want Flynn.'

Melva chuckled and leaned over to drape her frail arm around Reggie's shoulders. 'That's my girl.'

Feeling happier now that the decision had been made, Reggie had a cleansing shower, realising she would need to head out to the shops at some point to find something to wear to tonight's auction. She surveyed the bright scarlet underwear Flynn had sent as part of her overnight care package. No doubt he'd called one of the department stores where they'd gone shopping last week, asking one of the personal shoppers to gather a few things together and courier them to Melva's apartment.

At least she hoped that's what had happened because even thinking about Flynn, standing in the lingerie section, searching for the perfect matching set of underwear for her…and such a delightfully wicked colour as well…made her cheeks suffuse with colour.

Would he take the time to personally do such a thing for her? Had he left the hospital and gone straight to the department store? He had told Bergan he had things to organise. Had he gone to such great lengths *just* for her?

And that wasn't all. During the course of the morning the doorbell rang twice and each time Reggie's heart pounded with scared excitement at the thought that it might be Flynn. Instead, there were more parcels being delivered, the first a small but perfect Christmas tree, along with a box of decorations. There was a note with it that simply said, 'Enjoy your day.'

A few hours later, once they'd erected the tree and dressed it with baubles and tinsel, the second package arrived.

'This really *is* like Christmas.' Melva giggled as Reg-

gie signed for the parcel. This one, though, wasn't like
the others. It was a long dress bag, with a smaller box
inside. When she opened it, both she and Melva gasped.
There, inside, was the most beautiful scarlet-coloured
dress, perfect to match the underwear she presently had
on beneath her new pyjamas. The bodice was tastefully
embroidered with beads and a few sequins, the skirt
was full and came to just below her knee. The small
box at the bottom of the bag contained a perfect pair
of matching shoes.

'Good heavens. This must have cost hundreds.'

'And then some,' Reggie murmured, instantly falling in love with the dress. It would be wrong of her to
accept it, wouldn't it? Was Flynn trying to lavish gifts
on her in order to buy her forgiveness?

'I should send it all back. The dress, the underwear—'

'But not the decorations. Look how homely they
make this new apartment look,' Melva said instantly.

Reggie surveyed the brightly coloured room and
nodded in agreement.

'And why should you send it all back?' Melva continued. 'The man isn't trying to buy you off, Reggie.
You're far too strong for him to even attempt it. All he's
doing is showing you how much he appreciates you.
He's wooing you. For heaven's sake, girl, let the man
be romantic. Now, off you go to the spare room and try
on that dress. I want my own personal fashion parade
of dress and shoes so we can decide on your hair and
make-up—which I'll do for you. Now go. Shoo.'

She did as Melva had bidden her and they had a
lovely time deciding on make-up and exactly how she
should wear her hair. When the doorbell rang a third

time, Reggie was all in a dither. Dressed in her pyjamas again, she almost raced to the door, filled with excitement to see what Flynn might be sending her *this* time.

When she opened the door, expecting to see a delivery man standing there, waiting for her to sign for the next parcel, she almost tripped over her own feet to see Flynn.

'Flynn!'

She stared at him and he stared at her, both of them drinking in the sight of each other as though they'd been starved for years.

'Hello, Reg.'

'Uh…' She was at a total loss for words, unsure whether to invite him in or just stand there, or whether she should change into her clothes or thank him for all the gifts or… 'What do you want?' she blurted, instantly wishing her words hadn't come out sounding so confronting.

'I…um…' Flynn looked down at his hands, as though completely forgetting why he was here. It was then he seemed to realise he was holding a thick white envelope. 'I wanted to deliver this one. In person.'

'Oh, yes. Sorry.' Manners and a smidgen of coherent thought began to return. 'Er…thank you for all the—'

'It's fine.' He waved away her words with a hint of veiled embarrassment. 'I actually wondered if I could… read this to you.'

'Read it?' He was clearly nervous and it only made him seem more endearing. It was difficult, seeing him standing there—looking incredibly sexy in his blue denim jeans and pale blue shirt, casual but, oh, so delicious—really difficult to remember that just yesterday afternoon she'd seen him kissing another woman.

'Yes.' He dragged in a breath, as though pulling himself together. 'I have a lot of things I'd like to say to you, Reg, and all I ask is that you listen. I'm not looking for an answer or anything. No pressure. Just…please…will you listen?'

Reggie nodded and indicated for him to come inside but he shook his head. 'Here is good.' And without further ado he flicked open the envelope and pulled out a few sheets of paper. 'I wrote everything down, not only so I didn't forget the important things I need to say, because heaven knows that when I'm around you, Reg, my mind tends to turn to mush and all I can think about is holding you close and…' He trailed off and found himself staring at her yet again.

Didn't she have any idea just how adorably perfect she looked in those pyjamas? All soft and cuddly and so *his* Reggie?

'Anyway,' he went on, giving himself another mental shake. 'Here goes.' He cleared his throat. 'Oh, and I'd appreciate it if you didn't interrupt. Just let me get it all out.'

'OK.'

'Good.' He paused, then launched right in. 'Dear Reg.'

'Strong beginning,' she murmured.

'No interruptions.' He glared at her and she nodded again. He tried again. 'I want to apologise for not telling you more about my divorce. I guess as it's a topic I've learned not to discuss in public, I keep forgetting you don't know what really happened all those years ago. Rest assured that Violet and I are just friends.' He stopped and looked directly into her eyes. *'Friends,'* he reiterated, before going back to reading his letter.

'We've always been better friends than anything else. She is also happily married to my cousin, Colin. The child you saw me holding, Ian, is their son.'

'He's not your son?' Reggie whispered, hope filling her voice as he continued to read further.

'Violet and I should never have allowed ourselves to be bullied into the marriage, especially as she'd been in love with my cousin all along. She had broken off her relationship with him, just as I had done with you. Duty and family and all that guff was rammed down our throats and so we did as we were told, desperately trying to make a go of a marriage but instead only succeeding in making each other—and you and Colin—miserable.

'Violet and I secretly separated very soon after the marriage, more than happy to live our own lives, and it was then she began to see Colin again. When she fell pregnant, we all decided it was best to end the farce so that Violet and Colin could stand a chance of being a proper family unit.

'We all knew none of our parents would be pleased with the outcome but we did what we had to and now not only have they had five wonderful years together but Violet just told me that she's pregnant again with their second child. That was why she wanted to see me, to tell me the news in person. Unfortunately, Colin is overseas at the moment and wasn't able to join us.

'Reg, please believe me when I say that there is nothing romantic between Violet and myself. It is *you* I am most desperately in love with and it is *you* I wish to spend the rest of my life with.'

Reggie gasped and covered her mouth with her hand as he looked into her eyes.

'My heart has *always* been yours and I was a fool to

have let you go once. I won't make that same mistake again.' Flynn was no longer reading from the page but instead was staring intently into her eyes. 'I love you, Reg. More so now than I did six years ago.'

She wasn't sure what to do, what to say. What was she supposed to do? She did love him back with all her heart and she wanted desperately to tell him, to let him know that he wasn't standing out on that big scary ledge of emotion all on his own, but somehow, for some strange reason, she couldn't get any of the words past her lips and her feet seemed permanently glued to the spot.

'I know this is a lot to take in,' Flynn continued, clearly not expecting any sort of response from her. 'Hence why I've written everything down. Take this letter, Reg. Read it over and over. Process it. Take your time. Don't rush but, please, believe me when I say that at the moment there's only confusion between us because that's all it is—a silly misunderstanding, and I hope my words have helped clear all that up.

'I'm really looking forward to seeing you tonight at the auction and one simple look from you, a gesture, a word even, will let me know whether or not you accept my apology and my love.'

Then, as she stood there, she watched him fold the papers, putting them back into the envelope with his clever, sure fingers. He held the envelope out to her and with numb fingers she took it...watching in surprise as he bowed his head to her then turned and walked away.

Reggie blinked, several times, wondering if she was still lying in bed, dreaming. Had she fallen and hit her head and was hallucinating? The envelope in her hands was evidence that it was neither and after she'd somehow managed to get her body to function yet again she closed the door, then slumped down into a chair, trying to take in everything that had just happened.

Flynn loved her. Flynn had just stood there, before her, declaring his love for her, letting her know that not only did he love her now but that he'd *always* loved her and always would. He was hers. His love was hers to have...if she wanted it.

'I do. I do want it.'

And yet he hadn't pressured her, hadn't come inside, hadn't talked at her, but instead had read the love letter out loud, sharing with her his thoughts and deepest emotions. He hadn't wanted anything from her, hadn't demanded any sort of response, hadn't forced her into anything.

'But I want him. I love him.' As though it was just too much for her to contain, she raced back to the door and flung it open, staring out into the street to try and see if he'd really left, but there was no sign of him.

'What's going on?' Melva called. 'Is there *another* person at the door?'

Reggie headed back inside and sat down again, surprised to find tears of happiness streaming down her face, a wide grin on her lips. She brushed the tears aside, her heart lifting in complete and utter delight to know that Flynn loved her, that he still loved her, that he'd *always* loved her. She laughed out loud, unable to believe how light and glorious it was to be loved back by the person you loved.

She unfolded the letter and read it again, just to reassure herself that this was really happening, that this was really true. He really *did* know her so well, wanting to ensure she wasn't pressured in any way, and that knowledge made her love him all the more.

'But he doesn't know I love him.' The words tumbled out of her mouth in a rush and she looked around anxiously for her phone. With trembling fingers she dialled his number, heart pounding wildly against her chest as she waited for it to connect. She wasn't quite sure what she was supposed to say; her mind had gone blank. The phone switched through to his voicemail, which meant he was probably driving. She waited for the message to end but when it was time to say something she opened her mouth to tell him that she loved him back, that she loved the dress and the other presents he'd bestowed on her, that she couldn't wait to see him tonight, that she was sorry for being such an insecure ninny and having a big freak-out…but no words came out of her mouth.

She quickly disconnected the call and realised what she must do. She must look her absolute best for tonight. Let Flynn see for himself just how much she loved him. She stood and checked the clock.

'Only three hours to get ready! Come on!'

Flynn stood, dressed in a tuxedo, not caring if he was slightly overdressed for tonight's auction or not. He wanted to look his absolute best when he saw Reggie, hoping amongst hope that his gifts and his letter of explanation, his letter of love, had proved to her that he loved her and that she could trust him. He fiddled with his tie as he stood near the rear of the small stage.

So far, the night had been going for a good twenty minutes and there was still no sign of Reggie. Was she coming? Had something happened? Perhaps he should have organised for a car to pick her up but then he thought she might consider that too controlling and the last thing he wanted was for her to think him controlling. He wanted to cherish her, adore her and love her for the rest of her life, and as he rubbed his sweaty palms down his trousers again, checking the door for the hundredth time, almost wishing her to burst through, he heard his number being called.

'And next up we have bachelor number five. Ladies, he's the latest addition to Sunshine General's surgical department. Please welcome Flynn Jamieson,' Mackenzie, who was the MC for the evening, announced into the microphone. Flynn looked at Mackenzie as if to ask where Reggie was. Mackenzie's answer was to shrug apologetically as Flynn took centre stage, standing beneath the plastic mistletoe hanging from the ceiling.

'Who would like to get the bidding started?' Mackenzie asked, and wasn't surprised when a plethora of hands went up, bids being called out. The previous bachelor had raised well over five hundred dollars and although Flynn wanted to raise money for the hospital, he didn't care if someone only bid five dollars, so long as that someone was Reggie. Where was she?

Mackenzie was taking bids, the price going past one hundred dollars, past two hundred, then three, then four. Up and up the price went, getting to seven hundred dollars. Ingrid Brown, the general surgical registrar, was in a battle with Clara from the outpatient department. Flynn couldn't believe someone would pay that much just to have dinner with him but then again it really was for a good cause.

'Do I have an increase on seven-fifty?' Mackenzie called. 'Seven-fifty going once. Seven-fifty going twice.'

'One thousand dollars!' came a loud female cry from the back of the room and everyone turned to look, turned to see Reggie standing there, dressed in the most glorious scarlet dress and matching shoes, her short dark hair spiked out a little, giving her a radiant appeal. People around her clapped; the hospital's administrator whooped with delight.

'Sold!' Mackenzie called, banging her gavel and ignoring Ingrid's frown. 'Step right on up, Reggie, and claim your Christmas bachelor,' she called. Reggie kept her gaze glued to Flynn's as she made her way through the ballroom, not tripping over a chair or a tablecloth and not overbalancing in the five-inch heels.

Soon enough, she was standing before him. 'Sorry I'm late,' were the first words out of her mouth. 'The taxi broke down and I had difficulty getting another one.'

'You look…' Flynn stared at her, not caring that everyone else was staring at the two of them. As far as he was concerned, there was no one else, no one else except Reggie. 'Stunning.'

Her smile increased as she looked up at him, then motioned to the mistletoe above them. 'Look where you're standing, Dr Jamieson.'

He nodded and moved forward, sliding his arms about her waist and drawing her close. Wolf-whistles came from around them as well as a lot of cheering. Reggie didn't care. She wanted everyone in the world to know exactly how she felt about Flynn.

'Do you think we need it?' he asked, and she slowly shook her head from side to side.

'Thank you for your letter. It was perfect.'

'I hope you don't think I was trying to buy your affection by sending you the things I did.'

'I don't think that. I think you were trying to romance the woman you love.' She slid her hands slowly up his chest to link them behind his neck.

'I do. I do love you, Reggie, so very much. I've never loved anyone like I love you.'

'That's very good news,' she replied, her brand-new heels making her tall enough to lean in closer and line up her lips with his.

'It is?'

'Yes, because I've never loved anyone like I love you either.'

Finally, Flynn smiled at her, a small, secret smile that let her know that, finally, everything really would be all right. 'Marry me?' he asked, their lips only millimetres apart.

'Yes,' she replied instantly, and sealed their new deal with a kiss.

The room erupted into a frenzy of clapping and cheering as the two of them stood beneath the mistletoe, kissing each other with perfect delight.

'I'm sorry this proposal isn't as romantic as the last one,' he eventually said as they made their way out of the ballroom via a side door, not caring about anything at the moment but each other. With the moon above them, the stars twinkling in the night sky and Flynn's arms around her, holding her close, Reggie kissed his gorgeous, loving mouth.

'I like this one best, especially as I now own you.' He raised one eyebrow playfully at her words. 'Don't you realise that spread out over the next fifty years, you would only have cost me twenty dollars a year!'

'A definite bargain,' he returned, kissing her once again.

'Who said money couldn't buy love?' She giggled and allowed Flynn to keep on kissing her...forever.

EPILOGUE

'ARE YOU READY?' Sunainah asked.

Reggie stood dressed in a beautiful white wedding dress that had an asymmetrical split up the side, revealing a generous amount of her shapely legs. Ruffles seemed to be everywhere and as she looked at herself in the mirror, her three friends nodded in approval.

'That dress is *so* you,' Bergan said.

'I love it,' Reggie agreed. 'Almost as much as I love Flynn.' She giggled before turning to face her friends, looking at each of them in turn. She was surrounded by the people she loved and waiting for her in the communal garden area of the cul-de-sac stood the man of her dreams. 'Do you think I'm ready?'

Bergan, Mackenzie and Sunainah looked at each other for a split second before looking back at Reggie. 'Yes,' they said in unison.

'Only you would get married in a car park,' Bergan grumbled good-naturedly.

'It's not a car park. It's a lovely little garden that we all tend and love—'

'Which is right next to where guests usually park their cars when they come to visit,' Bergan added.

'Well, Mackenzie did want me to be part of the cul-de-sac crew and I think this definitely makes it official.'

'Just one more thing,' Sunainah said a moment later, and bent down to pull a rectangular parcel from a bag. It was wrapped in plain brown paper with no other adornments. 'This is for you.'

'Really?' Reggie accepted the parcel and looked at her friend in delight. 'I like presents.'

'I hope you will like this one.' Sunainah, Bergan and Mackenzie all grinned at each other as Reggie ripped the paper off with a touch of impatience and what she saw there made her stare at her friends in wonderment. There, in her hands, was a framed picture of herself and Flynn, standing on the beach in the Caribbean, sipping drinks with little umbrellas, the sun setting behind them.

'You told me to get rid of it but...I could not,' Sunainah confessed.

Reggie shook her head in wonder, then put the picture down and launched herself at her friends, hugging them all. 'Oh, this is perfect. This is the picture from our first real date. Oh, Sunainah, thank you for not listening to me and keeping it safe all these years. You three really are the best friends ever.'

'I am also pleased you decided not to wait and to get married *today*,' Sunainah added, as she set about fixing Reggie's dress once more. 'Christmas Day. Surrounded by everyone that you love most. It is perfect.'

'Yes.' Melva and her other neighbours would be part of the party and after the ceremony they were having a progressive Christmas wedding feast, going from one town house to the next. Reggie had wanted everyone to be included because everyone here was *her* family, the family she'd built around herself and the one in which Flynn now shared.

Since the auction Reggie had met Violet several times, wanting to include her in the planning of the wedding.

'I'm so glad you and Flynn have finally found each other again,' Violet had said when the two of them had been alone. 'He loves you very much. Always has.'

'I know. The past is the past,' Reggie said. 'We can't do anything to change it but what we can do is accept it and plunge right on in to a newer and happier future.'

Violet had laughed. 'Flynn told me I'd like you and he was right. Thank you for making him happy.' The two women had hugged and when Flynn had returned, finding them laughing together, Reggie had seen true happiness reflected in his eyes. They weren't his future wife and his ex-wife, they were the love of his life and his surrogate sister…and they liked each other.

'OK,' Bergan said a moment later, bringing Reggie's thoughts back to the present. 'It's time to go because I have a feeling Flynn isn't going to wait too long for his bride to appear.'

'Right, girls,' Mackenzie said, marshalling her daughter Ruthie and Sunainah's daughter, Daphne, together. 'You come with me.'

'And boys,' Sunainah said, taking her son Joshua's hand and then offering her other hand to Violet's son, Ian, who Reggie had wanted to include in their wedding party. 'You are with me.'

'Out you come,' Bergan said, opening the front door to town house number three and waiting for the bride to precede her. As Reggie was an orphan, she'd decided she didn't need to be walked down the aisle by anyone.

She would stand tall and walk towards Flynn by herself, offering herself to him, her three closest friends and the children behind her.

She accepted her bridal bouquet of bright red poinsettias from Bergan and smiled. 'Yes,' she said to them, before looking towards the garden where Flynn stood waiting impatiently for her. 'I'm ready. Ready for my normal, everyday life to begin. My life with Flynn.'

And with that, beaming brightly she walked towards the man who held her heart, giggling at his expression when he finally saw her, his jaw dropping in gobsmacked delight. Both Colin and Violet were standing in as his 'groomsmen' and with Richard, Elliot and John, as well as the rest of the extended families visiting for Christmas, it was almost difficult to find the wedding celebrant in the mix.

As soon as Reggie stood beside Flynn, she smiled up at him and gave a little shimmy, the ruffles on her dress shaking with the movement. 'Ready to get hitched?' she whispered.

'To you? Absolutely,' he replied, and took her hand in his. 'Now, this is a Christmas tradition I can get behind.'

Reggie laughed, unable to believe she could ever be this happy and it was all thanks to Flynn.

* * * * *

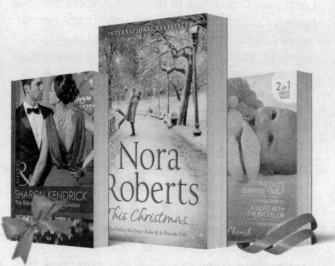

The World of
MILLS & BOON®